Praise for the Novels of Katharine Ashe

I LOVED A ROGUE

"Passionate, heart-wrenching,
and thoroughly satisfying."
All About Romance, Desert Island Keeper

"Rich and inventive, unexpected and
smart, and she doesn't pull any emotional
punches. . . . A blissful read."
USA Today

I ADORED A LORD

"A riotous good time . . . Delicious."
Publishers Weekly

I MARRIED THE DUKE
Historical Romance of the Year
Reviewers' Choice Award nominee 2014

KISSES, SHE WROTE

"Smoldering."
Library Journal (★Starred Review★)

"Finished it with tears in my eyes.
Yes, it was that good."
Elizabeth Boyle, *New York Times* bestselling author

MY LADY, MY LORD
RITA® Award Finalist 2015
Romance Writers of America

HOW TO MARRY A HIGHLANDER
RITA® Award Finalist 2014
Romance Writers of America

HOW TO BE A PROPER LADY
Amazon Editors' Choice 10 Best Books of 2012

WHEN A SCOT LOVES A LADY

"Lushly intense romance . . . radiant prose."
Library Journal (★Starred Review★)

"Sensationally intelligent writing and
a true, weak-in-the-knees love story."
Barnes & Noble "Heart to Heart" *Recommended Read!*

IN THE ARMS OF A MARQUESS

"Every woman who ever dreamed of having
a titled lord at her feet will love this novel."
Eloisa James, *New York Times* bestselling author

"Immersive and lush . . . Ashe is that rare author
who chooses to risk unexpected elements within
an established genre, and whose skill and magic
with the pen lifts her tales above the rest."
Fresh Fiction

CAPTURED BY A ROGUE LORD
Best Historical Romantic Adventure
Reviewers' Choice Award winner 2011

SWEPT AWAY BY A KISS

"A breathtaking romance filled with sensuality."
Lisa Kleypas, #1 *New York Times* bestselling author

The ROGUE

A Devil's Duke Novel

Katharine Ashe

AVONBOOKS
An Imprint of HarperCollinsPublishers

AVON BOOKS
An Imprint of HarperCollins*Publishers*
195 Broadway
New York, New York 10007

Copyright © 2016 by Katharine Brophy Dubois
Part title/chapter opener art copyright © Emre Tarimcioglu / Shutterstock, Inc.
ISBN: 978-0-06-241273-7
www.avonromance.com

First Avon Books mass market printing: March 2016

Avon Trademark Reg. U.S. Pat. Off. and in Other Countries, Marca Registrada, Hecho en U.S.A.
Avon, Avon Books, and the Avon logo are trademarks of HarperCollins Publishers.
HarperCollins® is a registered trademark of HarperCollins Publishers.

Printed in the U.S.A.

10 9 8 7 6 5 4 3 2 1

To
Marcia Abercrombie,
Sonja Foust
&
Lee Galbreath—
friends, artists, angels.

The exercises of chivalry produced two effects, physical and mental. Physically, they produced graceful and vigorous bodies; mentally, they tended to courage, generosity, and truth.

—COLONEL THOMAS H. MONSTERY
The Spirit of the Times (1877)

THE FALCON CLUB

THE MISSION
To find missing persons and bring them home.

The Director
Anonymous

The Agents
Colin, Viscount Gray—Peregrine,
Secretary of the Club

Lady Constance Read—Sparrow

Leam, Earl of Blackwood, heir to the
Duke of Read—Eagle (retired)

Captain Jinan Seton—Sea Hawk (retired)

Wyn Yale—Raven (retired)

Their Nemesis
Lady Justice, pamphleteer

PART I
The Maiden

Prologue

The Danger

April 1815
Fellsbourne, estate of the Marquess of Doreé
Kent, England

*O*f the dozen men in the room, he was the only man she should not be staring at. He was not a lord. Not an heir to a fortune. Not a scion of impressive lineage or a favorite of the prince. He wasn't even really a gentleman.

Yet she could not look away.

It shouldn't have mattered; a hidden niche was an excellent place from which a young lady could spy on a risqué party. Until someone else discovered it.

Unless that someone else were the right someone else.

For four nights now no one had noticed her peeking from a door that could barely be called a door in the corner of the ballroom. These passages had been fashioned in an earlier era of rebellion, and everybody had long since forgotten them.

Except her.

And now him.

A quality of familiarity braided with danger commanded the breadth of his shoulders and the candlelight in his eyes as he watched her. Yet she did not duck back into the dark passage and escape. She had no fear that he would know her. Like the women who had actually been invited to the party, her mask hid the upper half of her face. Anyway, she knew no one in society. Her father had not yet taken her to London, only deposited her here at Fellsbourne, where he imagined her safe in the company of his dear friend's family. Where she had always in fact been safe. Teased, taunted, treated like an annoying younger sister, and very carelessly acknowledged. But safe.

Until now.

Not removing his eyes from her, the stranger unfolded himself from the chair with predatorial grace. He moved like a hunter, lean and powerful and aware. *Not entirely human.* Even at rest he had watched the others, disinterested in the amorous flirtations of the other men and the women here to entertain them, yet keen-eyed. Like an elven prince studying mortal beings, he observed.

For four nights she had wondered, if she were one of those women would he be interested in her? Would he seek her attention? Would he touch her as the other men touched those women—as she longed to be touched—held—told she was special—good—beautiful?

She was wicked to her marrow.

Wicked to want a stranger's notice. Wicked to relish the thrill in her belly as he walked

straight

toward

her.

Under normal circumstances her tongue was lithe enough. But normal circumstances had never in her wildest misbehaviors included a man with eyes like his—green, clear and shining, moonlight cast upon the waters of a forest spring. Perhaps he was *not* entirely human. This wasn't Scotland. But England had its fair share of mystical beings too.

When he stood within no more than two wicked feet of her, her tongue failed.

"You were staring at me," he said in a voice like fire-heated brandy—rich, deep.

"You were staring at me." The low timbre of her own words startled her.

"One of us must have begun it."

"Perhaps it was spontaneously mutual. Or it was coincidence, and both of us imagined the other began it."

"How mortifying for us both then." The slightest smile appeared at the corner of his mouth that was beautiful. *Beautiful.* She had never thought about men's mouths before. She had never even noticed them. Now she noticed, and it did hot things to her insides.

"Or fortunate," she ventured. She was grinning, showing her big teeth. But she couldn't care. A young man was smiling at her, a young man with sun-darkened skin and whiskers cut square and scant about his mouth, like a pirate too busy marauding to shave for a day or two. *Not* very mystical, true. His hair was the color of ancient gilt, curving about his collar and swept dashingly back from his brow. A military saber hung along his thigh, long and encased in dark leather. Its hilt glittered.

He was staring at her lips, and so she stared at his. Giddy trills climbed up her middle.

Kisses.

His lips made her think of kisses. *Want* kisses. Kisses on her mouth. Kisses on her neck like those that the loose women got from the other men. Kisses wherever he would give them to her.

Wicked wicked wicked.

"Dance with me," he said.

She darted a glance into the ballroom. All of the women wore costumes, scanty, sheer, slipping from shoulders beneath gentlemen's bold fingertips. Jack was throwing a masquerade for his friends and these women. Women she should not envy.

She should not be here. She should be at the dower house a quarter mile distant, where Eliza had drunk whiskey with dinner and now snored comfortably by the parlor fireplace.

"I cannot dance tonight," she said with more regret than she remembered ever saying anything.

"Cannot? Or will not with me?" His tongue shaped words decadently, as though the syllables were born to kiss his lips and taunt her with what she could not have.

"If I could, I would only with you."

He seemed to study her face: her too-big eyes, her too-small nose, the mouth that was too wide, brow that was too spotted, and cheeks that were too round. She knew her flaws, and yet he seemed to like studying them.

"What is your name?"

"I haven't one." Not that she could tell a stranger with elven eyes and pirate whiskers.

He smiled, and it was such a simple unveiling of pleasure that her heart thumped against a couple of her ribs.

"I will call you Beauty," he said, then his brow creased. "But you have heard that before."

"Then I suppose I must call you Beast," she replied. She liked the tingling tension in her belly that he had deposited there with only his smile.

"For what I'm thinking now, you should," he said quite seriously.

"What are you thinking now?"

"That your lips are perfection."

She could not control those lips; they wobbled, smiled, disbelieved.

"Men have told you this before," he said.

No one had ever looked at her mouth except to strike it when she misspoke.

"Why do you care what other men have said to me?"

"Because I wish to be the first, the most eloquent and original. Yet I cannot be that. And so I fail before the battle has begun."

"Battle?"

"For your attention."

"You have my attention. Entirely. This seems obvious to me." She *tried* not to smile. "But perhaps you are slow-witted."

"Undoubtedly," he murmured and abruptly seemed closer, taller, larger. She could *smell* him, a scent of sun-warmed leather and bergamot that she could reach out and swallow.

"I would like to kiss you," he said.

The explosion of excitement in her belly took her breath.

"I must go," she whispered. But she did not go. This was wrong, wicked, *disloyal* in so many ways. But her feet would not obey her. She wanted to stay. She wanted to breathe him in and in and in.

His eyes gleamed with candlelight. "You haven't been invited to this party. Have you?"

"No."

"Are you a servant in this household?"

It was on the verge of her tongue to declare, "Yes!" and let him continue staring at her mouth and saying outrageous things. But something in his eyes said that he would know if she lied.

"I *must* go." This time she did, darting back into the darkness. She made her way swiftly along the narrow corridor, her slippers silent upon the floorboards, counting the steps in the complete dark to the exit. Many times she had hidden from Jack, Arthur, and Ben in these walls, spying on them, longing to be on the other side of the wall, longing to be welcomed into their games. Often she had climbed into shadowed corners in order to be near them without revealing herself. Whenever they discovered her, they ran. Boys will be boys, her nurse had said, to which she had replied that if that was so then boys were hurtful.

The stranger's boot steps sounded behind her in the passageway.

"Don't go. I beg of you," he said into the blackness.

She obeyed and he came upon her in an instant.

"What did you hope to accomplish by entering that room?" he said and seemed close, the sound of his shoulders brushing the walls to either side, as if his frame filled all of the empty spaces in the corridor and inside her. Her head spun.

"I wanted to see it. I—" She could not lie, but she knew that she would be every kind of fool to reveal anything about herself. "I needn't tell you."

"You have been barred from the company," he said with certainty. "No wonder."

"No wonder?"

"Wolves prowl this place tonight. You are a lamb."

She did not feel like a lamb. She felt like a Jezebel.

"Hardly. I have just turned eighteen," she replied.

"Ah. A veritable crone."

She liked his teasing. She liked it that he wished to tease her, that *he* followed *her*, and that he now stood too close.

"Your tongue is delightfully noble, sir. I am all gratitude."

The air seemed to shift, to loosen.

"I cannot see you." His hot-brandy voice was smoother now. "Have you just curtsied?"

"Of course. That compliment deserved it."

"Compliment?"

She laughed. "You called me a crone."

"*Did* I?"

"Indeed you did."

"No. I couldn't have. That must have been the other fellow in this blackened crevice with us. The lout. But fret not. I will dispatch him when we are finished here."

"Finished?" *Not so soon.*

"Why did you stop when I asked you to just now?"

"You did not ask. You begged. I pitied you."

Abruptly the tension returned, the air humming upon a delirious edge.

"Do you know you might be in danger from me?" he said at least several notes lower.

"If I were in danger from you, wouldn't you now be endangering me rather than warning me of it?"

He seemed even closer—his heat and scent, his eyes that could not see her, and his mouth from which she wanted to drink kisses.

"Perhaps I will endanger you yet." He spoke with a roughness that shimmied up her insides.

"You won't," she said, her fingers bunching in her skirts.

"How do you know that?"

"Because I want you to. And I could not be so fortunate for once to have such a wish fulfilled."

"Girls like you . . ." He seemed to hesitate. "Girls who play at danger get hurt."

"What if I'm not playing?" She could barely breathe.

He said nothing, and the silence wrapped around her.

"What can you be about, I wonder," he finally said. "Were you spying in the ballroom?"

"Yes."

"Who was the lucky man?"

"What if I only intended to peek through that crack in the door?" The first night. The first night she had been merely curious. "What if I had been watching it all in disappointment and increasing boredom, on the cusp of relinquishing my vigil in favor of the book on my bedside table?"

"*Boredom?*"

"Just because I have never before seen debauchery doesn't mean I know nothing about it." He needn't know that the first night she had been a bit sickened watching Jack's party, eager to return to the dower house and Eliza's familiar company.

He chuckled. "Then what, oh easily jaded one, held you back from the superior enticement of your book?"

"I saw you." And she had felt things inside of her that she had never before known she could feel.

Wicked.

Wanton.

"Now I will kiss you," he said a bit urgently, "and be damned for it."

"Why? Is it a sin to kiss a woman?"

"A woman, not typically. A girl like you, yes."

"Then pretend I am only a woman tonight." She spoke upon a tightrope.

"And tomorrow?"

"Tomorrow . . ." She went onto her tiptoes, tilted her chin upward, and leaned into his heat. She would seize this delirium for only a moment, a forbidden moment that felt like the most honest thing she had ever done. "Pray for us both."

She thought he would kiss her. Some of the other men had walked straight up to the loose women and kissed them on the lips without even asking. Instead she felt the briefest brush of his arm against hers, the heat of his hand momentarily near her face.

Then a tweak of pain.

She jerked her head forward.

"Ouch!" The half-mask fell away from her face and she was naked, her face entirely revealed. But in the blackness he certainly could not see her.

"Forgive me," he said, not particularly contritely.

"You caught my hair." Happiness bubbled in her. "You might have asked, you know."

"Do you need it again?"

"The mask or my hair?"

"If you were mine, I would buy you combs inlaid with diamonds to adorn your hair." The words caressed.

"Can you afford diamonds?"

"Mm . . . No."

"Combs?"

"No."

"Wildflowers, then."

"Wildflowers?"

"Adorn my hair with wildflowers and I will dance for you upon the meadow. Like a faery maiden." With her prince. "Would you like that?"

"Quite a lot, I suspect." She heard him breathe deeply. She had never listened to another person breathing before, not like this, in the darkness, hearing so acutely because she could not see. It was deliciously intimate.

"I think I should like to linger for a moment now in this imaginary scene on the meadow," he said.

"Would you?"

"But I need more details. For instance, what will you wear for this performance?"

"It will not be a performance. Rather, a celebration of freedom."

"Freedom from what?"

"From everything." *From loneliness.* "So I will probably wear something shockingly immodest. White. Sheer. You know the sort of thing, I daresay."

"I'm beginning to understand how the scene in the ball-room bored you. Who *are* you?"

She had gone too far. She knew it. She *reveled* in it.

"Just a girl, as you have said." She tried to sound breezy. "A girl who wants her first kiss to be with you."

"I am glad to oblige you in that."

Yet still he did not kiss her. Instead his hand closed about her shoulder and she inhaled sharply. His touch felt warm and strong through the fabric of her gown. Then a single fingertip traveled slowly to the gully at the base of her throat. A shudder rippled through her.

"*Oh.*" She ached, wanting more of this touching in a deep well of wanting she barely recognized.

"Tell me to stop," he said like the rumble of a storm.

"No man has ever—I've no' been touched." She was re-vealing herself, the naïve innocent who could be easily se-duced. But it was too late. With a few words and a single caress he had already seduced her. She was the greatest wanton alive. "I cannot believe this is happening to me," she whispered.

"Then we are as one in disbelief." He was close, so close.

His lips brushed across hers and heaven descended. Dawn broke. Stars showered. From lips to knees she awoke in an explosion of tingling wonder.

"Sweet heaven," she rasped and grappled in the dark for him.

His lips were soft, his arms hard as she cinched her fingers around them—male and alien and thrilling. And very swiftly all she wanted was *more*. More soft lips and hard arms, more of their breaths mingling, more of a young man in her hands and on her mouth. *This* man, whose hand cupped her face and urged her mouth against his, whose lips grew firm and tasted good. *Tasted*. She had never known a man had a *flavor*. Or *textures*, soft and firm and rough and smooth all at once. She had never known the caress of another person's breaths on her cheek.

She had been missing a *lot*.

Climbing up his arms that were wonderfully muscled, her fingers clenched around his shoulders. So unfamiliar the smooth wool coat against her hands, so alien his fingertips stroking the edge of her hair, so strange and delicious and intoxicating and she wanted more.

She pressed her lips harder to his, but it did not suffice. She still wanted more, *much more*. Something was missing . . . Something would be better if . . .

She opened her mouth.

And felt it *all*. And understood why the men and loose women at the party embraced each other as they did—why there was nothing better than this—why she would never, ever get enough.

She made sounds, noises from her throat, without meaning to; they erupted on her breaths that he was taking with his kisses. He didn't seem to mind. Both of his hands wrapped around her face and he drew her up to him and she went onto her toes and their mouths were fused, giving and taking and melding and melting and hotter each moment. She was hot all over, in her throat and thighs and *everywhere*. The power of his arms beneath her palms made her wild inside. She could *eat* him, taste him and seek him like this, deeper with each breath, more desperate to have, to possess. *All* of him. She felt the tip of his tongue touch the edge of her lips and she moaned aloud.

"Tell me to stop," he said harshly. "Push me away."

"I cannot." Her lips sought his again, demanding his kisses. "You must take yourself away. For I find that I cannot make you go."

He did not take himself away. He held her in his hands and the universe became him—his mouth, his heat, his tongue caressing her lips, her teeth, her *tongue*. She whimpered, gripped his shoulders, and let him inside her.

And then they were apart, he was putting her away, and she was standing alone in the blackness with damp lips and frantic breaths and empty hands.

"I've got to go," he said firmly.

"I know," she cried. "I *know*. Will you . . . ?"

"Will I . . . ?" He sounded oddly choked.

"Will you be sorry?"

"For kissing you?"

"For *leaving* me?" she said a little desperately.

"Yes. So, perhaps you should leave instead."

"If you suggest that because you believe I won't be as sorry to leave as you, you are mistaken, sir."

She heard him shift, and the sound of his taut breathing.

"We are already having our first disagreement," he said. "That's a poor sign, you know. Clearly we are doomed right from the start. Probably best to end it straight off."

She laughed. "All right. Though I thought we might allow it another ten seconds."

"It?"

"This."

"This? Standing in blindness? Not touching? I won't survive another ten seconds." He sounded certain.

"How do you know that?"

"I have the wisdom of age and experience to guide me."

Oh. Oh.

"Experience," she mumbled, the joy slipping away. "With women, I suppose." Of course. She was immeasurably silly.

"I say to you now," he said in a new voice, "with complete honesty and in all sincerity, with no hope of anything at this moment beyond being heard: in this thorough darkness your face is more clearly etched upon my memory than that of every other woman I have met."

He was immeasurably silly too, it seemed. And *perfect*.

"Half of my face." She smiled.

"Granted." His voice smiled back at her. "And your eyes."

She chewed on her lip. It tasted raw. "It *cannot* be true that you see my face and no others now."

"I tell you it is God's truth."

A tiny ray of hope lit her insides. "Really?"

"Go," he growled like the beast she had called him. "Now. Go."

She must. She thought perhaps that he was trying to be good. Trying to stop them from kissing again. Kissing more. Kissing too much.

She never wanted to go.

"All right." Touching the walls to either side, she backed up. "Good night, sir." Then she had to turn away, because the ache inside her was no longer pleasurable.

In the darkness he found her wrist. He took it, lifted it, kissed it.

She sighed.

He kissed her palm, the tips of her fingers, and she could not breathe, could barely stand on knees that had turned to jelly. Sensation ripe and hot and wonderful overcame her.

He opened his hand, allowing her freedom. She made her feet move, made herself draw her hand away, trailing her fingertips across his callused palm until she felt him no more.

"Good night," he said.

Then she was alone again, walking swiftly through the darkness. Alone with a secret and a painfully quick heart-beat and a new ache of loneliness in her throat and chest that in all her eighteen years of solitude she had never imagined possible.

Stealing through shadows, she made her way out of the big house and then walked the quarter mile along the wooded path to the dower house. The moon was bright and her lips felt especially soft, and she knew she ought to feel guilty but she did not.

Later in her bed, sleep did not easily come. He was there now, at the big house. She knew every room in Fellsbourne. She could find him tonight. Go to him. If she dared.

And do *what*? She wasn't that girl. She was many awful things. But she was not that girl.

She wasn't really sure what being that girl entailed, anyway.

When morning came she arose before dawn, bleary-eyed and subdued. Strapping on her bow, she saddled Elfhame and rode to the woods. Eliza wanted hare stew, and hares were aplenty at the edge of the woods. She knew well enough the usual habits of the men who attended Jack's parties. No one would leave the big house before noon. Today she would not be discovered.

When she reached the woods, she dismounted and teth-ered her horse to a sapling. Through the mists that rose from the earth in soft clouds, she swiftly espied her prey. At the edge of the trees, it feasted on clover. She halted and watched it.

Innocent creature. It had no idea that it could be eaten for dinner.

Drawing an arrow from the quiver on her back and set-ting her stance with silence born of years' practice, she lifted her bow and nocked the shaft. Siting her target, she pulled back the bowstring.

A stick crackled nearby. The hare's ears popped up. Abruptly, it bounded into the underbrush. She leaped for-ward but it was too late. Wise little creature after all, to rec-ognize danger and react so swiftly.

Blowing out a frustrated breath, she pivoted to the ruiner of her hunt. And every sleep-deprived mote of her body came to life.

In the misty dawn he seemed even more like an elven prince than by candlelight, his eyes silvery and fixed upon her with great intensity. Not merely a prince. *A warrior.* He wore the same coat as the night before, a bit wrinkled now, and his gilded hair was tousled. The sword at his side looked so fearsome and his stance so powerful and certain, that he seemed at once like the most ordinary man and the most extraordinary god.

"You were not a dream," he said—ridiculously, wonderfully.

"I am not a dream," she replied, smiling, and knew that it would be the simplest thing in the world to pretend now that she was not in danger.

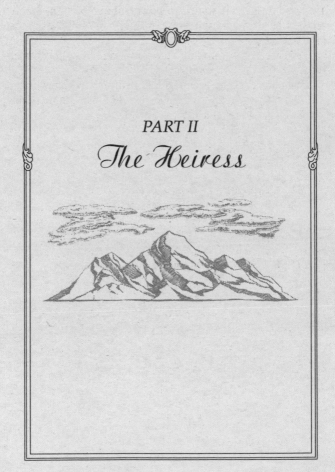

PART II
The Heiress

Chapter 1

The Rustication

22 Febr. 1822

Sparrow,

I have not heard from you in too many weeks. Do check in.

Peregrine

28 February 1822

Dearest Peregrine,

As All of Society knows, I have lost my One True Love (rather, my Second True Love, but who's counting?) to another lady (whom I adore, which is positively delightful) and in (supposed) grief have exiled myself to the North to avoid all mention of their bliss (although they set sail last month for the East Indies and will not return for a year anyway). So you see, I am very busy Rusticating at present and haven't the time to write tomes to you.

I am certain, in any case, that you would rather amuse yourself in trading correspondence with Lady Justice, as always. I understand that her current project to Improve Britain is to press Members of Parliament for married women's rights to legal and financial autonomy from their husbands. I applaud her. With your seat in the Lords, you might consider aiding her rather than antagonizing her. But alas, I believe you thrive on that antagonism. Whatever would you do if Madame La Justice *ceased writing pamphlets that condemn our Club and you no longer had the excuse to trade barbs with her? I think you might simply cease to exist.*

In hopes of that day never arriving, I am ever yours,
Sparrow

Chapter 2

The Swordsman

March 1822
The Sheep Heid Inn
Duddingston, near Edinburgh, Scotland

*F*rederick Evan Chevalier de Saint-André Sterling could hold his sword, liquor, and woman with equal skill. Unlike any other man Miss Annie Favor had enjoyed in her nineteen years, he could do so all at once.

Fond of weapons in the bedchamber, Annie welcomed the sword dangling from Saint's hip when he threw her upon the bed in a tangle of skirts and laughter and got to business. It wasn't every day, after all, that a man with shoulders like a cavalry steed's and eyes as green as the Queen's own emeralds came into the Sheep Heid Inn in the little village of Duddingston.

"Good sir," she sighed some time later as he rolled away from her and sat on the edge of the bed to tug his breeches over his tight bum. "Will ye do it again? An' again?" she said with satisfaction, watching him pull on his boots.

Lean muscles in his back and arms twisted beneath a sheen of moisture. She could not see now the scar that stretched across half his chest and waist. But she knew it was there and it gave her delicious chills. She trailed her fingertips down one impressively taut arm as he drew on his shirt.

"I want to be able to tell my father all aboot it come Saubath," she said. "Just after he preaches on the evils o' fornication."

Slowly swiveling to face her, he set his emerald eyes upon her. Like a river beneath sun, they glittered. Annie's tongue got abruptly dry.

"I've never seen such eyes," she whispered. "Be ye a demon come to steal my soul?"

The mouth that had moments earlier made her shout into the rafters now curved into the Devil's own smile.

"Sweet, sweet Annie. Your father is a man of the cloth?"

Relaxing back against the pillow, she grinned. This was her favorite part.

"He be the vicar o' Duddingston Kirk." She allowed her eyelids to droop. "I'm vexed to say, he's a birsie one. Why, the last man he found me with, he scourged up an' down the causey. But he couldna find his walkin' stick, so he used a carriage whip."

For a moment he regarded her with those eyes of otherworldly intensity. Then he threw back his head and laughed.

Annie did not know quite what to do. No man before had ever laughed.

She let her fingers slip from his waist to the sword he strapped anew to his hip, caressing the hilt. "Have ye ever used this on a woman?"

His laughter halted. Quicker than a single breath, the blade whipped free of its scabbard and laid flat across her throat. Heavy and cold, it pressed into her flesh. She tried to scream but found no air for it.

"Not yet, Annie, my girl." His voice was deep, husky, just like when he'd been inside her. He leaned down and his next words brushed over her gasping lips. "Never been suitably tempted."

When he went from the room, he left a gold coin on the table and a curse curling off of her tongue.

"Speed in all else, but with the ladies always a gentleman," drawled a man of dark locks and ale-colored eyes from the taproom chair in which Saint had left him earlier. "That, despite the drink. You put the rest of us to shame, cousin."

Saint settled into a chair but did not take up his glass. The girl's enthusiastic ministrations had not filled the icy hole in his gut. More whiskey would not either. His brother, Torquil, had always accused him of having a hollow leg, or alternately that he was so quick he could toss the contents of a glass under the table without anyone noticing.

Tor might have been right about the hollow leg. For, despite how much he'd drunk in the past two days since they crossed into the Borders—in the two months since his brother had died—he was not intoxicated.

His inestimable cousin, Dylan, Lord Michaels, however, was.

"That redheaded minx upstairs is not a barmaid," Saint said. "She is the progeny of the vicar of this village," playing a game of *How naughty can I be before Papa whips my lover with a stick?* The games women played never ceased to astonish him.

Dylan's glass arrested halfway to his mouth.

"Good God, Saint. Don't say you've docked a preacher's daughter? For an entire hour, no less! Hell's fire, he'll drag you to the altar for it."

"I daresay in this case he would account an hour or a minute all the same."

Dylan cast drink-soaked eyes at the other tavern patrons and said in a hush, "You're a duck waiting to be shot here now. D'you want to be leg shackled to a Scots jade?" He tried to stand, but wavered. "Tor would've quit this place the minute he learned the strumpet's secret."

"Come now. You did not think her a strumpet an hour ago, when you imagined her a girl of the trade."

Dylan nodded. "True. But, the modesty of a gentlewoman . . ." He waved his hand about. "Strong appetites ain't the thing for a lady. Tor could spot a strumpet from leagues away."

Saint settled more comfortably into the cushioned leather and lifted his glass. "To my brother, the smartest son of a bastard this earth has known."

"Nossir," Dylan slurred as he fell back into his chair, all danger from irate Men of the Cloth apparently forgotten. "Won't toast to that rakehell. Rather, to my cousin Saint, the finest son of a merchant this side of the Atlantic. Both sides." He swallowed the remainder of the spirits then set down the glass with a clunk, and peered at a letter on the table beside it. "Read wants a tutor for his ward," he said abruptly.

A slow heat bloomed in Saint's gut, dead center of the ice. "Read?"

"Duke. 'S got a nephew or grandson or some such. Favor to Blackwell, don't you know. Rather, no . . . Black*wood*, that is. Damn whiskey."

There was no making sense of Dylan when he was foxed. But this merited clarification.

"The Duke of Read?" Carefully, as though it were a directive from a general, Saint pinched the sheet of finely pressed paper between thumb and forefinger.

"'My uncle, presently in residence at Castle Read,'" he read aloud, and then to himself. When he finished, he looked up at his cousin. "What is this?"

"Th' reason we're here, cousin," Dylan said.

"You gave me to believe that there was a girl in Edinburgh," Saint said perhaps too languidly. "A girl you intend to court. A girl whose family would not bring her to licentious London again on account of their Puritan ways. A girl who had promised her hand to you in secret and whom you wish to marry."

Dylan sighed. "A pearl of a girl."

Saint set the letter down on the table.

"It's a *favor*," his cousin said. "Debt of honor. Played cards with Blackwood. Years ago. Lost. Emptied the coffers to pay him, but it wasn't enough. Said I'd make it up to him someday."

"Presumably you have not yet?"

"Couldn't. Can't."

Dylan's estate was entailed, his lands secure, but poorly productive; he never had money to spare. Tor had been the best of them at making gold hand over fist, because he had made it illegally.

"Blackwood said th' old duke needs a tutor for his ward." Dylan's curls wiggled over his brow. "Can't refuse."

"A tutor? How awful is this boy that a duke cannot keep an actual tutor employed? You are a baron, for God's sake, Dylan. Not a schoolteacher."

"Not sums and French. *Fencing*. Boy's got the rudiments. Needs technique. A few months, s' all. Brief stint."

Saint frowned. Sums or swordplay, this did not add up. "Dylan?"

His cousin offered him a saturnine frown. Above his lavender coat, it lent him a decidedly clownish air. "Well, he don't want *me*, of course."

Years ago, when Saint had been running between bullets on battlefields, Dylan had taken pleasure in sending him letters from country estates all over England. The young Lord Michaels, it seemed, was accounted one of the finest fencers in the land, sought after at house parties for his entertaining showmanship with a blade and his charming company. For the first time in their lives, since that day in the cane fields when Saint had picked up that old sword out of the dust, everyone thought Dylan was the best.

"He asked for you," Dylan said now.

Slowly Saint curved his fingers around the carved

wooden arms of his chair. A moment ago he had been enjoying this chair, thronelike and so ancient that it looked like it had lived in this pub since Creation. He had been enjoying the flavor of malt upon his tongue and the sweet laughter and plump thighs of Miss Annie Favor until she revealed her intention of having him scourged. He even liked the little medieval village of Duddingston despite the new threat of its vengeful vicar. He had been enjoying this entire holiday to Scotland with his cousin, upon which Dylan drank heavily to ease the grief of losing the man they had both loved, and he considered his next step in life.

Since burying his brother at sea, he had been at a standstill. He hadn't the funds to found a fencing school. Every reputable *salle* in London had made him offers, but he could never live there. This little journey to Scotland had seemed the ideal diversion until he decided what to do next.

"Why me?" His fingers played about the wooden armrest. "Why not Faucher or Accosi? They are both in England."

"Read wants an Englishman. You're better than both of them anyway. And you're my cousin, the great-great-grandson of a baron, for pity's sake," Dylan added. "A drop is enough."

Yet a drop of noble blood had not been enough six years ago. And now the Duke of Read wanted him. The irony of it would be sublime if it weren't unwelcome.

"Had you intended to tell me the truth before we actually walked into the duke's castle? Or did you plan to simply turn me over to the major-domo and hold your palm out for the commission before heading off to cards in the drawing room?"

"It ain't my choice that you won't let that blasted solicitor read Tor's will. Must've left a fortune to us, the blackguard. I wager you'll be through with teaching for life once you accept that money's yours to use as you like."

Not an option.

But he had swiftly discerned the essence of Dylan's plan. "And while I am teaching the gentlemanly arts of foil and saber to this young branch of the noble tree of Read, you will be courting the pearl-like Miss Edwards while residing in the castle of a wealthy duke."

Dylan grinned, his face to no greater advantage than when he was pleased with himself. "Ideal accommodations for launching a campaign, what?"

"And what of her father's conviction that you are a drunken, penurious Corinthian? Will that simply evaporate?"

"He likes me," Dylan mumbled. "He just don't know it yet."

"'Holiday in Scotland, cousin. Take a month or two to celebrate Tor's rakehell life.' Hm."

"Well, if I could've done it the old-fashioned way and forced his hand, I would have! But I ain't handsome enough to make the girls drop their drawers at the crook of a finger, like *some* fellows." He gestured to Saint and then rolled his eyes. "Oh, stuff and nonsense." Abruptly he brightened and tipped his glass forward. "You'll see. No better patron than a duke."

This was true. He wanted out of England. His own reputation and the patronage of a duke with foreign connections would ensure that wherever he founded a school it would be a success. To secure this exalted patronage, for a few months he must live in the last place he wished to be.

Dylan was wrong. Some girls did not drop their drawers for him at the crook of a finger. With some girls he had been too fool-besotted to even ask. Rather, with one girl. Only one girl. The girl whose house six years ago he would have given everything he had to gain entrance to. The house he had now been invited into as an employee.

This would be a good moment to be drunk.

He lifted his hand to summon the tavern keeper. "If you intend to court a lady shortly, you had best sober up."

"You'll do it? Great gun, Saint! I knew you would." The barkeep set a plate of mutton pie before Dylan. "You'll see," he said around a mouthful. "This'll be just the thing you need to set you right. By God, it'll set us both right. Tor would be proud."

If he were alive now, Tor would split his sides.

How his brother had laughed at him six years ago and called him a fool—a fool for not getting what he had wanted before he knew who she was, and a fool for making another attempt a year later. But Torquil Sterling had lived life without honor. A cheating, Machiavellian, woman-chasing slave smuggler, he had never missed an opportunity to celebrate the pleasures of life while manipulating it all to his advantage.

Saint could still hear his laughter when he'd told him about that ill-fated fortnight in Kent six years ago. Now he was gone, and with him the last person who knew.

Except her.

But she lived in London. So he told his cousin he would accept the post.

Castle Read
Home of the Duke of Read
Midlothian, Scotland

"I need a husband," Lady Constance Read declared, tumbling into the velvety interior of her father's carriage. "Immediately."

"Well, this is an abrupt change of heart," said Eliza Josephs from the opposite seat as the carriage drew away from the cloth mill.

"My heart has nothing to do with it, of course." It hadn't in years. Affection for five men Constance had aplenty: four now blissfully married, and the fifth so devoted to the secret government agency he headed that he hadn't time for anything else. She loved these men as friends, as brothers. But only one man had ever stolen her heart—a man she could not have. After that, the single time she had tried to give away her heart again, she made the greatest mistake of her life.

She was neither fortunate nor wise in love. Now affection must be enough.

"Make haste, Rory," she said to the coachman and pulled her cloak from about her as the door closed. "It will have to be the duke," she directed at her companion, tugging her hair out of its heavy coils.

"The duke who is an abductor of maidens?" Forty years Constance's senior, a widow, and an aficionado of fermented brews, Eliza tilted her frizzled head. "How adventuresome you are, dear girl."

"That is all gossip and rumor." Constance bound her hair into a tail at the nape of her neck. The countryside passed swiftly by. There were few miles from cloth mill to castle. She still had time to snatch a ride before dinner.

Eliza proffered a pile of soft velvet. "You are depending upon your memories of Loch Irvine when you were bairns."

"I am." She accepted the clothes eagerly. During her childhood at the castle she had worn skirts suited to riding astride and bodices and sleeves for shooting. Today, however, she had dressed demurely. A lady just up from London could not go ferreting out clues to a horrible mystery looking like a hoyden.

"Boys change when they become men," Eliza said darkly.

"Not *that* much." The boy she had known twenty years ago could not possibly have become a monster. "I must discover what happened to those girls."

"Gossiping with mill workers will not accomplish that." There was a *tut-tut* quality to her companion's voice.

"But it already has! A man of low appearance ordered a dozen white robes from the mill not a sennight ago, to be delivered to Sir Lorian Hughes at the house he has just let in Edinburgh." Her fingers worked at the buttons of the gown she had worn to take tea with the villagers. "A *dozen* robes, Eliza. And here is the astonishing detail: half of them were to be suitable for men, the other half for women."

Eliza's birdlike hands folded in her lap. "Sir Lorian Hughes needn't intend the robes for a devil-worshipping society at which they sacrifice maidens, child," she said primly. "He might intend to throw a masquerade."

"We shall see." She lifted her hips to tug the gown down her legs. "I must find a husband. Quickly."

"You should have remained in London. Candidates dropped from the trees when you walked through the park."

"When I left London I did not yet know I needed a husband, of course."

"I cannot believe that you actually intend to marry Loch Irvine in order to enter a secret society."

"Well, I cannot enter it *un*married."

➤ "Your devotion to subterfuge is impressive," Eliza said archly now. "I think you are enjoying this horrid mystery."

"I do not find pleasure in tragedy." A fortnight earlier she had held Cassandra Finn's mother in her arms and felt her heaving sobs against her breast, and she had recognized that grief. She had wept like that when she was fourteen and her mother disappeared. She had not been able to save her mother. But if Cassandra Finn and Maggie Poultney were still alive, she would save them. And if memories of her mother weren't sufficient, her own fresh scars would compel her to rescue innocent girls from danger at the hands of a villain who hid behind a polished veneer.

"I must remove to Edinburgh and begin investigating." Only twelve miles distant from town, Castle Read might as well be twelve thousand.

Eliza's lips pursed. "The Edinburgh police—"

"Have not done enough. I can." For five years in London she had performed her role as the reclusive Scottish duke's heiress with perfection: riding decorously, flirting subtly, gossiping cleverly, all for the sake of cozening information from others to help her fellow agents in the Falcon Club. She would do whatever she must now too, this time alone. Here, amidst rich green hills bathed in stripes of mist and sunshine, she was, after all, accustomed to solitude.

Shaking her head, Eliza assisted her into the wide skirt. "Your father expects you for tea. Dr. Shaw and Libby arrive today."

"And I am eager to see them. I promise not to be long."

Eliza lowered her chin. "You are going *there* again, aren't you?"

"Not all the way there."

"This is not wise, Constance."

"No one will see me, Eliza."

"You should have at least brought a suitable shirt. This shift is insufficient to cover your bosom. You look a fright. An heiress should not go about the countryside as you do."

Constance laughed. "It warms me, darling, that you take more care in my appearance than in my safety."

"Impertinent girl."

"And yet for all of these years you have stayed with me," she said with a grin. "There must be hope for me yet." Leaning forward, she bussed her companion on the cheek. Then she threw open the carriage door. Rory had brought them along the road directly to the stable block. But even at a distance the impressive mass of Castle Read dwarfed all else. A solid medieval keep of golden brown limestone topped with a dozen pointed turrets of gray slate and fronted by a low forecourt wall, it both beckoned and warned, "Walcome," it seemed to say, "but anly if ye be allies."

It was a heathen place. No gardeners cut the lawn. No one touched the rose vines that had gone feral about the forecourt gate. No industrious clippers tamed the ivy that snaked up the fortress's walls.

She adored it. It was solid and strong and wild all at once, and she had missed it.

The carriage continued to the forecourt where Eliza would disembark, and Constance entered the stable. Her skin was too hot, as though it had sucked all the heat within her and threw it to the surface to battle the late-winter air. But inside the stable fashioned of ancient stone, her mind quieted. At the sound of her footsteps, her horse turned its head.

"Good afternoon, Elfhame." She stroked the mare's milky brow, then saddled and bridled her.

A short canter brought her to the river and another thirty

minutes to the apex of the hill from which she could glimpse the hulking pinkish tower of Haiknayes Castle, present home of Gabriel Hume, the Duke of Loch Irvine.

The Devil's Duke.

All over the countryside, at tea tables and in shops, gossip boiled: The enigmatic Duke of Loch Irvine was the head of a secret society. A selective society to which only rich and wellborn married couples received invitations. A society dedicated to the Dark Arts. And in this society's lair somewhere in Edinburgh, the practitioners of this evil religion sacrificed maidens.

The police had yet to solve the mysteries of the disappearances in September and December of Cassandra Finn and Maggie Poultney: unwed girls of marriageable age, only Maggie's bloodied cloak discovered upon the bank of the loch near the Duke of Loch Irvine's Edinburgh residence, and marked with a six-pointed star that bore three symbols: a flame, a wave, and a mountain peak. The same unique star was carved into the lintel over the main portal of Haiknayes Castle.

Some whispered that during his years sailing the seas as captain in the Royal Navy, the mysterious Duke of Loch Irvine had become a practitioner of native magicks, a worshipper of Satan, a fiend. The villagers that Constance had spoken with at the cloth mill that morning had called him *Christsondy*: the Devil.

But she would not find answers staring at his castle. She must meet the duke again and learn the truth of it from him.

Shadows cut swaths across the hills as she walked Elfhame home. She would tell her father that she intended to move to the house in Edinburgh for the spring. After allowing her to live with only Eliza in London for years, he would not deny her.

In the stable, she gave her mare into the stable hand's care.

"They be some fine animals visitin', my leddy. I'll gladly volunteer to put that bay through his paces."

"Have Dr. Shaw and Miss Shaw arrived already, Fingal?" She whipped off her hat and gloves. "Am I that late?"

"No' the doctor, my leddy." Fingal gestured along the stable. "These belong to the gentlemen visitors."

"Gentlemen?" She moved toward the unfamiliar horses.

And her steps faltered.

The two animals in the stall did not belong to Dr. John Shaw or his daughter. Beside a pretty chestnut stood a bay with such a rich brown coat that in the shadows it looked nearly black. It was gorgeous, with long legs and a powerful neck, ears pointed forward, and intelligent eyes watching her. She recognized it. Its beauty and breeding made it unique. And she recognized its tack. Its bridle of supple leather was surmounted by a brow band imprinted with two black, crossed swords. The saddle was of finely tooled leather, with holsters for the scabbards of two swords sewn carefully onto either side so that the weapons would not disturb the animal's gait.

She knew this animal because eight months earlier she had spent three silent hours tucked into the corner of a public stable in London watching it—watching, and waiting for its master to return and claim it. When he had, he had settled into that saddle with the ease and grace of a warrior.

Cheeks hot and hands unsteady, she swept the train of her riding skirt into the crook of her arm and left the stable. The castle forecourt was empty, but two dozen windows stared down at her like eyes that seemed as shocked as her frantic pulse. She crossed the threshold and pretended not to hold her breath.

In the hall, her father's voice came down from the balustrade, quiet and firm, stone wrapped in felt.

"Castle Read was built in the early fourteenth century as a fortress, with little concern for comfort. Each of my predecessors made additions to it. There are plenty of guest rooms now. I shall have my housekeeper make up the finest for you, my lord."

"Terribly decent of you to take me in uninvited." A man's voice, light, jaunty. "I'm much obliged."

Not . . . *not him*.

Air seeped back into Constance's lungs.

Then deserted her entirely.

Upon the stairs beyond the chandelier descended two feet encased in knee-high boots the color of earth. Two legs clad in leather breeches that shaped the muscle like carved stone. Two hands, ungloved, strength apparent in the sinews. Two shoulders to which she had once clung like sunshine to a stained-glass window. And one long, steel blade upon which the remaining light of day seemed to gather.

Then his eyes—eyes that captured a hundred ancient incantations and turned them into magic, that had once thrust her world upside down. Now he turned them upon her. How the touch of a man's gaze could seize everything inside her and lock it into paralysis, she had never understood. Certainly not then. And not now.

She stared.

Behind him, her father and the other man appeared on the stairs.

"There is my daughter now. Constance, I required your presence here for tea. But I see you have been riding."

"I have been to the ridge to see Haiknayes." She hardly knew how she spoke.

"I see." Displeasure sat upon his tongue like a cockerel. "Constance, I present to you Lord Michaels and Mr. Sterling. Perhaps you and his lordship have crossed paths in London."

They had not. She had intentionally avoided him.

She curtsied. "My lord."

A dimple dented Lord Michaels's cheek as he bent at the waist. He was an attractive man, nattily dressed in a nip-waist coat and shiny Hessians, as though he weren't now in the Scottish countryside but paying morning calls in London.

"Truly delighted, my lady. I hope you don't mind that I have imposed myself on your hospitality."

"Of course not."

"Do tell us," he said, "how was your viewing of Haiknayes Castle?"

"From a distance only. Are you acquainted with it?"

"Rather, with the duke himself. In fact, I had reason to pay a call on him at the Christmas holidays only a few months ago, at Port Leith."

During the Christmas holidays Maggie Poultney had gone missing.

"Did you?" she said.

"Yes, indeed. He's a capital fellow." But his smile faded.

Then she must turn her gaze to *him*.

Hand resting on the guard of his sword, he bowed. "Good day, ma'am."

Hot brandy. The same. She had remembered it well. He had changed little. Six years ago his face had been perfect to her, the features strong and handsome. Now a slender scar ran the length of its right side, making a slash in her cheek along the line of short, neat whiskers, to his jaw.

She could not curtsy. The velvet train lodged in her elbow felt weighed in stone and her legs were foolishly unsteady. Quite acutely she felt now cool air upon the skin of her neck where she should have donned a shirt. But he did not look at her neck. He looked into her eyes, as he had all those years ago. She had never met a man before or since who looked at her like Frederick Evan Sterling did, as though he cared only for what he found in her gaze.

She dragged her attention to Lord Michaels. "What brings you to Scotland so soon again, my lord?"

"Truth be told, I am hanging on to my cousin's coattails."

"I have engaged Mr. Sterling as a fencing instructor," her father said.

"My cousin wields a dashed clever blade." Lord Michaels pointed a smile at the man Constance had spent six years not trying very hard to forget.

"But you know how to fence, Father." Every word crawled over the next with awkward haste.

"The lessons are not for me," he said without pleasure in his eyes.

"Oh." She felt foolish, her cheeks a flaming apple orchard and her tongue useless. Gone was the London belle who flirted with ease. Gone, the lady of fashion sought after by hostesses from Mayfair to Kensington. Two minutes beneath the gaze of Frederick Evan Sterling, and she was again an impetuous girl struggling to steady her frantic pulse. It didn't help that her father had not warned her of this. But he would have no reason to think she needed warning. No one but Eliza had ever known—no one except Jack, and Jack was dead.

"I see," she said. "I am sorry for your trouble, Mr. Sterling, My nephew was visiting us here, but he departed a sennight ago. Your pupil has already returned to his parents' home."

"I did not engage Mr. Sterling to teach young James," her father said. "He will teach you, Constance."

Chapter 3

The Bribe

S aint turned from the beauty whom he had not thought, hoped, or wished to ever see again to the Duke of Read. "I beg your pardon?"

But the duke's attention was still on his daughter.

"Me, Father?" she said. "But, whatever for?"

"Your interest in swords has not gone unnoticed by me, Constance."

"My *interest*?"

The duke peered down his patrician nose. "Did you imagine that each time you sent another package here from London, I simply handed them over to Mr. Davis without taking note?" With a gesture he indicated the walls of the hall in which they now stood. From floor to ceiling, weapons adorned the wood paneling, most of them sabers and smallswords, and a number of very old and fine rapiers, but also daggers, knives, bayonets, and bows, as well as other tools of war. Upon entering the castle an hour earlier and seeing this collection, Saint had finally made sense of the duke's wish to hire an expert to teach a mere boy. Clearly the duke was an enthusiast.

Apparently not only the duke.

"But, 'tis merely a collector's curiosity, Father," she said, the soft music of Scots slipping over her tongue. Years ago, that lilt had only appeared in her voice when—

When he touched her.

Now her cheeks were not pink as then, but ivory.

"I never thought of learning to use them," she said.

"Now you may," the duke said.

"I knew nothing of this," Saint said. As he had known nothing of her presence here. For five years she had lived in London exclusively, which had been sufficient reason for him to make his residence anywhere else—Bristol, Plymouth, Dover—wherever he would not encounter her by accident. He had been wise to do so. She was astonishingly beautiful now, more so than he had imagined she would someday become, with golden hair, ripe lips, and those same vibrant eyes. The softness of youth had fled from her, revealing beauty sculpted by a master.

Years ago she had fidgeted, as though she had not known how to rest in her own skin. And her eyes had been everywhere on him at once. She had looked at him then as though she stood before a banquet, famished, yet did not know how to eat. That gaze, both hungry and confused, had turned him inside out.

Now her gaze was aloof as it came to him.

"You did not?" she said.

"No." He turned to his cousin. "Did you?"

"Not I! Lord Blackwood's letter said you were to teach his grace's ward."

"I beg your pardon, Mr. Sterling," the duke said with a cool absence of sincerity. "My nephew must have misunderstood my instructions."

"Well, now that we all have the true story," Dylan said cheerily, "it sounds like a capital plan. What say you, my lady?"

"I won't do it," Saint said.

"You won't?" Her eyes snapped wide. "Do you doubt that I am able to learn the sword?"

"Yes."

"Why?" she demanded as she took a step toward him, her chin tipping upward. A stray wisp of gold falling over her brow marred the perfection, and she was breathtaking. "Do you think women incapable of skill and strength?"

"I think women capable of most anything they wish."

"But then—"

"I think *ladies* capable of skill with flirtation and strength in demanding that their wishes be met."

Her lips hardened. Even so they were beautiful and he still remembered how soft they had grown beneath his.

"Do you intend to insult me?" she said.

"If you find insult in my words, I advise you to consult your guilty conscience."

Her mouth shut abruptly. And, by God, *it pained him*— irrational, idiotic—it pained him to see her chastened, even by his own words. But this was no innocent before him now, with seeking eyes and unpracticed touch. This was a stunning woman who by all accounts made men the length of Britain slaver after her while she gave none of them satisfaction.

"If you truly wish instruction," he said, "I will write to an acquaintance of mine in London who will, I am certain, be happy to teach the martial arts to the daughter of a duke. He would consider it a coup. I would not. Shall I contact him on your behalf?"

"I already know the other martial arts. I shoot like a man with both bow and pistol. Can you believe that?"

Swiftly he inspected the set of her shoulders, her arms that were more toned than rounded, her solid stance.

She was staring at him as though he had undressed her— here, before her father and his cousin.

"Perhaps," he said.

"I am gratified by your assessment," she said like the softest cream sliding over his skin. And then she curtsied.

For the first time in months he actually wanted to smile. "Do you wrestle too? And box?"

"I have struck a man's face with my fist. Does that count?" Laughter glimmered in her eyes.

"I should think so. What did he do?"

"Before or after I struck him?"

The pleasure in Saint's chest died.

"Why not, cousin?" Dylan said. "If his lordship is for it, and Lady Constance likes the idea, I think it fitting enough, especially now that we're already here."

Dylan only thought of the bald opportunity, and he would happily prostitute anyone else to serve his desires.

Saint could not oblige him. He backed away from the woman who had, six years ago, taught him a lesson he had not wanted to learn.

"I will write to my friend in London," he said to the duke. "I apologize for the misunderstanding. I will depart immediately."

"Mr. Sterling," the duke said, "I should like your company for dinner tonight. As the sun is setting and frost is expected, travel is not advisable. You must remain the night at least."

"Yes, Mr. Sterling." Her bewitching mouth twitched. "Do remain the night."

AFTER SEEING THAT his horse had been watered and fed, and combing the tangles from Paid's mane while a barn cat peered at him from atop a stall door, Saint returned to the castle. A servant in the hall gave him a swift perusal, frowned, and snatched a brush from a brass bucket.

"Place your foot upon this, sir." He gestured impatiently toward a chair. He had small black eyes and a thin disapproval about his face.

Saint glanced at his muddy boots. "I can clean my own shoes."

"Foot on the chair, sir. Now."

He did as bidden and watched the fellow buff the leather to a shine. "I am obliged, friend. What is your name?"

"Mr. Viking." The servant straightened. "And I am not

your friend. I am only ashamed that you would enter his grace's private chambers looking like an oaf."

"His private chambers?"

"You are expected immediately. Come."

Saint followed, wondering if Scottish dukes had the power to hurl a man into a dungeon for verbally abusing their daughters. Not his finest moment. But he was no one's servant, most especially not hers.

Stairs rose up a tight, round tower, and he ducked his head to pass through the doorway to the second story and into an antechamber decorated with mammoth paintings of a hunt. Towering over his dogs and mounted upon his steed like a general, the hunter wore a crimson coat with epaulettes. The eyes of the mighty stag he pursued showed white with terror.

Viking led him into a chamber of dark brocaded burgundy, polished wood, and the scent of foreign spices— cardamom, frankincense. A half dozen dogs reclined about the floor. Comfortably lit and warm, the room boasted two chairs by a hearth and a table laid with a chessboard.

A dog rose and came to Saint, sniffing the stable on his boots and breeches. The duke did not rise. Seated before the chessboard, he studied Saint with eyes like his daughter's, brilliant blue and intelligent. A man of six decades, with a hard mouth, he had exchanged his coat for a dressing gown threaded with gold.

"Do you play, Mr. Sterling?"

"I do."

With the tips of two fingers inclined toward the opposite chair, the Duke of Read invited him to a game. Saint sat. Whether Read wished to shame him by beating him or to cajole him by letting him win mattered little. To the nobility, a game was a game.

The duke led with a knight. "I understand that you returned to the stable to see to your horse. How did you find it?"

Aha. This was the moment Read would inform him that his bed for the night had been transferred to a stall there. "Exceptional." He moved a pawn into play.

The duke took up a rook. "I have recently had the building renovated. It was high time. The block was erected in fifteen twenty-eight, more than a century after the construction of the castle itself."

Now he was meant to be awed by the family's ancient lineage. He shifted a knight across the board. "Your coachman told me that you breed horses."

"Hunters. Do you hunt?"

He allowed himself a smile. "No."

"Your horse is an extraordinarily fine animal, and still young enough to be trained to it. From whom did you purchase it?"

"It was a gift."

The duke lifted a bishop. "From a patron?"

"From a friend who believed he owed a debt of gratitude to me."

"What had you done for your friend, Mr. Sterling?"

He slid a pawn toward the duke's queen. "I taught him how to defend himself against those who wished him ill."

"I see." The duke moved his queen aside. "You were hard on my daughter earlier. You are skeptical of her potential as a student."

"I am skeptical of her application to the task."

Read's hand paused over the board. "My daughter does not tease, Mr. Sterling."

Clearly the duke did not know his daughter well. "I don't take your meaning."

"If she wishes to learn to fence, she will put her best effort toward it. She is an extraordinarily adept student with a formidable tenacity." Read now held his gaze.

"With all due respect, sir, you cannot intimidate me into accepting this post."

A serving man entered with trays of covered silver dishes and arranged them beside the chessboard. The duke dismissed him. Ignoring the food, he took up a crystal carafe.

"Wine?" He poured without waiting for Saint's response. "So you will teach her."

"I have no intention of doing so."

"Delay your departure for a day or two. A sennight. Come to know my daughter's character before making a decision."

He already knew her character as well as he could bear.

"There are other teachers."

"But none better, I understand. Nevertheless, I found your history perplexing. Why is that, Mr. Sterling?"

"I suspect you already know."

"For nearly two years you went by another name in England, your own, but not Sterling. I know the reason." The duke set his elbows on the chair arms and made a steeple of his long fingers. "I offer you my condolences on the loss of your brother."

"Thank you." Saint waited for the blow.

"I am aware of certain ventures of his that, were they to be carefully examined, might not bear the full scrutiny of the law."

"I haven't any knowledge of my brother's business."

"It seems, however, that Lord Michaels invested in several of your brother's ventures, and benefitted from those investments. It would be unfortunate if they were revealed as not entirely legitimate. That sort of thing can ruin a man. A shame. Such a pleasant young man, your cousin. But alas, the young are prone to make careless mistakes."

Saint stood up.

The duke unfolded from his chair and went across the room. A sword case rested atop a chest. Inlaid with wood fashioned in the shapes of tiny bees, the box itself was valuable: Italian, of the house of Barberini. The duke set the box on the table and opened the latch. Upon a bed of dark velvet glimmered a long, silver rapier. He withdrew it.

"Have you ever seen anything so beautiful, Mr. Sterling?"

Gleaming in the candlelight, it was lithe in design, despite the length of the blade preferred by men of centuries past.

Saint nodded. "No. But beauty is only part of a sword's allure."

The duke offered it to him. Its balance was perfect, the blade ideally weighted to the hilt. He wrapped his palm around the grip. It fit his hand as though fashioned for him.

"What do you think of it?" Read said.

"It is magnificent."

"My daughter purchased it from an Arab trader in Dover. Why she was in Dover, I haven't the least notion, except perhaps to add this to her collection. And yet I don't believe she even removed it from the case before sending it to me. With each weapon she sends, she includes the same letter: *Father, Here is a gift for you. Do with it what you will.*" Standing beside the chessboard, he reached down and absently moved a piece. "I have never been particularly clever with a blade, Mr. Sterling, but I do like to look at them. So I have put them about the house, as you have seen. But this one . . . this is special." He settled again in his chair, a king upon his throne. "I would like you to have it."

Saint returned the rapier to its case. "I am an honest man, sir. I don't care for bribes, nor for those who offer them to me."

"You refuse to address me as I think you know you ought." Read's eyes were sharp. "I don't care for that."

"It must be my French blood. Revolutionaries, all of us, you know." Saint glanced at the chessboard. "Thank you for the game." He went to the door.

"This sword is not a bribe," the duke said behind him. "It is a gift. A man would be a great fool, Mr. Sterling, to hide such a precious treasure away in a remote castle when the ideal candidate for it stands before him. I am well aware of your skill and the use you have put it to. It is impressive, to say the least."

He laughed. "I am not a girl to have my head turned by flattery, nor a child to be chastised . . . *Your Grace*," he added with a smile.

"Of course not. Still, I trust you will accept this. Putting it in good hands will go some way toward assuaging my disappointment over your refusal to instruct my daughter.

Mr. Davis," he called and the butler opened the door to the antechamber. "Convey that sword case to Mr. Sterling's room."

The man carried it past Saint and departed.

"You needn't keep it," Read said. "Only consider it, if you will."

"Good night." Saint left the room, crossed the antechamber and reached for the door handle. The panel swung open and abruptly she was before him, her cheeks flushed and lips parted. She had changed her hair and wore jewels about her bared neck now. The lamplight set them aglitter, like the candid blue of her eyes. She practically glowed.

She was an heiress, a woman of beauty and wealth and rank who had in her youth engaged in a careless flirtation with an idiotically susceptible young man. She was no grand villain. No matter that he'd spent years avoiding this moment, now he saw only the soft, quick surprise of that girl with whom he had spent one forbidden fortnight, the girl he had not for one day in six years forgotten.

Chapter 4

Unpredictable & Invincible

*H*er chin tilted up. "Did he read you a setdown?"

"For refusing to teach you?"

"For insulting me."

Saint had to smile. "Not exactly."

Her gaze slipped over his face slowly, settling upon his mouth.

"My father is . . ." Delicate nostrils flared. "Unpredictable."

"To my advantage in this instance, it seems."

"That is an impressive scar. How did you come by it?"

Unpredictable. "By the tip of a blade."

She met his regard again. "Then it seems you are not the invincible warrior my father believes you to be."

"Ah, but you mistake it. A man's invincibility is not measured by the impenetrability of his skin, rather, by the imperviousness of his heart." He bowed. "Good night."

He passed by her so close that Constance felt the brush of his sleeve against her bare arm. Then he was through the door and gone, leaving her unbalanced as he had earlier.

Impervious.

If he could claim imperviousness, so could she. Willing away her nerves, she knocked on the door to her father's rooms.

"Come," he said from within. With a glass of wine cupped in his palm, he was seated before his chessboard.

"Why have you done this, Father?"

"Mr. Sterling departed without making his next move. I would have you finish his game, but I like to see how a man plays to the end. I must await his return."

"His return? But . . . I thought he was leaving."

"I believe he intends to stay on for a few days. He cannot be comfortable departing in the middle of a game, after all."

She must know if he had told her father the truth: that they were not strangers. But she could not ask without revealing it. And now her father was playing his favorite sort of game, the sort that left her confused and frustrated.

"I should like an answer."

Finally he raised his eyes to her. "I thought it would please you."

She gripped the back of the chair his opponent had vacated. "If I wanted to learn to fence, I would have hired a fencing master in London."

"Have a seat, if you will."

"Why?"

"Because I am your father and still in command of your future."

She lowered herself into the chair. From habit, her eyes studied the arrangement of pieces. Every conversation of any significance with him had taken place over this chessboard. He was a man of quiet pursuits, and since her mother had died he had changed very little about how he lived: he remained in this castle most of the year, eschewing his houses in Edinburgh and London which his wife had disliked, and he still allowed his only child to go on in most any manner she wished with only the companionship of an elderly widow.

"I would like to remove to Edinburgh, Father. I have

instructed Davis to see to hiring servants and preparing the house. I intend to go with Eliza within the month."

"That suits my plans well," he said.

"I—I am glad to know it," she said in some surprise.

"Constance, you will marry before your birthday."

"Before my birthday? In five weeks? I—"

"Loch Irvine has made his interest clear to me, and I think him an ideal candidate. His holdings are large and productive in barley, wheat, and wool, and his mercantile activities ensure additional income."

Loch Irvine. "I—"

"Your cousin, Leam, has informed me that Alvamoor suits his family, and that he does not intend to move here when I am gone and he ascends to the dukedom. Haiknayes is close enough so that when that day arrives you can remain chatelaine of this castle on your cousin's behalf. In this way, the breeding herd needn't be sold unless you and Leam agree to it."

"But you are in good health, are you not?"

"Dr. Shaw assures me that my health is excellent."

"Then I don't understand why—"

"Loch Irvine will be in Edinburgh next month, allowing a fortnight for the two of you to become reacquainted and for the banns to be read before your birthday."

"Father." She grappled for words. Here was what she wanted, what she had hoped. "This is unexpected."

"Since Jack Doreé's death, I have allowed you virtual autonomy. In the five years since your mourning ended, you have refused offers from a number of suitors who applied to me and, as I understand it from Mrs. Josephs, directly to you as well."

"But, Ben and I—"

"I have long known that you and he never intended to wed. He suggested it to me more than once."

"He did?" This struck her painfully. She had trusted Ben never to tell anyone that they had agreed not to wed, that their extended courtship was a sham to allow them each to pursue their own interests in London. "I see," she said.

"I have not pressed you to wed because none of your suitors satisfied my wishes for you."

"The Duke of Loch Irvine does?"

"Yes. More importantly, time has run out. According to the terms of your mother's dowry, on your twenty-fifth birthday your portion from it will be folded into any marriage contract you enter into. I would prefer that this money remain in your control. If you marry after your birthday next month, along with your dowry of twenty-five thousand pounds, this money will also become your husband's."

"My *mother's* dowry?" This was news indeed. "How much money?"

"Fifty thousand pounds. Not a trifling amount."

"*Fifty* thousand pounds? But that is a fortune. Why didn't you tell me this before? Years ago?"

"After Jack's death I had no desire to see you marry in haste merely in order to collect that money."

"You wound me, Father. I would not have done so."

"Perhaps. But that concern is now moot. You must marry before your birthday. Loch Irvine will do." He stood and his dogs lifted their heads from their paws. "When he arrives in Edinburgh he will inform me. Until then, I have a number of matters to attend to here. I will advise Mrs. Josephs that she should see to your trousseau. You will marry from the house in town." He snapped his fingers and six sleek spaniels followed him through the door to his dressing room, tails wagging.

Constance stared at the chessboard, the pieces carved in the East Indies from marble. The game was advanced, with white and black perfectly matched, neither at an advantage yet. Mr. Sterling, it seemed, could hold his own against a chess master. Perhaps an impervious heart helped him with that.

She stroked a fingertip along the white knight's mane. With this set, her father had taught her to play the game, carefully instructing her how to maneuver and plan tactics and outflank. He had shown her that to gain a king a player must sometimes sacrifice other valuable pieces, and that she must always anticipate her opponent's guile. Yet, six months ago, she had not heeded those lessons. She had trusted a man she thought was a friend only to discover that he was not.

If her father knew how Walker Styles had played her for a fool, he would despise her.

She did not understand her father. She never had. She had never asked him for anything, but he had always been generous. Generous and untouchable, when she would have given every gown, horse, and London luxury for a moment of his affection.

Now he intended her to wed Gabriel Hume, the duke everyone believed to be a monster. And yet hiring a master to teach her fencing was even more surprising.

She would use it to her advantage. If the Duke of Loch Irvine was the Devil rumor claimed, her father was giving her precisely what she needed to learn to defend herself.

Invincible. Six months ago, she had been far from invincible. Now she could become so. It seemed only fitting that Frederick Evan Sterling would be her teacher, the man who had misled a naïve girl into believing that men could be trusted.

Bracing two fingertips against the corner of the board, with a single thrust of her arm, she pushed. The board jerked to the edge of the table, teetered, and fell, scattering marble and teak across the floor. She stood up and left the room.

"Lady Constance is positively stunning." Dylan was sprawled in a chair in Saint's bedchamber. On the ground floor, it was a sizeable room with arched ceilings painted white and a massive recessed fireplace that must have once been a kitchen hearth. Narrow slits cut through the thick outer wall proved the room's former utility; he could aim a rifle or crossbow directly through any one of them.

"Stunning, I say," his cousin repeated.

Stunning.

Confident. Brazen. Direct.

Breathtaking. She halted his lungs and turned his insides out with the briefest caress of her gaze. Still.

"Is she?" he mumbled.

"Good Lord, yes. Are you blind?"

He wished he were. Even so, the music of her voice would plague him to distraction.

"And what a delightful dinner companion! It's a shame the duke entrapped you. Mrs. Josephs is an amusing conversationalist too. And Dr. Shaw, Read's bosom bow, as I understand it. His daughter dined with us as well. Fifteen. Bookish. They've come for a lengthy visit. Shaw is a good enough fellow. Too taciturn for my tastes, of course. But Lady Constance ensured an entertaining evening all around. Why, she's been in Scotland for nearly two months yet knows all about what everybody's doing in London this very week."

"Gossip?"

"'Pon my word, she never uttered a salacious phrase. Mostly praise of this fellow's new high steppers and that lady's musicale. You know the sort of thing."

Dylan always spoke to him like this, as though he fluttered about from clubs to drawing rooms every day too. A man of good nature and little thought, Dylan had never entirely understood the difference between his life and his cousins'. Throughout their childhood Georges Banneret, the baron's steward in Jamaica and the man who taught them the sword, treated them all as equals. It had made a permanent mark on the baron's heir; Dylan was thoroughly egalitarian in spirit and entirely oblivious to his own actual privilege.

"Both Shaw and his daughter dote on her," Dylan continued. "The servants, too. She's a favorite here, as she's always been in London. How else would she have been able to go around for years without a wedding ring?"

Perhaps by giving everyone she encountered the intimate perusal she had offered him in the duke's antechamber, and instantly rendering them senseless too. He scraped a hand over his face, but with his eyes closed he still saw her.

"If my heart weren't already lost to a pearl," Dylan said, "I would make a play for that diamond. Read likes me. I had a tasty glass of claret with him before he sequestered you for dinner. And he's a civilized man, not a screwy Methodist like Edwards. Rich as Croesus, too. Saltpeter, of course. Come to think of it, Lady Constance's fiancé, Ben Doreé, was an East India Company man. *Is* a Company man, rather. *Was* her fiancé. He married another girl recently, elegant redhead, nothing to compare to Lady Constance, though. No girl is."

Saint didn't usually mind Dylan's ramblings. Tonight he did.

"Peculiar . . ." Dylan mused, "Doreé passing up a beautiful heiress for another girl, especially after a betrothal of years. I wonder which of them held the thing up for so long? His elder brother, Jack, perished in a tragic accident along with their father. Did you know?"

"I believe I had heard something of it." This was unendurable.

"Ben inherited it all, including Jack's bride-to-be. But I'm sure that was years ago, and he only just married that other girl in January." He tapped his fingers thoughtfully on the bowl of his glass. "They say Lady Constance was devoted to her first betrothed."

"Is that what they say?" He tugged at his neck cloth. The room was too hot. He looked to the hearth where the fire was barely embers.

Dylan scrunched up his brow. "Perhaps Ben finally decided he'd rather not play second fiddle to his dead brother for the rest of his life. I certainly wouldn't want to."

Saint stood up and went to the sword case. "You don't have a brother." He opened the case.

"It cuts me to the heart to hear you deny me so," Dylan said dramatically and came to his side. "What's this?"

"Read gave it to me."

"As payment? Good God, cousin, I didn't realize you were so expensive."

"As a gift."

Dylan took it up, running his fingertip half the length of the blade and around the tip. "This is a fine piece. Dull as a butter knife, though."

To keep a blade of this caliber in such an impotent condition was a crime.

"Tomorrow I will find a smithy and see what can be done with it."

Dylan's head came up. "You've accepted the post, after all?" He grinned. "Great g—"

"I haven't."

"Damn it, Saint." He raised the sword between them. "I would use this on you if I thought it could cut through a jelly."

"I dare you to try."

"You cur." The sword drooped downward, mimicking Dylan's posture. "She invited me to Edinburgh. But the house there isn't ready yet. Repainting and furnishing and what not. The move won't happen for some weeks, I imagine."

"She?"

"Lady Constance." He returned to the chair and slouched down into it, fondling the sword in the manner of a boy with a toy he had already tired of. "Haven't you been listening? She's the veriest darling. And she's a brilliant hostess. She'll entertain everybody who's anybody, politicians, churchmen, precisely the prosy sort of dullards Edwards likes. He couldn't possibly refuse me then."

"Lady Constance invited you to reside in her house in Edinburgh? With her?"

"And her father and Mrs. Josephs. And Dr. Shaw and Miss Shaw, I believe. She said we'll have a merry time of it." He sent a narrow frown across the room. "Don't tell me you disapprove? What, have you reformed since that preacher's daughter put one over on you the other day?"

"I have no idea of what you are accusing me."

"Never believe those jealous old biddies in London, about

that arrangement she had with Doreé. It's all nonsense. She's far too fine a woman for those sorts of games. I don't care what you've heard—"

"I have heard no gossip about her, no more than you yourself have told me."

"Then why the dark brow? What's to prevent me from taking advantage of a beautiful heiress's generous invitation to put up at her house for a bit?"

Nothing except his wish to protect Dylan from the unhappy fate she was entirely capable of offering to a man heedless enough to court it.

"When I depart tomorrow," he said, "take a room at a hotel in Edinburgh."

"I've made it clear to everybody here that I'm bound to your side. It's my dratted excuse for coming along. If you don't stay, I cannot."

"What of the Duke of Loch Irvine? You said earlier that you called on him in Edinburgh at Christmastime."

"He's up north at present," Dylan grumbled, "at his principal estate." He jolted from the chair, tossed the sword into its case, and went to the door. Pausing there, with an unusually grave face he said, "I am in love with an exceptional girl, Saint, and I want to make her mine. I don't guess you know what that feels like, or what it's like to be thwarted in it. But I'm asking you to take pity on a fellow and help me."

He went out, leaving Saint with a sword worth hundreds of pounds and an ache in his gut.

Chapter 5

A Plea

The Viscount Gray
Grosvenor Square
London, England

Dearest Colin,

Join me in my joy as I share wonderful news: I am to be wed. He is a duke and very rich, although possibly a Very Bad Man. But I am certain we will be deliriously happy together. I do hope you will attend the wedding.

Fondly,
Constance

Lady Justice
Brittle & Sons, Printers
London

*Dearest Lady (without whose attention I languish,
and without whose sweet condemnations—offered
so generously—I would barely know myself a Cretin
and instead be called, mistakenly, Man),*

*I write to you in dismay, for I have received news
of a Most Distressing Nature: The last remaining
member of my Club is to marry. When marry, how,
and to whom, I will leave to your journalistic per-
spicacity. Know only this, that in anticipation of the
event I am bereft. For upon that day when bells chime
in the church tower to announce the vows are said, I
will be left alone. The Falcon Club that was once five
will be only one in number: me.*

*And so I write to you with this plea: Do not aban-
don me as my companions have. Remain with me (in
such a manner as you have allowed this concourse
betwixt us), give me your counsel (as you are ever
eager to do) to relieve my dejection, your wisdom (im-
mense, quick, and astonishing) to calm my lonesome
fidgets, and your bosom (metaphorically, of course)
as a cushion for my cheek when I need the most simple
comfort—the comfort of knowing that I am yet in the
mind and heart of one inestimable Friend.*

*I claim this succor of you knowing that your gen-
erosity in giving it will only confirm in my breast that
Profound Admiration that I have had for you these
five years of our correspondence.*

Ever Yours,
Peregrine
Secretary, The Falcon Club

To Peregrine, at large:

My cheeks are free of tears for you. No man who deserves friends has cause to fear their loss. Moping is the privilege of the pampered classes. Boredom that you inflict upon yourself is your true enemy. I recommend that you find some useful employment worthy of a Man rather than a Mob Cap.

—Lady Justice

Chapter 6

A Lesson, of Sorts

In a blacksmith's shop not a mile from the castle, the smith examined the rapier and then produced a small stone the color of sunset. The stone was warm and fine, perfect for the sword.

"I'll take no payment for it, sir. Leddy Constance sent word that I was to aid ye with whatever ye wished. I'm happy to do a good turn for her."

Saint tucked the whetstone into his pocket and returned to the castle along a road bordering the vast wood flanking the pastures and hills of the estate. A wall ran the length of the forest, breaking to dip into the estate grounds beyond where one-time formal gardens now grew wild.

Walking Paid along a path at the tree line, he saw her.

Facing at an angle away from the wood, with the breeze pressing her skirts around her legs, which were braced slightly apart, she lifted a long bow with an arm as straight as her spine, nocked the arrow, and shot. With a thwack that sounded across the lawn, it pierced the target dead center.

Without pause, she reached for another arrow, settled it against the nocking point, drew her arm back smoothly, and let it fly. It embedded flush with the first.

A third time she fit an arrow to the bow and pulled the taut string back with the ease with which most women unfurled a fan.

"Ten pounds says you cannot split them," he called across the grass.

She swung around toward him, released the string, and a breeze brushed his cheek before the arrow sank into a tree trunk behind him.

"Goodness me," she said, lowering the bow. "I missed the target. And I so wanted a new bonnet. Ah well, I will continue practicing and then I might win that ten pounds. But will you offer the wager again?"

He pressed his mount forward. "Your aim was off just then by at least two inches."

"I thought you might like a matching set." She wore a leather hand protector and her gown was plain and fitted snugly to her upper body and arms. Tall and lithe, with ample breasts and straight shoulders, she had a beautiful form. He wondered how many men had seen her dressed like this—revealing her shape so bluntly, so decadently—and if she intended Dylan to see her now.

"Thank you, but I will pass," he said.

"But men with scars are so mysterious." She was smiling—barely.

"The more scars, the more mysterious?"

"Naturally."

"Then I prefer less mystery. And a bit less levity about it too."

She turned again toward the target, lifted the bow, and took up another arrow.

"If you cannot make light of injury, Mr. Sterling, perhaps you should pursue a different profession." She let the arrow fly. It impacted the target's outer ring.

"Lost your concentration, have you?" he said.

Swiftly she nocked another arrow and shot. The arrow joined its two mates in the bull's-eye.

"Apparently not," she said, and hoisted the bow again. "I thought you were leaving."

"Shortly."

The bowstring twanged and the arrow soared upon a wobbly trajectory to the target. It dove into the straw a hair's breadth above the other four.

"I see that your boast about shooting was justified," he said as she took up the empty quiver and walked toward the target. He urged Paid forward. "What is your range with a pistol?"

"Fifteen yards with perfect accuracy. At twenty yards, one in two."

"Then given my aversion to acquiring more scars, I am glad to have encountered you with the bow."

He reached the target before her, dismounted, and pulled the arrows from the fabric. When she approached, she accepted them and dropped them into the quiver.

"I did not actually intend to hit you." She slung the strap of the quiver over her shoulder, and turned in the direction of the stable. "If I had intended to, I would have."

"I have no doubt." Drawing his horse by the reins, he followed her, enjoying the vision of the curve of her hips and her gait that remained steady even over knobby grass. From beneath a brimmed straw hat her hair lay in a long, thick plait down her back. She carried the bow at her side like she'd been doing so since it was taller than she.

"How do you come to be such a fine shot?" he asked.

"For nineteen years I had little to do but amuse myself on this estate. Needlework, books, and the pianoforte could not fill all the hours. And I was . . . restless. When I discovered shooting, I liked it. My father's huntsman and my cousin gave me instruction." Before the stable door she pivoted to him. "Why won't you?" Color stood upon her cheeks and her lips were a lush garden of temptation, but the hat brim cast the top of her face in shadow.

"Remove your hat," he said.

"Why?"

"I want to see your eyes clearly."

"My eyes?"

"Eyes are windows onto character. If you intend to fight a man, you must first look him in the eye."

She set down the bow and untied the ribbon beneath her chin, then drew off the hat. "I am not a man, of course, and I do not intend to fight you."

"The moment you take up a sword, you invite combat." He walked toward her. Her hair was damp against her brow, wisps escaping the bindings and caressing her cheeks.

"When you shoot," he said, "you do so at a distance. There is safety in that distance. Between you and your opponent might be obstacles behind which you can hide. Or your enemy might find himself without ammunition. Arrows and bullets are finite." He dropped his horse's reins and went the remainder of the distance separating them. "When you fight a man with a blade, you haven't the advantage of remaining aloof."

Her eyes were steady upon him. "Aloof?"

"From physical contact. You can be an expert marksman with bow or firearm and never come within arm's reach of your target." He halted before her, close enough to see the dilation of her pupils, the depths of ebony within the brilliant blue. "When you fight with a sword you feel your opponent's strength and you discern his skill in your own body. You experience him not only with your eyes and ears, but also in your flesh."

She was breathing quickly but trying to hide it.

He snapped the brim of her hat from her fingers and tossed it on the ground. "Show me your hands."

This time she did so without question, turning them face up between them. No fool to show him the backs, she offered him the palms, the seat of her power. But he had long since known she was not a fool. That award went to him.

"Remove the glove."

She untied the protective leather from her left hand and let it fall beside her hat.

"What are you looking at?" she said.

"The hands of a woman who hasn't done a day's labor in her life." He met her gaze. As it widened, he moved around her and into the stable, his horse trailing him inside.

"Of course I haven't," she said.

"An hour with a sword in your hand," he said, leading Paid into a stall, "and you would not be able to feel your arm for a week, except the pain." He slipped a halter over the animal's head and released the bit from its mouth. Hanging the bridle on a peg, he turned to her.

She stood at the threshold of the stall. "I don't suppose the children you teach begin with calluses on their palms."

He went to the door. "I don't teach children."

She arched a brow. "We are particular in our students, are we?"

"We are very good at what we do and needn't take on students who do not suit us."

Bow in hand again, with the full quiver of arrows slung against her back, she blocked the stall door.

"I don't want to learn how to fence. My father's idea is foolishness." Frustration carved lines in her brow. This close her scent of winter roses was all about him, as warm and intoxicating as he remembered.

He bent his head and said quietly, "Then why are you standing in my way now?"

"I—" Her throat constricted in a jerk, rippling the fabric hugging her neck. "I would like to know how to hand fight. With a dagger."

He straightened. "A dagger?"

"You know how to use a dagger, don't you? Or a knife?"

"You want to learn how to fight like a street thief?"

"Yes."

"And you imagine I could teach that to you?"

"Couldn't you?"

"I could. But that hardly answers the question of why you wish to learn it."

"Does it matter?"

He tilted his head and seemed to study her seriously, as he had assessed her while she was shooting. His clear, dark eyes had never seemed entirely mortal to her, rather from the faery realm. Sometimes during those forbidden hours they had spent together she had imagined that with magic he could see past her words and actions, directly into her soul.

Now the touch of his gaze took her breaths away in little bunches of useless air. The pale sunshine filtering through the window at his back painted a halo around his silhouette, like an image of Saint Michael, with his hard, bellicose beauty restrained only by art.

Abruptly he stepped forward, and she jerked her shoulder back so he passed through the door without touching her.

"You need no dagger. You have sufficient weapons at your disposal already," he said as he strode away.

"I want to learn how to injure a man at close range," she said to his back.

He looked around. "And how, I wonder, do you imagine that statement will now inspire me to teach you?"

"You have seen how well I shoot, yet you doubt my application to the task."

"Your determination seems clear enough. It is the fever in your eyes when you speak of injuring another person that concerns me."

"I see. Like most men, you fear a woman's strong emotions."

"That depends on which strong emotions she is expressing." He almost looked like he would smile. He smiled easily, she remembered, more pleased with her company than anyone had ever been before. After that first night, when they met at dawn by the wood, she had made him promise not to touch her again and to not seek to discover her identity. For fourteen days he had held to his promise. But the way he had smiled at her had driven her mad with desire she barely understood at the time. Many times she had had to stop herself from closing the distance he kept between them. She had wanted his kisses far too much.

Now he crossed his arms comfortably over his chest, his stance nonchalant yet so coiled with strength that he seemed at once perfectly at ease and entirely dangerous.

"Do you have one man in particular that you wish to injure," he said, "or is your prey simply men in general?"

Her stomach twisted.

"How vastly amusing you are, sir," she said lightly. "In refusing to teach children and women, do you hope to defend your sex from injury at the hands of your inferiors?"

His sudden laughter was deep and warm. "If women are men's inferiors, the moon is made of marzipan."

She smiled. "I suppose you are right about that."

Unfolding his arms, he again turned away.

"Don't leave today." She stepped forward. "Lord Michaels and Mrs. Josephs have planned a game of charades for this evening. Dr. Shaw and his daughter as well. I would not want to disappoint them. Will you remain one more night?"

"I'm not much for games," he said.

"I noticed the chessboard after you and my father played last night." She took another step toward him. "He invited you to play to intimidate you into acquiescing."

"He is a formidable opponent. But I am not easily intimidated."

"Oh. I understand. You have now seen that I can be an apt pupil." She gestured with her bow. "But pride will not allow you to recant your refusal to him."

"Pride has nothing to do with it."

"Give me a chance, an audition, as it were. My father needn't even know. Meet me in the ballroom tomorrow at dawn before all arise. I will show you that I can apply myself to learning how to wield a dagger with cool dispassion worthy of any man."

"No, I don't think I will," he said thoughtfully. "I've met you at dawn before, and it ended poorly for me. I have no wish to repeat the experience."

Her heart tumbled over. "You admit to it?"

"It?"

"The past. Our past."

"Why not? I haven't suffered amnesia or any other un-likely fate that wipes memory clean or makes a man deny history."

"I thought you meant to pretend amnesia. Since yesterday you have behaved to me like a stranger."

"We are strangers."

This was not true. From the moment they met he had never seemed like a stranger to her. Alien in his unfamiliar mas-culinity, yes—but never a stranger. Swiftly and naturally he had taken pleasure in her company as no one else ever had. And like no other person alive, he had spoken with her like an equal. A friend. She'd gotten drunk on him, and she had believed that perhaps he had been a little drunk on her too.

"I'd thought you craven," she said.

"Merely courteous in not wishing to expose you." Hand on the hilt of his sword, with a gleam in his eyes he bowed. "My lady."

My lady. Six years ago he had thought her an upper ser-vant, perhaps a lady's maid. But he had called her his lady and promised to be her champion, her protector, her blade to wield as she wished. The moment he discovered her name, that she was a noblewoman, that she had allowed him to believe otherwise, the ardor in his eyes had died.

Now he made light of it.

"Mockery is not courteous," she said.

"True," he admitted. "How deplorably unlike a chevalier I have turned out to be." He cocked a half smile. "Despite my vow."

There was such a foolish ache in her chest that she wanted to curl her fist into it and press it away.

"It ended as I warned you it would," she said.

"Given the encouragement you offered me, I would have been one man in ten thousand to believe that warning."

"I was very clear."

"An unwise man hangs hopes on gossamer thread."

Just as then, when he had spoken to her like this, directly, honestly, she wanted to be close to him. But she was no longer a girl. She had learned about men since then. Now she needed him for one purpose.

Ignoring her spinning nerves, she went forward until she stood before him.

"Do a woman's words have no weight to you?"

His emerald eyes narrowed. "I admit myself confused."

"By?"

"I don't think you are a flirt. I don't think you intend to seduce a man, then disappoint him, not in the usual manner. It does not suit your nature. But, then, I don't understand why you do this."

"You wanted what you could not have."

"I did." He backed away. "But not this time. Forewarned is forearmed."

"Then what harm will it cause to teach me to fight with a dagger? Please. At least teach me how to hold it correctly."

For a stretched moment he only looked at her.

"What are you doing?" she finally said.

"I am reconsidering."

Reconsidering. She drummed her fingertips on the bow. "It is taking too long."

He lifted a brow. "Impatient, are we?"

"We haven't much time before we are expected at our toilette to change clothes for lunch."

"The huntswoman's leather must give way to the lady's lace," he said. "Alas."

"Alas? You would rather I wear boots in the dining room?"

"Alas that I cannot be present at your toilette."

She *must not* smile. Not so easily and swiftly.

"What about 'forewarned is forearmed'?" she said. "A moment ago you were determined not to flirt with me."

"That wasn't flirting. I really am disappointed I haven't an entre into your boudoir."

She bit back her smile as he walked away. As always, watching his body move did things to her insides, spun gravity in the wrong direction. But he was leaving.

"Where are you going?"

"Into more light." Removing his sword and placing it aside, he halted in a splash of sunshine from an open stall window. "Set down your bow, Diana, and come here."

Diana. He had called her Diana that day in the wood, the virgin goddess of the hunt who would not allow herself to be captured by any god or mortal man.

"Now?" she said. "Here?"

"If you would rather not, my horse is still saddled. I can—"

"*No.* Yes, now," she said, elation bubbling. She moved toward him. "Is this because we have spoken of the past and settled it? Bygones and such?"

"Not quite. But now I am thinking of your boudoir and something must be done about that."

The quiver slipped from her fingers, strewing arrows upon the stable floor.

"I am only a man," he said simply. "Distraction is sometimes necessary." He reached into the top of his boot and drew forth a dagger with a blade perhaps five inches in length.

She stared. "You carry daggers in your boots?"

"Just the one, and only in this pair." He approached her and took the bow from her slack hand. "Unlike the daughters of dukes, apparently, I don't find that I need quick access to a dagger on a daily basis."

Not on a daily basis.

Nightly.

He was so close she could breathe in his scent and feel the reaction to it in her body.

"What a staid life you must lead," she managed to say, watching him set aside the bow with the same grace with which he always moved. She had known spies and lords, but she had never known a man like this. Her friend Wyn Yale carried the shadows with him when he wished. Ben's subdued elegance was unmatched. And Colin Gray declared authority in his very stance. But Frederick Evan Sterling made no statement of dominance, and he had no desire for stealth. With every muscle trained to serve him, he simply moved and it was poetry, art, beauty.

"Do you see where the handle of this dagger touches my palm?" He spread his hand.

"Yes."

"Watch as I grip it." His fingers settled again into place. She mimicked the clasp with her empty hand, then spread her fingers. "Your hands are unusually toned for a gentlewoman's," he said. "Supple. Do you shoot often?"

"Every day."

"Why doesn't your skin show it?"

"My maid files away the calluses."

He looked up at her face.

"Every day?"

"I am the daughter of a duke. A gentleman does not expect to take a washerwoman's hand when he asks me to dance."

Without warning he cupped the back of her hand and rolled the dagger handle into her palm. "Take care," he said. "It is quite sharp."

Six years. For six years she had remembered the warmth of his skin, the moment when she had fled his caresses in the dark because she had been afraid of what she might do—what she might willingly give him. Now he held her and she wondered that she'd had the strength to flee.

"How sharp?" She could not command more than a whisper.

He moved away. "I use it to cut saddle leather."

"How often do you find the need to do that?"

"Not often." He folded his arms over his chest again and a smile teased the corner of his mouth. "That is why it is so sharp."

The dagger felt light in her grip, well balanced and natural to hold.

"I am surprised this is so comfortable for me. Your hands are much larger than mine."

"It's a good dagger." His voice was odd—low and somewhat hoarse.

"Now you must show me how to use it."

"You said you wished to know how to hold a dagger correctly. You are holding it correctly. Lesson over. The road awaits me."

She rolled her eyes. "Come now—"

"*Sharp*"—he took a quick step back—"blade. Do refrain from speaking with your hands when you are wielding a weapon, my lady."

My lady, said without mockery.

"There. You have just taught me a second thing," she said, readjusting her grip on the handle. "Stay for another thirty seconds and I'm sure I will learn all I must to whittle a stick, spear a fish, and skin a hare with this dagger."

"I have never speared a fish with that dagger." He moved close again. "Only a man's quadriceps."

"Really?" she exclaimed. "Is that how fencing masters spend their leisure?"

"He was poised to impale me with a bayonet. It seemed appropriate at the time."

"I daresay."

"But I have in fact used it to skin a hare."

"How did it taste?"

"It wasn't mud. So, I would say rather good."

"That was in Spain. Wasn't it?" Six years ago he had just returned from the Peninsula. She had wanted to know everything about him, and she had asked and asked.

"Yes."

Neither of them moved. They stood close and she stared at the dagger in her grip.

"Why do you carry it in your boot now?"

"So that I have it handy to teach ladies whom I encounter in stables, of course."

"You did not encounter me in this stable." She turned her face up to meet his gaze. "You followed me in here."

"It is the place one puts a horse, which I happened to have with me." Pleasure glinted in his eyes that traveled over her features.

"What else will you show me with this dagger now?"

"How to give it over safely to its owner so that neither of you get cut."

"No." She backed up. "I want to learn more."

"The 'please' seems to have gone astray. Interesting."

She smiled. "Please."

"This is a single-edged dagger. The edge is sharp, but the weapon is principally intended for stabbing rather than slicing, though it can be used for either."

"Did you slice or stab the bayonet man's leg?"

"A bit of each. You are a bloodthirsty girl, aren't you?"

"I am not a girl."

His gaze snapped to hers.

"Not any longer," she said.

"To fight like a street thief," he said, watching her face, "your movements must be swift and decisive." He took up an arrow and gripped it mid-shaft, pointing the fletching toward her. "Imagine this is a knife coming at you. Knock it away." He thrust the arrow forward and she tapped it aside with the dagger.

Both bronze brows rose. "A *knife* is coming at you and you bat at it like you would a fly?"

She tightened her grip on the handle. "Do it again."

He did so and she smacked the arrow away.

"Better," he said. "Now again, but quicker and with all of your strength. You are fighting for your life, recall."

She slapped the shaft aside. Swiftly he thrust it toward her again.

"Ten times now, without pause," he said.

With the dagger she knocked away the arrow shaft, the clacks louder and sharper each time. After ten, he paused and she flexed to relieve the tension in her shoulder.

"Feeling the burn?"

"Yes."

"Adjust your stance."

"How?"

"You are standing as though you intend to shoot. Loosen your knees and center the weight of your body over your feet. Tuck in your hips."

She felt his eyes upon her. "This is a defensive action."

"Effective if done swiftly."

"What if the assailant comes from behind?" she asked.

"There are other maneuvers to defend against that."

"What about offensive moves?"

"A good defense is the best offense." If a man is not afraid of being killed, he has less reason to kill."

Her arm halted then slowly lowered to her side. She was breathing far too swiftly for the small effort she had just put forth. The sunlight cast her eyes in an ethereal aura.

"Show me an offensive move."

She was determined, and he had seen these eyes before: in the face of a courier he had run with, before the lad had set off for what became his final mission, to the front line.

"All right."

"Wait." She set down the dagger and began gathering up her skirts between her knees.

"What are you doing?"

"Making it easier to move." Sweeping fabric back, she tucked it into the sash around her waist. The lightest stockings protected her legs from the chill air and he was staring. And as swiftly as he studied their long, lithe beauty, just as swiftly he wanted them wrapped around him.

"You have done this before," he said. "The cinched skirts."

"When I wish to ride astride and haven't dressed for it," she said as though the sudden need to ride frequently overcame her before she could reach for a sidesaddle. But perhaps it did. There was a radiant impetuosity about her here, away from the house and his cousin and her father, that reminded him of that girl six years earlier—the girl who had not been afraid to meet a stranger in a wood at dawn every day. Alone with him again now, she was a glorious mix of that girl and the heiress refined by London. And he was making a colossal mistake to remain in her presence for a minute longer.

She took up the dagger. "Now show me, please."

He showed her. Instructing her how to readjust her grip on the handle and her stance so that the power of her arm came behind the dagger fully, he tried to ignore while he illustrated the simplest slice.

"Am I aiming for the chest?" she said, practicing the cut.

"There are four principal targets: the face, hands, groin, and Achilles heel. What you choose to strike depends on where you carry your weapon. Assuming it is at your hip, what target would you choose?"

"The groin?"

"Yes. Even a shallow slice there will impair an opponent. And if severed, the femoral artery bleeds swiftly. Try that movement, slowly first."

She set her hand at her hip then slashed the dagger forward.

"Good," he said, moving behind her, studying the angle of her hips and the sweet curves of her calves. "Now, swiftly. If you are smaller and weaker than your opponent, your greatest asset is surprise. Drop your shoulder. Throw the force into your forearm."

She swung again.

"Too low," he said. "Imagine an actual person before you."

"You won't allow me to use you as a target, I suppose."

"Certainly I will, the next time I wish to be gutted like a fish." The strength in her arm was impressive, the flush upon her skin beautiful, and he was hard as iron. "Or emasculated," he muttered.

She laughed, dropped a step back against a stall door, and surprised the cat sitting there. It howled and leaped forward, and she started, stumbled, and tripped on a drape of skirt.

Saint lunged. Hand clamping over her wrist, he grabbed her about the waist, yanking her body away from the dagger.

She fought him.

Wrenching out of his hold, she pulled herself over him, her thighs clamping about his hips, her left hand jamming against the base of his windpipe. The dagger quivered in her right hand a breath from his cheek.

He clamped his hand around hers and she shouted in surprise. But her grip held tight and her eyes were wide with terror.

He could break her fingers to dislodge the weapon. If she were a man, he would not hesitate. If she were any other woman, he would not be in this position. He had dropped his guard with her—*again*.

She hung above him, hair framing her face, her eyes now clouded as he stroked his thumb from the base of her palm upward.

The pressure on his neck relaxed, and he sucked in air through his bruised windpipe. Again he stroked from her wrist across her palm and along her thumb, cajoling the wild thing she had become, and he choked back the fury rising in him. This was the response of a woman who feared an attack—who *anticipated* attack.

She was still breathing hard. Once more he caressed her hand holding the dagger, trying to loosen her grip with gentle probing.

Her eyelids fluttered, a downward tick, and her pupils seemed to lose focus. The dagger dropped to the floor and her hand slipped away from his throat. Her palms flattened on his chest.

She rocked her hips into his groin.

Lashes dropping low, her lips parted. With her hooded gaze in his, she rocked against him again.

Then again.

The sigh that issued from between her lips swept his anger away.

Dipping her head, she caught his lower lip between her teeth. Before he could seek her, she released his lip and threw her head back. Her eyes were nearly closed. With a perfectly intentional thrust, she ground into him—once—twice—her body undulating. And she sighed again.

He grasped her hips and jerked her to him. Upon a soft moan, she went with it, pushing harder. Then faster. He helped her, working her tighter against his cock, feeling her against the base and the tip and entirely. She rode him, quick breaths bursting from her, surprised at first and then desperate, punctuated with short, delirious moans.

He felt it when her release overpowered her, the loosening of her body, the shudders. She whimpered, her cries soft and thick with relief. There was pleasure in her voice, her eyes tightly shut, a pink flush suffusing her skin.

His heartbeats were a cacophony of lust and astonishment. Gulping in air, he slid his hands from her hips to her waist.

Her eyes snapped open.

For an instant she seemed disoriented. Then aware.

She clambered backward and off of him, and stumbled to her feet. Grabbing up the bow and quiver, she fled.

Chapter 7

The Condition

There was no sound in the stable for some time except the usual snufflings of horses and the rustle of barn swallows. When Saint finally drew his hands away from his face and sat up, he discovered the cat perched again where it had been when Constance startled it, now cleaning its paws.

He climbed to his feet and tried not to think of whether she had returned to the house with her skirts snared up behind her and speckled with bits of straw. He tried not to think of her at all as he sheathed the dagger in the inner pocket of his boot and batted the dust from his own clothing. He failed. He thought of her sighs and moans, the strength of her thighs, and her hands gripping his shirt, and had little success at defeating his arousal. But some discomforts must be endured. He had learned that with this very woman years ago.

The duke's daughter required a word from the duke's hired employee. But not yet. A man should not enter into battle with a chest full of anger. Instead, he saddled his horse again and set out to cool off.

"DOCTOR, YOU ARE a sharp." Lord Michaels slapped his cards onto the table and chortled. "How do you do it?"

Dr. Shaw gathered the baron's coins. "I am humbled by your praise, my lord."

"Papa does not like to boast." Libby offered a nod that was far too wise for a girl of fifteen.

"Stuff and nonsense, Miss Shaw! Lady Constance, tell this sawbones he shan't cozen me with talk of humility. If I am to lose, I prefer losing to an arrogant man. At least then I can imagine myself bested only in game rather than in character as well."

"I won't tell him any such thing, my lord." Constance lingered by the bookshelf, trailing her fingers across leather and gold bindings. Here she could partially face the door. The man she had attacked in a stable had disappeared, and despite the rain that had begun to fall with dusk, he had not returned for dinner. "Dr. Shaw is truly humble."

Dr. Shaw pocketed his winnings. "Thank you, Lady Constance."

As long as she could remember, he had been a frequent guest at the castle. With a handsome smile and a measured mind, he was just the sort of man she liked best: the sort that did not turn her inside out.

Years ago she had felt that sort of admiration for Jack Doreé, her intended from birth. With his boyish teasing and careless affection he had bruised her tender feelings any number of times when they were children. But he had never made her want to abandon everything proper and plunge into delirium. He had never made her feel any strong emotion at all—never until that morning a month before their wedding when he discovered her on a footbridge toe-to-toe with another man. Then she had felt shame deeper than Hades.

In the stable, Saint had barely touched her and the need she had taught herself to deny awoke into full, spectacular wantonness. Apparently she had in fact changed very little in six years.

"Lord Michaels, I should like to measure your cranium." Libby scribbled in a small notebook. The manner in which she bent her golden head over her task was entirely reminiscent of the Duchess of Read. With the same guinea curls and pale blue eyes, Libby exactly resembled the portrait of Constance's mother as a girl that hung in her dressing room. Yet no one ever spoke of it.

"Whatever for, Miss Shaw?" Lord Michaels said.

"I am doing a study."

"Ah, I see," he said thoughtfully, then winked at Constance. "Are you studying men's heads only?"

"Women's too." Libby dipped her pen into the inkpot. "When I was here at Christmastime I measured everybody in the castle and the village. I should like to add your measurements and Mr. Sterling's to my calculations."

"Where *is* my cousin?" Lord Michaels looked toward the door. "I could win a pony off of him tonight and recoup my losses."

"Does he lack talent in card games?"

"Rather, he lacks interest in games in general," the baron said. "Except of course swordplay. Has he agreed to your father's proposal, my lady?"

"Not to my knowledge." *Not likely.* Not after the stable.

"Terribly sorry he didn't show for dinner," he said, frowning. "Too used to coming and going as he pleases, I suppose. But he's an unpredictable fellow at best. I've been thinking, and it occurs to me that if my cousin continues in his nonsensical obstinacy, I would be delighted to show you a fencing trick or two."

"Are you also proficient with the sword?" Libby asked.

"I'm not nearly as fine a swordsman as my cousin. But no one is. Still, if Saint doesn't relent, I'll be happy to stay on for a bit and share my humble skills with you."

"If you're not very good, I don't know why she would take you up on the offer," Libby said.

"For courtesy's sake, Miss Shaw." His smile broadened and he added sotto voice, "Ladies don't like to wound a gentleman's pride, what?"

"I am for bed," Dr. Shaw said, rising. "I delivered twins before dawn this morning and am fading swiftly. Libby?"

His daughter rose too.

"I am dreadfully fatigued as well," Eliza said, abruptly rousing from a sitting slumber. "Constance, come along." She linked an arm through Constance's and they went out.

Before the tower, Constance released her. "I will say good night here, darling."

Eliza grasped her elbow. "I shall accompany you to your bedchamber."

"Thank you." She tugged away. "But I do know the way."

"Does the route you prefer require you to accidentally encounter any of your guests?"

"I have forgotten my book in the drawing room. Really, Eliza. You speak as though I could not have misbehaved in London all the many times you left me alone with men over the past five years. Why your particular concern now?"

"Because *he* is the only one you have wanted in all five of those years. Rather, six."

Constance stared at her. "I thought you had forgotten."

"You nonsensical girl. How could I have? Constance, I shall not mince words. I firmly believe that you will be better served if he leaves at once. Let us hope that then your father will turn his attention fully to your impending nuptials and forget his latest autocratic whimsy. Fencing lessons, *indeed*."

"*Now* you think I should marry the duke? Because Father demands it?"

"Of course not. But removing to town will allow you to consider other suitors. If you choose a suitable gentleman, I suspect your father will not deny your wishes. Now go to bed, child."

She watched Eliza disappear into her bedchamber then returned to the empty drawing room. Crossing to the sofa, she took up her book and heard a step behind her.

He wore the same breeches and coat from earlier, now sodden. They accented his lean frame and the breadth of his shoulders, and his damp hair was swept away from his brow as though he had run his fingers through it. She wanted to do that—run her fingers through his hair. And then all over him.

He came directly to her and she thought he meant to grab her. But he halted just shy of her, surrounding her with the familiar scent of rainy Lothians nights that she loved.

"I thought you meant to depart without speaking to me," she said.

"Earlier, in the stable, that was not well done of you." Reflecting the firelight, his eyes were jewels. "I am not an object to be used at the whim of a coquette, then abandoned as swiftly. I am a person, with wishes of my own, and I haven't a fondness for being used like a slave."

Her throat was tight. "Haven't you?"

He tilted his head, uncertain now.

"You were aroused," she said.

"I would have had to be dead to be otherwise. But how an unwed woman of your status should know such a thing—"

"Come now. I am no longer a downy girl to be transported by a longing glance alone. My father has allowed me considerable liberty."

He didn't like that; his eyes retreated. "Liberty?"

"Liberty to learn what I should not," she finished more quietly than she intended. But her tongue would not obey her entirely, nor her lips that once had learned an innocent intimacy with his.

He stepped back from her. "Forgive me, madam, but I have no right to these confidences, nor interest in them."

"And yet you began it. You must have heard the gossips' speculation about me."

"I ceased seeking news of the inestimable Lady Constance Read five years ago when I was barred from her door."

She found she could no longer look at him. "I was in mourning."

"I knew the very hour you came out of mourning. From

an impatient yet respectful distance I had anticipated that moment for a year. But I would like to know now, finally, if it was by your order or another's that I was not permitted to call upon you then. Your father? The marquess?"

"They never knew." The old shame pawed at her.

"I see." He nodded, slowly. "But the past is done with. Over. Today's adventure, however, is another story. I have no complaint with a woman taking her pleasure where she will. In truth, I am flattered." His eyes scanned her face. "But if you aim to accost a man, ask first. Or at least give him some warning. Then allow him the tender palm as well as the sharp claws."

"Claws?"

He bent his head, so close that she felt the air stir upon her skin.

"I shouldn't have minded the teeth if you had offered the lips as well," he murmured. "If I am to suffer pain, I would like to enjoy the pleasure too."

She jolted back from him, and her cheeks became ghosts, her eyes like in the stable when she had been startled.

"What have I said?" He had expected raillery from her, more taunting, brazen flirtation—not shuttered fear.

She went around him and swiftly toward the door. "I will inform my father that you will depart tomorrow morning."

Watching her walk away from him was its own unique blend of respite and torture.

"I will teach you." His throat felt strangled. "I will teach you how to fight with a dagger."

She pivoted around. "You will? Despite my claws?"

"I will." This was a mistake. Only a day in her presence and he was again putting himself at her mercy.

"Why this change?"

Because the memories of his mother's body covered in bruises would never leave him. "A woman—all women should know how to defend themselves."

Relief came into her eyes, tentative but sincere enough to clear away any doubt.

"You understand?" she said in a whisper.

"I think I do. But I have one condition."

She was silent a moment. "I suppose I should have expected this, after what I did today."

"What do you expect?"

Moving again to the door, she spoke without feeling. "If you are no slave to be used by a coquette, I am no prostitute to trade my body for your acquiescence. Good-bye, Mr. Sterling."

Good God. What had she been through?

"That isn't my condition," he said.

She turned to him.

"I am willing to teach you upon the condition that Mrs. Josephs, my cousin, or a servant be present at all times."

Her eyes widened. "A chaperone? Isn't it too late for that?"

Six years too late.

"I cannot be alone with you," he said.

"You don't trust yourself."

"I trust myself entirely. I don't trust you." He went to her because it was too difficult to remain at a distance. "You are an unpredictable, complicated woman, Constance Read. But I needn't understand you to teach you what you wish to learn."

"You disarm me," she only said.

"Beginning tomorrow, I mean to do the opposite."

"A pun now?" Her lips curved just a bit. "You aren't truly angry with me, about earlier, are you?"

"Admittedly, I am ambivalent. It was the best time I have ever had in a stable, after all."

Her cheeks were pink and the light had returned to her eyes.

"After you breakfast," he said, "meet me in the hall."

"The hall? But—"

"Here is your first lesson: a student does not ask impertinent questions of her teacher."

"Then I'm certain I meant to say yes, of course, Master

Sterling, tomorrow after breakfast in the hall. Shall I hang my head now like a chastened schoolboy?"

"Yes." He allowed himself a smile. "If you know how to."

She curtsièd, pressed her book against her midriff, and went to the door. There she paused.

"I mean to become invincible, you know," she said.

"You will." Even if it killed him.

Chapter 8

Calmness, Vigor & Judgment

*B*efore breakfast, Constance rode with Lord Michaels and tried to gently pry from him details of his visits to Edinburgh the previous autumn and at Christmastime.

"Saint's brother did business with Loch Irvine. Shipping and that sort of thing," he said with a vague wave of his hand. "Thought I'd buy into Tor's business."

"Were you able to call upon the Duke of Loch Irvine at that time?"

"Oh, well, he wasn't in town except for a few days or so. But how do you like Sir Walter's latest? I didn't know what to expect after *Ivanhoe*, I'll admit. What a tome! But that story about the monks was smashingly good, don't you agree?"

The entire conversation went frustratingly thus. By the time Libby appeared on her horse, Constance had abandoned all hope of learning anything useful from the baron this day. Returning to the castle to change her gown for her lesson, she was eager to poke at something with a sharp stick.

When she reached the hall, she knew she must be mad to have wanted this. Simply looking at him from across a room—cross-armed, leaning against the opposite door, entirely in command of himself—made her marvel that she had even dared to touch him the day before. No wonder she had lost her head.

"Good morning?" He made a show of looking about the empty hall.

"Mrs. Josephs—"

"Has arrived!" Eliza announced as she hurried in, embroidery bag in hand. "I cannot agree with this program. But as you are determined to it, I am glad that at least *someone*"—she looked pointedly at Saint—"seems to have his wits about him."

He pushed away from the wall and came forward. "Thank you for sparing your time, Mrs. Josephs."

"As though I had any choice." With a crackle of starched skirts, she seated herself in a chair set against the wall beneath a stand of crossed axes.

Constance ventured further into the room. "My companion does not want me to learn how to threaten her with a weapon at close range."

"After my near encounter with a blade in your hand yesterday," he said, "I don't think I blame her."

"Good morning." Libby stood in the doorway, her hair tied in a hasty knot. "What are you all doing?"

"Constance is taking instruction in fencing from Mr. Sterling. Sit here beside me, child."

Libby obeyed. "I thought you dead set against it, Mr. Sterling. Lord Michaels even offered to teach Constance in your stead."

"Mr. Sterling has relented." Constance made herself walk to him. "Have you insisted we meet here so that I will be awed by this array of weaponry?"

"We are here because you must choose your sword."

Sword? "But—"

"I don't particularly like your father," he said quietly to her. "But he has hired me to teach you how to fence."

"He will not know if you do not."

"But I will." He allowed that to sit for a moment. "After you have learned the fundamentals of fencing, if you still wish to learn the use of a dagger, I will instruct you in it before I depart."

She glanced at the walls. "Shouldn't I learn with a wooden sword first? For practice?"

"No need to dally with toys when we are both eager for haste. I will blunt the tips, in any case. Which of these will it be?"

"Among them all?"

"The saber is a cut-and-thrust instrument. We will leave it aside for the time being—"

"Since I have no plans to fence from horseback."

"Or to join the army, presumably. Unless that is in fact your ultimate object?"

"Not currently. One never really knows, though." She felt ridiculously buoyant. But speaking with him like this had always made her feel this lightness inside.

"Choose from the swords with straight blades and hilts like this." He touched a sword attached to the wall. "This is a smallsword."

"A gentleman's weapon?"

"Yes," he said with a slight smile. "I haven't the expertise to teach you the Highland Claymore, and frankly you haven't the heft for it."

"Really?"

His gaze slowly scanned her body and she felt flush from her toes to her teeth.

"Perhaps a longsword," he said, decided huskiness in his voice.

Across the room, Eliza cleared her throat.

"I meant, haven't you expertise with a Claymore?" Constance managed to say.

"A man cannot be an expert at everything."

"Said without any sincerity whatsoever. You do know how to wield a Claymore."

"A bit." His gaze dipped to her lips. "But there is nothing on earth that will entice me to place a weapon of that blunt power in your hands."

Eliza cleared her throat louder. "I have eyes, sirrah."

"Eyes that wield a dagger superbly, it seems," he said to Constance, with a smile.

"And *ears*," Eliza shouted.

"What are you sewing, Mrs. Josephs?" he called across the room. "Manacles suitable for a man's wrists, perhaps?"

"If it suits the man."

He laughed. "Your companion hasn't any idea that I am not the party she should be concerned about here, has she?"

Constance's throat was dry. "You are no gentleman."

"I don't recall ever claiming that I was. But then, you are not much of a lady, are you?"

"I thought we settled that last night."

"I am still listening!" Eliza cried.

"So am I," Libby said with a little frown. "But I don't understand the half of what you are saying. It is as if you are speaking in code. Are you a spy, Mr. Sterling? Are *you*, Constance?"

"I am not, Miss Shaw, but I cannot speak for Lady Constance." His gaze remained firmly in hers. "We did settle it," he said in his hot brandy voice. "But I like seeing you blush."

"Woe to you, sir, for the day your instruction takes root and I employ my new skill in silencing your tongue."

It was the wrong thing to say. The easy amusement in his eyes became, in an instant, heat. And the desire in her responded.

"Haven't you swords that you typically use to teach?" she said in a voice like the bleat of a new lamb.

"I do. But as you are not a typical student, I am allowing you this choice."

"Are you treating me as an eccentric?"

"An unwed duke's daughter of twenty-four years taking up fencing? Of course not." He gestured to the walls covered with weapons. "You bought them. You choose."

She chose her favorite, a slender blade with a hilt fashioned of gold and silver and formed into the shapes of wings on either side.

"Wise choice." He detached it from the wall and gave it to her. It was much heavier than she expected, but the handle was comfortable in her palm.

"Pinch the grip between your thumb and forefinger," he said.

"That was a test, wasn't it?" She watched his face as she adjusted her fingers. "You wanted to see if I would choose a sword suitable to me."

"I did."

"Did I pass it?"

"You have chosen an épée. Favored by the French. It is a man's weapon." He gestured to another sword. "It is heavier than a foil, which is more appropriate for a woman to wield."

"Are you saying that I cannot manage this sword?"

"No. You have both height and strength. And you want to fight. You are unusual for a woman."

"The desire to fight is not unusual for a woman."

"The desire to use your body aggressively, however, is." He smiled slightly, privately. Inside her, something shifted, tightened, and tumbled over itself in a mess of confusion. How he could do this—be so direct, tease, and yet play no games—she did not understand. She had never known a man who did not keep secrets or pretend to be what he was not. And she had never fallen apart from any other man's smile.

"Teach me," she said, and hardly knew whether she wanted him to teach her how to fence or how to be honest.

ELIZA'S USUAL HABIT after breakfast each day was to nap in the parlor. This daily nap did not require a chair; the cushioned bench at the edge of the ballroom to which they had all moved seemed to suit her just as well. Not an hour into Constance's lesson, soft snores sounded across the floor, mingling with the patter of raindrops on windows. Libby had long since gone off in search of Dr. Shaw and Lord Michaels, and Constance had not seen her father since before dinner the previous night.

They were alone.

He said nothing of this flaw in his condition for teaching her. His focus seemed entirely on instructing her how to stand, hold her sword, and extend her arm so that the tip of her sword hit a padded wooden mannequin where he directed. Her focus might have been on these things too if she weren't distracted by the evident strength in every movement he made.

"I admit that this is more difficult than I anticipated. And tiring," she said after some time practicing the simple arm extension that he demonstrated with such ease—and missing the target on the mannequin nearly every time. Each time he grasped her blade to readjust her position, it made her nerves jerk.

"If it were easy, everyone would do it," he said.

"Will you now insult me further?"

"Would you like that?"

"Excessively."

"Then I will not."

"You are unobliging."

"And you are leaving your arm and hand open to attack. When fighting with a dagger or knife, any vital region might be the target. But in this your opponent will seek first to disable your sword arm." He moved to face her, switching the sword into his left hand. "Look at the angle of my blade in *en garde*, the position of my hand and arm and how the guard protects them from your blade. Study them."

Men had begged her to stare into their eyes as they declared their devotion. They had entreated her to admire their horses, phaetons, dogs, estates, and occasionally even their drawings and paintings. No man had ever told her to study his body.

"Do you have a picture of it now?" he said.

She could only nod.

"Now, imagine that you stand before a mirror and that I am your reflection. Follow my movements." He extended his sword arm, and she mimicked him.

His blade tapped hers back into place.

"Wasn't that right?"

"No. Again."

Her fingers and wrist ached. She repeated the extension. Again he readjusted her position with his blade, then his hand.

"Again."

Watching him so closely and ignoring what it did to her insides made her tongue sharp. "You move too swiftly."

"This is not swift."

"It is to *me*."

Eliza's snore jolted, then subsided into a regular pattern anew.

"A swordsman's calm is his greatest asset," he said. "Anger, frustration, even fear will make you clumsy, hasty, and careless. Whatever your opponent's skill, if you meet his attack with calmness, vigor and judgment, you are more likely to win."

She pulled a long breath between her teeth. "I shall keep that in mind."

"Mimic my movements. Imagine it just as when you were a child and you played the mirror game with other children."

"I never played a mirror game with other children."

"No?"

"No."

"Ah," he said. "Your parents imagined you too good for the local urchins."

"No. My mother did not like other people in our house. She was . . . ill."

"Your cousins, then?"

"They lived at a distance."

He seemed to consider his next words. "Your former betrothed? Both of them? You told me once that you spent every holiday of your childhood at their estate."

"They did not play with me. They ran away from me." She tried to smile, but it slipped. "I was not betrothed to the present marquess."

He went still. "Never?"

She shook her head.

"And you had no playmates as a child?"

"I had my horse. Now may we continue with the lesson?"

He said nothing, and then after a moment: "Watch, and do what I do." He switched the blade to his right hand.

"Just now," she said, "you used your left hand as easily as your right. Are you ambidextrous?"

"Not naturally. My master insisted that I become proficient with my left hand as well as my right."

"How?"

"He instructed me to use only the left—at all times—fencing, eating, writing. Each time I accidentally favored the right, he struck it with a switch made of sugarcane."

"Motivation, indeed. How long before you became proficient enough with your left hand so that he ceased the punishment?"

"Three hundred and fifty-one days."

The urge to seize his right hand and press her lips to it was too strong.

"That is barbaric," she said.

"Rather, civilized. I was born the son of a merchant of little character and empty pockets. My teacher wished to make me a gentleman. He told me to learn how to use my left hand as well as my right in the event that I should ever lose the use of my right hand. So I set for myself the goal of one year. I considered those fourteen days short of a year a victory." He took the sword into his left hand and flourished it. "I am still more accurate with the right hand, and quicker.

But my teacher was wise. He knew a man is only weak when he allows himself to be unprepared."

"Invincible," she said. "You seem to have learned that lesson well."

"Well enough. We are finished for today." He withdrew the épée from her hand.

"Will you disappear now as you did yesterday, not to be seen again until midnight?"

"Yesterday I had good cause to disappear." His gaze seemed to drink her features one by one. "Even if I did do the same today, it should not matter to you."

"As my father's hostess, it is my business to see to the comfort of his guests."

"I am not a guest. I am a servant in this house, paid according to my service to your father's wishes. Beyond this sword we have nothing more to say to each other now than we did six years ago, had I known it then."

"Your words say one thing and everything else about you says another. One moment you are the teacher and the next you are . . . *this*, standing closer to me than you should, looking at my mouth as though you intend to kiss me."

"In the competition for inconsistency, I have here a worthy challenger. One moment you are the woman in that stable yesterday, and the next moment the girl who had not yet been kissed," he said roughly. "I hardly know what to make of you."

"Perhaps you needn't make anything of me. Perhaps that is an impossible task."

"What do you want, Constance?"

She wanted to reach up and stroke the scar that grazed his cheek, to feel it beneath her fingertips and to learn how he had received it. She wanted to feel him.

"I want a husband," she said.

Chapter 9

The Terms Change

*T*he rain on the windowpanes, Eliza's snores, and Constance's tight breaths filled the silence.

"I must marry within the month," she said. "It is imperative."

He studied her eyes, then her cheeks and again her lips, the perusal at once intimate and questioning.

"And you tell me this now," he said slowly, "so that I will teach you how to force an offer from your chosen suitor at dagger point?"

A smile pulled at her lips. "You imagine that I could not secure a fiancé otherwise?"

"I would think that depends entirely on the man you have in mind."

"Ah. Here you are." Her father's voice carried from the doorway. "You have accepted my offer after all, Mr. Sterling. My daughter is persuasive, is she not?"

Saint stepped away from her. "She is."

"Mrs. Josephs?" her father said.

Eliza's eyes popped open like a bird's, abruptly alert. "Your Grace?"

"The Duke of Loch Irvine has sent word that he is in residence in Edinburgh. We will advance our departure by a sennight."

"Good heavens." Eliza went to him in nippy strides. "You expect miracles of me!"

"I cannot fathom, madam, how preparing my daughter for her wedding should cause you distress when that has been your sole task the past five years."

Constance's gaze shot to Saint. He was looking at her father, his face impassive.

"There are gowns to be fitted and arrangements to be made," Eliza said, "and—"

"Make it so. We will depart in a sennight. Mr. Sterling, you will accompany us to town, and Lord Michaels as well, I trust." Without awaiting a reply, he disappeared through the doorway.

"Your Grace." Eliza hurried after him. "You must understand that there simply is not sufficient—" Her words were lost upon the stairs.

Saint moved to the sword rack. His stance was easy now, the tension gone, only the waiting, vigilant grace now in his limbs and shoulders that made her breaths seem to come from somewhere in the soles of her feet.

"What sort of sportsman is the Duke of Loch Irvine?" he said.

"I don't know. Why do you ask?"

"A duke must be well enough occupied with the concerns of his estates that he has little time to spare for amusements," he said as he came toward her again. "Or perhaps such a man has so many minions doing his bidding that his days are in fact filled with amusements."

"What are you saying?"

He touched her chin with his fingertips and all the air collected in her throat.

"You have the husband you want, it seems." He spoke quietly and not quite steadily.

"Not yet," she whispered.

"Perhaps after you are wed he could see to your education in swords and daggers. Then I might be free to depart."

"You don't want to depart. If you did, you would already have gone. What holds you here?"

He looked into her eyes as though her thoughts were penned upon the irises and woven through her lashes. "Not this game you play."

"I play no game. I have told you the truth. I wish to learn how to wield a dagger."

A dart appeared between his brows. "To use against Loch Irvine?"

"If necessary."

His thumb stroked her jaw and the warmth of full summer went through her.

"You could refuse his offer," he said. "It would be simpler than stabbing him in his sleep at night."

"I daresay."

He released her, ran his hand over the back of his neck, and looked about the ballroom. "Where is that damn chaperone?"

"We are alone. And you touched me. You have broken your own rule."

"I did notice that."

"Are you so easily swayed from your convictions, then?"

"I am, it seems, when in the presence of your lips."

She couldn't help smiling. "Just my lips?"

"The rest of you too. But the lips are the greatest challenge at this time."

"Shall I wear a veil over the lower half of my face like women of the East do?"

"That would probably help." His eyes were mystically bright. "I will remain here. I will go to Edinburgh with my cousin in your party. I will teach you. But my terms have changed."

"Changed? How?"

His big hand surrounded the back of her neck, his fingers spreading into her hair and forcing her face to turn upward. Their lips were a breath apart.

"If you tease, if you flirt, if you come too close or touch me," he said, the heat of his words upon her skin, "I will take what I want."

"What do you want?" she said with little breath.

"I want your lips. I want the rest of you as well, beneath me, welcoming me." His fingertips stroked the nape of her neck, releasing hot remembrance deep inside her. "And this time I will not be hesitant about seizing it."

"Won't you?"

"Not a moment's hesitation. But know this: Whatever happens before you are wed, the moment you say your vows, I will be gone. You will never see me again."

Never.

"Are we clear on these terms?" he said.

"Yes."

His hand fell but he did not move away.

"Tomorrow," he said, "come here prepared to work. I will make you ready to stab your husband through the heart on your wedding night, if you wish." With exaggerated formality, he bowed. "Good day."

She watched him leave, her heart and stomach a twisted mess of pleasure and pain.

EACH MORNING HE met her in the ballroom, always accompanied by Lord Michaels, sometimes Libby and Dr. Shaw, and often Eliza, and he taught her the use of the sword.

From his post at the side of the room, the baron called out encouragement and cheerful praise. But the fencing master's only words to her were instructions: the hand must move in this direction, the feet in that, the tip of the blade there, the hips tilted thus, the elbow there, the eyes not fixed on her target but everywhere at once. Sometimes he remained at a distance as she performed the endless repetitions he demanded, correcting her frequently, and watching carefully with his gaze that could see beneath her skin. When he did touch her, to correct her hand or blade, it was swift and mechanical.

He donned a padded coat and mask and taught her how

to maneuver around his blade to hit him. He stood still for these demonstrations, like the wooden training mannequin, except for his sword, which she attempted to knock aside again and again without any satisfaction. And still it was a challenge to actually connect the tip of her sword with his body.

"Concentrate," he said again. "You have lost your focus."

Her focus was on him too closely, on the hard line of his jaw and the firm set of his mouth.

"Fencing is a conversation with swords," he said. "Your attention does not drift away in the midst of tea table chatter. It should not here."

She parried and did not respond. She wanted to tease him. To flirt with him. Especially she wanted to laugh with him. Laughing with him had always been as natural as breathing. But his threat sealed her lips.

After their lessons each day he disappeared from the castle. With obvious affection, Lord Michaels said that since the war his cousin preferred solitude.

"Too many horrid cramped quarters in muddy tents, I daresay," the baron commented with a chuckle that made Libby frown, Dr. Shaw nod, and Constance lose her appetite. When she had first met Saint, he told her how the simple scents of civilization—beeswax candles, fresh water, and her perfume—were like heaven.

At night, exhausted in every muscle, she fell onto her bed upon her back, ran her hands over her sore body, and tried not to think of him. Thinking of him made her ache in places she should not ache. Six years had changed nothing. He was still forbidden to her. Only now it was by his own choice.

Chapter 10

A Pink Parasol

The Duke of Read's house in Edinburgh smelled of fresh paint, wood varnish, and the bouquets of spring flowers that adorned tables throughout. Elegant and classically austere on the exterior, it commanded an enviable position at the center of a row of homes perched upon the long ridge across the valley from the cramped medieval city. Gorgeously appointed within and newly refurbished in haste, the house bespoke wealth and luxury and a hint of London style.

Her father loathed it. Upon entering, he gave the renovations a swift perusal, then immediately went off to his club. Miserable in every bone and muscle from a week of demanding lessons followed by hours in the carriage, Constance took dinner in her bedchamber and fell into sleep.

As she entered the dining room the following morning, Dr. Shaw greeted her.

"What a remarkable improvement you have had made to this house since your return to Scotland, Constance," he said as she took a cup of tea.

"Thank you." She sipped, unable to sit or eat. Soon she

would recommence her investigation into the disappearances of Cassandra Finn and Maggie Poultney. She would pay calls on Edinburgh's most avid gossips and the police inspector heading the investigation, and await her meeting with the Duke of Loch Irvine.

But the true cause of her twisted stomach now appeared in the doorway to the dining room as comfortably as if he had been born in a duke's house, watching her now with a predatory air. A pink lace parasol was propped against one broad shoulder.

"You mustn't mind that your father does not like the place, child," Eliza said. "His memories of it are all of your mother. Like you, she was far too beautiful. Men do not like to be thwarted by beautiful women."

"Too true, Mrs. Josephs," Saint said, his gaze never leaving Constance. "I see that town hours have made you indolent already, my lady. It is past time to begin your lesson today. Will you thwart me this morning, and eschew instruction in favor of the enticements of the city?"

"And raise my instructor's ire?" she said. "Certainly not." She went to the door.

He shifted only enough for her to pass by and said quietly, "It is not my ire that you raise every day."

She ignored the heat that bathed her face. There was nothing to be done about it. No one had ever spoken to her like this, so bluntly, so plainly expressing his desire for her. Men flirted, courted, requested dances, rides in the park, strolls. They escorted her to picnics, balls, supper parties, even to the races. They praised her eyes, her gowns, her horse, her parties, her skill on the pianoforte. They wrote poetry to her, sent posies, flattered Eliza in hopes of gaining an ally, went to their knees with offers of marriage, and promised her undying adoration.

Only this man told her directly and honestly that he desired her. He had told her this from the beginning, giving a name to the intensity of heat and yearning she had felt as she stared at him from her hidden place in the ballroom at

Fellsbourne. He told her, kissed her, welcomed the wanton in her. Then he had showed her how a man driven by desire needn't be controlled by it.

Now he followed her across the foyer and to the back of the house.

"How is it that the ballroom in this house is more spacious than that at the castle?"

"This house was built for entertaining." She paused at the door to the ballroom. The expanse of oaken floor shone with polish, and tall windows along one side shed spring morning light upon the white walls. "The ballroom at the castle was an afterthought."

"Medieval lairds preferred chain mail to silk knee breeches?"

She turned to him. "And swords to dance cards. Like you, I suppose."

"You haven't seen me dance." In his eyes was simple pleasure she had not seen for a week. It carved out a haven of pleasure inside her too.

"At all of those balls we have both attended," she murmured.

"Did you miss me at those balls? Each time a paunchy fellow in collars up to his ears requested your hand for the quadrille, did you sigh and think, 'How I wish that handsome soldier sought me now instead of this uninteresting fop. I wonder where that soldier is? I wonder if I will ever have the opportunity to dance with him after all?'"

"Yes." *Yes.* "At every ball."

His smile was slow.

She glanced at the parasol. "Are you intending to take a stroll? I'm not certain that particular shade of lace suits your waistcoat. But I don't suppose anybody here will mind it, especially if you avoid the most fashionable promenades."

From the handle of the parasol, he drew a thin, gleaming blade.

"This is a sword stick." Slowly he slid it back into the handle. "It fastens here and requires only the simultaneous depression of fingertip and thumb to release it. Take care in doing so. Like a smallsword, it is a thrusting weapon, but the blade is not dull." He demonstrated the release and then the catch that secured it in place inside the handle.

"I think I have never felt quite so lightheaded watching a man wield a parasol before."

A smile hovered about his perfect lips. "Have you ever seen a man wield a parasol?"

"If I have, this has blotted out all other memories of it."

"Flatterer." He offered it to her. "That was flirting, by the way. Do you even know when you're doing it?"

"I have exhibited great discipline for many days." She took the parasol into her hands and put her fingers to the clasp. "At present, however, I am overcome by awe of this remarkable device. And your abruptly high spirits have distracted me. My vigilance slipped."

"Bad habits die hard, hm?"

"You are the only man I know who considers mild flirting a bad habit." She explored the fastening mechanism. It was nearly indiscernible. "This is *my* parasol," she said in surprise. "Eliza gave it to me for my birthday last year."

"I requested it of her."

"Why did neither of you tell me?"

"I have never made a sword stick of a parasol. I didn't know if I would do so successfully."

"It seems you have succeeded splendidly."

"I had help. A bladesmith in the old town."

"I wonder what he thought you wanted with such a thing?"

"He did not ask." He crossed his arms. "But I don't recall him becoming lightheaded when I wielded it."

She squeezed her thumb and forefinger together on either side, and the blade snapped free silently. "This is truly wonderful."

He seemed to be watching her, both her face and her hands.

"Grip it as I showed you how to grip the dagger, with

your thumb toward the blade. But perhaps succeeding events wiped that detail of that day from your memory."

"You wish to make me uncomfortable, don't you?"

"No. I wish to reinspire you."

Her tongue went abruptly dry. "All week at the castle you were aloof."

"Rumor below stairs has it that your ducal suitor is soon to make an entrance. The time for opportunity grows short."

She turned her eyes up to him. "I flirted with you only moments ago. I broke your rule."

He bent his head and said by her ear. "You did not realize you were doing so. It does not count."

She laughed and felt full of stars. "So, I must flirt, tease, or touch you intentionally?"

"I count on it." He gestured her into the ballroom.

She went but her nerves were awhirl. If she touched him, he would kiss her. He would wrap his big hands around her hips again and draw her close, and *kiss her.*

He was looking at her hands. "Have you ever wielded a Scottish dirk?"

"Never." She loosened her fists. "I purchased several. My father put them on the walls."

"I saw them. Using a blade of this length requires similar maneuvers to a smallsword, but as with a dagger the hand is unprotected by a guard, so lengthy engagement is unwise, especially for a novice." He held out his hand and she passed the blade to him. He returned it to the parasol handle and set it down. "For now, we will put this aside—"

"But—"

"And continue with the épée until you have perfected your parries."

"When might that be?"

"Anytime before you wed, my lady." His voice was steady but low.

"You taunt me with what I cannot have." She nodded at the parasol.

"Turnabout is fair play." He seemed to draw a deep

breath, and peered over her shoulder. "Now where is your chaperone?"

"I am here!" Lord Michaels called as he hurried in, coffee in one hand and muffin in the other. "Miss Shaw will be along shortly. She is determined to regale me with her latest examination of the human brain. It seems we men have smaller brains than you women, Lady Constance. Not much of surprise, is it? My cousin's requirement that I sit here each day is proof of it."

"He wishes to protect my virtue," she said so primly that Saint nearly laughed. But there was some trouble in her face that he did not like.

"By setting *me* as watchdog?" Dylan cracked a laugh. "Why, if you'd been with us the night—"

"We will spend another day practicing parries." Saint moved to the sword rack. "After that I will teach you an attack to the groin."

"You see, my lord," she said, turning a smile upon his cousin that had everything of dissembling in it, "he intends to make of me a true menace to the male population of Scotland."

"England and Wales too."

Dylan rolled his eyes. "Why a woman can't be satisfied with menacing poor, unsuspecting fellows with her beauty alone, I will never understand."

"Swords never fade, Lord Michaels. I believe Mr. Sterling interrupted you a moment ago. Do tell me about that night—"

"Good day, everybody." Libby came into the room with her sketching notebook.

"Good day, Miss Shaw," the baron exclaimed. "I am all eager curiosity to hear about the inferiority of the masculine brain." He winked at Constance.

She took up her sword. "*En garde— Oh.*" She straightened. "I have torn my hem again." She tugged at her skirt by the knee and a portion of it draped over her foot. "This is the third already. I will run through gowns before I am perfect at parries."

He set the tip of his blade to the floor. "Is this an excuse to shirk your lesson?"

"I have no wish to shirk my lessons. They are my favorite part of every day."

For a moment he could say nothing. "I give you leave to go off and change your gown now."

"Too much of the morning is already advanced, and I have calls to pay later. Today I will train in torn muslin and tomorrow I will seek a solution to stepping on my hems." She offered him a smile with her eyes. "I am not so easily defeated, Mr. Sterling."

Because he had to, he said, "Nor am I, my lady."

Chapter 11

The Ensnared

Lady Justice
Brittle & Sons, Printers

Dearest Lady,

I will make my case more plainly to you: I have lost my friends. Each of them, one at a time, has fallen into Hymen's choking snare, and I mourn for them as well as for my loss of them. For marriage—as you, a lady of Violent Independence, must agree—is but a prison to subjugate both body and will to the whims of another. Woe to the ensnared whose betrothed in courtship is all charm, laughter and generosity of spirit, but who after the vows are exchanged is revealed to be capricious, vain, and greedy for attention.

We all know, of course, that this is more common than not.

*With great respect,
Peregrine
Secretary, The Falcon Club*

To Peregrine, at large:

You have lost your senses, even those few that you might have previously possessed. That said, at long last I find myself in agreement with you on one matter: marriage is a prison. But not for men. The Law does not bind husbands, rather, wives. Even the sacred vows instruct a woman to love, cherish and obey while a man must only love and cherish. Why must a wife promise to obey when a husband must not?

Therefore, as ever, I am unimpressed with your woe.

—Lady Justice

Chapter 12

The Rules, Broken

$\mathcal{T}$he following day, Constance awoke to daybreak and dressed quietly, then went on stockinged feet to the ballroom. According to Mr. Viking, the footman who had come with them from the castle and knew everybody's business, Saint greeted each day in the ballroom and remained there until her lesson. This morning she had good reason to find him early, and not to alert Eliza or Lord Michaels.

On the ground floor she could hear the clink of pans and the rumble of hushed conversation in the kitchen below, where the servants were already at work. Today she would instruct Cook to bake poppyseed cakes, favorites of the ladies she had called on yesterday afternoon, whom she expected would return the visit soon. None of them had spoken openly about the disappearances of the two girls. But when news of the Duke of Loch Irvine's arrival in Edinburgh entered conversation, sideways glances abounded.

She had navigated the treacherous currents of London gossip for five years, learning tidbits of information that helped her fellow Falcon Club agents solve mysteries. Someone in Edinburgh must know more than they were saying as yet. She would encourage gossip and pretend to confide and bide her time, and she would solve this mystery.

Opening the door to the ballroom with a silent turn of the handle, she peeked inside.

In the dim light of dawn that carpeted the ballroom floor, he moved with a grace at once poetic and powerful. He wore only breeches and his skin gleamed with moisture. Shadows and light shifted upon him with each twist of muscle, each thrust and advance, each moment of stillness that became action. The sword in his hand caught the morning upon its steel and, in a dance of violence and beauty he transformed the dawn into tiny, glittering miracles.

"Enough now, Viking," he called across the room. "You cannot require more than five minutes of rest. You are barely forty."

The footman arose from shadows in the corner of the room. Dragging a foil at his side, he went to the sword master. He wore a padded coat, mask, and gloves.

"While your taunting provides me with a chuckle, sir," the footman said without any evidence of amusement, "I am not a sportsman like yourself and haven't the stamina required to rise before dawn in order to be a target for an expert."

Saint laughed. "No excuses, man. As I recall, you volunteered for this."

"Only because I wearied of scrubbing the mud from your boots after every extended walkabout. This method of expending your energy seemed preferable." He sighed and wiped his brow with a kerchief. "But it seems that you are indefatigable."

Saint folded his weapon beneath his arm and bowed. "Your fortitude does you justice, Viking. But I would not trouble you if you weren't such a damned fine sparring partner. You keep me on my toes."

"And yet you do not wear mask or jacket while we spar,"

the footman said skeptically.

"I fight better when in danger. You should try it."

"You might practice with Lord Michaels. I understand he is a remarkably good swordsman."

"Whose mornings begin no earlier than ten o'clock, on his good days. Who taught you how to fence?"

"My former employer, Professor Oliver Highbottom, emeritus master of classical archeology. Until he passed away several months ago, I was his sole companion and he demanded it of me for years before he grew too feeble for it. Who taught *you* to fence?"

"The murderous husbands of women I bedded, of course. A man learns swiftly by example when he is bleeding," he said with a slash of a grin.

"You, sir, are a scoundrel. I cannot fathom why His Grace welcomed you into his house."

"That makes two of us. Now, villain, *en garde*."

Mr. Viking lifted his sword and they saluted each other. Then steel met steel, the sound carrying across the room with clinks and the footman's occasional gasps, while the maestro called the touches.

Constance watched, peculiarly, wonderfully hot. She had heard his skill praised, and during their lessons he demonstrated maneuvers for her to learn. But she had never seen him fight—not like this, not an actual opponent, even in practice. His did so with confidence and exceptional speed. He was astonishingly fast, yet without any appearance of haste or even urgency. Grace and ease marked his movements, as though Nature had fashioned him for this with some secret purpose of her own.

The bout was quick. When they lowered their swords, Mr. Viking bent over, gasping. Saint turned toward his clothing on a chair, and like that night years ago, across the ballroom he noticed her.

"Good morning," he said with the shadow of a smile. "This is a surprise."

Swiping a kerchief across his face, Mr. Viking bowed.

"My lady."

She walked into the room and Saint's gaze dropped to her body. She had worn men's clothing many times before when training her horse. The stable hand, Fingal, was nearly her size, and she had first borrowed breeches, shirt, and waistcoat from him. After that she had a set made for her.

But Rory and Fingal's appraisals had never made her feel quite so *unclothed*. And yet Saint's body was actually unclothed. Upon the honed contours of his chest that was damp with sweat, among other smaller scars, a long slash ran from his ribs downward to cross his waist.

"I thought we could begin early today," she said.

"No chaperone?"

"They are all still abed. Perhaps Mr. Viking will serve."

"Viking," he threw over a bare shoulder, "stay for a bit and watch her ladyship hit me as you never can."

"I hit you because you stand still and allow me to," she said. "What was that leaping forward you were both doing? It seemed more than a regular advance."

"The French call it an *elonge*. A lunge. Impossible for a woman wearing a narrow skirt. Not today, however, it seems." He scanned her legs and his sideways smile appeared again.

The footman came forward. "I am terribly sorry, my lady, but I have a dozen tasks to complete before breakfast. Shall I summon Mr. Aitken?"

"No. Lord Michaels or Mrs. Josephs will be along shortly."

He set his foil in the rack and departed.

"Neither your companion nor my cousin rise before nine o'clock," Saint said.

"It is best if fewer people see me dressed in this manner, of course." She moved past him to the sword rack.

"I should no doubt be included among the many," he said.

She turned around and discovered his gaze upon her behind. Slowly he lifted it to her face, the languid caress moving over her hips, waist, and breasts.

"Don't look at me like that."

"Like what? Like I would enjoy eating you for breakfast?"

"Mr. Viking was right. You are a scoundrel," she said with wretched unsteadiness.

"But a scoundrel with rules. And you are breaking all of them."

Now he did not look at her body. He looked at her eyes, and the amusement had disappeared from his.

Her lower lip was tender between her teeth. "I think you want me to break the rules."

"Clearly I am a glutton for suffering."

Suffering. There was bleakness in the taut lines of his face. He turned away and took up his shirt.

"Shall I go now and change my clothes?" she said, watching the cloth fall down over his back.

"Into what?" He pulled his waistcoat over his shoulders. "A kerchief? Or perhaps a shawl draped about you, like Salome dancing for King Herod?"

"Would a nun's habit do?"

"Then we would truly be in trouble. I would imagine you my confessor and unburden myself of all sorts of sins." He took up a cane and her pink parasol, and came toward her.

"I would not mind that."

He halted before her. "Yes, but then my dashing mysteriousness would be all in pieces. We cannot have that, can we?"

"I guess not. Did you come by that scar on your face in the manner you said to Mr. Viking?"

"What did I say to him?"

"That cuckolded husbands wounded you in duels."

"You heard that?"

"Yes. Is that how you received that wound?"

"No, that was chaff," he said. "I have only ever fought for the honor of one woman, and this particular scar was not my reward for it."

"That long scar. On your chest?" Her gaze dipped to where his shirt gaped at the neck, and Saint felt it—upon his skin, in his blood, and clamoring through his groin. Snugly contained in a pristine shirt and waistcoat, her breasts pressed against the fabric. Her sleeves were tight, like the breeches that clung to her thighs and hips. He was half hard, half helpless, and entirely angry.

"Not that scar either." He offered her the parasol. "Work. Now." Words were a luxury he hadn't the tongue for at present. Or the brain.

"With this?"

"Yes."

"But you said—"

"My time in your father's household grows short." *God willing.* Chloe Edwards had not been at home yesterday. But Dylan would call upon her again today and renew his courtship. "If you wish to be prepared to defend yourself against unwanted attention, we must speed up this instruction. How much time do you have here this morning? Or do you intend to take my cousin about to all of your friends' houses again today?"

"Could you be jealous?"

"Not at all. I have enjoyed more than enough of his company over the past three decades. He may share his time with anybody he wishes now."

"That isn't what I meant."

"I know it isn't. What do you want with him?"

Her chin ticked up. The curse of it was that defiance only made her more beautiful. When she was uncertain, he wanted to ease her confusion. But when her confidence came to the fore, he simply wanted her.

"I am fond of his company that you so blithely cast aside," she said. "He is vastly diverting."

"Not to you. I see you with him. I hear you speak to him. He isn't clever enough for you, yet you allow him to believe he is. Why?"

Her lashes dipped down a bit. "For the opportunity to become better acquainted with his friends."

She was telling the truth. Over the course of a fortnight

six years earlier he had memorized every one of her smiles. Now he had come to know the tones of her voice as well: the brightness of her amusement, the brittle edge of her anger, the silken chords of her teasing, and the clarity of her honesty. Still, she hid something behind those golden lashes now.

"Aren't they also your friends?" he said.

"I have spent little time in Edinburgh since my childhood. Lord Michaels has visited twice in the past year."

"Constance, don't tease him. For all that he is often an idiot, he is a good man, and his heart is already claimed."

"I don't want his heart," she said, lifting her gaze to meet his squarely, and that unruly organ in Saint's chest turned over.

"Be that as it may, if he sees you in this ensemble"—he gestured to her breeches—"it will confuse him."

"Confuse him?"

"Men are easily addled by lust."

She pivoted, walked to the ballroom door, and closed and locked it.

"There. Now no one will be addled by me today." She palmed the handle of the parasol and set the blade free. "Shall we begin?"

"You have just locked yourself in a room with me."

"I have. Yet I am tranquil. Of the two of us, really, I am becoming convinced that you, not I, are the flirt. I don't think you meant your threat to me. Or perhaps you are simply a sad failure at following through on your ultimatums." She flexed the short sword before her experimentally. "Now, pray show me how to use this instrument to wound a man."

He could not move. "You speak of wounding a man like it means nothing to you."

"On the contrary. It means everything."

There it was again in her voice: the sharp edge of fear coated in determination.

"Have you?" he said.

"Wounded a man?"

"Wounded the man that you wish to wound?"

Her throat constricted in a movement so jarring that it swept the air from Saint's lungs. He hated that she had been hurt. He hated the man that had hurt her. He hated that he had not been there to protect her then, and that he had no right to protect her now.

She did not reply.

Tucking the cane beneath his arm and lifting his hands to button his waistcoat, he went toward her.

"A sword stick is not a gentleman's weapon. Like a hidden dagger, it is a weapon of stealth and surprise."

"An assassin's tool," she murmured.

"We will begin by learning how to employ the entire parasol as a weapon to defend against an attack by knife or sword. Then I will show you how to release and withdraw the blade from the handle in a manner that allows you to strike with it as swiftly as possible."

"Awkwardly fumbling with one's parasol is not an effective method of defending oneself?" Her lovely eyes smiled tentatively.

"I wouldn't think so," he said, the tension beneath his ribs easing. "But never having had a parasol of my own, I cannot speak to the issue with confidence."

"You should."

"I should what?"

"Carry a parasol."

"To protect my delicate complexion from the sun during my strolls through the park on Lord So-And-So's arm?"

She chuckled. "Of course not."

"Then—"

"To make me lightheaded."

Quite swiftly, without any effort whatsoever, Saint imagined several things he could do to her to make her lightheaded, and none of them involved parasols.

"Focus," he said. "Now."

She offered him a smile not of flirtation, but of real pleasure, and he nearly walked out of the room. This Constance was much harder to resist than the flirt.

Diligently she applied herself to practicing parries and attacks with the parasol until she performed them with ease. She mastered the quick release of the blade swiftly, and the safe, active grip of the handle with a bit more application. As the sunlight crossing the ballroom floor grew brighter, he taught her how to hit with it.

"What? No endless series of defensive maneuvers that I must first master?" Strands of golden hair dangled to her neck and cheeks, a single lock draping nearly to her eyes, which shone now. He already knew she enjoyed challenging herself and that it made her radiant. But each time he witnessed it, he lost a little of his mind again.

"A cane or parasol or similar object is useful for defense. But one does not deploy a hidden sword unless one intends to abruptly attack another," he said.

"I daresay." She brushed the lock from before her eyes and it slipped entirely from the binding. She tucked it behind her ear. He stared. He could swallow her whole, then he might feel inside him the simple happiness that she seemed to feel at moments like this, like the humble floorboards deliriously lapping up glorious sunshine.

"Fret not," he forced across his tongue and lifted his sword. "There will be plenty of grueling repetition to dull the brief pleasure of learning this attack."

Upon a dramatic sigh, she set her stance. "Real pleasure must always be fleeting, mustn't it?"

"Not if you're doing it right," he mumbled.

Her eyes snapped to him. She blushed, a swift splash of brilliant pink sweeping up her sublime neck and over her cheeks to the very tip of her nose. Parting her lips, she released a short, audible breath. And the partial arousal that Saint had been battling for two hours became partial no more.

After that, he depended on two and a half decades of familiarity with the sword and the conditioned reflexes of his muscles to teach her what he had promised. For his thinking

brain had gone on holiday.
  Addled.
  Worse than addled.
  Considerably worse.

HE BECAME AN unforgiving taskmaster. Swiftly Constance came to regret having ever said a word to him since she entered the ballroom, and most grievously the words that had transformed her lesson in wielding a deadly parasol into military training.

He did not spare her. Instead of donning the usual padded coat and commanding her to hit him, he set before her the wooden mannequin and instructed her to advance and retreat endlessly, sheathing the blade each time then snatching it out to attack the wood over and over again. Then he ordered her to back up and he taught her how to lunge. Within an hour she could not feel her hand or wrist. But her thighs and calves provided misery enough for the entire rest of her body anyway.

"My arm is lead." She dropped back into *en garde*.

"Again, swiftly," he said.

"Quite literally." She whipped the blade free of the parasol and thrust it into the mannequin and her hair, damp with sweat, fell again over her eyes. "If I were to make an incision in my skin, beneath it would be a metalsmith's dream."

"Count aloud upon each strike, to ten, and then begin again. One, two, three—"

"Four." She thrust. "Five." Again. "Six—this repetition both exhausts and bores."

"It is necessary if you wish to master the skill." He had instructed her to direct her attention forward, toward her invisible assailant. Now she saw her teacher only in the periphery of her sight. He had retreated to a distance and spoke now to her as he had at the castle, dispassionately.

"I have learned the positions," she said, striking the mannequin yet again. "Why can't I try to hit you now?"

"The movements must come without thought. For this,

your muscles must know them as well as your mind. How long has it been since you had to think of the actions needed to slow your horse from a gallop, or to turn her midstride?"

"A lady never reveals her age."

"You told me your age within minutes of first speaking to me."

Pleasure tingled through her screaming muscles. "You should not have remembered it."

"Social niceties have never been my concern," he said in an altered tone, lower, not quite even.

"Seven . . . eight . . . I will never master this."

"You have."

She halted, dropping her weary arm to her side. "I *have*?"

"You will." His arms were crossed over his chest, the linen pulling at his wide shoulders, and his mouth was set in a hard line. The green of his eyes was like a forest at night, forbidding.

"If I am doing well, why are you glowering?"

He unfolded his arms and started toward the door. "Continue without me."

She swiveled about. "Where are you going?"

He reached for the key in the lock. "Elsewhere."

"You cannot leave yet." She did not want this to end yet. She did not want it to end *ever*. "My lesson is not over."

"Practice as long as you wish."

"If you leave, how will I know that I'm doing it right?"

Silence crossed the ballroom.

He released the handle and strode toward her. He halted so close that she could see the texture of the scar where it diverged from his whiskers to rise toward his cheekbone.

"The instant you saw me approach, you should have raised your weapon again. Harm comes to a victim who fails to react swiftly to a threat." The rough syllables ignited her exhausted nerves like sparks.

"I did not know that you intended me harm."

He wrapped his arm about her waist and dragged her to him.

Thigh to thigh, hip to hip, he held her securely as his gaze swept her face and everything inside her erupted in heat. The perfection of his mouth mesmerized her. Once upon a time she had kissed that.

"The pull of fabric here"—his hand curved with purpose around her shoulder, then smoothed firmly beneath her arm and, with aching slowness, caressed the side of her breast— "and here"—his palm arced along her waist, over her hip to surround her buttock—"is how you will know that you are doing it right. And this"—he tugged her hips tightly to his, and the hard length of his arousal pressed into her—"is how you know that your lesson is over."

For an instant there was not enough air in the world. Then the panic rose. Swiftly. The crawling dread. His hands on her were strong. Powerful. Locking her in place.

"According to your own accusation," she forced across her sticky tongue, "shouldn't you have asked permission to hold me like this? Or at least given me warning?" Her voice was thin. "Hypocrite."

Abruptly he released her.

The ballroom door swung inward. The butler stood in the opening.

"My lady, His Grace requests your presence in the upstairs parlor. The Duke of Loch Irvine has arrived."

"So early?" Her hand was slippery on the grip of her sword. "I must change my clothes. Tell my father I will come shortly."

"Very good." He withdrew.

Saint stood motionless, his eyes steady upon her.

"Are you all right?" he said.

She could say nothing that would not reveal herself entirely. She nodded.

"Go ahead, now. Your duke awaits you."

Setting down the sword stick, she went.

Chapter 13

The Duke

Constance's first thought upon entering the parlor was that Gabriel Hume looked remarkably like he had twenty years ago, when he still had a father and an elder brother and did not expect to inherit the dukedom. He was considerably taller, of course. And the prominent nose and severe jaw that had made him a homely boy now rendered him a shockingly attractive man, albeit in a saturnine fashion, with ebony hair and gray eyes and an air of earthy gravity about him. He wore his black coat loose and his cravat tied in a simple knot. He appeared to be scowling at her. But perhaps that was merely the cast of his brow.

An intelligent brow. Intelligent eyes.

From beside her, Constance heard Eliza's slow intake of breath. *Indeed.* If appearance were all there was to a man's identity, the Duke of Loch Irvine could easily be the leader of a Satanic cult.

Surrounded by his dogs, her father made the introductions.

"Good day, Your Grace." She curtsied low.

Loch Irvine frowned. But he bowed in a perfunctory manner that made her want to laugh.

"You're as pretty as you were when we were bairns," he said. "'Tis inconvenient."

"I am honored that you remember me." She gestured to the footman for tea.

"The duke has only a short time for this call," her father said. "Given the purpose of it, I will leave the two of you alone to become reacquainted." He gestured Eliza toward the door.

"Oh, no, Your Grace, I could not leave my lady in a gentleman's company without chaperonage," Eliza said, disregarding the last several hours during which she had napped while Constance was alone with her fencing instructor. "I will remain here."

Her father nodded at Loch Irvine. "Sir, until tomorrow." Flanked by his dogs, he left the room.

"Tomorrow?" Constance said, moving to the tea table. "Have you and Father plans for an outing?"

His dark brows dipped. "I'm to host a party tomorrow night."

"Will there be whiskey punch?" Eliza asked.

"My friend is trying to shock you. You are advised to ignore her. Have a seat, do."

He peered down at her. Then he moved forward and took a seat so close to her that she could see where his valet had nicked his chin while shaving him.

She poured tea. He took it up in his ridiculously large hands but did not drink. His fingers were stained with black that was not ink. It looked like pitch. He said nothing, and after a moment bounced the teacup in his palm until it splashed onto his breeches. He seemed not to notice this, but studied her even more closely.

"Would you care for a stronger beverage?" she asked. "Claret, perhaps? Brandy?"

"No." He set the cup on the table. "Your father has offered a remarkable price for you. Now I understand why. Your beauty is unmatched."

This time she did laugh. "I am gratified to learn that the price suits the mare."

His eyes squinted, revealing shadows beneath them. "But you're long in the tooth to be yet unwed. Tell me now, lass, be you a maiden?"

"Well, it seems I needn't have had concern over my companion's conversation after all."

At the door, the footman announced, "Lord Michaels."

The duke rose to his feet like an anchor being hauled from the sea, and now she saw quite clearly his weariness. He was awkward and uncivilized and most certainly exhausted.

"Your Grace!" Lord Michaels said with a broad smile. "What an honor to see you again so soon."

The duke's dark brow cut down. "'Tis a tragedy, your cousin."

The baron nodded soberly. "Thank you."

"Your cousin?" she said.

"Saint's brother died at sea in January."

"I—" *His brother?* "I am so sorry."

"If I had known what lay in wait for him on that voyage I would have gone too. Saint knew, I think. Clever fellow. Not quick enough to halt a bullet, though."

Her hands were numb around the porcelain. Saint had said nothing of it to her. That this omission stunned her only proved that she was still misguided enough to believe she could ever know a man.

"How does business go along these days, sir?" the baron said more lightly now.

"I feel the lack o' your cousin acutely."

"Were you in business with Mr. Sterling?" she asked.

"Aye. Of a sort." Abruptly, he stood. "I'll be taking my leave now. Will you come tomorrow eve?"

She rose and went toward the door with him. "Would my answer to your earlier question determine whether or not you welcome me to your party?"

His eyes cut to her face. Then his mouth tightened.

"I am a man of few words, lass, and even fewer bonnie words."

"I do not require bonnie words. Merely courtesy."

He stared down at her with a black frown. "If it's courtesy you want, you'd best be seeking a groom elsewhere."

"I daresay," she said, then smiled. "But I will no doubt enjoy your party tomorrow anyway."

Something that might have been humor glimmered for an instant in his eyes. Then it was gone, and he departed.

Lord Michaels sat again and plucked up a cake from the tea tray.

"Peculiar fellow. Though if you're to wed him, I shouldn't say such a thing, should I? Rather, what a capital sort, the duke is!" A grin filled his face.

She returned to him at the tea table. "My lord, you are incorrigible."

"Been told that before. Lady Fitzwarren said it. She likes to put a man in his place." He took up another cake. "Are wedding bells in the offing, my lady, or am I precipitate to ask?"

"You are precipitate, and outrageous."

"I am." He leaned back and spread his arms along the back of the sofa. "It's why all the ladies like me. No brooding angst here. Why, we've only known each other a fortnight and we are such good friends already that here I am guessing at your wedding plans." He twisted his lips till his cheeks became hollows. "So . . . are they? The wedding bells?"

She took up her cup. "You may presume outrageous familiarity with me, my lord, but I needn't return the compliment."

He released a breath that sounded like relief. "Then they're not. At least not yet, I'm guessing. That's fine then. Just fine." He folded his hands in his lap.

"You seem happy about that."

"I am not *unhappy*."

"My lord." She set down her cup. "Do you know unsavory news of the duke, perhaps, from your cousin's—that is, your deceased cousin's former business dealings with him?"

"Not at all." His eyes shot wide. "Deuce take it! I forgot

to attend your lesson with Saint this morning. No doubt you called on Mrs. Josephs in my absence." He craned his neck about. "Mrs. Josephs?"

She awoke with a start and looked about. "Has that big slab of granite gone already?"

"He made a swift assessment, it seems," Constance said.

"Well, a fellow don't have to look for more than a moment to see something he can like here." He grinned. "Was just saying that to Saint the other day, in fact, right about the time I was wiping myself up off the floor after sparring."

The image of Saint sparring with Mr. Viking earlier came to her abruptly and her entire body got hot.

"How did he come to be an expert swordsman?" she said.

"Practice." He snatched up another cake. "A great lot of practice, since we were little chaps. From the day he found that old sword in the dust alongside that cane field, he never put it down. Mustn't have even been seven at the time." He chewed thoughtfully. "And we had a splendid teacher."

"But he is not . . ." What he had done in the ballroom, touching her like that—she had not anticipated it. "He is not an aggressive man." *Usually.* "I would think a man must want to hurt someone to become so proficient at being able to do so."

"Oh, he does, believe you me," Lord Michaels said with utter assurance. "It's just that he directs it all into that sword. No need to bluster about pushing everybody around when you know you can skewer them through quick as lightning, what?" He grinned.

At the door the footman said, "Her ladyship, the Baroness of Easterberry, and Mrs. Westin and Miss Anderson."

"Good day," Lady Easterberry said as she swept into the room. Edinburgh society's greatest gossip, her circle of friends was wide and her interest in everybody's business insatiable. "Maude, Patience, I must have a private tête-a-tête with Lady Constance. Do entertain Lord Michaels."

Miss Anderson, a pretty girl of no more than seventeen, stammered and blushed. But she accepted a seat beside the baron, and her elder sister sat too. Lady Easterberry linked her arm through Constance's and drew her toward the window.

"My dear," she said in a hush, "it was not a quarter hour after you and Lord Michaels departed my home yesterday that I heard the most extraordinary news."

"Do tell, my lady." Constance ducked her head to come closer to the baroness's furtive whisper. She was a small woman, like her daughters in both height and the glow of her cheeks.

"But first I must ask." She released Constance's arm. "Was that the Duke of Loch Irvine I saw riding away from this very house just now?"

"It was."

She clasped her hands together. "Then the rumors are true. He is courting you."

"How any rumor of that could exist when he has only called upon me for the first time since we were children, I am at a loss to know," she said with a smile. "But do tell me your news, my lady. You have peaked my curiosity."

"In fact it is news of the Devil's Duke!" she said in a whisper and leaned closer. "I spoke with Lady Melville only an hour ago and she insists that Loch Irvine is *not* the man we have all been imagining him."

"Oh?"

"Oh, indeed. She says we should all be pointing the blame for the disappearances of those girls at another man entirely, a *lowborn* man."

"Lowborn?"

"She has cause to believe that the person who absconded with those poor innocent girls was a *merchant*." Her mouth twisted up in a grimace.

"How interesting! What sort of merchant?"

"Oh, well, whatever sort is the most depraved, of course."

"I see. Does Lady Melville have this man's name?" Or any reason to blame him for the missing girls.

"That is the most remarkable thing, for she learned it

from her housekeeper who overheard it at the fish market in Leith. Filthy, smelly place. I have never been there, of course."

"Naturally. What did her housekeeper overhear?"

"A man whose ship came into port only twice last year, in September and then again in December, happened to be letting Loch Irvine's house here in town on both of those occasions. He departed Edinburgh mere days after that girl's cloak was found by the loch. Do you see? Everybody *assumed* the duke had something to do with it, but in fact another person altogether was living in his house."

"Good heavens. That does seem like damning evidence." If one discounted the merchant's captain, crew, and servants who would have been in Edinburgh at the same times, as well as every other sailor and merchant who made port in Leith then, not to mention Lord Michaels and Sir Lorian Hughes who had both been in town on those occasions. "What is the merchant's name?"

"*That*," she whispered, casting her daughters and the baron a quick glance and lowering her voice further, "is the most distressing piece of it all. For, naturally, I sent my page early this morning to the dockyard to discover it. The merchant in question, Lady Constance, is a man by the name of Sterling. He is our dear, charming Lord Michaels's cousin!"

Chapter 14

A Hidden Knife

On the fourteenth of January, Torquil Sterling had perished aboard his own ship sailing from Newcastle-Upon-Tyne. His brother, a passenger on the vessel when bandits beset it, laid the merchant to rest in the sea, and traveled onward to London where he informed their cousin of the tragedy.

Torquil Sterling had indeed resided in the Duke of Loch Irvine's house in Edinburgh while doing business at Port Leith in September and December. But Lady Melville's information was not entirely accurate. Torquil Sterling had not let the house; the duke had invited him to stay there as his guest while he was absent.

Constance learned this from Lord Michaels through subtle probing after Lady Easterberry departed. But the baron seemed distracted, and soon excused himself.

"Remarkable," Eliza said, pouring whiskey into her teacup. "Do you think Torquil was as handsome as his brother? Cheekbones like that are family traits, you know."

"You doubt it?"

"That the biddies of Edinburgh have outdone themselves this time? Oh, no. I accept that entirely."

Constance stood up. "I will ask him."

"What exactly will you say, child? 'Dear Mr. Sterling, although I cannot manage to take my eyes off of you when you are in the room, I wonder if you can tell me whether your brother was an abductor of innocent girls before he died in your arms?'"

Constance left her. Many times she had been upon the verge of telling her companion about the Falcon Club. Never more so than now did she wish to explain precisely how successful she had been on numerous occasions at stealing information from people who never knew they were being robbed.

But Saint was different. With him, untruths unraveled upon her tongue. She could not lie to him.

But he could not be found. None of the servants had seen him since morning, and when she went to the mews she learned that he had taken his horse out hours ago and had not yet returned.

He never dined with her family, although her father had invited him to do so. After dinner, she went to bed, remembered the thrill of feeling his body against hers, and found sleep elusive. In the morning she would send a maid to inform her fencing instructor that she would not appear for her lesson. If he thought her craven, so be it. She had an appointment to keep with Maggie Poultney's mother. Innocent girls, after all, were the reason she now pursued the Duke of Loch Irvine.

"HE BARRED THE door to me!" Dylan sprawled on his back on his bed, an arm thrown across his face.

"With an actual bar?"

Dylan uncovered his eyes and raised his head off the mattress to scowl at Saint. "With a pistol clutched in his fist." His head plunked onto the counterpane anew. "He threatened to shoot me if I tried to see Chloe again. *Me.* I am a *baron*, for God's sake. What must a man do to impress a damned member of the provincial gentry?"

"Hold on to his monthly income longer than an hour, I suspect." He ran his fingertips along the edge of the rapier, testing the sharp edge. The fine whetstone had worked wonders.

Dylan sat up. His face was a splotched mess of despair. "I must see her soon. But how? Where?"

"Perhaps you will encounter her upon one of your many social calls."

"If *only* . . . But, wait, that's it! I will ask Lady Constance to beg Loch Irvine to send Edwards and his family an invitation to his party tomorrow night. The old curmudgeon won't refuse an invitation to a duke's house."

"Except, apparently, this duke's house while you reside in it."

"Edwards won't put it together. He doesn't know Loch Irvine's courting Lady Constance. It's rumor, of course." He moved to the edge of the bed. "Which puts me in mind . . . She asked me about Tor today."

"Who asked you?"

"Lady Constance, you noddy. Don't you listen to me when I'm speaking?"

"Hardly ever."

"P'raps her father wants to expand his ventures and he's set her to investigating opportunities. She could do it. She's frightfully intelligent for a woman. But by God, she's a beauty. Loch Irvine was speechless seeing her today. Couldn't string together more than five words of sense at a time."

He should see her wearing breeches. Although, if things went Loch Irvine's way, he would see her wearing nothing at all.

Dear God, he had to get out of this place.

"If he is as eloquent as all that, you and he must have had plenty to talk about." He climbed to his feet and went to the door.

"You are a regular wiseacre, cousin." But Dylan's voice had altered yet again. "Do you know what they're saying about Loch Irvine?"

"As I am not a party to the calls you make among Edinburgh's best and brightest, I do not."

Dylan waved that away. "Servants talk. My man spoke of it to me this morning."

Saint did not bother noting that he hadn't a "man." Nor had he ever. And in his exalted position in a noble household—reserved for dancing masters, drawing masters, and tutors—the only others in the house who spoke to him with any freedom were the butler and housekeeper, as well as the coachmen because his very fine horse made him worthy of notice. But those upper servants were above gossip.

"Well, aren't you curious?" Dylan pressed.

More than he wanted to be. "You seem eager to share."

"They say he's got a club." The words sounded peculiar, at once breezy and forced.

"Don't men like you have multiple clubs? I thought you took membership in at least three."

"His *own* club, muttonhead. Head of it. But this one ain't a sporting club, or even a scholarly thing." He peered askance at Saint in the manner he used to look at Monsieur Banneret when he was guilty of some misdeed. "It's, well, it's the sort of club a fellow don't talk openly about over tea. The sort Tor would have liked quite a lot, I suspect."

"Not you?"

"Nossir!"

Saint showed his skepticism.

Dylan shrugged. "Not since I met my pearl." Abruptly transformed, he lay back on the bed, arms akimbo. "I'll engineer her invitation to Loch Irvine's party. And then tomorrow night after I've held her in my arms again . . ." Staring up at the canopy, he heaved a dramatic sigh. "You've never seen a prettier girl, Saint. And she'll be mine."

The contentment on his face was so real, Saint had to

smile. Dylan's infatuation was a simple thing, complicated only by her father's disapproval. Once that was overcome, the pair's happiness seemed assured.

He deserved that happiness. Abandoned in the West Indies by parents who preferred to enjoy life unburdened by a child, Dylan had been raised by servants who barely tolerated him. Only the plantation's steward, Georges Banneret, had paid the baron's young heir any attention. Yet despite it all, he had an innocent, childlike appreciation of others that required only merriment and fond fellowship. Now, with Chloe Edwards, he would have that.

Tomorrow night, after the lovers' reunion, Saint would bid his cousin good-bye and leave them to their happiness.

THE EAST ROAD to Leith departed beyond the royal palace and bent toward the port to the north. Partway there, a westward turn into cultivated fields wended to the Duke of Loch Irvine's house.

Night had already fallen when the Duke of Read's carriage joined the crush of vehicles before the house to disgorge the elite of Edinburgh. Torches illumined all, and jewels glittered upon ladies' necks and gentlemen's fingers as they eagerly passed through doors flanked by footmen in smart livery.

Constance accepted Lord Michaels's hand to step onto grass damp with a smattering of snow. The house was lit from every window, sparkling gold and welcoming. She had not imagined the duke capable of such a festive show, and after so few days in town. Quite clearly he wished to impress. But whom, exactly?

The event was all anyone had spoken of around tea tables and in the parks all day. The enigmatic duke had never before hosted a party, not at either of his two castles or here. He might never again. No one dared miss it.

Amidst the chatter, Constance had heard the names of Maggie Poultney and Cassandra Finn whispered. She wondered if the gossips imagined the duke had a horde of maidens imprisoned in his house that they might accidentally discover during the evening.

Her prospective betrothed stood at the base of the stairs in his foyer, dressed in a black coat and stark white shirt and neck cloth, torchlight casting his features into harsh angles. He crossed through his guests to her and her father.

"Sir. My lady. Doctor," he said with a shallow bow, entirely ignoring Lord Michaels and Eliza.

Her father perused the crowd. "A fine turnout. My compliments, Loch Irvine," he said and moved off.

Their host returned his attention to her. "You're lovelier than an angel."

She disliked it when men called her what she was not: angel, goddess, occasionally savior.

"And yet you look positively diabolical. What a pair we must appear."

"Aye, you've a tart tongue between those teeth."

"Do I? I thought I was merely being honest. Lately I am trying very hard to be so."

He peered at her with scowling eyes. "This—" He gestured curtly. "I've done this for you. You understand?"

"For me? How kind of you. I do like a good party." Considerably less than she liked a hard ride or an hour with her bow and a quiver full of arrows. "Thank you."

"I know less than half o' these folk," he grumbled.

She tucked her hand into his arm. Beneath her fingertips was thick, hard muscle. It felt alien. She thought of Saint's lean strength and how easy yet impossible touching him had always been, and she got weak with longing she could not cast off even as she was taking another man's arm.

"Shall I make you acquainted with your guests?" she said.

Nodding, the duke allowed her to lead him about.

MUSIC, CONVERSATION AND a great quantity of fine food characterized the Duke of Loch Irvine's party. He was not entirely taciturn; although he seemed not to enjoy the conversation of most of his guests, he spoke with Dr. Shaw at length.

After several hours, Constance left him to make her way from guest to guest at her own pace. But she sought out one man in particular.

Sir Lorian Hughes was thirty-five years old, with sandy hair, long, poetical sideburns, and an impressive physique. She knew he boxed in London; once he had boasted to her of his conquests at Gentleman Jackson's. At the time, he had been dangling his comfortable fortune and good looks before hopeful maidens. When she made her disinterest clear, within the sennight he offered for Miranda Priestly.

Lady Miranda Hughes was now nowhere to be seen. Instead, in a corner of the drawing room Sir Lorian spoke with a young lady of black curls and rosebud lips who Constance recognized as the daughter of an Edinburgh family of no pretentions.

A hand on her elbow arrested her. Constance turned.

"Oh, dear." Miss Anderson's cheeks turned crimson. "Mama told me not to be so forward. She says I am all *hands*."

"No worry." Constance clasped the girl's fingers in quick reassurance. "I am not as starchy as I should be either."

"You, starchy?" Miss Anderson giggled. "Oh, Lady Constance, how I would someday like to be like you, so—so—*graceful*."

"What a dear you are." Sir Lorian was leading Miss Edwards toward the dining room now. "Was there something you wished to speak with me about?"

"Yes. That is . . . everybody is saying that Mr. Sterling is among your party. No one among my friends has yet made his acquaintance. I hoped you would not mind making an introduction."

"Mr. Sterling?" *Here?*

"Yes. He is . . ." The girl's cheeks turned even pinker. "*Compelling*. Why, look. He wears a sword when no other gentleman does. Is it not *illegal* to do so?"

He was here. That she saw him every day in her own house mattered nothing now. This was public. This was reality. This was the world they had never been in together. This was the world in which they were not allowed to be together.

"He is an accomplished swordsman," she managed to say.

"Is he?" Miss Anderson's eyes rounded. "How utterly *romantic.*"

She had once thought so too. Fool that she was, she still did. "I will be glad to introduce you," she said with a smile. She did not want to introduce him to pretty girls, not even girls he could not possibly court, like this daughter of a baron.

And then he was walking toward them and, like the girl at her side, she could only stare. He wore a dark coat of very fine cut and the same partial smile upon his lips that had driven her mad from the first night she had ever seen him. He looked like a gentleman. With the naked sword at his side glimmering in candlelight, he looked like more of a gentleman than all the other gentlemen in the place, thoroughly handsome and quite possibly dangerous and perfect. *Perfect.* The way he looked at her now, as though there were no other women in the room, the house, the entire world, made her want to scream.

He bowed. "My lady." Then he turned his attention upon Miss Anderson.

Maude smiled prettily, stammered a bit, complimented him on everything she reasonably could—his sword, his coat, the buckles on his shoes—and when he thanked her with an economy of words, she launched into a monologue about everyone she had yet spoken with at the party.

He listened attentively, smiling a bit each time she paused for acknowledgment. Finally Lady Easterberry appeared with her other daughter, Patience Westin.

"Maude, you are monopolizing Lady Constance's attention. She must wish to speak with others tonight as well." She gave Saint a guarded appraisal.

Constance introduced them all. With a transparent excuse

and another wary glance at him, Lady Easterberry swept her daughters away.

His eyes were laughing as Constance turned to him.

"How fantastically amusing," he said, looking after the Easterberry ladies.

"The scar deepens when you smile like that."

"Does it?"

"It makes you look like a cutpurse."

"And you have a vast acquaintance with those, I guess."

Her lips betrayed her; they twitched. "Some."

"Are all young noblewomen that wonderfully scatter-brained? Present company excepted, of course."

"You are wearing a sword at a party."

He offered her a lazy smile. "Not done, is it?"

"She is taken with your dashing disregard for morality. She has lost her wits."

"Ah." He folded his hands behind his back. "Then she has my sympathy."

"Why are you here?"

"Your father demanded that I attend. Remarkable, I know. I declined, but he insisted. He is accustomed to getting what he wants, clearly. And it seems he is loath to pay me if I do not obey his every command."

"Do you need the money so much?"

"Well, I don't have any at present. So, yes. Must feed the horse or he won't go, you see. But I was under the impression that ladies of your estate never acknowledge lowly trifles like actual money."

"Oh, we don't. Sometimes, however, when I am carried through town on a chair by my four Ethiopian eunuchs, the peasants toss flowers at me, and in return my little pageboy throws coins at them. So I have actually *seen* money."

"How affecting for you that must be."

"I enjoy consorting with the plebes," she said airily. "As long as they don't actually come too close, of course."

"Naturally." His eyes swept her hair, bared shoulders, and the dip of her bodice. "You are breathtaking tonight. I am happy to have the opportunity to see you in your evening finery."

"Thank you."

"But I prefer the breeches."

This was impossible. *He* was impossible. She did not want to jest about the divide between them. It was real, and she despised it now just as she had six years ago, when for a fortnight she had pretended because pretending was all she could have of him.

Sir Lorian was now in close conversation with Lord Michaels. Nearby, Lady Hughes was speaking with Mrs. Westin.

She would begin with Lady Hughes, tease out the reason for the white robes. Then she would flirt with Sir Lorian. It made her ill to anticipate it. But Mrs. Poultney's tears this morning were reason enough to proceed with yet another charade like those she had practiced dozens of times for the Falcon Club.

Saint's eyes glimmered like his sword now, sharply, as he watched her.

"My wits, however, are not lost," she said. "Please excuse me—"

"Constance."

She paused, and abruptly wished there were no mystery to solve, no missing persons to be found, nothing but his voice caressing her name.

"I came here tonight for two reasons," he said soberly now. "I have written a letter of resignation to your father and intend to depart before light tomorrow. I wanted to say good-bye to you. And I wished to see this duke that you will be marrying."

The air deserted the room like a vast fire had sucked it all up, leaving a vacuum.

"You are leaving," she said too weakly.

"He looks better than I imagined he would. But so did your first fiancé. And your second."

"I never had a second fiancé. I still do not."

"You will shortly, then the husband you seek, and I admit that I haven't the stomach to remain here and watch that happen." His gaze traced her features and she struggled to make her lungs function.

He was leaving.

Of course he was. Nothing had changed in six years. She was still the daughter of a duke with a fortune to inherit and he was still the son of a colonial merchant, a man who earned his wages teaching. *Forbidden.*

"And perhaps if I leave now," he said, "my cousin will find other lodgings and cease ending each day disconcerted by you. I don't know exactly what you asked him yesterday, or why you need bother him with questions he clearly does not wish to answer. But at least I won't contribute to your ease in doing so any longer."

"I asked him nothing untoward." Only questions she could not ask *him* about his brother because she could not bear to hurt him any more than she already had. "I won't pine away for you after you have left, you know."

His throat moved in a rugged jerk. "I hope not."

"I should not delay your departure further," she forced out. "Good night." Fighting the prickling heat at the backs of her eyes, she crossed the room swiftly. Desperate for distraction, purpose, *anything* but this ache of loss yet again, she sought out Sir Lorian in the crowd. He had disappeared. But Lord Michaels stood alone, shoulders bunched up, chin low. Casting his eyes about in a furtive manner that should have made her chuckle, he hurried toward a closed door, opened it, and slipped through.

She followed. The door led into a small antechamber that let onto a gallery. A narrow room, it seemed to run the length of the house, with windows on only one side. Dark portraits of men glowered down at her and against either wall were various pieces of furniture: a high wooden chair backed with engraved bronze, marble busts on pedestals, and a glass-fronted display case. Except for moonlight, the room was dark, and it smelled of dust and age.

The Duke of Loch Irvine had not, apparently, cleaned up his entire house for tonight's party. How many other rooms were there in this vast house? And why had Lord Michaels snuck away into this closed portion when his friends were all enjoying themselves elsewhere?

With a click, the door to the antechamber behind her opened. It closed, again shutting out the sounds from the party. Constance ducked behind the tall display case and pressed her back against the wall.

It was her curse to have spent more than a sennight listening to the sound of Saint's footsteps upon a wooden floor, of learning the confidence of his stride—yet more details about him that she would never forget. He did not now try to hide his presence in the gallery. She pushed away from her hiding spot.

"You won't make this easy for me, will you?" he said.

By moonlight she could see his unsmiling face.

"I will." She moved toward the opposite door. "I will recommend that if you leave immediately, you will not see anything you cannot like."

He followed her. She reached the door and tried the handle. *Locked.* But Lord Michaels must have come this way; there was no other exit to the gallery.

Reaching into her hair, she plucked out a pin from the coils. As she had done many times before, she unfastened the lock and opened the door.

Saint grasped her shoulder and loomed over her. The naked shock in his eyes took her breath.

"For God's sake," he said harshly—raw, as though it hurt him to speak. "What do you want with him?"

His fingers gripping her shoulder were not rough. Rather, they were far too gentle given the pain she saw in his eyes. Even now, he would not harm her, even now when he believed her to be doing wrong to a man he loved.

Placing her palm upon his chest, she closed her eyes and spread her fingers and pressed them into his strength, and felt the pleasure in her body. No panic, no fear like in the ballroom when he had grabbed her. Only longing, pure and simple, like the longing she had always felt for him.

He said nothing now, but the uneven cadence of his breathing revealed him. She drew her hand away and opened the door with unsteady fingers. Beyond it was a high foyer, perhaps a rear entrance to the house, dominated by a stairwell that led both up and down, with carpeted steps. A finely carved wooden railing ran in both directions into darkness.

"You needn't be jealous," she whispered, moving onto the landing.

"I'm not jealous. I'm worried."

She looked back at him. "For me?"

"For my cousin."

She moved up the steps. "Let me go after him, and I will explain later."

"Explain now." He made no effort to quiet his voice. Shrouded in shadow, he was a dark silhouette, but she could see well enough his right hand resting upon the hilt of his sword as though he meant to draw.

Her heartbeats stuttered in the emptiness.

"You cannot mean to threaten me," she said in disbelief.

"No?" There was the rawness again underlying the single word, like the desperation she felt inside.

"Do you imagine I fear you?"

"I imagine you want me," he said. "Rather, I know you do."

She gripped the railing. "Your arrogance renders me all submission, sir."

"If that were so, I would not need to threaten you, would I?" His voice had changed. It sounded almost as if he were smiling. And his hand had fallen to his side again.

"Do you threaten me, or don't you?" she said. "You contradict yourself."

"Perhaps because you make me insane. Tell me what you want of my cousin."

She moved down two steps, to within his reach if he wished to touch her.

"There is evidence to suggest that the Duke of Loch Irvine is connected to the disappearance and possible murders of two girls in Edinburgh, one in September, the other in December. They were both last seen near this house and the cloak of one of the girls was found, stained in blood."

"Loch Irvine," he said slowly. "Your betrothed?"

"He is not my betrothed."

"If you suspect him of murder, I should hope not."

"It seems he may be associated with a secret society. Some say that at the meetings of this society the members engage in dark rituals. Rumors suggest that he is the founder and responsible for the girls' disappearances." And his brother, Torquil. But she could not share that rumor now.

"You are mad."

"Upon the girl's cloak in chalk was a symbol, a very particular six pointed star. In all of Britain, this symbol is unique to Haiknayes. I am not mad. There are too many clues bespeaking a chilling crime that must be stopped."

"Your preoccupation with daggers is suddenly much clearer. *You* aim to stop this secret society? You?"

"Again you doubt my abilities."

"Never. I only wonder at your interest. You might leave it to the police to unravel."

"The police have collected reams of information on the disappearances of the girls but have arrested no suspects as yet. Innocent girls have been snatched from their families, Saint. How can that not be my interest?"

He stared at her for a long moment. "What do you believe to be my cousin's part in this?"

"He came to Edinburgh twice in those six months, once at the time the first girl disappeared, and again when the second girl's garment was found. And he has admitted to his acquaintance with the duke. I believe he may belong to the secret society."

"He does not."

"How do you know?"

"I know the reasons he came here, both in September and December. Neither was for a satanic ritual, I assure you."

"Tell me the reasons."

"Last autumn he traveled here to convince my brother to cease smuggling and turn his talents to honest trade instead. In December he came to Edinburgh to court a girl."

"Which girl?"

"Chloe Edwards. She is the reason he wished to live in your father's home, to prove his impressive connections and make himself a more desirable suitor."

"Chloe Edwards? Black curls?"

"Yes."

"She was speaking with Sir Lorian Hughes earlier to-night, a handsome man with long—"

He ascended the steps and was upon her. "My cousin is innocent of whatever wrong you believe him."

"Why has he gone away from the party secretly, as though guilty of a wrongdoing?"

His gaze traveled swiftly over her face. "Perhaps he is pursuing a woman he should not be pursuing."

"Like you?"

"I am not pursuing a woman."

"I am not a woman?"

"You are plague."

"A *plague*?"

"A curse. A distraction. A preoccupation." He curved his hands around her shoulders and his thumb stroked the edge of her bodice. "An intoxication," he said huskily. He bent his head beside hers and the heat from his skin caressed her cheek. "A memory I cannot shake, though I try."

She tilted her head and her cheek brushed his and it was heaven again to feel him like this. "Will you kiss me now?" she whispered. "Finally?"

"My cousin is guilty of no crime, Constance. You are chasing the wrong man."

She broke away and clambered backward up the steps. "I will find the man responsible for those missing girls."

"I will prove you wrong about Dylan."

She pivoted on the step and pressed her fist to her chest. "I hope you will."

"You hope? You do not seek to find your villain?"

"I do. But I have no wish to see you hurt. I want what you love to be free of guilt."

His eyes arrested, and a muscle shifted in his jaw.

She backed up another step, and another. "Stay away from me, Saint."

"That is simply not possible any longer," he said in an entirely altered voice.

She reached the top and moved into the corridor, and heard his footsteps on the stairs behind her. He followed without speaking.

Lit by moonlight from a single window, the long corridor boasted several doors, only one unlocked. It opened onto a room decorated with a couch of sumptuous upholstery and a table bearing a silver washing basin, pitcher, and candelabra. Behind the draperies, however, the windows were boarded up.

Saint waited in the doorway, then went with her to the final door at the far end of the corridor. It opened onto a narrow staircase: a servants' stairwell, perhaps to an old, exterior kitchen, descending into shadow.

"You have no lamp," he said over her shoulder. "I will go first."

"You think I lack the courage."

"I think you seem too eager to throw yourself into danger." He moved around her swiftly and started down the stairs, pulling a knife from his sleeve.

"You have a knife hidden in your sleeve as well as a dagger in your boot?" she whispered, placing her feet carefully down each riser as the stairwell grew darker.

"I am not wearing boots at present. Thus the sleeve."

"I would like to have a hidden knife."

"You know, it isn't particularly wise to reveal one's weaponry to an adversary waiting in the dark below."

"There is no one below. But the next time we creep down a servants' staircase in the dark, you can provide me with a hidden knife and I won't speak at all. Agreed?"

As they came to the bottom of the stair, the blackness concealed them almost entirely. She felt for a door handle, and turned it, but it remained fast.

"A door to the exterior, most likely," he said, his voice muted in the close, chill space.

"Why would he have left the party secretively, if not to conceal something?"

"This is an unsafe position to remain in."

"No escape except from above," she agreed. "It seems increasingly that you believe in the danger."

"The stairwell is too narrow for me to draw freely. The darkness, however, provides ideal opportunity—"

"For you to kiss me."

"No. You are insane. I am not going to kiss you. We are adversaries in this, Constance."

"If you don't wish to, you should not, of course. And I don't want you to, anyway."

"That is a bald-faced lie. And I do want to kiss you. Quite a lot. Much more than kiss you. And I intend to. But not in the dark again. Not in secret. Never again in secret, do you understand?" His hand encompassed hers on the door latch, jerked it down, and the door sprang open.

Frigid air rushed in. A shadowy figure stood before them in silhouette.

"Constance? Mr. Sterling?" Libby Shaw's surprise sounded crisply in the night air. "What on earth are you doing *here*?"

Chapter 15

A Gift

*T*he moon was nearly gone, retreating beyond the mass of Arthur's Seat, visible to the south even at this distance.

"I stowed away under the seat and climbed out after Mr. Rory went to warm his hands," Libby said. "There are a great many hedges, so it was not difficult to sneak around the side of the house. I had no idea how I would get past all the guests and servants at the main door. I imagined I would be obliged to climb a trellis or drain or some such thing."

"I don't understand." Within minutes the snow had seeped into Constance's slippers, and she tightened her arms around herself. Saint had refused to remain in the indefensible position of the stairwell or to allow her to speak with Libby in the stairwell without him. Now she shivered in her gown that had been made for a drawing room full of people, not the back stoop of a house in March at midnight. "Why did you wish to sneak in at all? I thought you didn't care for parties."

"All the people in one place make me cross. I want to study the duke's collection of human bones. Yesterday when he was leaving our house I asked him if I could come see them, but he refused. I knew you would be taking the grand carriage to the party tonight, and I have stowed away in such places before. It seemed my only opportunity. I did not have a complete plan as to how to get inside once I was here, but then I found this door."

"Human bones?" Her teeth chattered upon the words.

Saint removed his coat and wrapped it around her shoulders. It was heavy, and warm from the heat of his body.

"Tell us about the duke's collection, Miss Shaw," he said.

"It's one of the best in Britain. The duke has specimens from all over the world. My father says there must be three dozen skulls alone. I would like to compare the size of male and female crania."

"Has Dr. Shaw seen this collection himself?"

"No one has been allowed to study it for more than a decade. But *your* brother lived in this house for weeks on end. I wonder if he was allowed to see the collection. Did he ever mention it to you?"

Saint frowned. "How do you know that my brother lived in this house?"

"Lady Easterberry told Constance yesterday. I am so sorry about him. Perhaps he would have been more forthcoming than the duke."

"My brother was not interested in science or antiquities, Miss Shaw. You said this door was propped open before?"

"With a brick from that pile." She pointed. "I went in and got as far as a parlor upstairs. But the other doors were locked. I intended to continue, but then I remembered that Rory had an augur bit in the carriage I might use to pick those locks."

"I have a new appreciation tonight for ladies' skill at breaking and entering," he murmured.

"I went back to the carriage," Libby continued, "but the door prop was gone by the time I returned here. I'm so happy you two appeared, or I never would have gotten back inside."

"You are not going back inside." Constance returned Saint's coat to him. "You and I are now going to the carriage and Rory will drive us home. I cannot blame you for wanting something that is prohibited, but this is not the way to achieve your goal. Tomorrow I will ask the duke and we will hope for a positive response."

"I will see Miss Shaw home," Saint said. "I'll send the carriage back."

"But—"

"You will not have your positive response from the duke tomorrow if you desert him in the middle of the party that he has given for you," he said, throwing Constance's stomach into tumbles.

"I am deeply disappointed." Libby's brow was stormy. "Deeply."

The chill sank beneath Constance's skin. It was not childish tantrum on Libby's face now. Through the tunnel of memory, she recognized this anger—it was the anger her mother had expressed in tears so often before the end, when her wishes were thwarted—her wishes for the house to be free of dust, the draperies drawn precisely, her dinner served in exact proportions, certain words never to be uttered, subjects never to be broached. When Constance, her father, and the servants had not done all of these perfectly, the duchess had raged. But mostly she had wept.

And Libby's crossness with crowds . . . it was the same, too. Until the illness consumed her, the duchess had been a loving mother. But she had never found the world an easy place to bear.

The memories moved Constance's feet forward, and her hands surrounded Libby's.

"My dear, I understand," she said softly. "I am sorry for this disappointment."

"But I *must* measure those skulls, Constance. My study will not be complete without those measurements."

"Yes, of course. You must be very frustrated," she said with the same soothing tone she had learned as a girl to speak to her mother. "We will try to see them tomorrow."

"How can you be certain that the duke will agree to it?

What if he does not agree? And what if he thinks me too persistent and becomes more vigilant about keeping them secret?"

"I do not have an answer for you tonight. But I promise that I will do my best. I promise, darling," she said, and waited for the explosion.

But Libby's lips shut tight. "I am sorry, Constance," she said thickly, her fingers digging into her own palms. "I will return home now with Mr. Sterling and wait until tomorrow."

"Excellent," she said gently. "I commend you on your patience. Now go along." She looked at Saint. "Good night."

He studied her without speaking.

"I won't," she finally said, shivering but deliciously warm inside.

"I don't believe you," he said.

"You can."

"And yet."

"What are you two talking about?" Libby said.

"I promise I won't do a thing," she said. "At least not tonight. Then it will not matter to you if I do or don't, will it?"

"If you think I still plan to leave, then you truly are mad."

And just like that, in an instant, Constance didn't care that Libby Shaw was what she had long suspected—her half sister, or that her father must know the truth of it, or that the man courting her had a collection of human bones hidden in his house. Tomorrow when she awoke, she would care. But for one precious moment she was happy.

"I will see you in the ballroom tomorrow after breakfast?" she said.

He gave her the knife. "You might want to find a place to hide that before you reenter the party."

With a smile, she drew the door open and tossed him the kerchief he had lodged in the handle. Then she retraced her steps. The door to the gallery remained unlocked. Moving swiftly across the long room, she paused to tuck the knife into the crack between the base of the display case and the floor. For the next visit.

Standing before the antechamber door to the drawing room, she pinched her cheeks so they would match her cold nose and rubbed her hands over her arms. She opened the door a crack and slipped through and into a group of guests.

"*Another* cloak?" the lady beside her whispered with round eyes.

"Rather, a coat," another lady exclaimed in a hush.

"Are you certain?" a gentleman muttered skeptically.

"Oh, yes! On the bank of the loch, not a stone's throw from this very house. The Devil's Duke has struck again. But this time he left the body!"

IN THE CARRIAGE on the journey home, no member of the Duke of Read's party had any conversation except the duke himself. Commenting on the wisdom of Loch Irvine to host such an event in Edinburgh given his intention of living at nearby Haiknayes, he appeared entirely unmoved by the furor stirred up during the last hour of the party.

The rest of the people in the duke's carriage as it climbed to the new town were silent: Eliza dour, Dr. Shaw thoughtful, and Lord Michaels white-lipped. Festivities had ended well past midnight upon a flurry of whispered conversations, hushed exclamations, and horrified stares at their host who, rumor had it, had received the news at his door directly from the men who had found the girl.

Driving their sheep to Lochend Toll, two shepherds had paused to water their animals and discovered her on the bank of the loch. One of the men recognized her; she hadn't been there above a day, he guessed, and her features were clear. Like the two missing girls, she was a local lass, and unmarried. And drawn on her coat in chalk was a six-pointed star.

CONSTANCE ARRIVED IN the ballroom after breakfast to find it empty.

"He is gone then," Eliza said. "It's for the best."

"My lady." Mr. Viking stood in the doorway. "Mr. Sterling

requested that I deliver this to you." He extended a folded sheet of paper.

The paper bore only four words penned in a bold, neat hand.

"Well, is it an apology for leaving without notice?" Eliza said when Viking had left. "Or a poem? How happy I was when that foolish poet ceased courting you. What was his name? Cicero? Virgil?"

"Lord Warbury?" she said, relief slipping through her. "He called himself Dante."

"His poetry was dreadful. So what is it? A sonnet or a ballad?"

She folded the paper and tucked it into her sleeve. "My cousin Leam is a poet, Eliza, if you recall. Quite a good one."

"I did not say all poets were dreadful. Only the poets that hang after you."

"Mr. Sterling does not 'hang after' me, of course. And it is not a poem. It is an address in the old town. A shop."

Eliza sighed. "With the snow, my rheumatism is wretched today."

Constance smiled. Eliza was only adamant about protecting her virtue when it was comfortable and convenient.

"Mr. Viking can accompany me."

She donned a fur-lined cloak and they set off. Cold wind cut across the Mound, which connected the newer part of town to the medieval city. The day before, she had taken this walk to find Maggie Poultney's house. Now she picked her way through icy puddles and along narrow passageways to the shop that Saint had indicated. The marquee above the door showed two crossed sabers split up the center by a dirk. Inside the room lined with racks of swords, knives, and daggers, the air smelled of leather and metal. The *clank* of a smith's hammer upon an anvil sounded from beyond a partially opened door.

The opening widened and, ducking his head to pass under the low lintel, Saint came into the room.

"Good day," he said to her, and, "Viking."

"My lady, do you wish me to remain?" Mr. Viking said.

"No. Mr. Sterling will see me home."

"Very good, ma'am." The footman departed.

She turned to Saint. "Mr. Sterling will see me home, won't he?"

"He will." He gestured to a stool. "Have a seat."

"You are very mysterious." She removed her gloves and hat and set them on the counter. "Is this your shop?"

"No. I am not a bladesmith. But if I were, I am fairly certain I would have mentioned it to you by now."

"Would you have?"

"I am not the one of us who keeps secrets, Constance. What you see is what I am."

Unaccountably, her heart did an uncomfortable shudder.

"But I know a fine bladesmith when I meet one," he said. "When we are finished here I will introduce you to Ian MacMillan—if, that is, the daughter of a duke is permitted to enter a smith's workshop?"

"The daughter of a duke can mostly do whatever she likes, really." Except marry as she wished.

"That is a weight off my conscience," he said dryly. "Sit, please. I have a gift for you."

"A gift?" She perched upon the stool. "My birthday is not for weeks yet."

"This cannot wait weeks." He took up an item from the counter and knelt before her. Constance's pulse quickened. He glanced up at her and his eyes were brilliantly green, like a woodland glade after a rain.

"Lift your skirts," he said.

Heat. Everywhere. In her abruptly labored breaths and in her cheeks.

"Scabbard." He brandished a finely cut flat strip of leather with two slender buckles. "Dagger." Upon his other palm balanced a small blade, perhaps four inches long, with a handle fashioned of ivory. "Your right leg, if you will."

She pinned her lips together; she did not trust her voice to not reveal her erratic pulse. Bunching up her skirts, she slid her right foot forward and bared her calf.

"Good," he said, and laid the leather against the side of her shin.

She closed her eyes and tried to breathe evenly as his fingers skirted her ankle, then higher. "Good?" she mumbled.

"This will remain in place securely over wool stockings like these." He glanced up. "Or bare skin."

She swallowed. "Oh?"

"When you wear silk stockings, fasten it just below the knee." Circling her leg, he ran his hand upward, his fingertips strafing her calf. "Over this bone." His thumb caressed. She caught a gasp between her teeth.

"With the scabbard here"—he stroked again—"the dagger will be more cumbersome to retrieve swiftly from beneath your skirts than when you bind it just above the ankle. But it will not slip down to your shoe when you are dancing." The caress came again, under her knee. On her thigh.

"Remove—" She dragged in a breath and looked everywhere but at him. "Remove your hand from my leg."

He drew his hand away. She pushed her skirts to her toes.

"This dagger should suit you." He offered the handle to her. "It is small, but lethal if used correctly. You will have to practice striking at lower targets: the tendons behind the heel and knee, ideally. But given your impressive trick with a hairpin and skill with the sword stick, I suspect you will master this soon enough too." He waited. "Take it."

"I do not wish to at this moment."

"Constance—"

"My hands are shaking, damn you."

A smile of pure roguish satisfaction crossed his lips. "Are they?"

"Why have you done this?"

"Because I have been fantasizing about touching your legs for six years," he said quite seriously.

Laughter broke from her beleaguered throat. She took the

dagger from him, drew up her skirt enough to reveal the ankle, and slipped the weapon into its scabbard.

He climbed to his feet. "After last night I don't care to imagine you sneaking about darkened corridors during parties without some method of protecting yourself."

She stood up and her hand moved toward him, but she pulled back before touching him. He followed the movement with his eyes.

"Thank you," she said.

"I beg your pardon for asking you to come all the way here for this. I wanted to make certain that it fit correctly, and to make adjustments immediately if necessary."

"You did not ask. You made me guess what I was meant to do. You were testing my wits."

"I needn't test you. I know you."

She went around him to the counter and took up her hat and gloves. "Am I to have the pleasure of becoming acquainted with Mr. MacMillan now?" Her cheeks were hot, her hands contrarily cold, and her stomach in so many knots.

He gestured her toward the open doorway.

THEY WALKED HOME without haste. Despite the cold, she had no wish to hurry and he matched her pace like a gentleman. Along the way they met people who had attended the duke's party the previous night. Every one of them only hinted about the girl found in the loch, as though speaking of it openly weren't suitable on the street.

When they again walked alone, Saint said, "A girl was found?"

"A body."

His gaze slewed to her.

She nodded. "Found in the same place the two missing girls were last seen, on the lake by the Duke of Loch Irvine's house."

"And the symbol from Haiknayes?"

"On her coat."

"The police have been told, I assume."

"For whatever that is worth."

"Do you believe Loch Irvine has done this?"

"He keeps a collection of human bones in his house."

"The man who stabled my horse in Plymouth collected dolls carved from corncobs. That doesn't mean he was a corn farmer. And what equally thin evidence can you bring to bear against my cousin?"

"None but circumstantial," she admitted. "I looked for him when I returned to the party. I did not see him until we mounted the carriage. Has he told you where he went during the party?"

"I haven't seen him today. I will speak with him."

"Perhaps you should not."

"So that you can continue to investigate him without his knowledge? No. I will not assist you in that."

"Saint—"

"Constance, he is innocent of these crimes."

"How can you know that?"

"Because I know *him*."

He had said he knew her, too. But he did not. They had come to the house and she went swiftly up the steps to the door.

"Wait," he ordered from below. "Why now? Why September, December, and now?"

"What do you mean?"

"What other reason might there be for these girls that would prove the coincidence of Dylan's presence here at those times?"

"I don't know. I will put my mind to it."

"Do so." He walked away. She did not ask him where he was going, or if he would teach her today. She had already had more of him than she could bear. The more she had, the more she wanted.

SAINT FOUND HIS cousin at a pub on Rose Street where they had drunk a pint days earlier.

"You know," Dylan said. "Those fencing masters of last

century—the Frenchies, I mean—half of them mulattos, of course—they wed impressively. The ones that *did* wed, that is." His tongue slurred every other word. "Some ended up on the guillotine before they had the chance to tie the old knot. Poor sods, loyal to Louis and all that. You'd think they would have known better. But complicated politics that, what?"

"What are you talking about?"

"Your wedding. Marriage. *Espousal.*"

"You are drunk." At two o'clock in the afternoon. Dylan hadn't drunk like this since they had first stopped in Edinburgh at that inn in Duddingston.

"I am." Dylan waved a hand about sloppily. "But that's neither here nor there with regard to your courtship of the *stunningly* beautiful Lady Constance Read."

"I am not courting her."

"'Course you are, whether you know it or not. She's taken with you. Entirely. Be-damn-*sotted*, my boy." He sucked down half the glass of ale. "*Unlike* some girls are with some men."

Saint watched his cousin's face. Dylan's jaw was slack, his eyes glassy.

"Miss Edwards?"

Dylan hung his head. "Left me high and dry. She was supposed to meet me at the party, alone, in secret. Know it ain't the honorable thing." He swung his face around and his brow was crumpled. "I wouldn't have overstepped the bounds. She's a lady. Just wanted to make a plan of attack with her."

"She didn't show?"

He swung his head back and forth. "Stood in the cold three quarters of an hour waiting for her."

"Where?"

"Stable." He shrugged. "Locked myself out of the house. Had to go around the front. She wasn't inside either, though." His chin grew tight. "Lorian was gone too. He'd been the one to set up the assig—" He swallowed hard. "Assignation for me. With her. Even told me where to find the key to get through a locked door. I thought he was doing me a good turn. Lying son of a . . ." he mumbled.

"You believe that Sir Lorian left with Miss Edwards last night?"

"Don't know how he could have. Her father and mother were there."

"Dylan, there are some who believe that the disappearances of the two girls, and the girl found last night, are connected to the Duke of Loch Irvine and his friends."

Dylan's head swung up abruptly, distress in his eyes.

"Is that what you did not wish to tell me the other night?" Saint said. "That the duke's club is responsible for the disappearances of those girls, and that somehow you know about it?"

"Good God, Saint. I wouldn't—That is, I'll—Oh, holy hell." He gripped his head.

"Are you a member of the club, Dylan?"

His eyes grew even wider. "I am not! What do you take me for?"

"Not a murderer."

"Then why this questioning? I'm drunk as an emperor, heart broken into bits, only wanting to see my angel again, and you're asking me if I've taken membership in a *devil*-worshipping society? Well, damn you." Hurt covered his face. "I might as well ask you if you returned to that public house in Duddingston the other night and did away with that saucy vicar's daughter who tried to play you."

"What?"

Dylan's mouth fell open. "You don't know about Annie Favor?"

"Know what about her?"

"Good God, Saint. Annie's the third girl. She's the one they found in the loch last night."

Chapter 16

A Dance, Finally

$\mathcal{T}$he police inspector questioned the Duke of Loch Irvine in his drawing room with enormous deference. They had never interrogated a duke before, they admitted, and hadn't any proof that he was connected to the death of Miss Annie Favor or to the two missing girls, either. He answered brusquely. Lord Michaels and Eliza said nothing. Constance reported only what she had heard and seen the night of the party. The police had proven themselves inadequate in uncovering the truth of Maggie or Cassandra's disappearances.

They were questioning the wrong people. For Edinburgh's society gossips were full of information. Lady Melville had furtively shared the news with Constance: two nights earlier, Patience Westin and her husband had been seen entering the Duke of Loch Irvine's house at nearly eleven o'clock. Who had seen them, it wasn't known; the news was too far removed from its original source already. But Mr. and Mrs. Westin had taken dinner that night with Sir Lorian and Lady Hughes.

Recalling Lady Melville's fevered recounting of the rumor, Constance felt nauseated. Lady Melville and Lady Easterberry were fond friends, yet one was willing to lay the other's daughter upon the altar of scandal to learn new information. Torquil Sterling's cousin and brother were, after all, living in Constance's house; Lady Melville was unsubtle in her probing.

The duke had not mentioned having the Westins to his house the night after his party. But he would not, of course, if he were the Devil.

When the police departed, Constance poured tea.

"Well, that was thoroughly unpleasant, what?" Lord Michaels said. "Dratted law, getting into everybody's hair. It's certainly not my business and I am sure it's none of yours, Duke. Or yours, Lady Constance." He eyed the biscuits.

"I beg your pardon for the paltry sweets," the duke said gruffly. "The cook gave notice yesterday."

"Would you like me to see to finding a new cook?" If she had access to the upper servants, she might learn something useful about the household.

"Aye. That'd be a help, lass."

She stood. "Perhaps I can have a chat with your housekeeper about it now."

He came to his feet. "She gave notice too."

"Good heavens. And your butler?"

"He's gone to Leith."

"Well, then, another day."

"Sir," the baron said, "Do assure us that you will attend the ball at the Assembly Rooms tonight. It's bound to be a frightfully good time."

"I'm not too fond o' dancing," he grumbled. It was a deep sound, and not at all unpleasant.

She placed her hand on his forearm. "I am very fond of balls," she said softly. "Do tell Lord Michaels that you will attend so he can rest easy."

The duke gave the baron a brief scrutiny, then returned his attention to her. "If you wish."

Lord Michaels pumped his hand, which the duke bore with a tight jaw.

"My lord," Constance said as the baron assisted her into the carriage. "You should not tease him so."

"But he is so famously amusing to tease. Dear Lady Constance, you really cannot marry him. I simply won't allow it."

"Sir," Eliza said archly, "I do not believe that you have any say over who my lady does or does not marry."

"Oh, don't I?" he replied with equal hauteur, then spoiled it by winking at Constance.

Either he was an extraordinarily good actor, or Saint was right about him. Saint—whom she had barely seen in three days, only for her lessons and only with Eliza and Lord Michaels in attendance. He was not cold; when he came near her she sensed the tension in him. But he did not touch her. Nor did he speak again of the matter that divided them. She practiced swordplay with him and alone in her bedchamber she practiced unsheathing the little dagger that he had given her, eventually managing to do so without tearing her skirts to shreds.

THE PUBLIC ASSEMBLY Rooms was a grand building on George Street, barely a stone's throw from the Duke of Read's house. But it was raining and Lord Michaels called the carriage.

"I don't care if Fingal must hitch up the team for a ride of a block and a half," he declared as she descended from her dressing room. "I refuse to allow the ladies I escort to a ball to be made uncomfortable at any moment of the evening. And I'm certain my cousin agrees. What, Saint?"

He stood in the dining-room doorway, and the familiar weakness of longing climbed through her. Evening dress suited him too well, his shoulders broad and square, his legs long, and the short, close whiskers on his jaw peculiarly unnerving. He looked like a gentleman, yet . . . *apart*, just as he had the night at Fellsbourne when she had not been able to look away.

"I do," he said to his cousin, but his eyes were on her. Appreciative. More than appreciative.

"No sword tonight?" she said.

"Prohibited in the Rooms," Lord Michaels said lightly. "Else I'd be wearing one myself. After that party at Loch Irvine's house, every girl in town is batting her lashes at this fellow. It's the sword," he confided to Eliza. "Ladies admire dangerous fellows, don't you know?"

"I know no such thing, you young scapegrace."

Umbrellas raised, they went to the carriage. By the step, Saint extended his hand. Constance hesitated.

"Go ahead," he said quietly. "I don't bite. That's your job, as I recall."

Fingers blessedly gloved, she accepted his assistance.

"Splendid of his lordship and the doctor to prefer chess to dancing tonight," Lord Michaels declared, slapping his palms to his knees. "More room on the seat." He smiled at everyone.

"What has you in such a high humor?" Eliza demanded. "It is enough to give a person a megrim."

"Oh, I do beg your pardon, ma'am! I shall endeavor to be staid instead."

But he did not. For two blocks he regaled them with the gossip heard at tea tables that afternoon. The duke's party and the girl who had been found that night seemed entirely forgotten in the anticipation of the first Assembly Rooms ball of the season. But Constance could not forget. She had plans tonight—plans that did not include the man sitting across from her in the carriage, his arms crossed, his emerald gaze upon her.

Her insides might betray her, but she was no longer the naïve girl from that night at Fellsbourne. She refused to be discombobulated by him.

"Do you dance, Mr. Sterling?" she said.

"A bit."

"Ha!" Lord Michaels snorted. "He's as light on his feet on the dance floor as a—well, as a fencer. Damn you, cousin, for being too blasted good at—"

"*Sir.*"

"Oh! A thousand pardons, Mrs. Josephs. I forget my tongue on occasion."

"You are forgiven, my lord," Constance said. "I forget mine as well." In darkened passages and stairwells, nearly begging a man to kiss her.

Saint was not quite smiling. "Will you spare a dance for me?"

She could not make her voice function, which had to be for the best. Nodding was safer. Then her tongue could not reveal her nerves that spun upon a six-year-old dream of dancing with him.

CONSTRUCTED ON A grand scale, with high ceilings and mirrored pillars throughout, the Assembly Rooms glittered with candlelight and hundreds of feminine adornments. Amidst the crowd, waiting at the door, the Duke of Loch Irvine greeted their party curtly.

Constance was gracious and soft-spoken with him, which made Saint grin. She had never spoken like that with him, not even years ago. But when the duke claimed her for the first set, and she tucked her hand cozily into his arm, Saint's amusement faded.

She glittered. Her gown was of some fine white fabric that shimmered like frost when she moved, her golden hair was swept up into an arrangement that allowed two locks to caress her neck, and her smile sparkled at her partner—a man she imagined was abducting and murdering girls. She was as unpredictable as the Scottish winds. But her warmth was constant, even when she acted the grand heiress.

He scanned the walls where young ladies of modest appearance and awkward mien stood with their chaperones. A girl with hair as fiery as Annie Favor's and orange spots across her nose stood at the edge of a group, staring at her toes.

He went to her. There were plenty of girls without partners in these rooms. It was a backward and too-late apology to Annie Favor for threatening her, even in jest. Rather, it was his penance. He would dance with every wallflower in the place tonight if it would atone for having even briefly teased a girl with violence.

Many dances later, he stood removed from the crowds, savoring a moment without small talk, when Constance's sweet lilt came at his shoulder.

"You have danced with every other woman here tonight. When will I be I allowed my turn?"

Her skin glowed as though in this place golden sunlight illumined it. He could not say to her that he had wished for this moment too many times. He could say none of the words that gathered upon his tongue now. Instead he extended his hand. With the briefest hesitation, she laid her gloved fingertips upon it.

"Good heavens," she whispered upon a thick inhale, her eyes on their hands, and it was all he could do to remain silent.

He led her into the set.

The dance gave them no opportunity to speak at length. But he had the pleasure at moments of the touch of her hand, and her bright gaze remained upon him throughout.

"You do dance wonderfully," she said when they met briefly.

"Fancy that."

She smiled, and he knew that this was what hell must be, endlessly wanting a woman yet having only moments and fleeting touches.

"I have been considering your question from the other day," she said and was parted from him.

"My question?" he said when the pattern brought them together again.

"About September, December, and now."

Dylan's supposed guilt.

"Not only considering," she said the next time they met. "Researching." This time she held on to his hand too long, and delayed the dancers behind her. With some scurrying, the others moved back into the pattern.

But they were watched now. In truth, she had been

watched since entering the Assembly Rooms. Everyone in Edinburgh high society was curious about the heiress who seemed pleased to be courted by the Devil's Duke.

"I determined the dates. Exact dates," she said quickly before they separated.

Shortly, the dance brought them together again.

"Equinoxes and the winter solstice," she said, the pleasure slipping from her features as she moved again away from him.

Seasonal rituals? Rituals of sacrifice. Not unknown in centuries past.

"I intend to examine the symbol," she whispered the next time they came close. "I have seen the symbol drawn on the cloak, and it is unclear. I—"

Another in their set took her hand and she glided away.

He watched her now, the buoyancy of her step, the color upon her cheeks. When she came near she said, "At the castle."

Haiknayes.

"No," he said.

"He is driving me there on Saturday." Her eyes flared with excitement.

He pulled her off the dance floor.

"What are you doing?" She glanced back at the dancers they had abandoned. "You cannot remove your partner from a set—"

"Are you going with him alone?" He released her hand.

"Eliza will accompany me, of course. And my father, I presume. Where did you learn to dance like that? I was the envy of every woman in the place just now."

"From the same man who taught me fencing, music, and philosophy. Your flatteries will not distract me. You must secure—"

"That was not flattery."

"—an invitation for Dylan."

The animation deserted her features.

"Gabriel is suspicious of Lord Michaels's teasing," she

said. "He is not a fool, Saint. Quite the opposite, I think." Her gaze slipped downward, across his chest, then back to his face. "And I think he wonders at your presence in my father's home. He asked about you earlier tonight."

"What did you tell him?"

"That my father's friend Dr. Shaw is passionately interested in learning how to fence, of course. You believe me now?"

"About my cousin?"

"About the girls. The secret society. The rituals."

"Constance." Music and conversation and laughter flowed around them, but he cared for none of it. "Do you want him?"

A sudden breath stole from her; he saw it in her parted lips and the jerk of her throat.

"I want to find those missing girls and the man responsible for murder," she said. "I imagine Libby and every other maiden in Edinburgh as his next victim."

He traced her features with his gaze, each curve and angle, each shade and texture fashioned with a master's tools, and the fevered spark in the blue of her eyes.

"Are you seeking danger?"

"No," she said quite sincerely. "But if I happen upon it, rest assured, you have prepared me to defend myself." She twitched at the hem of her skirt by her ankle. Then her shoulders dipped back. He followed her attention across the room as she moved away from him and walked directly to Sir Lorian Hughes.

He could not stop her from it, and he didn't particularly wish to. Just as she had been when they first met, she was still the intrepid girl prepared to meet the unknown without fear.

"Mr. Sterling?" A young woman stood beside him, black hair swept back from a face the perfect shape of a heart and her sweetly rounded figure on display in a gown that revealed the cleft of her breasts. Her dark eyes studied him with unmistakable appetite.

This was no wallflower. She was Sir Lorian Hughes's wife.

"Good evening," he said.

"I have heard ladies speak of you," she said, her gaze traveling over him. "But I did not understand until this moment quite how positively virile you would be."

He laughed.

Her lashes fluttered a bit. But her smile remained.

"I saw your last partner desert you. But some women are shortsighted like that. When Lady Constance has been married for a few years, she will sing a different tune, I suspect. Now, ask me to dance."

He smiled.

"Have I misspoken?" she said with another flutter of lashes. "How awkward. I beg your pardon."

"It is I who must beg yours," he said. "I am regularly diverted by the brazen incivility of members of your class. But I don't like to return that incivility."

"Incivility?" Slender black brows arched high. "I flattered you."

He bowed. "Forgive me, madam. I have had my surfeit of dancing tonight already."

"Perhaps another time." Her pout seemed more sweetness than contrivance. "You are refreshing, Mr. Sterling. I should like to see you again. Will you call upon me tomorrow? Three o'clock? I will close my doors to all others so that you and I can become better acquainted."

It was upon his lips to decline. But Constance's marked interest in Sir Lorian was certainly not idle. She was determined, single-minded, and it frightened him how he could look at the face of a beautiful woman now and still see only hers.

"I would like that," he said.

Lady Hughes walked away smiling.

Minutes later, Dylan found him. He had a crestfallen air about him.

"She's gone," he said. "Her father sent her to her aunt's

two days ago. The old bounder just told me with a triumphant smile. Said he'd keep her there till she comes to her senses or I leave Scotland, whichever happens first. Villain."

Sir Lorian had led Constance into the dance. A waltz.

"Why don't you discover her aunt's location and call upon her there?"

"Thought of that. Considered carrying her off to Gretna Green, or anyplace else. This is Scotland, after all. But you know, cousin, I've decided I'm not that sort of fellow. She'll be my wife someday. Till then I've got to behave like a man of honor with her *and* with the people who'll be my family, eventually. She's fond of her mother and sisters, even the obnoxious wart that's her brother. And of course her father. Never want her to feel she's got to choose between me and them."

Across the room, Constance smiled at her partner. Hughes held her at a distance. But her back was rigid, the muscles in her arms and the sinews in her neck strained. She was preventing him from drawing her closer as they danced.

"Perhaps she wants you to seek her out," he said.

"Then she'll send me a message," Dylan mumbled. "If she doesn't, well . . . She *will*. I'll wait. Edwards cannot keep her from me forever."

Sir Lorian's hand slid down from Constance's back to her waist, and she stumbled.

"By the way, Saint, I had an interesting conversation with Loch Irvine earlier this evening. Said he just went down to Newcastle-Upon-Tyne. Something about Tor's ship, the one you sent back north after—well . . ."

"After they did business together."

"Anyway, you know, that secret society . . . Do you think Tor was a member?"

The Torquil Sterling the world knew—perhaps. The man Saint knew—no. He was a carousing devil, but not a murderer. Saint had never understood how the brother he knew could so blithely trade in slaves. But there were piles of gold to be had in the trade, and Torquil had certainly loved gold.

"You know . . ." Dylan was looking askance again. "It might help my suit with Edwards to have a bit of blunt in my pockets. Do you think . . . might it be time to have that solicitor read your brother's will after all?"

"Why are you so certain he amassed a fortune?"

"Well it couldn't hurt to know for certain, could it? If he did, it would be impeccable timing for me to come into some funds." He grinned.

"All right." Ignorance of the truth did not change the truth. "When I am finished here."

Dylan glanced at the dance floor. "When do you imagine that will be, cousin? Ever?"

Sir Lorian was remarkably strong. And insistent. Constance kept her arms locked, her back stiff, resisting his urging to hold her closer. It was the most uncomfortable waltz she could recall.

"How are you enjoying Edinburgh, my lady?"

"It's delightful, all the museums and shops." She regarded him through her lashes. "But it is nothing out of the ordinary. Not after years in London. I wonder what one does for real *amusement* here. I suspect you know."

"I imagine I could invent some entertainment worthy of a lady of your sophisticated tastes." He smiled at her as though he owned her. "Speaking of which, I had the greatest pleasure of sitting in Parliament House beside a friend of yours."

Had.

"Oh?" She could manage no more.

"Lord Styles." He was watching her face closely. "A shame he was obliged to go abroad so abruptly. But those fellows who don't mind getting their hands dirty with merchant ships are forever negotiating deals."

"My father has been involved in eastern trade, sir." She

forced a tone of teasing indignation. "You mustn't dismiss it so entirely."

"Of course. But let's not bother with dull talk tonight. Let us instead turn ourselves to pleasure. I understand you are an avid horsewoman."

"My father breeds hunters. But I ride for diversion only."

"I'm fond of a satisfying ride. You and I must ride together sometime." His eyes were tight upon her. "Lord Styles intimated that you have a fondness for the crop."

Constance's stomach rose to her throat.

"I prefer the carriage whip," he continued, his grip cinching her waist. "The finest mares perform best when their driver does not spare them."

She felt her nostrils flare, her hands grow damp, yet could do nothing for it.

"It is a shame that you are unwed, Lady Constance."

"Is it?" she made herself say.

"My wife and I have membership in a private little society, you see. Only married couples are admitted."

"How singular," she choked out.

"It is a singular sort of society. For those of mature tastes." His smile invited confidences. "But perhaps you won't be long for the altar." Sir Lorian's tongue lingered on the final word. "Then I might secure an invitation for you to our little society, and take up your riding instruction where my friend left off."

The musicians drew the waltz to a close. Constance tugged out of Sir Lorian's hold, everything inside her flushing cold and then hot.

"Until our ride, my lady." He bowed.

She fled. In her head was a twisted sickness of panic and dread as she went swiftly from the ballroom and up the stairs to the ladies' retiring room. Cold water on her cheeks and the nape of her neck would help. Three minutes alone to still her pulse and calm her churning stomach. She could do this. She was no fragile miss. Rather, Diana, a huntress stalking her quarry. Athena, armed for battle.

This time she would win.

THE HOUR WAS late, the crowd thinned. Saint had no trouble following her from the ballroom and up the stairs. She went swiftly, her cheeks pale and fists sunk in her skirts.

On the floor above, women's voices came from beyond a partially opened door. Another narrow stairway led up into darkness.

She would not join other women now. She would never reveal her vulnerability.

He took the stairs three at a time and found her just beyond the turn, in shadow limned in lamplight from below. Back pressed against the wall, she opened her eyes.

He went to her. "It seems you are making a habit at parties of escaping into empty stair—"

She grabbed his hand. Her fingertips dug into his palm.

Sudden anger seized him. "What did he do?"

"Lend me your strength. For a moment, if you will, and I will recover." She brought them palm-to-palm, twining her fingers with his. The action, so trusting, so intimate and vulnerable, hollowed out his chest.

"My strength is yours," he said. "Say the word, and whomever has distressed you will know my displeasure upon the edge of my blade."

"What will you do, Sir Knight?" The barest glimmer of relief shone in her eyes. "Draw on him in the middle of the minuet?"

"If necessary. I have no concern for the rules of your society. I don't care if I am barred from every house in Britain."

"I was frightened," she said, memory twisting inside her. "This helps."

He held her fingers tightly and with his other hand he turned her face up so that she must meet his gaze.

"Before—" he said. "Days ago in the ballroom, you were frightened when I held you."

"Yes."

"Are you frightened of me now?" His voice was low, deep, and beautiful.

"No. Yes. I don't know. But I want you to kiss me anyway."

He took her waist in his hands, wrapping them around her with such secure certainty that a fragmented sigh stole through her lips. His palm smoothed downward, over her hip, capturing the silk of her gown in an exploration of her that was at once innocent and erotic. Then, releasing her hand, he cupped her jaw. With the stroke of his thumb across her lips and the emerald fire in his eyes, he did not demand; he asked a second time.

She breathed, "Yes."

He bent his head, his lips above hers so close. "You might want to close your eyes for this."

"No."

He drew away slightly. "No, don't kiss you?"

"No, I want to see it. The only thing I didn't like about kissing you before was not being able to see you."

A moment's silence became two. Then he said, "The only thing."

"The only thing."

Finally he kissed her.

Softly, his lips brushed hers once. Then again. As though he wished only to capture a trace of her essence, he kissed first her upper lip, then the lower, fleetingly, the hush of their breaths enchanting the silence between them. Then he brought their mouths together. She let him kiss her and she felt his desire in the beauty of this caress and in his hands that held her with such careful strength. She wanted to bolt and run and she wanted to stay and sink into him completely.

"Saint," she whispered.

"Don't make me stop," he said roughly.

"Don't stop." Fingers twining in his hair, she pulled him down to her and opened her lips to him.

Just as six years ago, he was perfect. He kissed her and pleasure stole sweetly and hotly through her. Tears prickled the backs of her eyes. Aching with relief and a nascent joy she could barely believe, she met his kisses with parted lips. Frightening and honest and delicious, exactly as she remembered it, his kiss sought her. He wanted her desire and she gave it to him. Circling her hands around his arms, she went onto her toes and she allowed herself to taste him with her tongue.

"*Constance.*"

He seized her lips and she let him inside, felt him, and lust arced through her. She had known he wanted this, and she had longed for it. But this was *real*—his skin and scent and heat—animal and beautiful and physical, like they had never allowed themselves to be, like they had always wanted since the first. She grasped his waist as his hands surrounded her face. Closer, urgently now, he took her mouth completely, not allowing time to breathe, or to think. Each stroke of his tongue drove pleasure deeper into her. Each caress opened her body for more of him.

He dragged her against him. She went into his arms willingly, hot, and eager. Clinging to him, with her breasts and legs she felt the hard muscle of his chest and thighs, perfect, *so perfect*. Beneath his coat, she pulled at his shirt and sought his flesh with her hands. His skin was smooth, taut, a masterpiece of male beauty. She raked her fingertips over him, needing the reality of his body in her hands, feeling it inside her with a wild desperation. She *needed* him. She needed him to touch her. She ached for it, for pleasure, honest pleasure.

Grasping his wrist, she drew his hand between her thighs.

A shudder shook him. He broke the kiss and pressed his brow to hers.

"Constance, I—"

"Touch me, Saint. *Please*. Help me feel—" She caught the words behind her teeth. "Help me."

He closed his hand around her.

Pleasure.

Sweet, sharp, forbidden.

Finding by her gasps where the pleasure was greatest for

her, he caressed her and she let herself feel it. He touched her perfectly, beautifully, making her arch to him and sigh and need more with each stroke. Beneath her hands his skin was hot, his muscles hard, and inside she was tightening, surging, and hungry for release.

She came against their interlocked hands with such relief that she could not contain her moan. He pulled his hand from beneath hers and sank it into her hair, and dragged her mouth under his. She let him bear her back against the wall, mad for this, for his hands on her body, his arousal against hers. Her palms swept up his back beneath his shirt. She had never thought she would feel this, that she *could* feel this—not like this, *never like this*. Digging her fingertips into him, holding him tight, she let him touch her everywhere.

A gasp sounded nearby.

"Good *gracious*! Maude, turn away!"

Constance's eyes snapped open to see Saint's, fevered, moving over her face.

"Mama, I think that is Lady Constance. I recognize her gown."

"No! It *couldn't* be. Go—go down the steps, Maude. Immediately!"

Saint's hands slid out of her hair.

"And Mr. *Sterling*?"

"Maude, *now*!" Lady Easterberry's demand came shrilly from the base of the stairs.

The steps creaked. Then, from farther away, came a flurry of whispers and exclamations. They faded quickly.

Constance flattened her palms to the wall behind her, biting her softened lips and tasting him there. He ran a hand over his face and around to the back of his neck, and took in a heavy breath.

"So . . . *not* secret," she said unsteadily. "It seems you have your wish."

Confusion then anger flashed through his eyes. "Do you think that I—"

She reached out and pulled herself against him.

"No," she whispered, twisting her fingers into his waistcoat and feeling him beneath it. One last moment of him. "Thank you." Releasing him, she went swiftly down the stairs.

Chapter 17

Vows

Dearest Lady,

You claim that a husband's marriage vows promise less than a wife's. And yet here is his vow: "With this ring I thee wed, with my body I thee worship, and with all my worldly goods, I thee endow." That is, he gives her everything he has. He worships her like a goddess.

What more, kind lady, can you expect a man to give?

In long-suffering affection,
Peregrine
Secretary, The Falcon Club

To Peregrine, at large:

No doubt it has escaped your notice from your height of privilege that—despite the sacred words that you quote—when a woman weds, the Law of this Kingdom places her income, belongings, indeed her entire person in the possession of her husband. She has no power or authority over her money, her property, her children, even her own body. She can do nothing without his consent, including leave him if he treats her with cruelty.

Marriage does not bestow upon a woman a devotee. It shackles her to a prison guard.

—Lady Justice

Chapter 18

The Offer

"It wasn't to be hoped they would keep it to themselves. Lady Easterberry is a sorry gossip and Maude is a peahen." Eliza picked threads from her embroidery one stitch at a time. "Her sister, Patience Westin, has a good head. If she had been the one to discover you, she might have been able to convince her flibbertigibbet mother to keep it mum."

"It isn't even noon yet." Constance stood at the window of the parlor, looking out onto the street. Rain pounded a steady beat on the windowpanes beyond which carriages and carts splashed puddles hither and thither. And yet her maid had already heard the news from a neighbor's maid. "Lady Easterberry and Miss Anderson must have gone calling at a shockingly early hour."

"Would you have remained at home until a more reasonable hour if you were brimming over with *that* news?"

"I do not spread gossip, Eliza. I collect it."

"Now you create it," Eliza said, and poked the needle through the linen.

Constance turned to her companion, putting her back to

the last place she had seen Saint, riding out before breakfast. She did not blame him for escaping. She had said nothing to him the night before in the carriage, and nothing again when they entered the house. There was nothing that could be said in the presence of others. But what would she have said even in private? That he was the first man to touch her like that? That she was hot and panicked merely recalling it? And that if she could turn the clock back, she would do it exactly the same again?

Still, she had not expected him to be gone all day.

"I must tell Father before he hears it from others."

Two riders halted before the house.

"Oh, good heavens," Eliza said, peering out the window. "But I suppose we should have anticipated this. He is unconventional, isn't he? Both of them, I daresay."

Alongside Saint on his magnificent horse, the Duke of Loch Irvine was dismounting before the house. A groom rushed out and took their mounts' reins, and the men ascended the front steps.

The footman who opened the parlor door announced only one man.

"His Grace, the Duke of Loch Irvine," he said, and admitted Gabriel Hume.

He had not removed his wet coat, and he swept his hat off brusquely in a shower of raindrops. The footman closed the door but the duke remained where he stood.

Constance curtsied. "Good day."

"Not much good about it now, in truth." He looked at Eliza. "Ma'am, would you be giving me a moment o' your lady's time alone?"

"Absolutely not," she said. "Whatever you have come to say, you must say it in my presence."

"Eliza," Constance said. "Please go."

With a narrow eye, Eliza snatched up her embroidery and went out.

"Sterling's told me that I'm certain to hear news o' you that I willna like. News o' the two o' you. Is it true?"

"It is."

His brow lowered. "We're not betrothed, and I'm not in luve with you. You've no cause to fret that I'll be throwing a mighty tirr."

"Thank you. I am sorry."

"I'm disappointed, though. You're intelligent, and I've need o' such a woman."

He had *need* of an intelligent woman?

"And your money," he added with an absent gesture of his hat. "But I canna allow my wife to carry on with another man, even one who's man enough to tell me the truth o' it himself. You understand."

"Of course." She sounded chastened because she felt it, in equal parts guilt and frustration. She had not wanted to hurt or shame him. But also, this would end their meetings. She would lose access to his house.

"I've no cause to tell your father the reason I'm withdrawing my suit."

"As you wish."

With an abrupt bow, he went to the door, then looked over his shoulder.

"The lass wished to see the collection in my house. My father's collection." For the first time since entering the room he sounded uncomfortable. "I will arrange it."

"That is generous of you."

"Well, she didna betray me, did she?"

He departed and Constance went to her father's study.

A portrait of the first Duke of Read dominated the room: a sixteenth-century kilted laird of advanced years and thick beard but the same strikingly hard blue eyes as her father. The present duke sat beneath it at his desk. Except for the dogs dozing about the floor, his study was pristine. Nothing but a pen, inkpot, blotter, and lamp adorned his desk, as well as a neat folio of papers upon which his attention was focused.

"Close the door, Constance."

"Father, I—"

"I have just heard the news." His voice was cold. "Dr. Shaw had it from a patient not an hour ago. It seems you are now a celebrity of the most deplorable sort. How long, I wonder, before Loch Irvine hears of it?"

"He called just now. He has withdrawn his suit."

Finally, he lifted his eyes to her. "Are you telling me that you were not able to convince him that you were not at fault?"

"I was at fault."

He stood, a tower of iron disapproval. "That hardly matters. How you choose to squander your modesty is not at issue here."

"It h-hardly *matters*?" Her words stumbled. "Does it mean nothing to you whether I acted voluntarily last night or involuntarily?"

"Of course you acted voluntarily. I did not raise a daughter foolish enough to make herself a victim. What is at issue now is the success of this union."

A victim.

Once upon a time, his steely anger had made her cower and run for her horse and the hills, the woods, anywhere she could breathe and forget that her mother was gone and he was all she had. Now, as a horrible chill invaded her, laughter welled up in her throat.

"You are a study in contradictions, Father. You insist that I wed before my birthday so that I can retain possession of my mother's fortune, and with it some autonomy in marriage. Yet you insist upon the man I marry. Is the latter to protect your consequence? Must your daughter be a duchess? If so, there are at least three other unmarried dukes in Britain, and more abroad. I'm certain we can scare up an aging widower for me in the next few weeks."

"This is not about your mother's dowry. It never was."

Her brittle amusement dissolved. "I—"

"After all of these years, do you understand so little of how I have cultivated you to succeed?"

The air seemed to go entirely still around her in the

manner of wild things that silenced in the moment before the break of a storm.

"Cultivated?"

"You were to be the best. I assured it. Your character from the earliest years showed too much eagerness to defy restrictions. But I knew that could be honed into an asset rather than a weakness, and I made it so. I ensured that you became self-reliant instead of rebellious. I gave you everything you required to excel, to become an extraordinary woman. For the most part you have done precisely what I wished. Until now. This was careless. I am exceedingly disappointed in you." His fingertips pressed against the surface of his desk. Constance stared at them. Here was a father she had not known, who by his own account had intentionally guided her rather than ignored her.

She could not believe it.

"Perhaps I have disappointed you, Father," she said slowly. "But the disappointment is mutual. I never intended to wed the Duke of Loch Irvine. I have allowed his courtship in order to get close to him. In doing so, I have learned that he stays quite alone and often makes short journeys away from home. I have not yet confirmed whether he is the Devil's Duke that rumor claims. But I am close to clues that will help me solve the mystery of the abductions of two girls over the past several months here in Edinburgh, and the murder of the girl found just the other night. So, you see, I have used your lessons in self-reliance to make something of myself. I only wonder that you are so ignorant of everything that goes on around you to have missed entirely that society believes the man you chose to be my husband is a monster."

His lips were a white line. "And now you have destroyed the single most promising opportunity of learning his secrets."

She could not have heard him correctly. "I have—?"

"As his wife you would have had the necessary access to him and his properties to discover the truth of his involvement in this business. Indeed, I depended upon him inviting you to participate."

"To *participate*?"

"Now that avenue is closed, unless you can convince him to reconcile."

"You *know* what people say of him? You suspect him of it yet you intended me to marry him anyway?"

"I am not interested in rumors circulated by idiots. Loch Irvine is not what he is believed to be. I have been watching him for some time and in January learned news of him that must be investigated. I have not idly allowed you to remain unwed, Constance. I knew there would come a time when it would be to our advantage. This was that time, but your actions last night ruined that."

"*Our*? Of whom else do you speak? For surely it is not I."

"You must marry now. That is without question. Your reputation has proven resilient in the past, but it cannot withstand this scandal. You will choose between Michaels or Gray. Michaels is a lackwit, but entirely benign and more importantly convenient at present. You will be able to control him. It is likely that he will never have any idea of your work unless you tell him. Gray will not be led by you, of course, but he will do as I wish in this. It is not my preference to diminish the Club's reach by binding agents together in marriage. But it could eventually prove useful."

"*What*?" she whispered.

"You have gone too far this time, Constance. Your friendship with Ben Doreé served its purpose in allowing you to remain unwed. But you cannot continue the work I intend for you if you are no longer received universally, which you will be if your name is unfavorably associated with a man of no rank. You will mend this now. Unless you believe you can convince Loch Irvine of your contrition, choose which you will have—Michaels or Gray—and prepare for your wedding."

"Lord Gray?" There was a twisting sickness in her chest. "Father . . ." She stared at his face. "Are you the director of the Falcon Club?"

"He is," Eliza said behind her. "And he has done a piss-poor job of arranging matters this time."

"That is enough, Elizabeth. I hold you equally account-able as my daughter for this travesty."

She turned her bony shoulder to him. "I never agreed with his plan to wed you to Loch Irvine. I attempted to dis-suade him from it more than once."

"You knew? All this time?" Memories tangled, criss-crossing and confused. Eliza had known about Saint years ago. "But—"

"I never approved of the introduction of Mr. Sterling into this household," Eliza said swiftly.

"You wanted me to learn how to use a blade so I would be able to defend myself against the duke if it became neces-sary," she said to her father. "Didn't you?"

"Your cousin assured me that you had become proficient with a pistol. But if Loch Irvine threatened you, it was nec-essary that you be able to retaliate swiftly."

"Retaliate? You imagined I might attack my own hus-band if he threatened me?"

"I did not prefer that scenario, of course."

"And yet you planned for its possibility. Without telling me." Cold and heat flushed over her in quick waves.

"There are a score of aging fencing masters you could have chosen to teach her self-defense, Angus," Eliza said. "You needn't have invited a handsome young man to do so. I am sorry now to have the opportunity to say that I told you so." She cast Constance a glance that said more: she had not told him about that fortnight at Fellsbourne years ago.

"Why did you choose him, Father?"

"His brother partnered with Loch Irvine in several busi-ness ventures. I hoped he knew details of those, but I have been disappointed in that. And I chose him because he is the best. In the finest *salles* in London, his skill is spoken of with awe, despite his refusal to teach in any of them. I have always provided you with the wherewithal to succeed. The Club is not the end game, Constance. It has been your training ground only. There is more at stake here than three girls. Someday you will understand that."

The world was turned upside down.

"My cousin," she said. "Leam. Did he know it was you all along? Did he agree with this plan?"

"No," her father replied. "He must be told now, of course."

"It's about time," Eliza clipped.

"And Lord Gray? He has communicated with you directly these past five years. Has he always known?"

"Yes."

Her friend, Colin.

And Eliza, her confidant, the only person she had trusted with her secrets after her mother died.

"What of Ben?"

"No. His interests often coincide with mine. But it never became necessary to inform him."

As he recited this litany of secrets, her grief transformed into anger. And then understanding.

"And Mr. Sterling?" she said. "Once he learned that I was to be his student, he did not wish to remain. He intended to leave. What did you say to him to make him stay?"

"He tried to bribe him," Eliza said, "and when the young man was immoveable in that manner, your father threatened him."

"You *threatened* him?"

"I suggested to him that I was more valuable as a friend than an enemy," her father said.

"Does he know? About any of the rest?"

"Of course not."

Bribery. Threats. He had stayed because her father had forced him to. It was too much to bear. She had no one now, nothing but herself, just as years ago when her mother disappeared.

"I will not marry Lord Michaels or Lord Gray."

His fingers pressed harder into the desktop. "You will."

"Drag me to the altar beside whichever nobleman you choose, Father, and then watch my naturally defiant nature in action. I have no intention of continuing as a pawn in your unfeeling games, unwittingly or otherwise. I choose to remain unmarried."

He moved, rounding the desk and coming toward her. Eliza hurried to her side.

"If you threaten this girl, Angus, I will make you very sorry you ever knew me."

He ignored her. "I will cut you off. You will have nothing. No house in London. No allowance. No carriage. No gowns. No horse. And no companion to allow you to remain in society unwed. Within the day Mrs. Josephs will find herself homeless."

Eliza grabbed her hand. "Don't listen to him, child."

"You would cast her out after ten years as a member of our family? Father, you outdo yourself."

"I will not have all the efforts I have lavished upon you wasted in a momentary fit of temper."

"This is not a fit, Father. It is who I am, that self-reliant person you crafted so carefully."

"I had thought better of you."

"While I had thought both better and worse of you. For my entire life. And I begin to think my mother's fifty thousand pounds is more important to you than you have said. Is it? Do you have a plan for that money that will be ruined if I fail to marry by my twenty-fifth birthday?"

His eyes were as hard as she had ever seen them.

"I see." She moved away from Eliza, folding her shaking hands before her. When she was on the other side of the room she turned to her father. "I am prepared to make a bargain with you."

"What is it?"

"It is this: If you allow me to marry as I wish, including the dowry that you offered to the Duke of Loch Irvine, I will do so before my birthday and you may have your fifty thousand pounds—entirely free of other conditions, except this one: upon my marriage you will remove permanently to Castle Read and I will take up residence here or in the house in London as I wish, and I will cease to pursue the Devil's Duke or any other mystery. I have no desire to continue to be involved in your web of secrets. Remarkably enough, it has all become distasteful to me of a sudden. Do you agree to my terms?"

"Who is your chosen groom?"

"Frederick Sterling."

Eliza gasped.

Constance held her father's gaze with all the serenity she had learned during years of trying to please him, to be a daughter he might love enough to pay her attention. She had never dreamed he had been paying attention to her all along, training her to hunt and fetch as he dictated. Like one of his dogs.

"Mr. Sterling it will be, then," she said into the silence. "Shall we shake hands on it, or shall I risk accepting your word alone?"

"If you do this solely to defy me, you will regret it, Constance."

"Astonishingly, I do this because you have offered me an ultimatum and I do not wish to entirely relinquish the life I have lived for twenty-five years." Her throat caught. She swallowed over it, hoping he had not heard. "And because he is a good man."

"Is he? A man who would compromise an unwed woman in a public place? Is that honorable, Constance?"

"I *begged* him to." Her breaths came hard but her voice remained strong. "I begged. These past weeks he has done everything he could to help me and yet remain aloof from me. Last night I was distressed, and when he offered me comfort I begged him to hold me. Does that disgust you, Father? Are you sorry now that you wasted so much effort on such an unruly specimen of femininity?"

"For pity's sake," Eliza choked out. "Constance, I have failed you. Both of us have."

"Father?"

"You are making a mistake in this, Constance," he said.

"I don't think so. I trust him. Quite a lot more than I trust you."

"So be it. Mrs. Josephs, send a footman for Mr. Sterling."

Stunned, she watched Eliza leave. It seemed a dream. Reality was scampering away from her, the revelations of these minutes leaving an echoing chamber of disbelief inside her.

By the time Eliza returned and Saint entered the room, her father had taken up the position behind his desk again. He wanted to appear forbidding and threatening, she understood now.

The swordsman seemed not to notice this display of power.

"My lady," he said with a graceful bow and eyes that showed both resignation and appreciation of her. He turned his attention on her father. "If you have summoned me here to chastise me, I beg you to save your breath. I told you weeks ago that I won't be threatened. And as you already know, I am even less amenable to scolds." He looked to her again. "Constance, I cannot be sorry for having been the cause for the end of your betrothal to a man you do not wish to marry. But know that if I could silence the mention of your name upon the tongues of gossips now, I would do all in my power to make it so."

"You can, Mr. Sterling," her father said.

"A public hanging is much more likely to encourage gossip than diminish it, sir."

"Ha!" Eliza cracked a laugh. "I said you were a fool to bring him here, Angus. Some men are not as easily intimidated as you like."

"In fact I am sufficiently intimidated, Mrs. Josephs," Saint said. "I have no doubt he could make my life exceedingly uncomfortable if he chose. I will depart this hour." He turned to her, and Constance felt as though the world was ending and beginning at once. "I only wished to first ask your daughter to give me leave to do so."

"She will not," her father said. "Mr. Sterling, I offer to

you my daughter's hand, including all the attendant benefits accruing from such a match—dowry, properties, privileges, etcetera. Do you accept?"

Silence seized the room, the only sounds a distant clatter of a carriage passing by on the rainy street and a servant's whistle in an upper chamber.

"I beg your pardon?" he said in a low, quiet voice.

"What do you not understand?" the duke said with an edge of impatience.

"What do I not understand?" Saint repeated, and then sharply: "Is this a—is this some sort of ruse, like the lie that brought me here initially?" He turned to her. "Is it?"

"No. He is sincere," she managed to utter.

"Mr. Sterling, the public sensation that my daughter and you have created has caused the Duke of Loch Irvine to withdraw his offer. She must wed before her twenty-fifth birthday in less than four weeks or forfeit a large sum of money. The latter is, of course, undesirable. But arranging another suitable match for her at this late date is not possible. The simplest solution is for the two of you to wed. If you agree to it, she will retain possession of that money, but her dowry, which is considerable, will be yours."

"I don't want it."

The duke frowned. "What sort of man refuses a dowry of twenty-five thousand pounds?"

His lips parted without speech. Finally he said, "The sort of man who never thought to have a bride upon whom a dowry of twenty-five pounds had been settled, let alone twenty-five *thousand*. I came here to earn enough money to feed and stable my horse through the year. You are offering me a noblewoman and a fortune. I need a moment, if you please. With Constance."

"Not until you are wed. Not a minute alone before that, or accompanied by Mrs. Josephs or Lord Michaels."

"Hmph," Eliza snorted.

Constance dragged her attention from the astonishment upon Saint's features to her father's implacable stare.

"Father—"

"Do you accept my offer, Mr. Sterling? I will not make it a third time."

There was a heartbeat's pause.

"I accept it."

A strange weakness rushed through her, crowding out the elation she had felt since stating her ultimatum. Saint's shoulders were rigid, and now he did not look at her.

"My man of business will prepare the contract," her father said. "There is still time yet for the banns to be read. That nod to propriety should quiet the gossips if not silence them."

"I must go to London to see to my brother's affairs," Saint said.

"Of course. The contract can wait until your return."

Left hand on the hilt of his sword, finally Saint turned his gaze upon her. "My lady."

Throat closed, she nodded. He departed.

"You have your wish," her father said. "I hope that you understand what you have sacrificed."

She thought of Saint's distant eyes before he left the room, and she understood entirely.

PART III

The Bride

Chapter 19

The Most Expensive Bottle in the Place

Baker & Chambliss, Solicitors
London, England

$\mathcal{D}$ylan opted to travel to London with him. "The old curmudgeon won't let me see my pearl anyway. No cause for me to hang about Edinburgh. And I cannot abide Read's frosty glowers."

"He doesn't glower." The Duke of Read rarely revealed any feeling. Saint wondered how his vibrant daughter had borne that steely parenting. But then he found himself thinking about her eyes hazy with passion and her hot mouth and her fingers scraping across his back, and forgetting the street he was looking for, and the reason he'd just ridden hundreds of miles, and his own name.

"'Course he does," Dylan insisted, doffing his hat to a pair of ladies in a passing carriage. "Hope it's not catching.

Wouldn't like to see you start glowering too, now that you're going to be a member of the family." His eyes twinkled.

"Enough already."

"Saint, my boy, you are the most peculiar fellow I know. Any other man would be shouting for joy that he'd just nabbed the most beautiful girl in Scotland—Britain! And twenty-five thousand pounds in the bargain. What your difficulty is with celebrating your good fortune, I can't for the life of me see."

The difficulty with his good fortune was that it was too good. *Unbelievably* good.

One kiss, and she was to be his? The heiress who had turned away men of rank and fortune? The stunning beauty with a thirst for danger who had engineered a courtship from a man she suspected of crimes so that she could investigate him closer? The passionate woman whose eyes flared with panic even as she reached for him?

He wasn't ready to celebrate. Not until he understood what in the hell was going on.

"Here's the place." Dylan gestured to a modest brass plaque on a door and drew his mount to a halt. "I won't play coy with you, cousin," he said less cheerily. "I'm damn glad we're finally here. Can't lay old Tor to rest entirely till this is done."

A narrow man wearing spectacles opened the door to them. "My lord." He bowed. "Mr. Sterling? I have been expecting you for months." He led them into an office furnished sparsely but expensively. "Tea?"

"I'll take a spot of claret, Chambliss," Dylan said.

The wine was poured, its year and bouquet appreciated, while Saint waited. He hadn't come here to chat with the solicitor over vintages. But Dylan would be Dylan. And he was in no hurry to learn the truth about his brother's business ventures. He was doing this only so that he would not bring Constance unexpected trouble.

"Shall we begin?" Chambliss finally said, opening a portfolio across his desk. "Mr. Sterling's holdings were not terribly diverse, but they were lucrative. I was instructed to withdraw all investments upon notification of his death—"

"He instructed you of this?" Saint asked.

"Five years ago. When Lord Michaels informed me of his death in January, I did as your brother instructed, leaving only one investment active, which is due to pay out in June. That is a shipping venture currently en route to Port-au-Prince. It should net a considerable sum."

"All right then," Dylan said impatiently. "Give us the grand total."

"Without including the investment that I have just mentioned, or the property in Kingston and the house in Devon, all told, Mr. Sterling, your brother's worth at the time of his death was eighty-four thousand pounds."

Dylan's face went white.

Saint closed his eyes.

"If you wish, I will be glad to find purchasers for both properties," Chambliss continued. "The Devonshire house is a fine specimen of Elizabethan architecture on a valuable parcel. According to the surveyors Mr. Sterling hired last autumn, it is also sitting on a cache of coal. It should bring a fine price. While property is not as sought after in Kingston as it was several decades ago, the warehouse will still interest buyers, of course. Those should be easy to convert to liquid assets. The two ships are, of course, also of value."

"Mr. Chambliss," Saint forced through his tight throat. "How much of my brother's money came from the sale of human cargo?"

The solicitor's brows peaked. "Sir?"

Saint leaned forward and placed his elbows on his knees. "Please. I have no intention of exposing you or my brother's associates to the law. But I need to know."

"None of it, sir."

"None?" Dylan exclaimed.

"My brother gave us to understand that his ships transported cargo that, on occasion, could not bear official inspection."

"The investments he hired me to oversee were all entirely legitimate. Your brother was a savvy investor, and astonishingly fortunate."

"He did have the Devil's luck at cards," Dylan mumbled.

"Could the ships have made journeys unknown to you?" Saint asked.

"Impossible. I will study the records again, if you wish, but for ten years I have followed them closely and I recall nothing odd in the itineraries. The *Queen Anne*'s route was regular between Boston and Kingston. And while the *Gladiator* occasionally took a turn through the North Sea, as you know, sir," he said with a frown, "its usual itinerary was Kingston to Portsmouth, and for the past few years since the treaty, occasionally Nantes. Neither ship sailed to African ports. I have no records of human cargo shipped from the West Indies, either. Only passengers."

"Passengers?"

"It is common for merchant ships to take on a handful of passengers to increase the gross earnings of a journey."

Dylan shifted in his chair. "While this is all as fascinating as rust on a carriage wheel, I would like to know the distribution of my cousin's gold."

"The land, houses, shop, ships, and warehouse all now belong to Mr. Sterling, and the liquid assets are to be divided into four parts: one to you, my lord; two to Mr. Sterling; and the fourth to a charitable institution that your brother designated specifically."

Dylan's breath exploded from him. He leaped up, grabbed the solicitor's hand, and pumped it up and down.

"Good show, Chambliss! This is cause for celebration. What say you, Saint, let's head over to that pub down the block, buy the most expensive bottle in the place, and get soused, shall we?"

Saint stood. "Take no action on the properties at this time, Mr. Chambliss. I would like information on that charitable institution sent to Lord Michaels's flat today, please."

"Yes, sir. Of course."

They departed, Dylan with a skip in his step.

"Twenty-one thousand pounds! This is a capital day. An exceedingly capital day! Edwards won't be able to deny me his daughter now."

Edwards: provincial petty gentry, reluctant to marry his daughter to a baron because of his lack of funds.

Read: a duke bestowing his heiress upon a man of no status with no more than fifty pounds to his name.

Not right. Read was not to be trusted. And his daughter . . . She would be his wife.

Chapter 20

A Wedding Night

After his journey, she saw him for the first time from the opposite end of the church. An empty aisle stretched between them, paved with stone, and cold beneath her silk slippers. Her hands were damp around the bouquet of roses.

They were white roses. That morning her bridegroom had sent them to her from the hotel at which he and Lord Michaels had taken rooms upon their return to Edinburgh. He sent them with no note, only his name. The name that would shortly be hers.

Her stomach hurt. Her mouth was dry. But amidst the colorful gowns, bonnets, hats, and coats of the guests packed into the church, she saw only his slight smile as he watched her walk toward him.

The ceremony was swift, his voice strong as he spoke his vows, and the touch of his hands as he slid the ring onto her finger warm but brief. When it was over she looked up into the otherworldly eyes of her husband and tears gathered in her throat. She swallowed them back and smiled.

At the church door, he entwined their fingers and held her

tightly as they walked through the well-wishers tossing rice. He did not speak to her, nor she to him.

She had never imagined her father would agree to her ultimatum. When Saint left for London, she had fully expected her father to cancel the bargain and level a threat at her fencing instructor that would banish him forever. She had never expected to see him again. She went into her own wedding celebration bemused.

He seemed at ease among their guests, whom he barely knew. Rarely was he not at ease, except when he held her.

"Well, Con, you are as stunning a bride as I always knew you would be." Silvery gray eyes appraising, her friend Wyn Yale studied her face. He had a sharp appreciation for farce, and she suspected he understood that this house now filled with gawkers and gossips and very few actual friends was precisely that.

"Thank you, darling," she replied. "I clean up nicely, don't I?"

"As nicely as your groom," Leam's wife, Kitty, said, and glanced at Saint across the room. "It is obvious to me why you chose him. Despite your nerves—"

"She does not have nerves," Wyn interjected, "rather, ambrosia running through her veins."

"Despite your nerves today," Kitty continued, "the two of you seem perfectly natural together. And really, Constance, he is positively . . . well . . . I cannot say it with Wyn and Leam listening."

Her husband grunted. "'Tis the sword."

"Ladies do like a nice hard weapon," Wyn murmured.

"*Wyn.*" Kitty laughed. "You are making the bride blush."

He eyed her. "Am I, Con?"

Constance could not quite manage a smile. "No. But thank you, Kitty."

"Still," Kitty said, "it astonishes me that your father has allowed this."

"Guilt," Leam growled. "He's been putting it over on the lot of us for years. He could not deny her now."

"It isn't guilt," the Viscount Gray said, entering their group. "Your uncle, Blackwood, never does anything without a carefully planned strategy. You should know that by now. Do you have any idea what his strategy is this time, Constance?" Dark-eyed and tall, with a natural air of authority tempered by gravity, he showed no contrition now for the secret he had been hiding from them all for years.

"I believe I do, Colin," she said. "But I will not be sharing it with you. How do you like it when the tables are turned?"

A shallow dent appeared in his cheek. "You are your father's daughter, whether you like it or not."

"We are all marked with our parents' stamp." Lady Emily Vale appeared at her best friend Kitty's side, and spoke directly to the viscount. "It is the manner in which we cast off those marks that defines us."

Colin's eyes took on a gleam that Constance had never before seen.

"Is it, then?" he said.

"It is true, of course," Emily added, "that some prefer to embrace their parents' mistakes rather than correct them."

Colin's reply was the shifting of a muscle in his jaw.

"Now, here's something I never thought to see." Wyn looked from Emily to Colin. "A man she likes less than me. Congratulations, Gray. I commend you on this accomplishment. What have you done to ruffle her? You're not the teasing sort, after all."

"Isn't he?" Emily said with obvious surprise.

"Not for eighteen years at least," Colin replied and turned to Constance. "Felicitations, my lady." He bowed over her hand. "I wish you happiness."

"I don't forgive you, you know."

"You will." With a nod to the others, he departed.

Wyn turned fully to Emily. "*Do* tell, my lady. Names, dates, places, anything necessary for me to understand the reason for your disdain of the inestimable Lord Gray. I want to write it all down and compare it to my list of deficiencies, and then crow."

"Stop, Wyn," Kitty said. "Pocahontas needn't explain herself to you or anyone else."

"It's clear at least that she needn't explain it to our redoubtable viscount. He seems to be in the know. And it's Pocahontas that you're going by now? Charming."

"You are a wart upon the foot of humanity," Emily said. "I don't know how Diantha bears you."

He grinned. "Currently by casting up her accounts daily—"

"I don't blame her in the least."

"—due to my child that she is carrying."

"It seems she has fewer wits than I thought."

"You two bicker like siblings," Kitty said with a fond smile and tucked her hand into Constance's. "Constance, it has been a delightful sennight here with you. And I have grown tremendously fond of Dr. Shaw and Libby. I should like to remain longer and become better acquainted with your husband too. But the two of you must want some time alone, and we should be returning home to the children tomorrow."

A footman offered champagne. Constance declined it. Her head was light enough without aid.

"I hope we can all gather this fall when Jinan and Viola have returned from abroad," she said. "I adored having Jamie at the castle in February."

"Aye," Leam said. "The bait that brought the swordsman to Scotland, with my unwitting assistance." Along with Ben Doreé, he was the closest to a brother she had, and now he looked upon her somberly. "Constance, take care. My uncle has been playing a deep game. I don't wish to see you hurt."

"Not to fret, darling. I'm sure I have nothing to fear."

Except her own wedding night.

CLOSE TO MIDNIGHT, after the Edinburghians departed and Constance's friends retired to their bedchambers, the servants went about dousing lamps. She stayed them from snuffing the last in the drawing room, and as they left they closed the doors. Saint remained where he stood across the room, his head bent, his back partially turned to her, his fingertips resting on a marble bookend carved into the shape of a horse.

"Well, *wife*." His voice was in shadow. "This is an interesting circumstance we find ourselves in."

"Do you think so?" she murmured, apprehension and excitement skimming up the back of her neck in a tangled braid.

"I am to be played like a pawn." He turned to her. The lamplight cast his hair into bronze and his eyes were sober. "Am I not?"

"Of course not."

He walked slowly forward. "Did you think me naïve?"

"I thought you avowed to protect me."

He came close and the tingles in her belly became fireworks. Taking up a strand of her hair draped upon her shoulder, he twined it around two fingers. "I have wanted to do this for six years."

She turned her chin toward his hand and felt a frisson of pleasure at the brush of her skin against his. "Now you may."

"It is a peculiar thing, on a day like this, to feel so certain," he said quietly.

Her heartbeats were wildly off kilter. "Certain of what?"

"That it will not last." He stroked his knuckles along her cheek. "And this. I have wanted to do this too, again."

"Yes," she whispered.

"When, I wonder, will it be? At the moment the threshold of the Devil's lair is crossed? Or will you wait until the next morning to demand that your father summon the bishop? When will I be annulled?"

She snapped her gaze up to meet his. "Annulled?"

"Surprise from my bride?" He studied her features. "And it seems so genuine."

"It *is* genuine."

His hand encompassed her shoulder and he bent his head.

"I admit, it will prove difficult." She felt his words against her hair.

She tilted her face to bring her lips closer to his. "What will prove difficult?"

"Forsaking my bride's bed. But if we are to do this thing right, we may as well play it honestly. I cannot very well stand before priest and Parliament and swear to the Almighty that I have not enjoyed the rewards of this marriage if in fact I have. Can I?"

"I don't know why you believe this." She touched her lips to his jaw and heard his breath catch, and she felt it all inside her—longing and desire and need for him. If only it could remain like this. Perhaps it could. Perhaps the cold panic would not come this time. "But supposing that this marriage is what you say it is, you will not take advantage of it even temporarily?"

"If I were that desperate to have a woman in my bed, I would find one who did not come with a prickly father and dangerous intrigue."

Her lips smiled against his chin. "You have found me out, it seems. I knew you would."

"You did mention some weeks ago that you needed a husband. And I don't think your reason for haste is the same as your father's. You, Constance, are an incorrigible schemer."

She nibbled his jaw, tasted him, and every spark of fire within her flamed. "I think I liked you better when you did not know who I was."

He touched his fingertips to her arms and gently, tantalizingly, stroked. "And I liked you better when you did not treat me like an object to be used at your convenience."

She whispered against his cheek, "I needed a husband."

"To breach the Devil's lair." His hands tightened around her arms. "But not Loch Irvine?"

"That would have been complicated."

"Marrying me was preferable to marrying a monster?"

"It seemed the better of the two options."

"That night, at the Assembly Rooms, when you bade me kiss you—touch you—had you already formulated this plan?"

"No." His lips were so close. "I wasn't thinking as clearly at that moment as I usually do."

"You knew your father would demand that you marry."

"He already had. That night I needed you."

His lips brushed her cheek, then her brow, and then, softly, her temple. "I don't know that I can entirely believe this."

"Why don't you believe what I say?"

"Once, some years ago, you told me that you were mine. A year later, you would not admit me to your house. That seems to me fairly good cause for skepticism."

"I am yours now. For better. For worse."

He looked into her eyes. "Let no man put us asunder?"

"Aye."

He lowered his mouth to hers.

There was no hesitation, no uncertainly, only deep satisfaction in the meeting of their lips. His arms came around her, their bodies came together, and heaven passed through her in hot, wonderful ripples of mingled joy and desire. He took her bottom lip between his and then claimed her lips fully, and she slid her hands into his hair, around the back of his neck. He kissed her thoroughly, deliciously. With each kiss she wanted him closer, deeper, *inside her*. His hands moved on her, felt her, from her shoulders down her back, drawing her to him, molding her against his chest so she felt him in her breasts and against her belly and thighs. She wanted to feel him. She needed him to touch her again. And again and again.

His mouth moved to her throat, marking her skin with heat, and his hands held her tightly to him. She ran her palms beneath his coat, his taut strength making her hungry, making her press herself against him.

"I won't make love to you, Constance."

"I don't want you to anyway."

"My God." He buried his mouth in her neck and she clung to him. "This farce makes liars of us both."

"Then at least we share that."

He laughed at the ridiculousness of it, of how everything

always seemed real, right, sublime between them, even when they were at odds. Then he kissed her deeper, tasting the sweetness of her mouth that he had dreamed of for years. Groaning, he swept her against him. "Tell me you cannot lie to me."

"I cannot lie to you. I have not."

Abruptly he put her away from him, holding her shoulders and looking down into her face. "You have not?"

"Never." She was trembling in his hands, the most delicate quiver of satin-covered steel. "You are quite likely the only man alive to whom I can say that."

"Likely?"

"You *are*. I am trying . . . desperately . . ." There was uncertainty in the brilliant blue of her eyes.

"Constance," he whispered, drawing her close again and pressing his lips to her brow.

"I am trying desperately to hold something back from you," she confessed. "Anything. The smallest, slightest, least important thing would suffice, and I would account myself a victor in this battle."

"The battle you wage against me?"

"Against myself." She pushed him off and staggered back. "Do not visit your bride's bed tonight. Any night. I don't want you in it."

"This is . . . unexpected." He ran his hand through his hair and drew in a steadying breath. "But welcome."

"Now you are lying."

"So are you. Congratulations. We are both of us remarkably clever at detecting lies."

She closed her hands over her mouth. "Saint," she whispered. "Pray for me."

A shiver passed through him. "Does your father still intend for you to wed Loch Irvine?"

Her eyes widened. "No. He could not. But this . . ." She gestured between them.

Saint waited. She did not look scheming or defiant. She looked frightened.

He went to her and pulled her into his arms where she was perfect. Determined, frightened, perfect, and *his*.

"You are trembling," he managed to say with credible composure.

"I am tired," she breathed against his collar. "Excessively. It has been a . . . fatiguing day, and I have not slept since the ball."

"The ball." His composure slipped. "Three weeks ago?"

"Well," she said with a catch in her voice that sounded like a smile, "I have never threatened my father quite like that before."

Threatened.

"And my newly betrothed disappeared immediately afterward." She spread her fingers on his chest. "That was cause for concern."

The reality of her hands on him was still too new, too unbelievable. She was touching him and he could barely breathe. He struggled to find his tongue.

"You must have known I would return."

She lifted her face. "How was I to know that?"

He could not summon words.

"But I will recover with a night's sleep." She made to pull free of him.

He swept her up into his arms. "To bed, then."

"No. *No.*" Her voice was panicked. Her hand twisted in his waistcoat. "Do not demand that of me. Not tonight."

"Hush." He spoke softly as he carried her from the room. "I have already said I won't stay."

She tucked her face against his neck. "If I allowed any man to stay, it would be you." They were an echo of her words that night at Fellsbourne, that first night in shadow when he had merely thought her an uncommonly pretty girl with a streak of daring in her soul.

A maid waited in her bedchamber, and he left her to undress her mistress and put her to bed. When the servant departed, he entered and closed the door. Constance lay on her side beneath the covers, her eyes half lidded. He went to the hearth and placed a new log on the grate. Then he removed his neck cloth and coat.

She seemed to sleep. Moving to a chair, he lowered himself silently into it. For some time he watched her, the gentle rise and fall of her shoulder, tracing with his eyes the dip of her waist and curve of her hip beneath the coverlet.

He could have that body now. It was his. In an instant he could be beside her on the bed, atop her, inside her. Enjoying her.

If I allowed any man to stay.

Allowed.

Even now, when by God's law and man's she was his to do with as he wished, she refused to submit. Edgy pride crowded his lust. She was magnificent. Inconveniently so, given his arousal. But he wouldn't have it any other way.

"Saint?" Her whisper was muffled against the palm of her hand tucked beneath her cheek.

He held his breath.

"I know you are still here," she said. "I can smell you."

He unbent from the chair, went to the bed and sat on the edge of the mattress. "How is that?"

Her eyes remained closed. "It is the cologne that you wore the night of the Assembly Rooms ball. And cigar smoke, but on your coat only. And whiskey on your mouth."

"I kissed you not an hour ago. You cheat."

"I observe," she murmured sleepily, but her lips curved. He wanted to caress their beauty with his fingertips, then to taste her on his tongue.

"Cologne, cigars, whiskey," he said. "And what else does that clever nose of yours discern now?"

"You."

"Me?"

"Your scent. Your skin. As though brilliant sun soaked through leather and only heat remained."

His heart beat too swiftly.

"If I had never met you again after Fellsbourne, Frederick Evan Sterling," she said, "I would have remembered the scent of your skin all my life."

He gripped the back of his neck with his fingers. "You know, this isn't making it any easier for me to forsake my husbandly rights tonight."

"I cannot stop you from claiming those rights."

He leaned back, propping himself on the mattress with his hand. "With such an invitation, how could a man resist?"

"Why do you resist?" Her eyes opened. "Why don't you claim your rights now?"

"Because as well as your flesh, I would have your consent. Your enthusiastic consent."

She stared at him. "You are so honest."

"Mostly."

"It confuses me." Her body seemed to vibrate beneath the coverlet. "I have lived in pretense for so long, kept company with men pretending to be who they are not. I know French, Italian, and German. I even read a bit of code—"

"*Code?*"

"And yet I hardly know how to understand you."

Her agitation robbed him of humor. She was like a deer frightened into paralysis by a hunter's approach. But he thought he understood. This magnificent woman, so certain of herself, mistrusted men. And she feared being touched. In the stable when he had reached for her . . . in the ballroom when he had held her to him . . . and her hands forcing him to give her pleasure at the Assembly Rooms. When she took, she did not fear. When he tried to take, she balked.

His chest was tight. "You did not scent me out like a hound a moment ago to say this to me."

"No. As ever with you, I have said too much that I did not intend to say."

"Not enough, in truth. But I am a patient man."

"Are you?"

"What will you have of me now, my lady?"

"Will you help me, still? Will you help me search for the Devil's lair now that you needn't?"

He regarded her for a stretched moment before he was

able again to speak. "What a peculiar idea of marriage you have."

"Do you mock me?"

"Was your attention elsewhere in church earlier? Did you fail to hear the bishop's words?"

Bewilderment clouded her eyes.

"You are mine, Constance." His voice scraped over the syllables. "To enjoy. To cherish. To protect. Whatever the duration of the vows we spoke today, and for whatever reasons they were spoken, while those vows endure I will honor them."

Her fingers tightened around the bedclothes.

"And," he added with a shrug, "I know you will proceed with your mission whether I assist you or not."

"I will."

"So you can understand my motive. A man has his pride to maintain, after all. Can't have my wife traipsing about Edinburgh's seamy underside while I'm reclining in ducal splendor, sipping sherry and growing gouty. What would people say?"

"That my father bought you." She said it baldly. "They would say that any man I should rightly have wed—a man like Loch Irvine—would not have allowed me to continue the scandalously independent life to which I am accustomed. But that you, penniless and easily persuaded, were happy to accept the terms of my freedom that I demanded of my father as a condition of my hasty marriage. They would say that as long as the portion the marriage contract promised to you was sufficient to keep you in brandy and shiny new swords for the rest of your days, you would allow me whatever rein I demanded."

He crossed his arms. "That about sums it up."

"You are a scoundrel."

"But a proud scoundrel." He grinned a little.

"Saint."

"Constance?"

"You should go now."

"Why? Are you on the verge of throwing yourself into my arms, despite your intention to remain a chaste spouse?"

"Yes."

He smiled.

"Damn you," she whispered, her eyes alight. And then she damned him in deed. She rose, the bedclothes falling to her waist, and she wrapped her arms around his neck, sank her face into the crook of his shoulder, and pressed her body to his. She was warm and soft—*dear God*, so soft—and lithe and strong, her hold on him certain. His hands found her back, his nose the fragrant depths of her hair, and he held her as she wished to be held, and as he needed to hold her, tightly to him.

"I don't think you understand that this is something of a challenge for me," he said, rather strained, caressing the cascade of her hair over the curve of her spine. Her breasts against his chest seized his reason and restraint and buried them both in his groin. "Beautiful woman." The woman he had wanted for years. "Scantily clad. In my bed." His hands slipped beneath her arms and he allowed his thumbs to stroke the voluptuous curve of her breasts. He groaned into her hair and felt her shudder.

"I have wanted to ask you something," she said somewhat breathlessly.

"Ask."

"Why did you go to Loch Irvine that morning? After the ball."

He laughed.

"*Why?*" she said.

"I didn't want you to marry him, obviously."

"Thank you," her lush lips whispered against his jaw, driving fingers of lust straight to his cock. "Thank you."

"Good God," he uttered. "You will make this impossible for me, won't you?"

She broke from him. Cheeks flushed, she heaved in tight breaths.

"Take me now." Her teeth clamped together. "Do it."

"Take you?" came from deep in his throat.

"Have done with it." Her eyes were full of fear.

He backed off the mattress and jerked to his feet. His hands needed the sensation of anything but her; he raked them through his hair.

"Actually, I don't think I will."

"*Do it.* I beg of you." A tear slipped down her cheek.

"Tomorrow, in the light of day, ideally from across a room, and from behind a screen where I cannot quite see you, and most certainly where I cannot touch you," he said slowly, firmly, "you will tell me the truth of this."

In the candlelight her eyes flashed. "You make me a fool. Would you prefer that I grovel? Shall I go to my knees?"

His aching cock responded too readily to the suggestion. "Constance—"

"You want me to be weak. In your power."

"I want you, yes," he said. "I have wanted you since before I knew your name. I have dreamed every scenario imaginable of having you. This was not one of them. Good night."

He went through the dressing room into the adjoining bedchamber. Dragging a wooden chair before the fire, he took up his sword and sat with his palm tight around the handle. When the flames faded, he refurbished the fire. He avoided the bed in this unfamiliar room. Instead he settled into the hard chair and wished for something to skewer.

Chapter 21

The Confession

Constance stood calmly as her maid buttoned her into her riding habit, arranged her hair in a chignon beneath a matching hat, and tweaked the collars on the crisp white shirt beneath her coat. Through the dressing room doorway her eyes followed the chambermaids' coy glances as they made up the bed. They would find no blood on the sheets, no evidence of her discarded maidenhood. But they would not have found that even if her desperate pleas had met with her husband's acceptance.

"Where is Mr. Sterling?"

"He's gone riding, milady. Mr. Viking laid out breeches and boots this morning."

The idea of Saint accepting a valet's ministrations was too delicious. She would like to see him disconcerted by servile attention.

She stretched gloves over her fingers and went to bid her friends good-bye. When they had all departed, with promises to meet again in the autumn, she retrieved Elfhame from the stable.

She found her husband along the Water of Leith, the new green of spring making a bower alongside the river. Mounted on his fine horse, he was a man at ease. When he saw her, a glimmer lit his eyes that reflected the verdant riverbank.

"Hail, Madam Sterling," he said in the hot brandy voice that had always unhinged her. "I trust that your chaste repose in our wedding bower satisfied you."

"And I trust that the haggard pale of your face now reflects an equally satisfying rest on your part."

He laid his palm upon his chest. "You cut me, lady."

"I do?"

"Women are not the only creatures dependent upon flattery. A man doesn't like to be told he is anything less than devastatingly handsome."

He was devastatingly handsome. Not in the manner of the men she usually knew, with their white skin and soft hands that were evidence of their aristocratic indolence. Frederick Sterling was hard, taut, and lean. There was nothing soft about him, nothing pampered or civilized—or even shaven. He wore the whiskers around his mouth like the men of her society wore signet rings proclaiming their noble family trees: like a badge of his masculinity.

"I have no doubt that your confidence remains intact," she said, "despite me."

He said nothing in response. The air between them hung with the fire-lit incompletion of the night.

"With those words, I intended you to recall my rejection last night," she clarified.

"I did understand that." He smiled slightly. "Your victory, however, is flat. Like my wife, my confidence remains unpricked."

She almost laughed aloud. "Does it?"

His eyes were lazy, self-satisfied, exaggeratedly so. "You begged."

"It was late." She gestured blithely. "I was delirious."

"You seemed lucid enough to me." He folded his hands over the saddle's pommel. "But what of today, wife? What responsibilities does my new role require of me?" His gaze slipped from her eyes to her lips, and then to the front of her coat where it lingered. "Responsibilities for which I am not already eager."

"You can say nothing that will shock me, sir."

"I am not trying to shock you. I am trying to arouse you. You look especially fetching in that ensemble. I would like to remove it from you piece by piece. With my teeth."

"What would you say if I told you that your teasing has the opposite effect of arousing me?"

"I would say that you need to practice truth-telling."

His tone did not alter, but she thought these words were not spoken idly.

"There will be callers today. Many," she said, urging Elfhame away.

"Callers who are to be held upon the grill of genteel prying?" His horse's hooves sounded on the path behind.

"At the Assembly Rooms ball Sir Lorian spoke to me of a private society to which only married couples are admitted. He told me that the members of this society enjoy especially sophisticated entertainments, and that when I wed he would contrive an invitation for me. It could be the club that everyone associates with the Devil's Duke. It is possible that Mr. and Mrs. Westin are also members. There must be others. We must tease them out."

"Ah. The fog begins to clear." The smile had disappeared.

"You should change your clothes before they arrive."

"The crème de la crème of Edinburgh society does not care for the aroma of the mews, I suppose. Not even the secretly deviant crème?"

She chewed on her lip. "We shall see, I suppose."

"Constance."

She turned in the saddle to him as he came beside her.

"You will not hide anything from me," he said.

"Hide?"

"Nothing of this investigation. Make me a confidant of the intimate secrets of your past, or not; that must be as you wish it. But of this charade we play for the sake of the dregs of polite society, and of what you learn, I will not allow you to withhold information."

"What good would it do me to withhold information from you? I would not have allied myself with you to begin with if I did not think your skills would be useful." She heard her father in her own words and they tasted sour upon her tongue.

He ran a hand over his jaw. "Not exactly the response I hoped for."

"You are distracted by your lust."

"I wish to protect you. I cannot do so if you don't tell me everything." He said it simply, sincerely.

She fought the warmth that he made inside her.

"There was a man," she heard herself say without any plan for what she would say next. "He—" The sounds of the woods grew agitated, bird cries shrill, whirls of noise and scents too strong. "I . . ." Over the frantic burble of the river, her heart throbbed. "He hurt me."

"Enough for you to fear me."

"I do not fear you."

"You feared me last night. Was it Doreé?"

"No. Not Ben. Never him."

"Tell me who he is. I would like to teach him a lesson."

"He is beyond your reach now."

He stretched out his arm and angled it as though testing the distance to the tip of a sword. "I don't know about that. My reach is really very impressive. Everybody says so."

A smile tugged at her lips. "Your humility is an awesome thing."

He studied her face, and she watched not his eyes but his mouth. His perfect mouth.

"Wife," he murmured.

"Why do you call me that?"

"To remind you that I own you," he said upon a smile. He gestured ahead. "Shall we continue home now, so that I can make myself suitably presentable for those whose souls are less presentable than the soles of these boots?"

She urged Elfhame forward. He would not insist on knowing more. Perhaps she could simply forget now. Perhaps it could be over. But when she glanced back, his eyes fixed on the distance were hard.

"HALT THIS INSTANT!"

Saint jerked the razor away from his jaw. Soap splashed across his coat.

"Damn it." Being a gentleman was proving inconveniently uncomfortable. He tore off the soggy neck cloth.

Viking, who had announced himself the previous day as "your personal manservant," now hurried forward.

"You will cut yourself," he exclaimed. "It is my responsibility to shave you. I demand that you give me that razor and sit."

Saint took the chair before the dressing table.

"It was my understanding that servants don't give orders," he said as Viking draped a cloth over his chest. "But perhaps I was wrong. I've only been at this for a day."

"Upper servants give as many orders as they wish, especially when their masters are ignorant colonials. Lean back, sir."

"I left Jamaica many years ago, you know."

Viking slathered more soap on his face. "You clearly spent years there. You are as brown as a sailor." He whisked the razor over Saint's cheek with the lightest touch. "You should have told me this morning that you intended to do away with this monstrosity. I would have prepared a warm compress before the shaving, then mixed a refreshing lotion to apply afterward."

Saint forbore laughing. He knew the danger of a blade in the hand of a man who wielded it well. When Viking had wiped clean his jaw, he perused him skeptically.

"You appear marginally more civilized, sir."

Saint ran his hand over the tender skin. He had always worn the whiskers spare, but he had not gone without them in years. He took up his coat. The valet snatched it out of his hands and produced a fresh cravat. By the time he descended to the drawing room, he imagined he looked something like he should.

Several callers had already arrived. Constance sat at the tea table, the women around her chatting merrily as they assessed her, each other, and him when he entered. Lady Easterberry had the gall to effuse over their wedding.

There were men aplenty among the callers. In especially high spirits since their visit to London, Dylan made introductions. Saint found Lady Easterberry's son-in-law, Mr. Westin, repugnant. From a modest family, he had invested wisely in coal and now anticipated a title. Soft of both chin and waist, he had the joie de vivre of mutton stew. Sir Lorian Hughes and his gorgeous young wife arrived mid afternoon. Expensively dressed and cocksure, Hughes spoke with an affected drawl and looked too long and too intimately at Constance.

After a bit, Lady Hughes drew Saint aside.

"I waited for you to call on me the day after the ball at the Assembly Rooms," she said.

"I was obliged to travel to London unexpectedly."

"Of course," she purred.

Everyone was pretending that Constance had not been on the verge of a betrothal to someone else. It was surprisingly amusing and he might have laughed if his bride would not have taken it amiss. But perhaps she wanted to laugh too. There was always a hint of laughter about her lips, even when her eyes showed fear, as though within her a battle raged, as she had said.

Lady Hughes followed the direction of his gaze. "I commend you on your conquest."

"I am a fortunate man."

"She is beautiful."

"Yes."

Mrs. Westin came to them and offered Saint a thin smile.

"Miranda," she said. "I must go to the shops tomorrow. Will you join me?"

"Certainly, darling," the beauty said. "Lorian demands new shirts and I haven't the energy to sew any part of them myself lately. I will enjoy an outing with you poking through linens." She swept him from chin to boots with her dark eyes. "Perhaps Mr. Sterling could escort us, if Constance can spare him?"

Mrs. Westin's cheeks flushed. "Do you care to join us, Mr. Sterling?"

"I would be honored," he said, and wondered how long he would have to endure this sort of thing before the end.

EVERYONE BUT TWO women departed, and they settled into a cozy conversation with Constance. Saint went to find his cousin. A footman had beckoned Dylan from the room earlier with a message; but he was a social creature and it was unlike him not to have returned.

Dylan stood in the foyer, his face ashen.

"I've just spoken with Edwards. He came here to find me—to speak with me—good God." He dragged his fingers through his hair and clutched his head. "What am I to do?"

Saint gestured him up the stairs and into his private chamber.

"Has Edwards rejected your suit, despite Tor's money?"

"No, God, Saint. He—He came here because he'd just heard I'd returned to Edinburgh. He'd thought I left her there—that I had taken her off."

"Taken her off?"

"Eloped with her! The morning after Loch Irvine's party, she went to her aunt's house, as I told you. Her parents have thought her there these past three weeks. But five days ago her aunt sent a letter wondering when Chloe would arrive." His eyes were wild. "She is *gone*. Disappeared! Edwards came here just now to beg me to bring her back. He said he'd let me marry her, that he only wants to know she's well. He thought I'd absconded with her. I'll admit I thought about it. But I would never *do* such a thing. She's a lady and she is to be my wife. My baroness." His voice broke.

"Her parents and aunt have no idea where she has gone?"

"None! I think I convinced Edwards that I didn't have her hidden away somewhere. But, good God, Saint, if I don't know where she is, and they don't . . . nearly *four weeks*. I could see my thoughts in Edwards's eyes. She is nineteen, just the age of those girls . . . *those girls*." His brow grew dark. "I will murder that diabolical duke. With my bare hands. Before this day is over."

Saint strapped on his sword. "We will go together."

THE DUKE OF Loch Irvine was away from home. No one answered the door and the butcher at a shop nearby said there hadn't been an order from the house in ten days. They went to the stable and learned from a hand that ten days earlier the duke had set out in his traveling chaise laden with luggage, his saddle horse in tow. He was not expected to return for several weeks.

"My God," Dylan said. "She could be off with him to God knows where! Or she could be—" He heaved breaths. "She could be *in the loch*."

"Not yet. The girls went missing after equinoxes and the solstice. It is nearly two months till the summer solstice. If she is a prisoner now, we will find her before then."

Dylan gaped at him. "What's that about?"

"Constance has been investigating the abductions."

"*Investigating?* After Loch Irvine broke it off with her? Woman-scorned sort of nastiness?"

"No. All along."

"Good God. This is grim." His brow pleated with misery. "What else haven't you been telling me?"

"Write to your friends in London. And Glasgow. York. Anywhere Miss Edwards might have gone. She could be with a friend."

"I will. But she's here, Saint. Close by. I can feel it."

He did not question his cousin's certainty. He understood it.

AS THEY ENTERED the house, the butler informed them that dinner would be served shortly.

"Make my excuses to the doctor and Miss Shaw, will you?" Dylan mumbled. "Can't abide the idea of chitchat tonight." He paused on the stair, his eyes desolate. "You'll tell her, won't you? And you will let me know what I can do—*anything*—to help?"

Saint watched his cousin ascend the stairs with heavy steps. Then he went to the parlor.

Dr. Shaw and his daughter were bent over a book.

"Constance's callers departed late," Libby said. "She went up to change, though I thought her afternoon gown pretty enough. Papa, I do not wish to change my gown three times a day. I like only this one. Perhaps I shall become a famous lady physician and never marry."

Saint went up, rapped on his wife's bedchamber door, and when he heard no response, turned the handle. Across the room, she stood with her foot up on a cushioned stool, entirely naked except for the stocking she was affixing about her thigh with a bright pink ribbon.

Every thought, concern, and piece of news hovering upon Saint's tongue evaporated into the ether.

The door clicked shut behind him at the same moment the maid appeared from the dressing room.

"Sir!" The woman's palm flew to her mouth, Constance looked up, and her ivory skin flushed as pink as the ribbon. She grabbed a garment from the maid and covered herself.

"Thank you, Carla," she said. "You may go."

The maid curtsied and passed by him to slip out the door. Constance held the linen over her breasts with one hand and cinched it at her lower back with her other.

"Well?" she said, the color high upon her cheeks and trailing down her neck.

"Well." He was obliged to clear his throat. "My entrance here was nicely timed."

Her intoxicating lips pursed and she rolled her eyes to the corner of the room then back to him. "You have, I presume, seen an unclothed woman before?"

"How you imagine that the answer to that question has

any relevance whatsoever to this moment, I cannot fathom. May I assist you with that stocking?"

Now the lips twisted. "Dinner will be served momentarily. I must dress." She glanced at his boots, then his breeches, pausing momentarily on the inevitable result of his timely entrance. "You too," she said less evenly. "Go now."

"You dismissed your maid." He leaned back against the closed door. "I will button you up."

"Then turn around."

"Absolutely not. I am being paid to fill this husband post, after all. It would be shoddy of me to turn my back on my duties so early in the game."

She narrowed her eyes, but her teeth played with her lower lip. "You shaved off your whiskers."

He ran his hand over his smooth jaw. "If I am to pretend to be a gentleman, I supposed I should look like one. But I feel downright . . ." He let his gaze travel along her partially exposed thigh and bared calf. "Naked."

"Do turn around now," she said firmly.

He folded his arms and smiled. "Dinner is getting cold."

With a distention of delicate nostrils like a vexed horse, she pivoted and moved into the dressing room.

Saint's heart did a thudding turnover and his smile flattened. He went forward and into the dressing room.

She snapped her head around. "What are you—?"

He grabbed her shoulders and choked down his rising horror as his eyes scanned her back. From her waist to the flare of her hips, straight, slender, brilliant red scars formed a series of parallel lines over the pale skin. Recent scars. No more than a few months old.

He swallowed, and swallowed again over the anger and sudden, searing grief.

"How did you acquire these wounds?"

Her knuckles were white around the fabric covering her buttocks. "I don't remember."

"You do."

She jerked out of his grasp and swung away, grabbing up a dressing gown and wrapping it around herself. "Go, please."

He had had so many fantasies of the moment when he would finally see her body. It seemed he would be continually exchanging dreams for nightmares. Her eyes were too bright and wide, the eyes of cornered prey.

"Constance."

"Does it repel you?" Defiance prickled across the words.

"No."

Her slender brows lifted. "No?"

"Look at my face. You know I bear other scars as well. I have so many scars from six years at war and twenty-five years of the sword that I haven't even bothered counting them lately. Now ask me that question again."

"But . . ." Her voice dipped. "I am a woman. I am . . ." Beneath her hands clenched in the silk of the dressing gown, her breasts rose and fell. "Beautiful."

"You certainly are. Did the man you told me about make those cuts on your back?"

"I am not a maiden."

The words fell into silence.

But from what she had told him in the stable at Castle Read—and what she had done there—he already suspected this.

"All right."

"Because of certain experiences I have had . . ." Her chin ticked up. "It is possible that I cannot share intimacies with a man." Her bright eyes remained firmly in his.

"I am fairly certain that you already have shared intimacies with a man," he said. "I was there. I remember it. Quite well. We are married because of it."

She blinked. Once. Twice. Then her brow creased. "You understand what I am telling you."

"Do you know for certain?"

The dart between her brows deepened. "Know?"

"Have you actually tested this theory? Have you invited a man inside you?"

She closed her eyes. "No. Not since." Her fist clutched over her middle, pulling the silk tight against her breasts. Her nipples showed taut through the fabric, but her lips grimaced.

"What's wrong? Are you unwell?"

"I feel ill." Her eyes opened. "You speak like this, so frankly, and I *want* you. I feel the desire, the heat and awakening. And my stomach churns. My throat crimps up. My skin erupts in cold sweat."

He blew out a hard breath. "Well, at least part of that is good news."

"This is *not* a laughing matter."

"Believe me, I'm not laughing." He bent his head and ran his hand over the back of his neck.

"I know you were wary of secrets when you agreed to marry me," she said. "But you did not expect this. You have sufficient grounds for an annulment."

His head came up. "*Annulment?* We have been married a single day and you are already speaking of an annulment?"

"We had been married only hours when you spoke of it last night."

"Clearly I was prescient."

Her gaze remained steady. Passionless.

"I see." He nodded. "Upon what grounds would I bring my case?"

"Upon whatever grounds you choose." She spoke without the music that made him hear her voice in every flutter of breeze through leaves and every ripple of creek water over rounded stones. For six years he had heard her everywhere, in everything. He had stayed far away from her, but his memory had never lost the music of her.

"Marriage under false premises?" he said.

"I suspect adultery would find more sympathetic ears from those who are already shocked that my father allowed me to remain unwed for so long."

"No. Adultery won't do."

"Why not?"

"What man wants to admit publicly that his wife has chosen another over him?"

"Then perhaps the truth: that I am spoiled. Unfit. Unwilling. Unable."

"Or too mad to bed. I could lock you in the attic and bring the bishop to witness you frothing at the mouth."

"It is cruel to jest about this."

"I suppose it is."

"We could separate. Quietly. I have no real wish to be married, and married men often do as they like anyway. I could remain here and you could live wherever you please, do whatever you wish. It would be more civilized than an annulment."

"I would rather lock you in the attic." He leaned a shoulder into the door frame. "Consider the advantage it would give me. All the maidens of tender heart would weep. 'Poor Mr. Sterling!' they would cry. 'He believed himself the luckiest man alive, to have the most beautiful and the richest wife in the land. Yet see how he is trapped now, bound to a woman who does not even know herself, let alone him.'" He smiled. "They would be competing for the chance to give me solace by Michaelmas."

She peered at him across the dressing closet. "You cannot."

"I cannot lock you in the attic?"

"You cannot *not* cast me off."

A sensation of disjointed certainty crept over him.

"Did you marry me yesterday knowing that this moment would come?" he said slowly. "That after gaining entrance to Sir Lorian's club you would make this revelation to me and I would repudiate you? Was that your plan?"

"No," she said, but her lips pressed together.

"The fog clears," he murmured, "then it descends again." He turned about in the doorway, this time putting his back to her fully and lifting a hand to grip the back of his neck. "What of Loch Irvine?"

"What of him?"

"You intended to wed him."

"My goal in allowing him to court me was specific. It was never to remain with him."

Abruptly he dropped his arm and pivoted to her. "I have given some thought to these options you have suggested, and I have come to the conclusion—"

"Some thought? Just now?"

"—that they don't entirely suit me."

"What option would suit you better?"

"Keeping my wife."

"No."

"My wife who is clever, beautiful, brave, passionate, and of course very, very rich."

"An annulment would bring you an ample settlement. More than ample."

"Not as much as I have as your husband. I've read the contract. I signed the contract." He shook his head. "No. I believe I will keep you. And don't think of running away. I have friends the length and breadth of Britain, not to mention abroad. I would enlist their aid and I would find you. Swiftly, no doubt. Women as beautiful as my wife do not exactly blend into crowds."

"*Saint.*"

"Wife?"

"This is not playacting. I have told you the truth."

He moved close to her. "You are mad. I will swear this to anyone, anywhere. But not in a church court. Not in any court. Drag me there and I will cut out my tongue before denying you. However, give me true reason for repudiating you, tell me you pluck the wings off butterflies, that you pinch infants to hear them wail, or that you are a witch bent on transforming me into a toad. Then I might take my case to a bishop. But this does not suffice." With his gaze he traced the tilt of her nose, the curve of her lips, the arc of her throat, and down to her hand bunched in the fabric over her breasts. "At this time, Lady Constance Sterling, I am keeping you."

"Your lust is dictating your decisions again."

"Partially."

"Saint." Her face remained immobile but her eyes glittered with tears she would not shed. "I don't want to be *touched*."

Carefully he stroked the pad of his thumb over her cheek, allowing his fingertips to linger. "You allow me to touch you. You make me touch you."

She drew her face away.

"Constance, trust that I will not harm you. I could not harm you."

"Will you allow me to dress in privacy now?"

He went into her bedchamber. "I will remain here to button and pin and tie and do whatever maids do," he said, sitting down on a chair by the fire and stretching his legs out.

"But you must change too," she said, muffled, and he imagined her body bared as she exchanged dressing gown for undergarment. "Viking will swoon when he sees the state of your boots. Or scold. And why are you wearing your sword in the house?"

He straightened up, rubbed his fingers into his eyes, and told her Dylan's news.

"Oh, no. This is worrisome." She came to the dressing room door wearing a gown of blue several shades lighter than her eyes, holding it together in the back as she had done with the shift.

"It is." He stood and went to her.

"We will make it clear to everyone that we hope to receive invitations to Sir Lorian's secret society," she said. "We should invite probable members here. Entertain them."

"How swiftly the bride forgets her own wedding celebration yesterday."

"That was my father's party." She turned around. "We will host parties with select guest lists."

One by one he fastened the tiny buttons that ran up the center of her back. He took his time, allowing his gaze to linger on the sweet curve of her waist and the nape of her neck.

"Your father departed early today, without bidding anyone adieu," he remarked.

She looked over her shoulder. "You cannot possibly be complaining about him leaving."

He watched her lips, so somber, unsmiling, and wanted to hear her laughter.

"No, ma'am," he said and, trailing his fingertips down the line of buttons along her spine, stepped away. He took up the dagger from the desk and unsheathed it. "Now, allow me to put a smile back on those lips."

She glanced warily at the blade.

For the first time in decades, Saint nearly dropped a weapon.

"I am off to the shops tomorrow with Lady Hughes and Mrs. Westin," he said, forcing lightness into his voice. "We made an appointment to purchase shirts, I believe." He extended the hilt to her. "Pray kill me now."

She laughed, and inside him it felt like honey and gold and a long, hard release.

"You are brilliant," she said. She came to him, laid her palm on his chest, and went onto her toes. He bent his head and allowed her to kiss him. He savored the momentary pressure of her lips on his, her scent filling him, and his body's deep ache. He withdrew and went to the door.

"Off I go to hide my dusty boots under the bed so Viking will not scold."

She did not smile, but he knew she watched him as he left.

Chapter 22

The Crème de la Crème

*S*aint returned from shopping the following day with news of buttonholes, gussets, French linen, and the certainty, he said, that Lady Hughes and Mrs. Westin were bosom bows.

Patience Westin was handsome but she was not a beauty or much of a conversationalist. Miranda Hughes liked to chat and adored beautiful people, like Constance's fencing instructor. Lady Hughes made this clear wherever they encountered her, drawing him away and putting her hand on him. Constance could not blame her. She longed to be alone with him and put her hands on him too.

Her birthday came and went without fanfare. She requested no celebration, only that Eliza accompany her to the bank to see to the transfer of her mother's fortune into her father's account, as they had agreed. Upon her return she found in her bedchamber a package of considerable size. Unwrapping it, she discovered a magnificent bow fashioned of polished wood that shone like a mirror. Twined about its string was a single white rose.

They continued her lessons in the ballroom. As he had at the castle, Saint drove her at a punishing pace, as though he still intended to depart soon and must teach her swiftly. He taught her to use the dagger with the sword. He said a dueler might wield a cloak in his other hand, or even a lamp if dueling before dawn, and that anything might serve as an effective companion weapon to a sword if a man had good technique. She asked if a woman might do the same, and he repeated to her that she had plenty of weapons already at her disposal. But this time he said it with a smile.

He remained warm and appreciative, but his flagrant attempts to arouse her ceased. They spent the days courting the elite of Edinburgh society, often apart from each other. After dinner each night he did not join her, Dr. Shaw, Eliza, and Libby in the drawing room for tea, but went out with his cousin to scour pubs and alleys for rumors of Chloe Edwards and the Devil's Duke. When he returned home each night he retired to his bedchamber. He did not again come to hers, and he did not again mention her scars.

Sometimes, when she met him in passing in the house, she considered grabbing him, pulling him into the closest room, and undressing him. She imagined him kissing her, touching her, giving her pleasure. Her husband. To whom she had told a secret that no one else knew. Then nausea would creep into her throat and shortness of breath into her chest, and instead she would greet him pleasantly and walk swiftly away.

But at night when she thought of his hands on her, she wanted more urgently to do what he had suggested: test her theory. Whatever pain came with it, at least she would know. They would know.

"Good afternoon, Mrs. Sterling," he said as she walked toward the mews behind the house. He had been out riding and he looked tousled and delicious. He stopped before her, the sun bursting through clumps of clouds and setting puddles from a momentary rain aglitter at their feet. "Or are you Lady Constance?" he asked with a smile. "Or Lady Sterling? My lack of breeding is inconvenient at times, you see." His gaze swept from her hat over her breasts and waist to the fall of her riding habit's skirt.

"I thought you preferred *wife*."

"I do prefer my wife, it's true. You are going riding, I see. With?"

"Gabriel."

Both brows lifted. "We are reconciled with our former almost-betrothed, are we?"

"We have been invited to attend a special exhibit of medical instruments at the museum. It includes a selection of tools used in torture and executions."

His face sobered. "Constance."

"He offered the invitation to Dr. Shaw and Libby. They are right behind me now. I am going along to assess his interest in the items on display, of course."

His jaw seemed to set. "All right."

"I have my little dagger."

"And I am certain it won't be a public sensation when you use it on him in the middle of the museum." He moved a step closer and for the first time in thirteen days he lifted his hand to her face. "How you do court danger, my lady." He stroked a single fingertip beneath her chin.

"It makes life more exciting," she said, not bothering to control her abruptly quick breaths.

"I have an anniversary present for you," he said, trailing two fingertips now along her throat. They were standing in an alley in broad daylight where anyone might see them.

"Anniversary?"

His fingers slipped along the edge of her collar. "We have been married two weeks."

Her lashes felt heavy. "A truly significant milestone."

"Given that after twenty-four hours you begged me to annul you, I consider a fortnight cause for real celebration." His fingertips trailed upward and she tilted her cheek into his hand.

"I am on tenterhooks," she murmured. "What is my present?"

"An invitation to an intimate supper party tonight at the home of Sir Lorian and Lady Hughes. For married couples only."

Her eyes shot wide. "The best present imaginable!" She grabbed his arms. "I could kiss you for it."

He smiled, very slightly. "Go right ahead."

And quite suddenly he was not a warm or amusing companion, or even a punishing instructor, but a man with every muscle in his body trained to lethal power and desire in his eyes.

"Papa has been delayed, Constance," Libby said as she walked from the house. "I think we should leave without him or we will be late. I do not want to make the duke unhappy, at least not before he invites me to see his collection of bones. Good day, Mr. Sterling." She passed them by on her way to the stable.

Saint backed away and bowed. "I hope your journey into torture is enjoyable," he said, his eyes dancing while Constance's lungs seized up.

Enjoyable torture.

Panic gripping her, she watched him walk away and wished she could shout at him to return and take her into his arms and still her shaking.

It was some time before she was able to steady her knees enough to mount Elfhame, so Dr. Shaw's tardiness did not matter after all.

AS EXPECTED OF a couple as acutely aware of fashion as Sir Lorian and Lady Hughes, their house was fitted out in the latest stare and the dining table laid with an exquisite repast. The other guests were the Westins and a pair Constance knew but whom Saint had not yet met: Lord Miles Hart and his wife, Clarissa.

"Lord Hart is a . . . ?" Saint asked her quietly as they went into the dining room.

"A baron, like your cousin. You should read the *Peerage.*"

"Now that I am hanging on to it by a golden thread?

But if I had, I would not have any excuse to lurk here at your shoulder, looking down at the expanse of beautiful breasts you are exhibiting tonight. This is an excellent vantage point."

"Hush. You will make me blush."

"That is the idea. Newlyweds, after all."

Newlyweds in name only. His hand rested on the small of her back so innocuously that she wanted to pretend he did not know about the scars beneath his fingers, and that they were regular newlyweds who, after tonight's party during which they cast each other furtive glances, would eagerly return home and fall into each other's arms.

Sir Lorian was watching her. Assessing.

"Newlyweds with sophisticated tastes," she whispered, and went toward their host.

AFTER DINNER THE women removed to the drawing room to drink tea and the men continued in the dining room drinking wine. Saint especially disliked this habit of the aristocracy. While Hart seemed a good enough sort, Westin and Hughes had long since begun to weary him. And separated from his wife now he could not look at her. He could not hear her speak or laugh, or watch the manner in which she drew a strawberry from a fork into her mouth, and fantasize about that mouth doing other things. To him.

This hanging about with men got tiresome swiftly when a man only wanted to be near his wife.

The gentlemen lingered and lingered, their conversation all hunting dogs and rifles, which might have been amusing if his eyes fixed on the candelabra in the middle of the table weren't still seeing Constance's cleavage. Chastity, when the woman he had wanted for years was literally within reach, was no picnic. Eventually he lost patience.

"Shall we join the ladies?" he interrupted, standing, not caring if he was breaking ten rules of etiquette.

Sir Lorian gave him a knowing perusal. "Eager to return to your beautiful bride?"

"Eager to return to a room full of beauties. I hope that does not make me unique here."

"They say you are a crack fencer, Mr. Sterling," Lord Hart said, coming to his side as they entered the drawing room.

"They say correctly, my lord." *Make friends with the noblemen. Become an intimate confidant. Learn the secrets of the Devil's Duke. Solve the abductions and murder. Be discarded by a wife who no longer needs the assistance.*

"How original." Sir Lorian refilled Saint's glass. "A colonial merchant's son with skill at a gentleman's sport. I should like to see that."

"I will be happy to oblige you, sir."

Constance moved toward him. "Saint—"

"Ah, the new bride wishes to protect her bridegroom," Sir Lorian drawled, his gaze traveling over her. "How delightfully sentimental."

"My husband is an expert swordsman, Sir Lorian. I should not like him to injure you," she said sweetly. "Or your pride."

Saint glanced down at her lips, set in a semi-smile, at her hand upon his forearm—her strong, supple hand that had held a dagger close to his face before she had taken her pleasure from him.

With slightly lowered lashes, she said, "You mustn't taunt poor Sir Lorian, darling."

Darling?

"I believe I am the taunted one here." He looked to their host. "Shall we have a go at it, Hughes?"

"I rarely lose a bout, Mr. Sterling."

"Then I shall try my best to be among the few." He set down his empty glass and, flourishing his left hand, said, "At your service."

Beside him he could feel Constance's excitement, the subtle shift of energy as Sir Lorian came to his feet and gestured to a footman.

"Bring my dueling foils and pads, and clear the parlor at once."

"Excellent idea," Westin said. "Always enjoy a bit of sport after a rich meal. All those French sauces make a man feel downright bellicose."

Everyone followed Sir Lorian into an adjoining chamber, where servants rolled a harpsichord toward a corner and pushed chairs and tables against walls.

Constance grasped her husband's forearm.

"You must win," she whispered. "Will you?"

His brow knit in comic perplexity. Then his gaze shifted to her mouth.

He unbuttoned his coat and peeled it off. She helped him and her temperature was too hot from only the sight of his shirtsleeves. His waistcoat, a fine garment of brocaded silk that she had not seen before, fit his chest snugly, emphasizing the breadth of his shoulders and his lean strength. She folded the coat over her arm.

"Thank you, madam." He offered her the half smile that always turned her inside out.

The others took chairs at the edge of the room. Lord Hart and a servant bearing masks and padded coats joined the combatants in the center of the cleared floor. The footman offered a coat and mask to Saint.

He glanced at it. "Thank you, I won't need those."

Sir Lorian's lips were tight. "Take them away," he said to the servant.

"Gentlemen," Lord Hart said. "I urge you to reconsider. At least wear the coats."

"If my host wishes it." Saint bowed.

"This is a friendly bout, Miles," Sir Lorian said.

"Without protective clothing," Lady Hart said, "couldn't they wound each other?"

"Nasty bruises, is all," Mr. Westin replied, leaning back in his chair. "They're using *point d'arrets*. 'Cept perhaps to the face. But Sterling's already got that scar so he wouldn't mind it, I'm sure." He chortled.

Lady Hart's eyes remained blank.

"*Point d'arret* means 'stopping point,'" Constance said.

"It is a three-pointed tip bound to the blade with twine. It snatches at fabric, so the tip will stick but not penetrate."

"Dear me," Lady Hart said. "How do you come to know all of that?"

"I must have gleaned a few bits and pieces of knowledge here and there." In grueling lessons that left her sore, exhausted, and thoroughly alive.

"Those chairs mark the end lines, gentlemen." Lord Hart pointed to either side of the room. "I will call the touches. No right of way. No hits below the waist, and given your refusal to wear masks, no hits above the neck, if you will. No blood, of course. Fence to five touches." He offered a sword to each man. "Agreed?"

Sir Lorian eyed his opponent indolently from beneath a poetic fall of sandy curls. "Agreed."

"As you wish." Saint accepted the weapon in his left hand, and walked several feet away.

On every surface of Constance's body, the tiny hairs stood on end.

The fencers saluted each other, pointing their blades upward before them then dropping the tips to the floor—Sir Lorian languidly and Saint with the same smooth grace with which he performed every action. Lord Hart called, "*Allez!*" and it began.

It went swiftly. Lord Michaels had often spoken of his cousin's prowess. She knew of his strength and speed, and she had seen him practicing with Mr. Viking. But she had never watched him face off against another man in competition.

He made it look as easy as strolling down the street. While Sir Lorian lunged and shuffled, Saint barely seemed to move, extending and parrying with such ease, advancing and retreating with such clean steps that she ceased holding her breath and instead allowed herself the pleasure of uninhibitedly watching him.

He was fencing left-handed.

Lord Hart called the points, the opponents disengaging

briefly after each successful touch, then reengaging. Neither showed any pain at being struck and she had to assume that neither was hitting as hard as he might. The first bout ended to Sir Lorian's advantage, five touches to four.

"Fine sport, gentlemen! Shockingly well matched, I say," Mr. Westin said. "Shall we demand another, ladies?"

"Oh, yes," Lady Hughes purred. "How I do enjoy seeing men in *action*. Don't you, Constance?"

Saint's gaze came to her, enigmatic. He was the better fencer. He must have allowed Sir Lorian to win.

"Another would be delightful," she said.

Sir Lorian smirked as he settled into *en garde*. "I was easy on you in that first bout, Sterling. This time I will make you work for it."

"I appreciate the warning," Saint said.

"*Allez*," Lord Hart said.

Lip caught between her teeth, Constance watched as with five quick, neat advances her husband destroyed their host. On the final swift attack, Sir Lorian gasped and his foil clattered to the floor.

Lord Hart called, "Mr. Sterling, lower your weapon."

"'Pon my word," Mr. Westin cried. "He's pinked him!"

Just above Sir Lorian's wrist on his sword arm, a circle of crimson soaked through the linen. His face turned nearly the same hue.

"Look at that," Saint said bemusedly, and glanced at the sharp tip of his blade. "I am terribly sorry, Hughes. I have no idea how that happened."

Constance stared at the spot on the floor where the *point d'arret* from his blade lay, still wrapped in twine.

"I inspected both of those," Lord Hart said with a frown. "They were secure. Mr. Sterling, you should have known when your blade became unprotected. I am surprised that a man of your ability would not have noted it. You have disregarded the rules of this bout. Sir Lorian, do you wish satisfaction?"

"Satisfaction?" Mrs. Westin's eyes were wide. "Do you mean a *duel*?"

"He's drawn blood unprovoked," Mr. Westin said as they gathered around the fencers.

"It is Sir Lorian's privilege," Lord Hart said grimly.

Every member of the party seemed paralyzed, except the one who had broken the rules of honor. He rested his palm atop his sword as though he were nearly bored.

"I am a mediocre shot, Hughes," he said without rancor. "If you choose pistols, you'll likely win."

Sir Lorian's fingers tightened over the nick on his forearm.

"Dear sir." Constance moved to their host. "I am newly wed. Should you dispatch my husband tomorrow at dawn, I am unlikely to find a replacement at short notice." She kept a playful tone. "And you see I was hoping . . . when you and I spoke at the Assembly Rooms . . . that is to say, I should like to remain *married* for at least a bit longer. Will you forgive this embarrassing mistake and shake hands instead?"

"Your wife is persuasive." Sir Lorian glanced at Saint, then briefly at the other men. "You are forgiven, Sterling," he said tightly. "But I will best you the next time."

Saint bowed. Constance took her host's arm and led him away in search of a bandage.

"You could have beaten him fairly."

He sat opposite her in the carriage, staring through the rain-speckled window at the shining street lit with lamps. He did not reply.

"Have you ever lost?" she said.

"Not in many years."

"How many?"

Finally he turned to her. "Fifteen. I lost to my teacher. I often did, so it was not remarkable in that."

"But it was remarkable?"

"It was the last time I fenced with him. The next day they beat him to death for the affair he was having with my mother." He said it with extraordinary calm.

"Who did?"

"My father's hired men." He turned his attention out the window again. "She was grateful to him for teaching me what my father would not. Georges Banneret was Dylan's father's plantation steward. He was French, an islander, and a great lover of civilized life. When war came to Saint-Domingue, he left. But he always regretted it. I think he enjoyed teaching us how to become gentlemen more than his actual responsibilities. My mother was also French. She admired him. But to my knowledge she never betrayed her marriage vows. My father was an ignorant, violent man."

"Was?"

"He died last year."

"I am sorry."

"Don't be. I hated him."

She could not respond. Even now, she did not hate her own father.

"He was discovered forcing himself on an unwilling girl," he said. "A slave. He had done so often enough. The man who found him with the girl told him to stop. He chose not to." His voice registered no feeling. "The world is better off without him." Streetlight cut across his jaw, illuminating the scar there.

"Have you ever killed a man?"

He set an elbow on the windowsill and stroked his clean-shaven chin with his fingertips.

"Six years at war, Constance. Why?" His gaze shifted to her. "Have you someone in mind? Other than the Devil, of course."

Looking into his unearthly eyes, she felt the distance between them acutely. "How can you tease about such a thing?"

"I'm not teasing."

"I asked you to teach me to defend myself, not to stand ready to murder a man."

He said nothing.

She allowed her eyes to trace his hand resting on his

knee. "I should have liked you to slice that grin from Sir Lorian's face tonight. You could have disarmed him more swiftly fencing with your right hand."

"I could have disarmed him immediately either way. I thought it best not to defeat him too quickly."

"Yet you wounded him."

"He irritated me. His skill is far inferior to his arrogance."

Lord Michaels's words hummed in her memory, how his cousin directed his aggression into his sword, how he did indeed have the desire to hurt another.

"So says the master," she murmured.

He slanted her a keen eye. "Your father's money has been well spent, my lady."

She was hot beneath his studying regard. Finally he turned his attention out the window again. Inside her, everything was twined and wound up and wanting him.

"It's a good thing you did not fight my fiancé six years ago," she said, watching him. "He liked to hunt. Birds, mostly. But he was not much of a swordsman."

"I did fight your fiancé. He acquitted himself well with his sword."

The words hit her like a punch to the stomach.

"He *challenged* you?"

"Yes."

"But—" She struggled. "He promised me he would not."

"He broke that promise."

"You met him? You *fought* him?"

"I'm not certain if I should take umbrage that you doubt this."

An awful silence echoed about the carriage.

"You did not lose," she said with certainty.

His eyes shone like a cat's in the darkness. "I withdrew."

"What does that mean?"

"It means that your betrothed was backed against a tree, his sword on the ground, his throat beneath the tip of my blade, and I quit the field."

Her thoughts moved slowly now. "He lied to me."

"Perhaps he believed your sensibilities too tender to endure the anxiety you must feel on his account."

"That day . . . after he discovered us . . . he was furious with me. He refused to see me. He went away, to his family's hunting lodge. He would not answer my correspondence."

"As remarkable as it may seem to you, I'm not particularly interested in the details."

"We were to have been married the following month. But then his brother Arthur died abroad. And then the fire. I never saw Jack again."

More silence, but changed now, like the silence of moonlight.

Finally he said, "Did you blame yourself? Or me?"

"Neither. He would not have been at the hunting lodge if it weren't for his anger with me. He would have been in London preparing for our wedding. But after Arthur died he might have gone there anyway. He adored Arthur, and the lodge was his refuge." Her tongue was dry. "He must have felt great shame over losing to you."

"He did not lose."

"You insulted him by withdrawing when you were winning."

"I was no one. It was not a profound insult to bear for a man of his rank and fortune."

But—*no*. "Then your cousin, Dylan . . . he must have been your second." And Jack's would have been Walker Styles.

"We agreed to do without seconds," Saint said.

Air rushed back into her lungs.

"For the sake of my reputation," she said.

He nodded.

"Why did you spare him?"

She saw in the tautness of his jaw that he did not wish to answer.

"You must tell me," she said.

"I spared him, as you so colorfully phrase it, because I thought perhaps you wished to wed the marquess's heir to whom you were betrothed. I did not fancy you forever after remembering me as the man who murdered your happiness."

She burned all over, with shame and grief and longing dragged from the past and tangled with desire.

"I asked him not to challenge you," she said. "I begged. On my knees. I had never gone to my knees before any man. I never have since."

"Racked with guilt, were you?"

"I did not want you to kill him."

"Your wish was fulfilled."

She looked at his profile. "I loved him. I had known him my entire life. He was like a brother to me."

He met her gaze across the space striped with passing light.

"I am sorry for your loss," he said, the edge gone from his voice. "I regret that the fire was not as merciful to him as I."

Her heart pounded. "Do you?"

His brow dipped.

Her fingertips dug into her palms. "I have never admitted this to a soul before. But I suppose if I admit it to anyone, it must be to you."

"What are you admitting?"

"I did not wish to marry Jack. I mourned the death of my friend but not of my betrothed. He was a fine man. But I did not weep when I learned about the fire. For the first time in my life, I was free of the unwanted destiny that my father had planned for me from birth. I was free."

He seemed to be considering her. "You knew that I was capable of killing your betrothed in a duel, didn't you?"

"Yes."

"You did not allow me even your name, but you discovered that about me?"

"Eliza did. She wanted me to understand . . . the danger."

"I see."

"I did not meet you because of what she learned."

"Circumstances conspired in your favor. Yet you begged him not to challenge me."

"I feared that you would be hanged for killing him."

"If I had killed him, it would have freed you from your betrothal."

"At the expense of both of your lives," she said, the euphoria and fear of those days pressing at her breast again now. Terror that she had put Saint in danger had sent her to her knees before Jack, frantic, apologizing, vowing fidelity. When he gave his word, her relief had been nearly as great as her heartache. But he had lied to her.

Saint's gaze upon her was unreadable.

"You think me a wicked thing, don't you?" she said. "Then and now."

"Not then," he said. "Not now."

"A manipulator who would use a man for her own desires, regardless of the cost to him?"

"Do you believe that of yourself?"

She thought of her father's plans, how he had defied convention and allowed her autonomy so that she would grow strong.

"A woman must do what she can with whatever resources she possesses."

"I am beginning to see that." He folded his arms over his chest and seemed to relax into the seat. "You played our hand well tonight."

Yes. Leave the past behind. Let there only be this moment in which they were allies. Not adversaries. Not strangers again.

"You, as well. Sir Lorian was as angry as a hornet. He will want revenge." She smiled. "I anticipate an invitation to the secret society arriving soon."

His eyes glimmered. "Let us hope so."

Her ribs felt too tight to hold the feelings inside them. "I like that, how you said *our* hand."

"Lonely little rich girl," he murmured almost tenderly. "Have you never had a partner in crime before?"

"Only once."

He tilted his head.

She shrugged. "Briefly, and it ended abruptly. I did not see him again for years. Six years."

After a moment he grasped the windowsill and moved to the seat beside her.

"And what," he said in a low voice, his head bent, "was your thought upon seeing him again after those six years?"

"That I hoped he had forgiven me, and that we could be friends, or at least not enemies. And that I wanted as desperately to kiss him as I did when I first saw him."

"So." He brushed the back of her hand with his knuckles. "More than one thought, it seems."

"Admittedly, my mind is often too active."

"About that last thought . . . kissing him." He traced the length of each of her fingers with the tip of his.

"Yes."

He smiled. "Yes, what?"

"I still desperately want to kiss him. I have considered waiting for him to kiss me again. But if he does not do so soon, I will have to take matters into my own hands."

"Beautiful hands." He caressed her skin. "Go ahead. Kiss him."

⋅ She turned her lips up to his. They met, and it was sweet and powerful and right—profoundly right. With the caress of his mouth his palm curved around her face, drawing her close, settling her to him as naturally as though she belonged in his hands. He felt right and smelled right and tasted right, his heat and mouth and body all perfectly suited to her, as though the heavens had produced him expressly for her. Need rushed up from her middle, a wave of hot, powerful feeling, surging into her throat, tangling with the panic lurking there. Choking her.

She jerked back.

He sucked in an audible breath, and his hand scraped over his face then dropped to grip the edge of the seat.

"All right," he said to the empty seat opposite. "Clearly not a good idea."

She felt cold, sick.

It mustn't win.

Gulping in air, she reached for him, clasped his face between her hands, and took his mouth beneath hers.

This—this was all she wanted—his lips parting, claiming hers instantly, the caress of his breath and his flavor of desire and heat. There was nothing like this, nothing like touching him. She kissed him, breathed him in, tasted him, and let him feed her. When his hands circled her waist she rose to him and wove her shaking fingers into his hair.

"I am sorry." She kissed his jaw, wanting the scratch of his skin against her lips, then his mouth again, needing to feel all of him at once. "I am sorry."

"Never apologize while you're kissing me." There was husky pleasure in his voice. "Never apologize to me at all." His hands were firm around her waist. He did not move to touch her elsewhere. It made her want to weep and kiss him until she forgot the world.

"Forgive me."

"For throwing yourself at me? I will not."

Laughter tumbled through her kisses. But she needed him to understand.

"Forgive me for hurting you then. Can you ever?"

"It is forgotten."

"You make me want to forget," she whispered.

"And you make me want to carry you off to that meadow you once spoke of to me, weave flowers through your hair, and watch you dance wearing the most immodest white dress you can find."

"Yes. Tomorrow."

She felt his smile against her lips.

"The moment the sun rises," he said.

She clutched his shoulders and wanted his hands all over her. This need was honest and thrilling and good.

"Before the sun rises." She laid her palms unsteadily against his chest. "Tonight. Now."

He looked into her eyes. Then he wrapped his arms around her and kissed her, deeper, fusing their mouths together, their tongues making love like she needed their bodies to. Stripped of secrets, she felt raw and naked and strong.

The carriage halted. She drew away from him. But he grasped her hand as he took a long breath. Then he lifted her fingers and he kissed her knuckles as though it were the lightest gallantry and not an arrow straight into her heart.

The coachman opened the door. Saint released her and climbed out. But he did not offer his hand to her. Men's voices sounded on the street, and the clop of shod hooves on cobbles.

"What is it?" she heard him say as she put her foot on the step. In the misty drizzle that lit the street with a confusion of amber and orange from torches, two men stood facing Saint, four more mounted. All of them wore the sober black coats of the Edinburgh police.

"Good evening, my lady," the officer closest to Saint said.

"What is happening?" she said.

"Mr. Sterling, if you'll come peacefully with us, we won't need to use those." He gestured toward the manacles in the hands of the officer beside him.

"For what are you arresting me?" he said as calmly as though he were accustomed to being met on a dark street by officers of the law.

"For the murder of Annie Favor of Duddingston."

"No," Constance said. "This is a mistake. He—"

Saint turned his face to her. In the eyes that moments earlier had looked into hers and made her want to fly, now there was nothing. No warmth. No laughter.

And no denial.

Chapter 23

The Truth

*C*onstance dressed carefully in a gown of sober gray with black kid gloves and a black hat with a veil that covered her eyes. Taking up the basket of food her cook had prepared, she went to the carriage, upon which two footmen and a coachman perched in full livery, including wigs. She would arrive at the jail in ducal splendor, and damn them if they did not cower.

Of recent construction and magnificently austere on the exterior, Calton Jail was dark, forbidding, and wretchedly cold within. A guard admitted her and Eliza and walked them the length of several corridors that smelled of the worst of humanity. Behind doors fashioned of iron bars, in cells no more than a few feet wide, men wearing slatternly garments slept on straw pallets. From another cell with a small, closed peek window came a bestial wail.

"Good gracious!" Eliza cried, lifting a kerchief to cover her nose.

They passed several empty cells with barred doors, then the guard halted before the last in the row.

"He's here," he said with a weary gesture.

Constance gave him the basket of food. "The tart and roast is for you and the other guards. The guinea under the roast is for you alone."

"Obliged, my leddy." He bobbed his head.

"If I promise not to approach the door, will you allow me to speak with my husband in private?"

"I dinna—"

"Do consider: if he is guilty of this crime, I haven't any wish to be within reach of him."

"Aye. I dinna suppose ye would." He retreated down the corridor with heavy steps. With a frown, Eliza followed.

Constance went to the barred door. The cell was empty of everything but a straw pallet and her husband. He stood facing her, morning light from a barred window painting him in shades of pearl and midnight.

"Good day, my lady wife," he said. "How pretty you are in your funereal gray."

"Don't." She peeled back the little veil over her eyes. "This situation is not amusing."

"I prefer comedy to tragedy." He did not approach the door.

She moved to the bars and laid her hand upon the iron. "Miranda Hughes called on me an hour ago. She did not know about this, I think. But she is worried about you. She told me that Lorian played cards two nights ago with a deputy advocate to the Solicitor General as well as a City Council member, and that he seemed cheerful last night after the party, despite your bout."

"Ah. Yes. Your noble pursuer." He stared off to the side. "You would think I would learn."

"Learn?"

"The last time I dared to dally with a lady of high estate I nearly met my end too." His gaze returned to her. "How careless of me to have repeated the misstep."

"He must have planned this before you beat him yesterday."

"But, do you know," he said as if she had not spoken, "I would do it again. Especially if I could be assured of that kiss in the carriage last night. And our enjoyable interlude at the Assembly Rooms. And in the stable at the castle—for all that I wasn't quite prepared for that one."

The bars were frigid beneath her palms. "You jest so cavalierly."

"I'm not jesting. In order to touch you, I believe I would risk any punishment anyone could invent."

"You cannot be sincere."

"Of course I'm sincere. Go take a long look in a mirror, Constance. It's about time you understood the truth of your allure. I am only a man."

Her throat was nearly too tight to speak. "You once said that you wanted to be with me even if you could not see me."

Finally he broke his immobility, but only to scrape his hand over the back of his neck. "You remember that, do you?"

She remembered everything from that fortnight at Fellsbourne, every word and glance and moment of stolen happiness.

"It is as if you are trying to turn me away from you," she said.

Slowly, it seemed, he drew several long breaths. The evening finery he wore accented his male beauty. No sword hung from his hip now. He was unshaven, hair rumpled, without a neck cloth, his boots scuffed, and his eyes revealed what his speech did not—pleasure in her despite this horrible situation. He was perfect and she wanted to press herself against the cold iron bars, touch him, and speak the words that had nearly tumbled over her tongue in the carriage.

"I sent for my father. He will arrive tomorrow, no doubt, and arrange for your release. The police have no evidence to connect you to Miss Favor, of course."

"They do."

The floor seemed to shift beneath her shoes. "Oh?"

"Yes."

"You were acquainted with her?"

"I was. In the interest of accuracy, I must add that it was a brief acquaintance."

Releasing the bars, she stepped backward. "How brief?"

"In the public house in Duddingston. There were a number of witnesses to the moment I met her, including my cousin, though none of course to the time I spent with her alone."

Her lungs would not seem to hold air. "Was it before our wedding? Or after?"

He walked to the bars and wrapped his hands around them. "Before I went to your father's castle. After Dylan and I arrived in Edinburgh he told me about your father's offer of a position. I was with her—once—for the first and last time—before he told me."

"But you must have known she was the girl found near the duke's house that night."

"Later, yes."

"Yet you did not *tell* me?"

"I had no reason to. The events were unconnected."

"Were your sword and dagger with you at the time you met her?"

"Always. Except now, of course."

Her limbs felt peculiarly numb. "Have they told you the details?"

"The details?"

"Of Miss Favor's death."

"They have told me nothing. Except for the guard that brought water and uttered no intelligible words, you are the first person I have spoken with since they locked me in here."

"She was cut with a blade. The examiner said the wounds did not seem accidentally or hastily inflicted. Saint, where were you at the times of the winter solstice and the fall equinox last year?"

For an instant he seemed confused. Then the light disappeared from his eyes. His hands dropped to his sides.

"Constance, you cannot be asking me this."

"And yet it seems that I am," she said through her choked throat.

He stared at her with eyes she had never seen before—disbelieving, shocked. Devastated.

But he did not defend himself.

"You cannot lie, can you?" she said, a fragile hope inside her crumbling. "You are incapable of it."

His chest rose and fell sharply with jerking breaths. For a minute that seemed an eternity he made no other movement.

"I want you to go." His voice was hoarse. "Now. Please go."

She approached the door but did not touch the bars that separated them.

"I will tell you a story now," she said, every syllable hitting the same note, as though struck upon one key of a piano. "It is of that man I told you about. The man who hurt me."

He said nothing.

"I pursued him," she said. "We had been close acquaintances for years and I felt confident he needed only encouragement. You see, I was watching my dearest friends marry, and have children, and I was . . . alone."

"You? Alone?"

"I cannot expect you to understand. You have seen so much of the world. But when I moved to London, I was frightened. I knew no one. I had lived so solitary, with my mother who could not keep company, and then with Eliza. In London when strangers sought my attention I did not know how I was supposed to be. Ben took me in. He taught me how to go along. I depended upon him, perhaps too greatly, and when my cousin Leam returned from abroad, him too. With everyone else I was the duke's daughter. But with them I was the girl who rode astride and hid in secret corridors."

Her hands clenched, but he did not speak.

"Then Leam married and left London," she said. "Last October, when Ben reunited with a woman he had known before, I knew so swiftly what would come of it. I saw in his eyes what I had once felt . . . years ago."

Saint's throat constricted visibly.

"It began abruptly," she said. "My acquaintance and I were both guests at a party in the countryside. At Fellsbourne." Where the footbridge at which she had met Saint each morning was still twined with honeysuckle vines. Where Jack's gravestone still seemed freshly hewn. Where the memories were so powerful she could not escape them. "Nearly everybody there was married, except us. I agreed to be with him. I did not know what he intended, but he assured me that I would enjoy it. I imagined myself a woman of the world, but in fact I was naïve. You—you were the only man who had ever touched me. You had done so with such respect. Almost reverence. I remembered it so well. I didn't truly understand that it could be otherwise."

"Constance—"

"No. Let me finish. I must." She drew a breath to steady her words. "When he told me that a woman's body must be tamed for a man to enjoy it fully, I said that was foolishness. But I trusted him. I allowed him to bind me. At the time it seemed like a harmless game." She stared at the cell bars. "It was not a game. I felt great pain and afterward I bled." The words came swiftly now; she was desperate to expel them. "The next time we met, I told him I would not allow him to touch me again. It was then that he said he loved me and only wished to give me pleasure. He admitted that my beauty had inspired him to seek the greatest ecstasy the first time, and he assured me that pain could make the pleasure sweeter. But he promised to be more careful. He produced a—a tool, of sorts."

Saint made a sound.

"He cut me," she said before he could speak.

"*Constance—*"

"I didn't realize what was happening until it was already done. I had trusted him. He insisted that he cared about me. He said I was precious to him and that there was no other woman he wanted to be with, to touch. It was as though he knew exactly what to say to deceive me. I had always longed to be touched, after all. You must remember. Even those women at Jack's party and the freedoms the men took with them had not repelled me. Instead, when I watched them I *envied* them."

Finally she looked again into his eyes.

"I did not tell you the truth last night. When my mourning ended I would not see you because I *did* feel guilt. Overwhelming guilt. When Jack died, I thought it was my punishment for having wanted you. I had never wanted anything as much as—as much as I wanted you. But I made a mistake and people I loved suffered because of it, because of *me*. For nearly six years I denied myself every feeling of desire, every longing, in penance for betraying him. I tried to forget, and I tried to satisfy that longing with friendship. But it was never enough."

"So you sought him."

"It ended at a ball. He led me to a darkened chamber and forced himself upon me. I had already told him he could never touch me again, and I fought. It was so painful that—" Nausea rose through her like a wave. "*Terrifying*," she heard herself whisper. "His strength—" She dragged herself from the memories. "I saw him only once after that, in a public place, and I finally learned the truth. He had used me intentionally, with guile, in order to injure my dearest friends whom he hated. But I could not allow him to win: I never told my friends how he hurt me. Only my maid knows of the wounds. Only you know, now, how I acquired them."

She returned her gaze to him.

"So you see, I am entirely capable of blinding myself to a man's true nature, even to my own detriment."

"Who is he?"

She shook her head. "Who is—?"

"Who is the man that did this to you?"

"Why do you wish to know?"

"Because I am going to find him and kill him. Tell me his name."

His eyes were full of a violent fury she didn't recognize.

While she spoke she had watched horror grow upon his face, and disgust. She had anticipated that. But not this anger.

"I sent Fingal to the castle at first light," she said, turning away. "My father will arrive soon to see to your release."

"My release?"

"A gentleman needn't be incarcerated like this, not upon such slight evidence. Your arrest and imprisonment in the manner it happened only prove that a man of influence engineered it. My father will set it to rights. You see, there are some advantages to marriage to me, even if not those you expected. The judge will allow you liberty until the investigation is complete. You will not be condemned unjustly."

He did not reply. Skin prickling with cold, she departed.

CONSTANCE DID NOT shut her doors to callers. Lord Michaels would not come to the drawing room, and her visitors remarked on his absence. But if she had learned any lesson while ferreting out hidden information for her Falcon Club friends, it was that appearances meant everything. If she treated this as a minor mistake by the police, others would come to believe it.

Her father arrived after dinner. Only pausing to change clothes, he went straight to the home of the Lord Advocate. A school companion of his from years ago, her father said, he would certainly assist them.

Evening crept to midnight. Certain she would not sleep, Constance rested her head on the divan in the parlor and awoke to the sound of a carriage. Dashing the sleep from her eyes, she went to the window. Her father descended from the carriage to the street. And then Saint.

She met them in the foyer.

"Good morning, Constance," her father said, drawing off his coat and giving it to the butler.

"Thank you for coming, Father."

"This is a temporary measure, of course. But I suspect it will all be settled shortly. Good night, Sterling." He nodded to Saint and went up the steps.

Servants were lingering in the foyer and peeking from behind doors.

"Mr. Aitken, a hot bath for Mr. Sterling, immediately," she said.

"Thank you," Saint said like the rasp of broom bristles upon a floor. "I was aware that I smell like a prison cell, but not quite so poorly to merit such haste."

"Everyone," she said, looking around at the hovering servants, "do follow us upstairs to ensure that you hear every detail." She went up as they finally dispersed.

"Don't be hard on them," Saint said. "It is a wonderful thing to have a bona fide villain in one's own house. I hope you have assured them all that I will be manacled from dusk till dawn. No need for any to fear they will be set upon while they sleep."

"You are vastly amusing. You must have put all of your cellmates in contortions of hilarity."

At his bedchamber door, he reached for the handle.

"Saint—"

"I wish to be alone," he said. "Not because this was a particularly unusual experience for me, by the way. I have spent plenty of nights in jail cells. Weeks, on occasion."

She could not hide her surprise. "Have you?"

"Yes. Which your father knew when he hired me. He and I have just spoken again of that history. It is likely to be held against me when this matter comes to court. Unfortunate, but so it goes. In any case, it is best if no one becomes accustomed to me being home—or alive. It shan't last for long." He went into the room and the door closed quietly.

Constance put her fingertips to the panel and heard his voice saying *home* as though it were the first time she had ever heard the word.

Chapter 24

An Invitation

"The accusation will likely be dismissed," her father said as they rode up the side of Arthur's Seat the following morning in a mist of rain striated with sunshine. Dr. Shaw and Libby followed on the trail behind. A rainbow made its reluctant way over the little mountain, allied with both rain and sun, yet without any enthusiasm.

"I spoke with the Lord Advocate at length," he continued. "He interviewed Sterling, both in my presence and privately. No witnesses saw him with Miss Favor on the day of her disappearance, the afternoon before the party at Loch Irvine's house."

"He was out all afternoon and evening that day," the day she had worn breeches to her fencing lesson and then left him to meet the man she was supposed to marry. She stared at the rocky heights rising to one side, Elfhame's steps sure upon the narrow track. "Alone."

"He said he rode into the countryside. The only call he paid seems to be at a bladesmith's shop. Unfortunately."

The shop he took her to two days later. "Unfortunate, indeed."

"Do you believe him guilty, Constance?"

"No. Do you?"

"If I did, I would not be making this effort to clear him of suspicion."

The hill rose gradually on one side, offering a view of the royal palace and the medieval city rising toward the castle. But at its center were steep hills and occasional depressions. In one, a church from centuries past lay in ruins. The far side of the mount descended abruptly to the village of Duddingston, where Annie Favor had lived.

"Thank you for coming, Father. I would not fault you for throwing this in my face now."

"Whatever ill you believe of me, Constance, I have only ever wanted the best for you."

Upon the crest, they looked down at the city.

"Father, did you create the Falcon Club before or after you found my mother?"

Slowly, he turned to her.

"I have known for years that Mama ran away," she said. "I know she was not at the house here, as you said at the time, but that you spent months looking for her. I always thought it had to do with Libby's father who, I think, cannot actually be Dr. Shaw. But now I am not certain of anything you have ever told me. When Mama disappeared, why didn't you tell me the truth?"

"It was not a truth for a young girl to know. I wanted to make you strong. Fear would have only weakened you."

"Libby shows signs of Mother's illness, but I don't fear for her. She has a strong mind and I believe she has already learned how to fight it, as Mother never did. I might have too, had I taken after her in that. You needn't have lied."

"I will not apologize to you, Constance. You became the woman you are because of the choices I made."

When they returned to the house, Saint and Lord Michaels had already gone out. Constance accepted callers. All were overjoyed to know that her husband had been released from his unjust imprisonment.

"Half of them think he is guilty," Eliza said. "The other half hope he finds the real villain and sticks him through with his sword."

Constance hadn't any patience with waiting for anyone else to find the villain. The following morning she paid calls, first to Lady Hughes, then Mrs. Westin, Lady Easterberry, Lady Melville, and every other gossip in town. While strolling through the park with Eliza later, she met Sir Lorian and Lord Hart. She smiled and laughed lightly and said how eager she was for the fencing rematch. That evening, the Lord Advocate sent a message to her father that he was needed in Glasgow and would return shortly to settle the matter of Saint's accusation. Lack of evidence pointed to a dismissal of the charges, but the police wished to be thorough.

Her father departed for the castle, taking the doctor and Libby with him. He needn't linger in Edinburgh, he said. The Lord Advocate would send him word when he returned.

The next morning as she breakfasted alone, Mr. Viking appeared.

"My lady, Mr. Sterling requests your presence in the ballroom at your earliest convenience."

Her earliest convenience? He hadn't spoken to her in days, yet now he thought he could summon her?

In the ballroom, he awaited her with sword in hand.

She halted at the door. "What are you doing?"

"Preparing you to fight." He gestured to her sword on the rack.

"You needn't do this."

"I am here expressly to do this."

"Not any longer," she said, weak inside—*damn him*. This was how it was to be, then, this distance again. "You have taught me the skills. I know them."

"You have never actually fought another person. You will practice doing so now."

"With you?"

"Of course not. With Viking."

The valet entered. "My lady, is this acceptable to you?"

"It is," Saint answered. He gestured to a mask and padded jacket. "You will wear those. Today you will practice two-handed."

She donned the protective garments as much because she wished to be with him, even in this manner, as because she wanted to learn. Standing at the side of the room, he instructed her by commands as she and Viking sparred. It was difficult and frustrating and thrilling to finally put her lessons to the test. She was clumsy with the dagger in her left hand, but her blood was jittery and she managed several hits to Viking's chest and arm with her épée.

When her attention darted to her husband, he said in a voice of steel that she must never remove her attention from her opponent, for any reason. In that moment's distraction, he said, she made herself vulnerable.

After some time, he told them to rack their swords and take their daggers into their right hands. When he called an end to it, she thought he would talk with her about it, review her performance. But he thanked his valet and departed. He did not return for dinner. The following morning she learned from Lord Michaels that his cousin had spent the previous afternoon with Lady Hughes and Mrs. Westin and the evening with him, out.

Each morning Saint supervised her sparring sessions with Viking, and after that left the house, not to return until late. On the occasions that he dined at home, he said little to her, and nothing that could not be said before others. Mostly he was silent. When she looked at him, she always found his eyes upon her but saw no pleasure there. The warmth was gone.

When she noted that her hands were blistering from the work, he bade her set down her weapons and demonstrated how to strike an opponent with the hand, the elbow, and the foot. He made her practice, at first on the wooden mannequin and then on his valet. Mr. Viking donned thick pads and accepted the blows with stalwart tolerance.

He taught her to fight now as though he must complete the task in a finite time. He could not leave Edinburgh until after the case against him either came to court or was dismissed. He was imprisoned now as effectively as he had been before, on all those occasions in his past that he had never thought to mention to her.

CONSTANCE SAT BEFORE her dressing table, fastening an earring of pearls and diamonds in her ear and looking out at the night sky suffused with the brilliant light of the full moon when her husband knocked on the door. Dressed for an evening out in a dark blue coat, black breeches, and shining boots, he was handsome and unsmiling and entirely remote.

"May I enter?" He had not come into her room since the day he had discovered her scars.

"Yes."

He extended a folded sheet of paper. "This just arrived, via a street urchin who ran off before Aitken inquired as to the sender."

Taking care not to touch him, she took the paper.

Sir & Madam,

The Master requests the honor of your presence at midnight this night at the Sanctuary for an intimate gathering of friends. Unaccompanied by servants, drive your carriage to the Peppermill, and don the enclosed. Your carriage and horses will be cared for.

The Reeve

"IT SEEMS THAT our efforts have finally borne fruit," he said, hands folded behind his back.

"Code names, even." She hardly knew how to feel. Triumphant? Excited? And yet a peculiar anger coated all else.

"Suitably medieval," he said.

"The enclosed?"

He held forth two pieces of carefully stitched black satin cloth.

"Masks?" she said.

"Blindfolds. Presumably so that we will not know where we are taken."

She could not stop staring at the strips of satin. The night they had first spoken, first touched, he had unmasked her in the dark. Yet the next day he had known her in the light.

"I promise not to pull your hair this time," he said with the first hint of warmth since the jail.

She looked up at him. "I don't want to fight Viking any longer. I want to fight you."

"You're not good enough to fight me."

"I will show you I am."

His eyes sharpened. "All right. If you insist. Tomorrow—"

"No." She stood up. "Now."

"I have an engagement just now." His gaze slid down her gown of sapphire silk embroidered with silver thread whose bodice cut low over her breasts. "It seems that you do as well."

"Then we will both be late." She went around him and out of the room.

He followed her to the ballroom. She went directly to the sword rack, pulled the padded coat over her shoulders and fastened it swiftly, then took up her sword. Without a glove, the hard grip against her palm felt good. Honest. The daylight had gone entirely, and only cool silver moonlight illumined the room.

"I know you will choose not to hit me," she said, "so I shan't bother with a mask. But I will hit you anywhere I can. You should wear protective gear."

He reached for his weapon. "You won't hit me."

"We'll see about that." She lifted her blade. "*En garde.*"

Chapter 25

The Duel

*U*pon her first thrust, her tip caught on his guard. In an instant he beat her blade aside, then he paused as though he meant to halt. But she dove at him again, lunging when he retreated, driving forward. He parried easily.

She advanced again, and his parry deflected her blade, but he did not counterattack. Again she thrust her arm forward, and again, redoubling and thrusting anew until he parried steadily, not pausing and not allowing her through, the swords clicking and sliding.

"What are you doing?" he said.

Lips pinched between her teeth, she extended, advanced, pressed him until he dropped back a step, then another, and yet another, deflecting her blows with an easy defense. Moonlight glittered on steel, and the sounds of metal clashing and her own labored breaths were in her ears.

"Advance," she said. "Attack, damn you."

"No."

"You want to," she grunted and her wrist jerked as his

blade beat hers away. Without the glove, her hand ached already. "I know you are angry."

"Methinks the lady should examine the plank in her own eye," he murmured and parried another advance with a quick click of steel against steel.

"Admit it," she said, her lungs tight.

"When will you learn to trust me?" His voice was low.

Springing from bent knees, with all her power she lunged. He parried, disengaged, turned his shoulder, and she stumbled past him, her legs tangling in her skirts. Catching herself up, she rounded on him.

The impassivity had gone from his face. His eyes burned.

"I don't know how to—" He dragged his free hand through his hair. "I *need* you to trust me, Constance."

Tip extended, she went at him.

He knocked her blade away with a parry that jolted her shoulder hard and jerked the handle from her fingers. Before she could readjust, he advanced.

It was no effort for him, she knew. The first hit to her shoulder came quickly, barely a tap. The next to her arm was the same, light yet smarting even through the padded sleeve. He did not halt with each hit, but blocked her counterattacks and advanced again. The tip of his épée struck her only on the coat, only where her skin was protected. But with each hit she felt his aggression contained by skill. This was not sport. It was a duel.

"Is this what you want?" he said, pressing her backward, his voice gravelly. "Is this the game you want to play?"

"It isn't a game." She thrust, parried, her mind spinning, lungs screaming.

"Are you certain?" He forced her into retreat, his blade sparkling coldly beneath the full moon. "Because I cannot do this. I will not any longer."

"Why are you still teaching me?" She tried to push through his advance, to recall every trick he had taught her. But he anticipated her feints, deflected her counterattacks. "Why have you been insisting that I spar with Viking?" she demanded, throwing all her remaining strength into her arm and legs, into each thrust and lunge. "Can you not bear to touch me even with a blade since I told you the truth? Is that it? Is that the reason?"

For an instant his face went slack and he paused, and she burst past his guard. She hit him. Her blade arced as his shoulder jerked back.

His eyes flared. His sword slashed and with a brutal jolt the handle sprang from her grasp. She shouted in pain and grabbed her wrist.

His sword clattered to the floor as he came at her. Wrapping his hands around her shoulders, he dragged her close.

"I have insisted because I don't want you to be harmed." His eyes were afire. "I could not bear it if you were harmed again. I could not *bear* it."

A sound of disbelief escaped her.

He brought his mouth down on hers. Her fists loosened, spread, her fingers sinking into his hair, pulling him to her, and she opened her lips to him.

The kiss was salt and heat and sweat, a seeking, desperate connection that wanted depth instantly. His hands covered her back, pinning her to him.

"You *hit* me," he said, pleasure in his voice.

"I did!"

"It *hurt.*" He sought her lips again and then her tongue, pulling her up to him with his hands, holding her against his chest. "It still hurts, damn it."

Laughter spilled from her throat. Breathing was a memory. He was crushing her to him and she wanted only this, his arms entrapping her, his mouth for her lips alone.

He kissed a line of delirium beneath her ear to her throat. She pressed against his body and a moan burst from her. His hands swept down her back to her behind and he held her to him.

"Do you want me, Constance?" he said against her skin. His kisses upon her neck were delectable and she felt them everywhere.

"I do. I *do*."

He looked into her eyes. "Then take me."

"Take you?" she whispered.

"Take me. I am here. Willing. Entirely ready. Take what you want."

He stunned her. She never anticipated him. She did not know how to anticipate him.

"But—"

"Don't deny this." His hands held her so tightly.

"What if I . . . *cannot*?"

"No fear. No expectations. Just us. You and me." There was such vulnerability in his eyes, such fierce longing.

She took him. Tearing off her padded jacket was time wasted, but removing his coat and waistcoat was unwrapping a gift. Spreading her hands across his chest, she felt his strength that he had never used against her. As she had at the Assembly Rooms, she pulled the shirt from his breeches and put her hands under it, on him, running them over the beauty of his flesh.

He shuddered. "*Constance*."

She allowed her hands to learn the shape of his chest, the heat and dampness of his skin. The shirt hampered her exploration.

"Remove this," she ordered, and he obeyed, discarding neck cloth and shirt on the floor.

So many scars. She kissed them all, trailing her palms over his skin, one and the next and the next, on his shoulder, his arm, his collarbone, and then the long slash across his waist.

She covered his arousal with her hand.

"Now." She lifted her face to his. "*Now*."

His hands encompassed her hips as if to pull her closer but then his arms locked and he made a sound in his throat. With the same discipline he had showed in their fight, he was letting her control this.

With trembling fingers she reached for the fasteners on the fall of his breeches. When she surrounded his naked flesh with her hand he went entirely still. His eyes were closed, the muscles in his jaw bunched.

"Saint," she whispered, uncertain now.

"My—" he uttered, his chest rising hard. "Tell me I'm not dreaming."

"Now. Quickly, please."

He opened eyes full of desire. "Come," he said, and went to his knees, gathering her skirts up as he drew her down to straddle him.

The first intimate contact of their flesh drove the air from her lungs. With slow, golden kisses upon her lips now, he settled his hands around her hips beneath her gown, strong and gentle at once. Then he moved her against him. He was hot and hard and she had not known to expect this pleasure in mere contact. Wrapping her arms about his shoulders and feeling his skin and muscles beneath her palms, she leaned into him.

"I don't want to stop doing this," she whispered into his ear as she moved on him.

"Then don't." He kissed her neck, her shoulder, his hands aiding her thrusts. "Do as you wish. Only as you wish."

"I want to feel you inside me," she said around a mountain of mingled pleasure and apprehension. "If it's possible."

"Give it a try, why don't you?" he murmured without urgency. But his heartbeat beneath her palm was thunderous.

She smoothed her hands over his back and lifted her hips a bit. "Help me."

He did so.

It hurt as she bore down on him. She buried her face against his neck. "*Saint.*"

Then he touched her with his fingers. Softly. Intentionally. The pleasure returned. Seeking his caress, slowly she eased down on him, taking more of him, stretching and feeling tension but no pain—only hot, hard fullness. Finally filled with him, flush to him, she saw the moisture on his shoulder where her tears had fallen.

"Everything all right?" he said, one hand flat over her

lower back, holding her to him. His voice was decidedly shaky.

She laced her fingers through his hair and kissed him. Again. Again and again. Sighs tickling her throat, she rocked her hips to his. His clever fingers on the center of her need and the hard length of him drove her to thrust harder, to rise and then take him in again as far as she could, and faster each time.

"Constance, if you cannot find satisfaction like this—"

"I—" she gasped, and moaned upon a thrust. Deep inside her he was touching her. She pressed her palms to his shoulders. "It shouldn't be—" It began, grabbing and constricting with delicious, coiling pressure. "*Difficult.*" It took her, releasing across her flesh as she strained to him. Both of his hands went to her hips, grasped tightly, and jerked her to him, giving her more, making it last in convulsions that tore the breaths from her. She pushed to him, seeking. His fingers dug into her hips and abruptly he held her still, his muscles hardening. Groaning, he shuddered.

For several moments, only the moonlight spoke. Then he kissed her. Hands around her face, he used her mouth fully, decadently, and she clung to him and began to laugh.

He drew back, kissed her cheek, her brow, her lips as she smiled.

"I presume this means that you are well," he said.

"Yes." She wanted to laugh forever. *This* was what it could be. This beautiful thing, this joining. Even holding him inside her now, her body trembling with satisfaction, was such pleasure. "Yes."

He stroked back a lock of hair stuck to her cheek and tucked it behind her ear as she laid her palms upon his damp chest.

"Except I think I have bruised my knees," she said. "And perhaps chafed my thighs on your breeches."

"Battle wounds." He nuzzled her jaw, then her throat, sending unbearably acute tremors through her.

"I must go change," she said, drawing away. As she

smoothed out her skirts she watched him fasten his breeches.
"I have a dinner engagement at—"

His hand curved around her hip and he scooped her up
into his arms.

"What are you doing?"

He started toward the door. "Taking you to bed."

"But, our previous plans—"

"I don't recall having previous plans. Do you?"

She circled her arms about his neck. "We cannot sleep.
The Master's gathering—"

"We aren't going to sleep."

Bare-chested, he carried her upstairs. In his bedchamber,
her eyes alighted on the bed and her pulse jerked into speed.

"No. Not—"

He set her on her feet then drew her into his arms.

"Tell me," he said close to her brow.

"Not this bed," she said. "Mine."

"Your wish, my lady." He took her hand and walked her
through the dressing closet that connected their bedchambers. Releasing her, he went to both doors and locked them.
Then he came to where she stood paralyzed and grasped her
hand again.

"We just made love on the floor of a ballroom after you
nearly skewered me with a sword. And yet in your own bed-
room you are terrified. Your hand is cold. What do you wish
of me now, wife? I am yours to command."

She went onto her toes and kissed his mouth, then his
neck, then the fierce red mark just beneath his shoulder that
was already turning purple.

"How is it that your skin is tanned here?" she said, caressing the bruise and muscle with her lips and feeling an
echoing thrill of pleasure within her.

"I have been on the loch."

She looked into his face. "Without a shirt?"

"When diving was necessary."

She pulled back. "Diving? Today?"

"Every afternoon for the past ten days."

"I thought you were paying calls, encouraging invitations to secret cabals."

"Briefly. Then Dylan and I went to the water and the surrounding fields."

"You are looking for the knife, aren't you?"

"For anything. Any clue that might help to locate Chloe Edwards."

"And prove that you had nothing to do with Miss Favor's death."

"It is a futile task, in truth."

She ran her fingertips lightly over the bruise she had given him, then across the strong collarbone and down the center of his chest.

"Then why are you pursuing it?" she asked, touching her lips to his shoulder.

"Well." His chest expanded. "That—that kiss just there—might have something to do with it."

"Because it will please me?" She spread her hands across his chest and smiled a bit. "I don't entirely believe you."

He grasped her wrists and plucked her hands from him.

"Constance, I will always tell you the truth. Always."

"Allow me to further inspire your investigations," she said, and traced her tongue around and over his nipple. Years ago she had made herself drunk on the sound and sight of him alone. Now she drank liberally of taste and texture. He remained still as her lips and the tip of her tongue explored him, his breathing uneven, but holding her loosely until her fingers came to the waistline of his breeches. Then his grip tightened.

She unfastened the fall of the breeches and pushed them down. He was fully erect and beautifully made in sex and limb. Her face was hot.

He cupped her chin in his palm. "My blushing bride," he murmured upon a smile.

"No."

"To which of those three words do you object?"

"This heat in my face is not born of innocence or modesty. I have neither."

"Then you have no complaint with the words *my bride*?"

She drew away from his hold. "You don't say what I expect."

"Perhaps because you expect me to be someone I am not."

"I require assistance to remove my gown and stays." Then with her hands she pulled his mouth down to her and kissed him.

His fingers were sure on the fasteners of her gown and on the laces of her petticoat and stays. When she stood before him in only a shift, she said, "Touch me."

He knelt on the floor before her and his hands came around her knees. In this way he raised the thin linen of her shift, his hands surrounding her thighs and moving so slowly upward that every half inch seemed a victory.

"You are so soft," he said as his hands curved around her hips, baring her to the glow of the moonlight. But he did not halt there. His hands continued upward, the fabric sliding with his touch, uncovering her waist and breasts. She lifted her arms and he swept the garment over her head.

His gaze took her in, from brow to feet, lingering upon her breasts and then her mouth.

"And yet," he said, lifting his eyes, "there is a hardness within you. Tempered anger. You would make a fine warrior, I think."

"Kiss me," she said.

He obeyed. His mouth moved to her throat, his hands to her shoulders, then down her back.

"At present, however, you are a banquet." His palms slid over her scars. "And I, a man who has been at sea for years." He kissed her and his fingertips played the striped welts like a musician upon a lyre. "And don't you dare critique my metaphor, or I will utter another even more trite."

She held tight to his shoulders. "Flames. The next metaphor must include flames. Or fire of some sort."

"I am certain I can come up with something suitable. Lie down." His hands marked every bit of her heated skin with need. But beneath it the cold was growing.

"I cannot." Her fingers dug into his arms. "I *cannot*." She broke away from him. "I cannot bring myself to it, even without bedposts."

"Bedposts?"

"Bedposts, bindings, facedown," she said upon a rush. "So that I could not see."

"I would like to hold you now," he said in an unremarkable tone. "May I?"

Her panic collapsed, leaving only shaking. She nodded. He drew her into his arms and held her against his warm skin, and she tucked her face into his shoulder.

"However much I am feeling inclined to murder at present," he said, "I am feeling considerably more inclined to making love to you." He lifted her face with his fingertips beneath her chin. "I don't need a bed, Constance. I don't need a chair. I don't even need the floor. All I need is your body on mine."

She smoothed her palm over his jaw and kissed him. She did not stop kissing him for quite a long time then.

They went to the floor, to piles of bed linens hastily strewn there with hands that were impatient to return to touching. Kneeling before her he kissed her breasts with such lavish attention that eventually she was obliged to climb atop his lap to satisfy the craving this built to unendurable intensity. Silver light filled the sky and candles illumined his skin in gold as, bodies entwined, they found pleasure together.

Afterward, he held her in silence and he kissed her tenderly on her cheeks and brow and lips. When finally she drew away from him, her cheek was damp though she knew she had not wept.

She summoned a maid, and he left her to bathe alone and went to dress for their outing.

Chapter 26

The Master

*E*xcept for the dip of her eyes that revealed her weariness, when he took his seat on the carriage box beside her, she did not look like a woman who had fought a duel with a man and then made love to him twice afterward.

"Wife, you bedazzle," he said as he snapped the horses into motion.

"I haven't any idea what one wears to devil-worshipping parties." She tucked her cloak about her gown of some glittering gold fabric. "I settled on dress suitable for a regular evening's entertainment." She tugged her hood up about her hair, which was bound again now in elegant coils. An hour earlier, before the fire, she had allowed him to unbind it and spread it over her shoulders and breasts. Now she would not take his arm or touch him in any manner, not even his hand for assistance into the carriage.

"You are sure to set the fashion now," he said.

"Tell me about your new friends."

"And who would that be?"

"Patience Westin and Miranda Hughes. Your cousin tells

me you have seen them every day since your sojourn in Calton Jail. You must be thick as thieves by now."

"I was a thief, you know."

In the lantern light, her face remained serene. "Thus your other such sojourns. What did you steal?"

"Nothing of lasting value, unfortunately. Bread, usually. Once I stole a live chicken. Difficult to hide beneath one's coat for any length of time, of course, and then it had to be cooked. Never tried that again."

"Could you not find work as an instructor?" Her voice was cool like the midnight mists falling now.

"I hadn't the heart for it. War can weary a man of weapons, which is a vast understatement, actually."

He felt her attention upon him now. "You ceased *fencing*?"

"For a time I could wield neither sword nor firearm. My hands shook too violently to do so. My commanders allowed me a leave of absence." During which time, eventually, he had found enjoyment in the sword again, in teaching fighting skills to a friend whose character was far superior to the lot he had been given in life.

"But you returned to war. When we met, you had just come home."

"I felt an obligation to the country that had given me solace after my mother's death. Also"—he smiled—"they expected me back. They were . . . insistent."

"You were the greatest swordsman the cavalry had ever known."

"No cavalry. I didn't even have a horse. I was a courier. I ran."

"You ran? From battlefield to battlefield?"

"From general to general. I was very fast. And intelligent. Thus their insistence. But I was still a boy, really."

"That must have been extraordinarily dangerous." Her voice was subdued.

"Everything at war is dangerous."

"Why didn't you use your skill with a sword, when you were able?"

"Because, Constance, I did not wish to kill anyone."

"But it was war. You—"

"My mother was French. My teacher as well."

Some minutes later, she pointed ahead.

"The Peppermill. You deflected my question before."

"Mrs. Westin is sensible and somewhat shy. Although she does not lack intelligence, Lady Hughes is nearly the opposite. They are an interesting pair."

"Have you enjoyed spending time with them?"

"I have. Did you hold back when you sparred with Viking?"

She turned to him abruptly. "No."

"And yet you hit *me*."

A smile transformed her face. "You inspire me."

"I will have a bruise on this shoulder for a fortnight."

"I didn't wish to injure you. I warned you should have worn padding."

He laughed. "Of course you wished to injure me. You have wished to injure me since the day I arrived at your castle."

The moon had disappeared and ahead in the darkness a muted lantern shone.

"There," she whispered.

"The moment I have reason for concern, we leave," he said, driving the carriage behind the building. "Do you understand?"

"You mustn't be overprotective," she said. "It would ruin everything."

"Trust me, I have great respect for your ability to defend yourself."

"Help me down." Now she allowed him to grasp her hand and assist her from the carriage. But she held on to him only briefly.

Two men came forward. One climbed onto their carriage and drove away. The other, of average height and frame, wore a hood obscuring his face.

"I'm Reeve," he said. "The carriage is this way." They

followed him to a vehicle without markings. The horses seemed fine enough. Reeve opened the door and Saint handed Constance in.

"The blindfolds, if you will," Reeve said. A moment later, the carriage jolted into motion.

When they halted, Reeve instructed them not to remove the blindfolds until they had entered the Sanctuary. They did so within moments. Reeve shut and locked the door behind them, and Saint swiftly took in the space. Constance's face showed no indication that she had ever seen these stairs or carpet or finely carved wooden railing before. She looked curiously about as though she had not stood on the landing above and told him fervently to leave her alone. It was the duke's house, just as it had been on the night of his party.

"This way." Lantern in hand, Reeve started up the stairs. He opened the first of the four doors on the corridor. It was a long parlor, dimly lit and warm from hearths at opposite ends. Like the rooms in the front of the house, the furnishings befitted a duke: fine wood, rich upholstery, elegant appointments. The people arranged about it were, however, a parody of polite society. Gowns were sheer. Postures were lax. And more than a few hands were in places they should not be, outside of brothels. But none of the duke's guests were prostitutes. Saint had taken tea with every titled woman and man present. The Duke of Loch Irvine was not among them.

"Welcome, darlings." Lady Hughes glided toward them. Her smile, usually sweet, was slack-lipped, her eyes heavy. From across the room, Sir Lorian watched.

Constance accepted a glass of wine from Lord Hart, her eyes assessing, studying. *Not for long.* There was no scent of opium in the place, but these people were not drunk; there was a placid lethargy about them that spoke of another influence. Saint watched her sip the wine that must be drugged and wanted to tear the crystal from her fingers.

Instead he accepted a glass and swallowed the contents. Reeve had not taken his sword or even asked him to remove it. The Master or Sir Lorian or whomever had sent their invitation must believe they were here eagerly. If he felt any effects from the drink, he could move before it overcame him entirely, with the advantage of surprise.

Constance played the part well. She smiled and flirted lightly, glittering, enticing, and he wondered how he had not seen it this clearly before: the vulnerable girl beneath this mask of gay sophistication she put on for others. Now he saw it and it made him ache.

Soon her eyes grew heavy and her motions slow. He took a seat in a cushioned chair and watched. Lady Hart came to his side, settled on the sofa languidly, and said nothing of interest.

He grew bored swiftly. The drugged wine in his veins softened the already dim lights, but his pulse remained regular. Then Reeve left the room through another door and conversations hushed.

"What's happening?" he asked Lady Hart.

"The Master has chosen," she replied with lowered lashes. Everyone it seemed had drunk liberally of the wine. "In a moment we will be free to do whatever we like. And I like you, Mr. Sterling."

Reeve reappeared and crossed to Lady Hughes. Rising, she went with him.

"What exactly has he chosen?" He readied his muscles for action.

"What a tease you are, Mr. Sterling." Lady Hart's half-lidded eyes perused him. "Have you anyone in mind, or will you await Miranda? I understand that you and she have spent time together lately."

He had heard enough. Miranda Hughes was not about to be sacrificed in a violent ritual, not if Lady Hart expected her to return shortly. Constance was moving toward him, her steps over-careful, her gaze firmly in his and—despite its hazy quality—definitely indicating that he was not to move. He waited for her to drape herself over the chair beside him.

"Here you are, darling," she said. "How are you

enjoying this d'lightful party?" Her tongue stumbled over the syllables.

"Delightful." For the twentieth time he scanned the room carefully, assessing the potential for taking her from the house without endangering her should they meet with resistance. "Constance," he said quietly. "Where did you hide my knife?"

"Gallery. B'neath the display case."

Shortly, the door to the Master's room opened. Into the candlelight came Lady Hughes. She wore a white robe that fell to the floor, the hood draped behind.

Constance's eyes flared.

With a slow, weaving stride, Lady Hughes went across the room. As she went, the robe parted at the front to reveal her petite, rounded, entirely nude body. Pausing before Westin, she stroked two fingertips along his shoulder. Without waiting for him, she drew the robe together again and walked out of the room.

Saint glanced at Hughes. His eyes were on Constance.

Westin rose and swaggered by them. "Care to come along, Sterling? If you're very good, I'll give you a turn with her."

"I will come." Mrs. Westin moved to her husband's side.

"That's right," Westin said with a pat on his wife's behind. "My good little Patience wants her turn too. But only because I'll be there, m'dear. You know the rules."

"The rules?" Constance said, her glassy eyes following them to the door.

"Once the Master has chosen, we ladies are free to choose whomever we like," Lady Hart murmured, lifting her fingers to stroke them along Saint's arm, "as long as at least one man and one woman are present in every room."

"For a man who keeps his club a secret," he said, "it seems the Master has fairly conventional standards."

"Disappointed? And I had imagined you the one-woman sort. Newlyweds. And so *unexpected* a match. You cannot think how surprised Hart and I are to see you tonight." Her fogged gaze dipped to his mouth. "Shall we summon my husband, Mr. Sterling, and see how unconventional you like it?"

He withdrew his arm. "Perhaps another night." He took Constance's hand and drew her to her feet. "It's time we depart."

"Wait," his wife said muzzily as he led her toward the door. "Just the other day Lady MacFarlane was going on and on about her sister's faithless husband. Now look at her over there ogling everybody. The hypocrite. I want to see who she chooses."

"Understandably. But that is not in the cards for you tonight, Madam Sterling." *Or ever.*

Reeve met them at the door. "Leaving already?"

"My wife is unwell."

Constance immediately sagged upon his arm.

Reeve had removed his hood and peered at her down a nose that had been broken more than once. Saint studied his unremarkable features. "Have your blindfolds?"

"Darling," Constance said with a giggle that was entirely charming and thoroughly false, "I am afraid you must tie mine. My fingers are numb."

Alone in the carriage she sat apart from him and did not speak. When they arrived at the mill he removed her blindfold and she took his hand only to dismount the carriage. But her steps faltered as they went toward their own curricle.

"You must put your arm around me or I will fall off the seat," she said, her eyes seeking purchase on his face but rolling away. "I do hope I won't be ill." He took the reins in one hand and wrapped his other arm tight around her, but she gripped the side of the seat, not him.

As they entered the house she said nothing, and when he set his hand to her lower back to balance her ascent on the stairs, she pulled away. Inside her bedchamber, with the door closed, she stood in the center of the floor and swayed. As he undressed her, her eyes remained closed and her face slack. He led her to the bed and covered her with a blanket.

He had seen plenty of drunks, both men and women. This was not Constance merely drunk or even drugged. She had withdrawn from him again, as soon as the charade had not been necessary.

He sat on the edge of the bed, bent his elbows to his knees, and covered his face with his hands.

"'Tis all remarkably distasteful," she mumbled, not opening her eyes.

"It is." A servant must have closed the draperies and removed the bed linens from the floor. Nothing remained of what had passed between them earlier except a fierce ache beneath his ribs.

"Or p'raps simply sad. Do you agree?"

He thought of Patience Westin's serious eyes. "I do."

"Good," she said upon a sigh. "B'cause I don't wish to share you."

Then she was asleep. She would remember none of this. So he savored the momentary satisfaction of hearing her claim him for herself alone. Then he went into his bedchamber, removed his gentleman's clothing, and slept for many fewer hours than he wished.

Chapter 27

The Principal Benefit of the Wedded State

Lady Justice
Brittle & Sons, Printers

Dear Lady,

I understand. You do not like marriage. Neither do I. From whichever direction one looks at it, it is a trap.

But, if you will, consider the principal benefit of the wedded state, which I cannot give a name to here (out of deference to your modesty), but which, assured every night, must be an advantage to both husband and wife. In rejecting marriage, are you so willing to relinquish that as well?

In doubt, yet most sincerely,
Peregrine
Secretary, The Falcon Club

To Peregrine, at large:

You seek to shock, or perhaps to titillate. You do neither. What antiquated, patriarchal notion of femininity suggests to you that a woman must first bind herself in marriage to enjoy that benefit which is readily available outside of the wedded state?

—Lady Justice

Lady Justice
Brittle & Sons, Printers

Dear Lady,

I can hardly write. My hand quivers so that the ink from my pen splatters on the page and I find myself obliged to blot it again and again.
I renew to you now my invitation to meet. Any time. Any place.

With hope,
Peregrine
Secretary, The Falcon Club

To Peregrine, at large:

In response to the invitation in your last letter, I offer three words: In your dreams.

—Lady Justice

PART IV

The Warrior

Chapter 28

A Bath

*C*onstance awoke alone with a mild headache and discovered herself naked beneath the bed linens. That was what one got, she supposed, when one's husband undressed one—a husband whom every female eye in the place had watched last night, and several pairs of male eyes too.

This had not surprised her. He was both handsome and a curiosity, a natural attraction to people with too much wealth and too little to occupy their imaginations. Sir Lorian's awful club proved that unhappiness led people who should want for nothing to the most peculiar lengths in pursuit of diversion. But she had learned that months ago.

Yet today she felt light.

She pressed her face into the pillow and allowed herself to feel the soreness of her body from their lovemaking. Not pain. Simply soreness.

Then she climbed from bed and dressed. The day was well advanced and she was late for her fencing lesson. But when she arrived in the ballroom she found it empty.

"They have long since gone," Eliza said. "When you loll about in bed all morning, everyone else will precede you from the house."

"He has gone with Lord Michaels? Where?"

"To hound down that poor Chloe Edwards, no doubt."

So many weeks gone, yet Lord Michaels did not relinquish hope.

Constance went to her writing table and began penning invitations. As midday turned to afternoon, Sir Lorian and Lady Hughes were her first callers.

"Darling Constance." Miranda squeezed her hands. "You are the most beautiful creature, even after an evening of debauchery. Isn't she, Lorian?" She laughed like tinkling bells.

"If debauchery halts at too many glasses of wine," she said, drawing Lady Hughes to a sofa, "then I am indeed debauched." She had taken only a single glass; she had certainly been drugged.

"You left so early, I did not have the opportunity to see to my responsibility." She kept hold of one of Constance's hands.

"Your responsibility?"

"Every woman who enters the Sanctuary must know the Master's rules."

"Lady Hughes, I admit myself bemused. We hadn't any idea, you see, that there were rules or . . . or . . ."

"A Master," Saint said from the doorway.

Sir Lorian mumbled, "Sterling."

"But I thought you both understood." Miranda's smile was like a blooming rose. "The Sanctuary is not a *regular* sort of party."

"My dear," Sir Lorian said, "I have a word or two to say to Sterling, about swordplay, of course. Why don't you explain the rules to Lady Constance and have that done with?"

Lady Hughes's hand was still firmly holding hers.

"Will you call me Miranda?" she said with a pretty smile. "Your husband does, after all."

He did?

"Thank you, Miranda. Now, do tell me, who is this

Master?"

"You must be able to guess," she replied with a coy smile.

"I truly cannot."

"None of us have seen his face. But all of the women have been summoned by him, and—"

"All?" This seemed unreal.

"Of course, darling." Her delighted laughter spilled over them.

"Forgive me, Miranda." She smiled with effort, the image of the surly Duke of Loch Irvine and sugary Lady Hughes entwined in passion robbing her of words momentarily. "I fear that after last night's wine I am far too slow today. Was that party typical of the Master's gatherings?"

"Oh, yes. We gather at midnight and the Master makes his choice within the hour. After that each lady is allowed to choose whomever she wishes to be with."

And yet Miranda had chosen Mr. Westin, the least attractive, least influential, and dullest man present.

"The gentlemen have no choice in their partners? None?"

"Isn't it positively wicked?" she purred. "Lorian is handsome, but naturally I hadn't any say in whether I wished to marry him or not. And do you know, he is a very poor specimen of a man." She wiggled her pinky finger.

Constance hardly knew whether to laugh. "The Master is not, I guess?"

"Well . . ." Lady Hughes buttoned her pretty rosebud lips together. She leaned forward and whispered, "I hope that what I am about to tell you will entice you to join our little club. What the gentlemen do not know . . . What none of us have ever told our husbands . . ."

"What haven't you told them?"

"He paints us."

"Who paints you?"

"The Master." Miranda shrugged prettily. "He doesn't touch us. He wears a mask and a robe that cover him entirely, and he paints us. He even wears a glove so that we cannot see his hand holding the brush."

"But . . ." How was this possible? "He doesn't—"

"No." Miranda giggled. "Not yet, at least. Not with me or any of the other women."

"He only *paints* you?"

"In the nude, of course. It is as sophisticated as any Parisian studio, I daresay. But he has never once touched me. He does not even allow Mr. Reeve to see us unclothed. Isn't it fantastic?"

Entirely fantastic. Hardly believable.

"Does he show you the paintings?"

"Yes, but only when he is finished. Oftentimes he requires many sittings to complete a painting. And he is a marvelous portraitist, Constance. Clarissa is so enamored of the picture he did of her that she begged to purchase it from him."

"Did he sell it to her?"

"He gave her no reply. He does not *speak* to us, darling. Not a single word. It is really the most diverting thing imaginable."

"And none of you have told your husbands?"

"It is our secret. Ours and his. And now it is yours too. You mustn't tell anyone, of course." Her gaze darted to Saint.

"But . . . why do you do it?"

For the first time since she had entered the room, the sparkle in Miranda's dark eyes dimmed.

"Constance darling, given your unconventional choice of a perfectly delicious husband, I suspect you will not entirely understand. But has it occurred to you that not every lady enjoys the liberty to openly choose a partner who suits her?"

The footman announced new callers and within a quarter hour Sir Lorian and Lady Hughes departed, with a private assurance that there would be another gathering soon.

Later, after the last caller left, Saint closed the door behind the footman.

"Dylan and I called at Loch Irvine's house this morning," he said without preamble.

"Without me? Why—"

"The duke is not in residence."

"Of course he is."

"No. He is absent, Constance, as I believe he was at the fall equinox and winter solstice."

"Have you proof?"

"Not incontrovertible. No one opened the door to us this morning, but the stable is empty. And not one of the shop-keepers recognize a man of Reeve's description."

"Edinburgh is not such a large place. We will find Reeve. And even if the Master is not the duke, he must know some-one is using his house."

"Like my brother used his house. That's what you are thinking."

"No. I am thinking that Miranda Hughes believes she was in that room with the Duke of Loch Irvine last night. Perhaps Sir Lorian knows the truth of it. When we—"

"We are not going back there."

"We must. Saint—"

"No," he said, his eyes moving across her features care-fully. "Nothing we saw last night proves that Loch Irvine or anyone else there is a murderer."

"But the ritual quality of the Master's little game does suggest that it is not beyond reason to investigate further. There was the white robe, like the robes Sir Lorian ordered from the mill. And today Miranda told me something ex-traordinary that you won't—"

The drawing room door crashed open.

"I have discovered a witness," Lord Michaels exclaimed. "Rather, I've spoken with a man who knows a man who saw her three weeks ago. Three weeks only! He's in Leith. I am going now to track him down. I'd like your help, Saint."

"Of course." With a swift, pointed glance at her, Saint followed him out.

THEY RETURNED SHORTLY before dawn. Curled up in a chair by the window, Constance heard the horses' hooves on the cobbles.

She met them on the stairs and pulled her sleeve across

her nose. "Good heavens, you smell wretched."

"Thank you, my bride. That is precisely what a man wishes to hear when he returns home at the end of a long day."

"Pig farmer," Dylan mumbled, then grinned. "He'd seen her, tho. Saint'll tell you. Bacon for breakfast every day from this day forward!" He disappeared into his bedchamber.

"This is hopeful news."

"It is." He leaned against the door frame.

"Go in." She gestured. "But do not *touch* anything, for goodness sake, or lie down on anything, or—well—anything. I will call up a bath." Grabbing the lamp, she went down to the kitchen to see to it.

When she returned, she found him lying on his back on the bare floor where the rug did not cover the wooden slats, asleep. Despite the stench, she felt all sorts of warmth and agitation seeing him stretched out like that. She knelt beside him and touched him on the back of his hand. His eyes opened and looked directly at her, into her, beneath every layer of skin and desire.

She helped him from his coat and waistcoat and filthy boots, and deposited them in the corridor as servants brought the first of the hot water to the copper tub in their dressing room. When the water was sufficient she dismissed the servants and woke her husband again.

"Good night, then," he said, reaching to close the door between them. She stopped him.

"I will bathe you. To make certain you wash off every bit of pig farm."

He looked down at her with half-lidded eyes and smiled. "You'll spoil that pretty gown."

"I have others." She pressed her palm to his chest and pushed him toward the tub.

She watched him climb into the tub, every muscle toned, and she could barely think for the agitation in her body.

She poured water over his head. It didn't help. He was just as gorgeous wet as dry.

"Soap, if you please?" He extended his palm.

"I said I would *do* it."

He opened an eye and looked askance at her. "If it is such a burden, you needn't. Not having servants care for my every whim my entire life, I can in fact bathe myself."

"It isn't a burden, of course." She removed her wrapper and pushed the sleeves of her nightgown up to her shoulders. She scooped a handful of soap. "The trouble is that I want to touch you intimately, and it is making me cross that I—"

He grabbed her around the waist and pulled her against his chest and covered her lips with his. She sank her soapy hands into his hair and let his lips command hers for a moment of decadence while water soaked into her backside. Then she broke her mouth free.

"—that I cannot control my lust," she finished. "Now you have gotten me all wet after all."

"Do this for me," he said over her mouth. "Don't try to control your lust with me." His hand curved around her breast. "All wet, hm?" His thumb circled the nipple, darkening the fabric with water. Then he bent his head and surrounded it with his mouth. She pushed into him.

"I feel this—you—everywhere," she whispered.

"That is the idea." His mouth rose to her neck and his hand dipped between her legs.

She dragged herself away from him.

"Bathe. Now," she said upon a short breath. "You smell like the worst sort of farm and I want to know what you learned today."

He lifted his hands to grasp the edges of the tub and closed his eyes once more.

"As you wish," he said. "But note that I am exhibiting a heroic force of will at this time that I hope will, at some point, be grandly rewarded."

She was certain her heart could not beat any faster.

"Noted," she said and gathered more soap and water to spread across his back. "Now tell me."

As she washed him, memorizing every contoured muscle

and each sculpted bone beneath her hands, he told her how they tracked the farmer to a house near the port. The farmer said he knew Miss Edwards well on account of her aunt having purchased from him a sow. He had seen Chloe one afternoon not far from the Duke of Loch Irvine's house. She had been with a man—he hadn't seen the fellow's face—and she called out in greeting. She had not seemed in distress. But when pressed, the farmer said she called her greeting two or three times, which in hindsight seemed peculiar.

Constance listened, tracing his scars with her fingertips and feeling the heat of his skin with her hands even as the water cooled. Finally she related what Miranda Hughes had said about what passed in the Master's chamber.

His eyes opened. "He *only* paints them?"

"According to Miranda, whose face is so wonderfully easy to read, I knew she could not be fabricating. Isn't it curious? None of the husbands know the truth, and the wives have a fine time keeping the secret from them."

"And yet you have just told me."

"Don't be silly."

"He paints them." His voice sounded thick again. "Extraordinary."

"I wonder what he does with the paintings?" She ran her soapy hands over his shoulders. "Private collection, I daresay."

"Mm."

"Now you must agree that we should return."

"No."

"Saint—"

"No," he mumbled.

By the time she finished, he was asleep.

She kissed him. He awoke with a start, then with a hand around the side of her face, his lips responding to hers without hesitation.

Reluctantly she drew away and offered a towel. Eyes hooded, he dried off, wrapped his arms around her, and took her mouth beneath his again.

"You are asleep even as you stand," she said.

"I needn't be awake to kiss you. I have kissed you so many times in my dreams, I am an expert at it," he said without opening his eyes.

"I must change my gown."

His hands moved up her sides. "Who needs a gown? Who needs sleep?"

She pulled him toward the bed. "We are having a party tonight. With many guests."

"I would rather have a party now with just the two of us."

She went to the dressing room, discarded her sodden nightgown, and pulled a fresh wrapper around her. On the bed, he slept as though he had fallen there. She drew the linens up around his waist, went to the other side of the mattress, and slipped beneath the covers. Curling up on her side, she laid her cheek on her palm and watched him.

"Saint," she said.

Not a lash flickered.

"Frederick Evan Sterling."

His chest rose upon each even breath.

"I need you," she whispered as the night gave way to pale sunlight filling up the room. "I need your kindness and strength and gentleness. I did not know that there were men like you." She stroked her fingertips on the counterpane between them, but she could not bring herself to touch him. "I love you."

Chapter 29

A Thin Sheet of Ice

*A*s she had once done from a hidden doorway in a corner, now Constance peeked, unseen, into a ballroom.

"Rapiers?" Saint stood in the middle of the room, his brow furrowed. "And a what?"

"A doublet, of course." Lord Michaels brandished his blade with a dramatic sweep of his arm. "Shakespearean garb, don't you know. But I refuse to wear hose or a codpiece. Dashed uncomfortable, those, what?"

Saint set the tip of his sword on the floor. "A codpiece." He seemed nonplussed.

"Mrs. Josephs insists, the sassy wench. But I defended my masculinity." The baron lunged dramatically at an imaginary Eliza.

"It is a costume party, my lord," Constance said, finally entering the ballroom, arms laden with cloth. "Not a competition."

"Everything's a competition, my dear lady, when a fellow's—er—*codpiece* is in question."

"I remind you, cousin," Saint said, looking at her, "to watch your tongue when speaking to my wife."

"Stuff and nonsense." The baron racked his sword and strode to her. Grabbing a plumed hat from the bundle in her arms, he swept a low bow. "Forgive my vulgarity, madam."

She snatched the hat from him and set it atop his head. "You will be a dashing knave, my lord. Now do go make yourself useful and tell the footmen where to place the decorations."

"Yes, mum." With a jaunty grin at Saint, he went out.

They met midway across the floor.

"I have brought your costume for tonight," she said.

"Not all of this, I hope?"

"Yours is on the top. The rest is my gown. Your cousin is in such fine spirits. He still has hope."

"You don't wish to disappoint him, do you?" he said.

"We must succeed."

"Why costumes, Constance?"

"Wearing costumes, people behave as they should not." She had once, after all. With him.

"They do so in the Sanctuary as well, it seems."

"But we are not returning there."

He removed the garments from her arms and let them fall to the floor, and drew her to him for the first time since the night before when he had done so wearing nothing.

"I am relieved that you have come to this decision." His hands spread around her waist. "I would not have allowed you to attend another gathering. But I was having a rough time of it devising a method for preventing you from going that did not involve tying you up."

She turned her face away. "You have just made my gorge rise."

"What every man longs to hear from the woman he is holding."

"Why are you intentionally cruel?"

"If you run from a foe, it will chase you until you stumble and fall, and it will overcome you. If you stand and fight, you have the power to defeat it."

She lifted her eyes to his.

"I will attend the party dressed as Viking!" Lord Michaels exclaimed as he entered carrying a stepladder, followed by Mr. Viking burdened with a heavy box. "He would not allow me to lift a finger to carry one of those dusty things. In thanks, I am trading coats with him forthwith. This one cost me a fortune. Viking, take that thing off now or suffer the wrath of my smallsword."

"My lord has clearly been at the whiskey already today, my lady. We shan't have a moment's peace until after the festivities tonight, I am sure," Mr. Viking said, opening the box and withdrawing a pile of satiny cloth as two maids entered the room.

"I should speak with Cook." Constance gathered up her costume and went out.

SAINT GLANCED AGAIN at the street address on the note Patience Westin had sent to him, then folded the paper and tucked it into his waistcoat pocket. There were many hours yet until the costume party. Casting the house a final glance, he gave his horse leave to go ahead.

LATER, CONSTANCE FOUND her husband in the private parlor. Not to be used during the party, it was free of preparations. Saint reclined in a straight-backed chair as though it were a commodious couch, his legs stretched out before him, eyes closed, and hand atop the blade of a longsword laid across his lap. Afternoon sunlight splashed the steel and his hair with gold.

As she sat down before her writing desk, she heard him stir.

"Do you know," he murmured, "I think I liked it better when we only met for two hours every morning at the edge of a wood."

She drew a sheet of paper from a drawer. "Oh?"

"Then I knew where to find you." His fingertips drummed slowly on the blade. "And when I did, we were alone."

"The pot calls the kettle black. I am astonished to discover you in this house at five o'clock in the afternoon." She cast him a glance, then regretted it. She found it difficult to look directly into his eyes. Mild estrangement was so much easier than encountering him like this. She had never had this domestic *familiarity* with a man. And, despite all, she still longed to touch him too much, more and more, as though tasting only increased her hunger. "Shouldn't you be off somewhere slaying dragons or rescuing maidens or some such thing?"

"I've just come from that, in fact. I am now taking a moment to recoup my strength." She could hear the smile in his voice, just as she had heard it in the dark years ago.

"One hundred and sixty-two guests have accepted, including all who attended the Sanctuary two nights ago. Your notoriety is to our advantage. Everyone wants to make merry with the accused."

"When did you decide I had not done it?"

She twisted around to face him. "At the jail when you said you would kill Walker Styles. But I never actually believed you did it. I was . . . frightened. Momentarily." She waited for him to berate her, to tell her she was a fool for her weakness.

"Walker Styles," he said. "That is his name."

She bent her head to the paper, her fingers tight around the pen. "We must catalogue the information we have collected."

"Shall I fetch Dylan?"

"Not yet. We need to speak freely about the Sanctuary. For all that I am immoderate in my lust, I don't care to discuss that party with your cousin. What is the sword you have there?"

"The bribe a duke offered me when I first refused to teach an heiress how to fence. I am carrying it tonight. Now let's talk a bit more about your lust, shall we? Better yet, let's put it into action."

"There is too much to do."

"Nothing more enjoyable."

She hid her smile. "Stay away from me, Saint."

"I've heard that before. Then you asked me to kiss you."

"I am listing what we know of the abducted girls beside what we now know of the Sanctuary. Unlike Maggie Poultney and Cassandra Finn, the women involved in the Sanctuary are not maidens. Like Annie Favor."

"Indeed."

She glanced at him. With a cloth he was polishing the rapier's intricate guard. He looked up from his task.

"I was not the first man to discover that, Constance."

She studied the words she had written. They blurred. "Only married couples are admitted to the Sanctuary, which is a peculiar stipulation for membership to any group, especially one in which the principal purpose of its founder seems to be to paint female nudes. He might hire models."

"Perhaps the painting is a guise to conceal his primary purpose."

"Which is?"

"Enjoying the vision of beautiful, wealthy women without their clothing."

"How odd that would be."

"I don't know about that. I found it remarkably enjoyable two nights ago." His smile was roguish.

"But you did not paint me, as he does," she said, biting back her pleasure. "And I am not married to someone else."

"No," he said in a low voice. "You are not."

She wanted to cross the room and climb onto his lap. The need she felt for him was too strong. "Why doesn't he invite them privately?"

"Perhaps he eventually hopes to paint their husbands too."

"And there is another peculiar detail of it. The men, who believe their wives are serving the Master's pleasure, do not seem to object to it."

"Rather the opposite."

"Have they no pride?"

He shrugged. "Pride falleth before unbridled orgy, I suppose."

Her lips twitched. "I don't care for the way you make me laugh in the midst of this."

He smiled. "How precious in your sensibilities you are, my lady."

She tapped the tip of her pen on the paper. "It seems silly."

"What it?"

"Spouse-trading in the guise of ritual. Why do they need the Sanctuary to exchange bedfellows? Everybody does it all the time anyway."

"Not everybody I know."

"How hopelessly unsophisticated you are."

"It's true. My notions of marriage lack that aristocratic patina of laissez-faire. In this matter I am sadly bourgeois." His tone sent shivers up her back.

"Mustn't you have money to be a member of the bourgeoisie?" she said airily.

"I do have money."

She looked around at him.

"I have your money," he said. "But we digress."

"The Sanctuary. In exchange for the perks of the arrangement, these leaders of society voluntarily allow themselves to be cuckolded. It is unfathomable to me."

He seemed to be studying her thoughtfully.

"Why do you look at me like that?"

"Some men, Constance, enjoy knowing that their woman is desired by other men."

"*Desired*, I understand. Actually allowing other men intimacy with their wives seems the opposite of manly."

"These men are giving permission, and they are using other men's wives in return. This makes them feel powerful."

"But who among the men in that room the other night would need to feel more powerful than they already are?"

"Some men's appetite for power is insatiable." He stared at the blade in his hands.

"Sir Eustace has an old title. Lord Porter has an

insignificant property but allies in the Lords. Sir Lorian and Lord Hart have comfortable wealth and fine estates. I wonder . . ." Her fingertips stroked the pen absently. "Why does the Master insist on at least one man and one woman in every room? To confuse the paternity of the children born of the unions at the Sanctuary?"

"It could be."

"But why would he wish that? Is it so that he can deny claims of paternity since in fact none of the children *could* be his? We must learn how long this club has been meeting, and how often. But what if offspring have nothing to do with it? There are so many questions unanswered, and now that we have seen the sorry banality of the meetings, all of it could be unconnected to the real mystery. Then we would have been wasting our time entirely with these people."

"Stop doing that."

She jerked her head around. "What?"

"With the quill. You are caressing it. I cannot think." His eyes were bright.

"Now?" she said. "In the middle of the day?"

"Around the clock."

"When the sun is shining?"

"Especially then." He set down the sword, stood, and walked to her. "For then no shadows obscure your face, your skin, each crevice of your beauty. The sun warms your flesh—"

"The Scottish sun? Surely you jest."

"I am waxing eloquent in this fantasy. Go along with me." He sat on the edge of the desk and stroked her hair back from her brow. "The sun glimmers in your hair and blinds me, so that the remaining four senses hasten to fill the deficit. Touch . . ." He stroked her cheek with the back of his fingers, slipping down the curve of her neck. "Scent . . ." He bent his head beside hers. "Sound . . ." His palm stole over her breast and she sighed.

"Taste," she said, and turned her lips up to his. She twined her fingers through his hair, he drew her mouth fully to his, and then she was in his arms.

At some moment between accepting his tongue into her mouth and his hand between her thighs, she dropped the pen.

Fingers pulling down her bodice, he was laying kisses upon her breasts above the fabric, leaning her back against the desk and caressing her through her skirts when words formed again on her lips.

"Did you like her?"

"Who?" He stroked perfectly.

Struggling for breaths, she clutched his shoulders. "Miranda?"

"Hm?"

"At the Sanctuary. Did you find her attractive? Her breasts? Her body?"

All movement ceased. All caresses. All pleasure. He lifted his head and stared at her. His hands fell away from her and abruptly he turned and walked across the room.

Stunned and aching, she stared at his back. Finally he turned to face her but he did not speak.

"I don't know what to say," she said.

"Then we are at an equal loss," he replied shortly. A muscle flexed in his jaw.

"That is . . . I do."

"Oh?"

"I want you to come back over here and continue kissing me now."

"I—" His voice broke. He stared at the ground and his hand scraped through his hair. He lifted bleak eyes to her. "I am terrified."

"Of what?"

"Of you," he said without air. "Of what you are doing to me. Of how much I want you."

"I need you to want me," came from her throat like crumpled paper. "I don't know how—I don't know how to *be* with you. But I need you."

He went to her, plowed his hands into her hair, and dragged her mouth beneath his. He kissed her deeply, and she met him entirely, needing to feel him, needing to take him into her, beneath her skin. The longing in her was painful. She let him bear her up against the wall and grasp her hips with his strong hands and make love to her standing, fully clothed, in the daylight that revealed everything.

"I feel like I am ice," she whispered. "A thin sheet of ice, and I am cracking."

"Don't," he growled against her neck. "Don't," he said again. She ran her palms up his chest, and his mouth on her throat and hands on her hips forced her pleasure. "Feel this," he said. "Feel me."

She closed her eyes and let his body urge hers toward more.

"I would say find a room," came Lord Michaels's voice. "But you're already in a room. You know, there are several bedchambers right around the corner." Standing in the doorway in full Shakespearean costume, he leaned to peer at her from behind Saint who had turned to face him, blocking her. "My lady, I beg of you, forgive the interruption. It was Viking's fault."

"It was *not*," Mr. Viking threw over his shoulder, his back to the doorway. "I merely opened the door. My lord chose to barrel in and make this scene."

"Get out of here, both of you," Saint said, gripping the back of his neck.

"Well, I would, but I am in desperate need of a pen and paper," Lord Michaels said, "and Viking assured me this was the place to acquire them. But it's a good thing I happened in. If you don't both get ready soon you will be late to your party. Tonight I aim to be a whirling dervish of information gathering."

Smoothing her hair, she walked with outward calm to the door, not trusting herself to speak as she departed, thinking that Saint's idea of meeting at dawn in a wood was a fine one indeed.

WITH THE HELP of her maid, Constance dressed in a silk petticoat with voluminous sleeves, a bodice that barely covered her nipples, and a heavy gown of slashed sleeves that was tied with laces up the center, making her breasts round above the square neckline. To complete the costume, Eliza set a jewel-encrusted tiara in her upswept hair.

"You should not be doing this," Eliza said with a disapproving eye at her décolletage. "Mark my words, if you continue in this manner you will lose him."

She gave her friend's stiff neck ruff a tweak and left to survey the preparations a final time.

Guests arrived with amusingly eager promptness. Footmen went about with trays of wine and musicians playing Italian dances filled the house with music.

Dylan's face was worried as he scanned the animated crowd. "What if he's taken her to the countryside? What if all of this is only wasting time while we should be searching elsewhere? Haiknayes, perhaps."

She tucked her hand around his elbow. "If we discover nothing here tonight, we will turn our search outward. We will not cease until she is found. Now come, help me greet our guests."

Saint was not present. She left her guests to the baron and went to find her husband.

He stood in the middle of his bedchamber, fiddling with his tight cuffs. The sleeves puffed out from a jerkin of indigo velvet that hugged his chest, and his breeches were tight to his legs. The antique rapier that she had purchased thinking of him—as she had purchased them all, for years—hung at his side from a long, doubled belt of gilded leather.

"You are very handsome," she said.

"Why do you think they call it the Sanctuary?" he said without looking up, his graceful fingers fumbling on the buttons.

"Have you been standing here pondering that since our party began?"

"And attempting to fasten these blasted things. Where is that damn Viking when I actually need him?" He extended his wrists to her. "Would you?"

She went forward, endeavoring to ignore the wash of feeling inside her at the sight of his hands—simply his hands spread before her.

"You are *not* going downstairs like that." His eyes were upon her breasts.

"I have already been downstairs." She finished her task and turned toward the door with a swirl of heavy skirts. "Come along, Sir Knight. Your guests await."

As she came to the landing, she went to the balustrade and looked down. The lights were low, the costumes sumptuous, and the breeze coming through the open front door heady with the scent of jasmine. Music rose to them, and laughter and the sounds of conversation.

"The solstice is but a month away," she whispered.

"We will find her," he said just behind her. "We will discover who is doing this, and I will put steel through his heart. And every other man down there."

"Every one?"

"If the villain is not one of these, why are you throwing a party for them? I serve at the pleasure of my lady, but I would prefer spending my leisure otherwise." His hand curved around her hip.

"Which leisure activities would you prefer?"

Air swished against her ankles. He was drawing up her skirts at the back.

"I daresay you can imagine," he said as the cool air touched her calves. She did not halt him and beneath the fabric his hand covered her buttock. She bit her lips together.

"What are you doing?" she breathed as his fingers cupped her.

"My wife," he said. "I should think that obvious."

Her laughter was husky beneath the murmur of voices and music.

"Someone will see."

"The light is below." He caressed the crease of her thighs. "We are in darkness."

Her fingers tightened on the railing and she fought the urge to ask him for more. She wanted his hands on her breasts. His mouth.

"It is too little," she whispered.

"And yet this brings me pleasure. Along with the hope that someday you will allow me to put my mouth here." He dragged two fingers across her most sensitive flesh.

"*Yes.*"

"Yes?"

She moved against him. "Anywhere. Everywhere."

He pulled her from the balustrade and swung her back against the wall. His lips hovered over hers, his eyes questioning and exultant at once.

"Anything," she said unsteadily. "How unchaste you make me want to be, Mr. Sterling."

His mouth found her throat, his body hers. Running her hands over his shoulders, she pressed to him and the pressure of his arousal against hers forced a moan from her throat.

"We *must* return to the party," she said. "I should go re-adjust my gown first."

"If you go anywhere near your bedchamber at this time, I won't be held responsible for your absence for the next several hours."

"If we never appeared for our own party, people would talk."

He released her, but his fingertips trailed along her arm as though reluctant to lose contact. "They would say that Lady Constance and her purchased man were too busy enjoying wedded bliss to show them proper hospitality." He moved toward the stairs.

"Will you not offer your arm to me, sir?"

"Constance, I am as hard as an anvil at present. Allowing you to touch me again will not help me reach the ground floor otherwise, and these breeches are damnably tight. If you wish, however, I am more than willing to display my desire for you to everyone below."

She glided past him, smiling. "It seems that I was right when I called you Beast."

"And you are my Beauty." He gestured for her to precede him down the stairs.

My Beauty. She went ahead of him and felt his gaze upon her all the way down the stairs.

Chapter 30

Pirate's Gold

*S*he moved through the crowds of costumed revelers, chatting, flirting, fluttering her fan over her decadent bosom as though every man's attention weren't already there. Saint did not approach her. Their purpose tonight was to show themselves eager for a lark, whatever that might be. He spent time with the women from Loch Irvine's house two nights earlier, and several of the men, but learned nothing of value except that the next meeting at the Sanctuary would celebrate the summer solstice. Their theories seemed on target.

Each time his gaze found her in the throng of guests, her eyes seemed brighter. And Dylan's mask of conviviality could not entirely hide his anxiety. Time was short. Tomorrow they must mount an offense.

As the clock began its ascent into day, Sir Lorian Hughes sauntered to him. He wore a long doublet of gold, wide pantaloons, and a smallsword.

"Splendid festivities the lady of the house throws, Sterling." He fingered the hilt of his sword.

"Doesn't she?"

Hughes's eyes were hooded. "You will hang for the murder of Annie Favor."

"I beg your pardon?"

"Read's petition to have the accusation against you dismissed will not meet with success. Do you know how I know this?"

"Enlighten me."

"I have proof that you killed her, proof that you buried a blade in her heart like it was butter and carved a mark on her face to match Loch Irvine's emblem."

"And what proof is that?"

"I have the knife that you used and the testimony of the man who sold it to you."

"That is hardly incontrovertible proof."

Hughes's mouth twisted into a smirk. "Given the present fear of every family with a daughter in Edinburgh, I do not need incontrovertible proof. Only a public square with you in the middle of it, and a mob."

So this was it. Now he knew. "And you call yourself a man of honor."

"Don't be naïve, Sterling."

"What do you want?"

"Her." Saint followed his gaze to Constance. "I tried to do this the easy way, through an invitation to that pathetic little gathering. But I understand from what others are saying tonight that you and she will decline the next invitation."

"The Sanctuary is not to our tastes."

"And yet she is to my tastes. So now it comes to threats."

Saint bit down on the fury building in him. "Could you be so sadly predictable? Your own wife is beautiful, and she is already yours."

"Don't tell me that a man of your talent with a blade does not understand the thrill of a hard-won victory? Has she told you that I offered for her?"

No. Along with all the other secrets she held close. "How intrepid of you."

"She refused me. She refused every man who offered for her. She preferred taunting us all."

"Pity for you all, then."

"She is a spirited filly. But perhaps she has had a change of heart. If she hasn't, it will be in your best interest to see that she does."

"Hughes, this is not a game you should play with me. You will come to regret it."

"She is far beyond your touch, Sterling, and everyone knows it but you." He strolled away.

CONSTANCE WATCHED SAINT'S spine grow stiff as he spoke with Sir Lorian. When they parted, he disappeared into another room.

She dove into gossip anew. As instructed, the footmen had refilled glasses liberally. But conversation continued exasperatingly dull. Most of her guests seemed unaware of the Sanctuary, and blithely optimistic regarding the accusation of murder hanging over her husband's head. It was wonderful and incredible and she wanted to laugh with him about it. But Lord Michaels's gaiety was forced, and when the guests trickled to a dozen, his face was grim as he retired.

Sir Lorian and Lady Hughes were the last to depart, lingering in the foyer over-long.

When they were finally alone, Saint grasped her hand and led her upstairs without words. He took her to his bedchamber, closed the door, and leaned back against it.

"Undress."

She put her fingers to her bodice and, from the top, unfastened the tight overdress. It gaped and she drew it off one sleeve at a time. Ribbons untied, the silky petticoat slid to the floor. Her stays were next. When she drew the shift up and off, she wore only stockings. She reached to unfasten the garters, rolled the stockings down, and dropped them on the floor. She stood before him nude and his elven eyes consumed her.

"Take two steps backward and lift your arms." He removed his coat and neck cloth.

She did as he demanded, and watched as he took up her stockings from the floor and came to her. Reaching up, he grasped her wrists and silk slithered around them.

"*Saint*—"

He ducked his cheek to hers and said quietly, "I will not harm you. I—" His fingers laced with hers. "Let me make love to you."

"You will cease if I say so?"

"The very moment." His lips touched the tender place beneath her ear. He drew the silk snugly over her wrist. "Yes?"

Tightness was gathering in her chest, of equal parts alarm and certainty. "Yes."

He tied her to the bedpost.

When his hands came down he put them around her waist. "Tug, and you can free yourself at any time."

She was cold with sweat. "I can?"

"Try it now."

She took a thick breath. "*No*."

His hands tightened on her waist. "You are magnificent."

"I am waiting," she whispered.

He kissed her neck, then her shoulders as he held her breasts in his hands and took every bit of breath from her. Then he kissed her breasts, marking a journey of teasing, languorous devotion on her skin. When his mouth closed around her nipple her fingers clamped around the bedpost. The knot was indeed no match for her; his teeth braised her nipple and she writhed and the stockings slipped away. But she remained stretched out for him, waiting, wanting. The ache was unbearable, the need to have him touch her and satisfy the craving too great.

Then he did, with his mouth. Soft, hot, wet, he kissed her, his hands parting her thighs so he could deepen the kiss. She had not known *this*. She had not known that a man could be this tender. She clung to the bedpost, her hips rocking to him, and begged him not to cease.

SHE WAS SHAKING as he took her up in his arms and laid her on the bed. He removed his shoes, then came to her side. She watched him with half-lidded eyes.

"Are you a pirate?" she said softly.

"Why? Have you found a hidden chest of jewels and gold doubloons in my private quarters?"

"Where did you learn to tie that sort of knot?"

"I ought to be shot."

"Because you stole a chest of jewels and gold? Then you are a pirate after all."

He wanted to touch her, to stroke the strands of damp silk from her cheek and trace the curve of her shoulder.

"Are you all right?" he asked.

"Quite all right. Will you do that again, sometime, but without the stockings?"

"This moment, if you wish it," he said less steadily than he liked.

She smiled, a sweet grin at odds with her unfocused eyes. "I think I might never have a wish other than that." Her voice quieted. "But not with the bonds."

"Shall I ask forgiveness of you?"

"No." She slipped a hand across the mattress and to his collar. Beneath her fingertips, his pulse was quick. "Why are you dressed? Do you have an assignation later, a meeting to plot diabolical rituals, perhaps? Could you have been so successful with our guests tonight?"

"Constance, you humble me."

She spread her fingers, five spots of noble pleasure upon his skin. "It was tiresome pretending to want everybody else's husband tonight. I don't know how those women do it all the time."

"They are not pretending."

"Everyone pretends." She stroked two fingers down his chest. "Except you." She laid her palm flat over his heart. "I should like to pretend right now that we are wed and that you wish to claim your conjugal rights of me immediately. Here. On this bed."

He turned her onto her back and took her into his arms. "No pretense necessary."

Her lips were welcoming, her arms tight around his shoulders, and her body open to him. He took his time giving her pleasure. When she cried his name, finally he allowed himself the release he needed.

He stroked a golden tress from her brow, watching her fall into sleep.

"Thank you for trusting me."

"My knight," she murmured.

She awoke to silver light blazing through the bedchamber window. He was there, sitting at the foot of the bed, his skin and every contour of muscle gloriously lit, and she thought she must be dreaming.

"Is it morning?"

"Not for several hours yet. You have slept only a short while."

"The moonlight is brilliant. Haven't you slept?"

He offered her a half smile that curled inside her.

"It seems I cannot," he said.

She pushed tangled hair from before her eyes and turned onto her side.

"Lady Hughes did not want to leave last night," she said, watching his face.

"I don't wish to talk about her. I don't wish to talk about any of that."

"I think she hoped you would invite her to stay," she said because his gaze upon her was so peculiar, at once longing and distant.

"If you had invited her to stay, she would have been even happier."

In a moment's clarity, the truth occurred to her. She leaned up onto her elbow. "Do you think that she and Patience Westin—"

"Yes."

"But at the Sanctuary, Miranda chose Mr. Westin."

"Choice is a peculiar thing, isn't it?"

"How cryptic you are. Miranda said something to me only yesterday about choice, too. She is flirtatious, to be sure. But Patience is so shy." She looked into his eyes and her throat abruptly tightened. "Oh, Saint. At the Sanctuary, Miranda chose Westin so that Patience would not be forced to be with *another* man."

"I imagine she did."

Tears leaped up behind her eyes. "She was protecting her."

"Yes."

"Sanctuary . . ." He had known about Patience and Miranda, or suspected, but he had not told her. "Will you share with me your conversation with Sir Lorian last night?"

"He believes himself slighted by you," he said.

"He said that to *you*?"

"He is determined to have you, Constance. You must take care with him."

A flare of panic stole through her. She struggled to sit, pulling up the bedclothes to cover herself. "You say that as though you will not be here to aid me."

"If I weren't, you are more than capable of defending yourself."

"That is not an answer."

"You asked no question." He came to her, and she knew her eyes were wide but she had no will to dissemble. "My wife," he said, kneeling before her and curving his hands around her face. "Let us for once not speak of these things. Let us for an hour forget them entirely. Shall we?" He stroked his thumb across her lips softly.

"Return to the edge of the woods at dawn?" she whispered, and felt that somehow he was saying good-bye to her.

He kissed her. She wrapped her arms around him and drew him close.

Chapter 31

Time

*W*hen the sky began to lighten, Saint dressed, sought food in the kitchen, where the cook and scullery maid were still wiping sleep from their eyes, and went to the mews. John Shaw was walking from the stable like a man who had not slept in days, medical bag in hand.

"Good morning, Mr. Sterling."

"Good morning, sir. Have you just returned to town?"

"Yesterday. The Lord Advocate sent for me to review the notes of the police surgeon who examined Miss Favor's body."

"You?"

"For a second opinion on the matter. And as a courtesy, I believe, to the duke."

"I see."

He rubbed a hand over his brow. "I am sorry to say that the evidence is inconclusive."

"In what manner?"

"I cannot share the particulars with you, of course. I have done my best to make sense of it, and I do hope it is to your advantage."

"Thank you."

"I'm for breakfast now, and sleep. Are you going in or out?"

"Out. But . . . may I ask you a question?"

"Of course."

"Has anyone else—anyone other than you—read the surgeon's report?"

"Not that I know for certain. The police officers that collected the body and the men who found her in the loch must have seen something of her wounds. That would all be included in the investigator's report of the incident, which I have not read."

"I see. Thank you, Dr. Shaw."

"Good day, Sterling." The doctor continued toward the house.

Sir Lorian Hughes might have gotten access to the reports of Annie's wounds. Or he might know of them firsthand.

Saint rode to the shop where he had fitted Constance for a dagger and scabbard for her ankle—her ankle that he now knew the shape and texture of with his mouth, and the rest of her body. The shop was closed. A sign posted on the door indicated that Ian MacMillan would be absent for some weeks.

Hughes must have gotten to him. There were few bladesmiths in the city, and Saint knew them all. It would not have required much gold to convince one of them to lie.

He had little time left. He would find Reeve. He would ride to Haiknayes and confront Loch Irvine. He would corner Lorian Hughes and slit his throat, if necessary, and then he really would hang. But she would be safe.

CONSTANCE MET DR. SHAW at breakfast in the dining room and her heart lurched.

"I did not know you had returned to town. Has my father too? Has he heard news?"

"No. Only I was called." He told her of his purpose in Edinburgh. "Constance, I don't know what conclusion to draw from it. But I think you should know, the knife wounds on Miss Favor's body do not coincide with anything we know of the girls who disappeared last year, except in one particular. She was stabbed peculiarly, but in such a way that the blade severed the artery leading from the heart. But her cheek also bears a mark. It strongly resembles one of the three details of the star symbol drawn in chalk on both Miss Favor's coat and Miss Poultney's cloak."

"Which detail?"

"The tongue of fire."

"Does the Lord Advocate believe Miss Favor's death is connected to the abductions?"

"He has not yet returned to Edinburgh. I will send him my observations tomorrow." He took one of her hands between both of his. "Constance, I do not believe Mr. Sterling is capable of such an act. If asked, I will support any theory that throws the blame for this terrible deed off of him."

She squeezed his hand. "Has Libby come with you?"

"No. She is too close in age to the victims. She will remain at the castle until this mystery is solved."

Leaving him, Constance went to find Eliza.

"I will take a footman," she said when her companion objected to her destination. "I must speak with her."

"You would be better off speaking with Loch Irvine."

"Until he returns, or until I go to Haiknayes, I cannot do that." She should have confronted him weeks ago, after his party. But she had not known how. Nothing in her life had ever shown her that direct confrontation solved anything, nothing until the man she had married showed her.

At the Hugheses' house, she and Eliza were admitted to an empty parlor. Sir Lorian appeared, grinning as his eyes perused her.

"I am delighted to see you, my lady."

"Is Lady Hughes in?"

"She is not. But I suspect you will be happy to converse with me instead, when you know what news I have to share."

"News?"

"For your ears alone, my lady."

"Eliza," she said, "please step into the foyer."

"I will leave the door open." Eliza went.

"Come," he said, moving to a sofa. "We will be much more comfortable here."

The door remained wide. She sat, and he beside her.

"What do you wish to say to me, sir?" She had finished with flirtation to achieve her goals.

Sir Lorian's smile reached only as far as his mouth. "I spoke with your husband last night. I am thrilled to say that he will not stand in the way of our affair." He stroked a fingertip along her wrist.

She drew her arm away. "We are not having an affair."

"Then you do not doubt his approval."

"I do not doubt it. I entirely disbelieve it."

"I assure you, his interest is elsewhere. Do you know that he has purchased a house not far from Tantallon?"

She stood up but he grasped her wrist.

"It is a small house in a remote village," he said. "Ideal for avoiding discovery."

She tugged away. "Sir Lorian, I flirted with you in the past because I wished to gain entrance into the secret society. It was a mistake to have done so, and I regret it. Good day."

Constance went toward the doorway.

"Dear lady, your certainty in your husband's fidelity disappoints me," he said lazily. "I thought you cleverer. But if you will not believe the truths I have already told you, then do believe this: I have proof that he wielded the knife that put an end to Annie Favor's life."

"You do not."

"I have the knife itself. And witnesses to the deed." He sat cross-ankled, his arm stretched across the back of the sofa.

"You would invent this—condemn an innocent man to death—in order to bed me?"

"I did not invent your husband's guilt." His fingertips

stroked the carved wooden frame of the sofa. "I merely uncovered it."

"I don't believe you."

"My lady," Eliza said at the threshold. "Come away now."

"Whether you believe me or not is immaterial now, isn't it?" he said. "Would you like to see the knife? Speak with the witnesses? Before I take them to the police, that is?"

Eliza bustled forward. "Constance—"

"What do you want?" she said. "Tell me exactly."

"A night."

"*One* night?"

"A single night. And your thorough compliance."

"Where is Chloe Edwards?"

His brows rose. "Who?"

"You know her. I saw you speaking with her at the Duke of Loch Irvine's party."

"My dear," he said, rising and moving toward her. "I cannot remember the name of every woman I speak to at parties."

"You know where she is. You know who killed Miss Favor, I think. Yet you prey upon my husband now. Why are you doing this?"

He smiled. "I need you."

She pivoted away and went out.

On the walk home, Eliza linked their arms together, held her close, and whispered curses intermingled with words meant to soothe. But it was too late for either.

HAIKNAYES CASTLE ROSE in a massive tower of dusky pink stone from the side of a hill barely twenty miles south of Edinburgh. Saint arrived as the sun dipped below the crest to find the master of Haiknayes absent, the fortress shut. Impregnable. The single shepherd he found was ignorant of any recent ducal visits: he thought the duke in the city.

Saint had not found him at Leith earlier in the day, and no one in the village by his house in town had anything of use to share. One girl said she had seen a finely dressed man with a hood over his head enter the duke's house the previous week. But when Saint asked her for details, her mother demanded his name, then she pulled her daughter away with fear in her eyes.

Sir Lorian's threat was not empty. The newspapers had been full of speculation for weeks, and full of his name. The people of Edinburgh were afraid for their daughters. No other man had been accused. They needed a villain to hang.

He rode fast and returned to town by the glow of the waning moon. Stabling his horse, he entered a silent house lit with only two lamps—in the rear foyer where he left his travel-stained boots, and on the table by his bedchamber door. Inside the room, a fire crackled. By the glow he saw Constance rise from the bed and come forward, garbed in a chemise of ghostly hue. Without words, she twined her arms about his neck and lifted her lips to his.

He held her, tasting the heat and sweetness of her, breathing her in. She pressed her body to his and slid her hand down his chest to his waist. The buttons of his coat opened swiftly to her fingers, then his waistcoat, and her hand slipped beneath his shirt.

"Touching you like this . . ." Her palm carved a path of need across his flesh. "I am hungry for you."

He removed his neck cloth and shirt and took her into his arms.

"You smell vaguely of horse," she said against his shoulder as her hands spread on him.

"Will you insist on bathing me again?" He ducked his head and caught her neck with his mouth.

Her fingers convulsed on his muscle. "No. There's no time for that." She broke away and moved to the bed. Turning her back to him, she pulled the garment over her head, dropped it on the floor, and looked over her shoulder. "Come now," she said.

Paralysis seized him and he could only stare. This was his. This woman with rounded hips and strong, slender arms and golden hair tumbling to her waist. The passionate, undaunted, tenacious girl he had dreamed of for years, standing at the end of his bed, beckoning to him.

Then she climbed onto the mattress on all fours and lowered herself to her stomach.

"Take me like this," she said so quietly he barely heard it. Curling her bent arms beneath her, she tucked her chin under. Preparing herself. *Protecting herself.* The scars shone dark upon her skin and her body was strung like the bow with which she was so proficient.

He struggled upon the surge of feeling that grabbed at his chest and rose to his throat. Moving to the bed, he unfastened his breeches.

"Turn over, Constance."

She looked around at him. "But I—"

"I don't want you like that. Not tonight," he said. "Tonight I want your hands on me. Your legs around my waist. Your lips on mine. Your clever, sensitive nose buried in my neck. Your eyes full of light when you find pleasure. Tonight I want all of you."

She turned and climbed onto him. Her hands were urgent, shoving his breeches down enough so that she could guide herself onto his cock. He pushed her onto her back and sank himself into her. Holding hard to him, she thrust her hips, driving him deeper, and she was all beauty and hot, tight need.

And then abruptly she stilled. With her eyes shut tightly, her fingers dug into his arms.

"Saint," she whispered.

His heart twisted. He wanted all of her, at once and forever.

"You are concerned about the chafing again, aren't you?" he murmured.

Her eyes popped open.

"Well, if you will make a habit of ravishing me before I have entirely undressed," he said, forcing a smile to his lips, "I'm afraid you will have to become accustomed to wool burn."

Laughter spilled from her, rich and free. Her hands smoothed over his shoulders.

"Battle wounds I will happily bear." Her eyes shone in the darkness.

After that, he found he could not speak. Neither of them did. There were too few hours until dawn and far too many words to be said.

The Brave Day

"Get up!"

Constance turned over, pushed hair from her face, and closed her eyes again.

"Just once I would like to wake up to my husband still in my bed." She sighed, smiling.

"There is a man here insisting upon seeing you or your father immediately." Eliza swept away the covers and tossed a shift at her. "And I don't particularly care to hear the details of your wedded intimacies."

The remnants of her wedded intimacies felt deliciously wicked on her skin. But no blood. Never blood.

"There is a love bite on your breast!"

"A what?" She peered down.

"And another on your neck. Cover those this instant." Eliza marched to the dressing chamber. "Your blue silk, with the high collar."

Constance bathed and dressed and went down to her caller. He stood far from the windows, holding his hat before him uncomfortably.

"My lady." He looked beyond her shoulder. "Is His Grace not receiving?"

"My father is in the countryside. How may I assist you?"

"My name is Ferguson. I am a clerk for the Lord Advocate. I have news he wishes to share with the duke before it becomes public."

"Please share it with me, Mr. Ferguson," she said as though the whole world weren't spinning about her now, "and I will see that my father hears it immediately."

His arms dropped to his sides. "Strong evidence has been brought to bear against Mr. Sterling that places him at the location of Annie Favor's disappearance. Additionally, a weapon has been discovered at the loch where the body was found. It was purchased by your husband on the day of the murder. The Lord Advocate asked me to express to His Grace and to you that he wishes it were otherwise, but that tomorrow upon his return to Edinburgh he will be obliged to indict Mr. Sterling for the murder of Miss Favor, with a public trial to be held as soon as a presiding judge can be determined."

"Thank you, Mr. Ferguson. I will convey this information to my father. We are grateful for the Lord Advocate's consideration in informing us first." Allowing the duke's son-in-law time to disappear. "Good day." She saw him out.

Lord Michaels stood at the base of the stairs, his face stark.

"Good God," he said shakily. "He didn't do it, Constance. You must know he didn't."

"Of course he did not. Will he go? Will he flee?"

"No. My God, *no*. He'll stand trial and insist on his innocence until the moment they pull the stool out from under his feet." He went to the door. "I'll find him, talk sense into him, tell him to take that bundle of money Tor left him and buy quick passage to someplace safe till the real villain can be found."

"Bundle of money?"

He jerked around to her. "He didn't tell you?"

She shook her head. "Find him quickly. Beg him to go. He hasn't much time."

He left and she went up to the private parlor. Sitting down at the desk she set a sheet of paper before her and took up the penknife. Her fingertip traced the blade. Then she set it against the goose quill and cut a perfect tip.

SAINT SPENT THE morning searching the old town, trying to trace Ian MacMillan's departure from Edinburgh, with no success. Finally he hired a rider, put a letter in his hand with a guinea, and instructed him to go with haste to Castle Read, promising another gold coin upon his return.

He returned to the house as Aitken was laying two envelopes upon a silver tray.

"Sir, these just arrived, separately," the butler said, proffering the notes, one which bore his name only. "Shall I take this one to her leddyship?"

"I will have them both."

The first was an invitation to the Master's Sanctuary this night. If they returned an acceptance with the boy who came for their response at dusk, they would be met again at the Peppermill.

The other was from Miranda Hughes, penned without care for neatness. It begged his company for a stroll in the park at his earliest convenience.

"Leddy Hughes's page is just without now, sir, waitin' for a reply," Aitken offered.

Saint found the boy perched on the stoop. She had not instructed him to secrecy or even subtlety. The lad leaped up.

"Tell her ladyship that I will await her in the park." The boy scampered off. Saint looked up at the windows above. Then he turned his feet toward the park.

LADY HUGHES CAME to him swiftly along the path. The skies had clouded over and the colors in the flower beds to either side were shadows of brilliance.

"Dear Mr. Sterling," she said, grasping his hands. "You are too good to meet me so swiftly."

He took her hand upon his arm. Gossip about them abounded already. But the desperate grip of her gloved fingers told him she needed reassurance.

"How may I help you, Miranda?"

She squeezed his arm. "You know, he does not call me by my name. He never has. Beneath that charming smile he is viciously cold, even when he—" Her voice dipped. "Do you know . . . I am increasing. I hope it is not his child that I bear. I want to love it."

"You will be free of him soon enough. And you will love your child." As his mother had, despite the man who had fathered her sons.

"You are too kind to me." She dipped her head. "I have not deserved it."

"Everyone deserves kindness. Now, tell me the reason you wished to see me."

"I think I know where Miss Edwards is."

He halted. "You know that I have been searching for her?"

"Lord Michaels called on me weeks ago suggesting that Lorian might know something of her whereabouts. He had seen them speaking at a party. Lorian denied it. But the night of the Sanctuary's last meeting, when I went to the room I have always gone to after the Master released me, the door was locked. It had never been locked before, not in a dozen gatherings. I mentioned it to Lorian and he said that Loch Irvine must have some other use for it now. But he grinned, as though he knew."

"Do you believe that Miss Edwards is being kept in that room?"

"Lorian is not a good man, but I have never thought him a monster. But a meeting of the Sanctuary has been called for tonight and perhaps . . . I know you don't wish to attend again, but you must make an exception tonight. After the Master has chosen, I will take you to the room with the locked door."

He nodded.

"Will Constance mind?"

"She won't be there."

"She must attend. Mr. Reeve will not admit you alone."

"It doesn't matter. I know that the Sanctuary meets at Loch Irvine's house."

"It does! How clever you are."

"I needn't wait for Reeve tonight. I will go as soon as night falls."

"Then I will arrive early as well, and if Mr. Reeve is there I will try to distract him." Her rosebud lips offered him a smile. "I am jealous of your wife. If it weren't for my Patience, I think I would hate Constance for what she has."

BY THE TIME Saint returned home, Constance had already received Sir Lorian's reply.

Dylan sprang from his chair. "Where have you been, damn you? I've been searching all over town for you."

"It seems to me that you are lounging at tea with a beautiful woman, actually. Good afternoon, wife," he said as she placed her hand on his chest and pretended to straighten the lapel of his coat which did not need straightening.

"Lady Easterberry just called. She saw you in the park with Lady Hughes and was eager to inform me. How is Miranda today?"

"Well enough." His eyes were warm. Like the rogue he was before they wed, he had not shaved today, and she wanted to stroke her fingertips across his jaw and feel everything he always made her feel. "And you?" he said.

She released his coat and went to sit before the tea table. Distance was better. Again.

"The Lord Advocate sent word that you are to be indicted tomorrow. Dylan and I think you should leave Scotland. Ideally, Britain. Tea?"

"I see." He sat beside her but did not accept the cup she offered.

Lord Michaels plumped down on the edge of a chair and gripped his hands together.

"You've got to flee, Saint," he said. "Ride. Sail. Whatever

you must. Just hide. Perhaps France. You speak French as well as your mother and Banneret did. Or perhaps cross the sea. Martinique, I daresay. Or some Spanish island if you must. No one will think to look for you there. Then when this has all blown over, we'll let you know."

"I am not leaving," he said.

"Knew you'd say that. So I've come up with a bribe. If you leave now, when you return I'll give you Harwood."

Saint laughed. "I don't want your house, Dylan."

"It's in the entail, of course, so I cannot really *give* it to you. But you can use it indefinitely. You've said you like it any number of times. I realize you've got that manor house in Devon now, but it's on all that coal." He scowled. "Read's castle is more impressive, s'truth, but Harwood's in Kent, more fashionable. Anyway, the castle will be Blackwood's someday—"

"Constance, I have written to your father and asked him to return to town. I told him of the Sanctuary and our pretense with Hughes and the others. I hope you will forgive me for doing this without your approval. I felt that haste was essential."

"I sent for him not an hour ago. It seems we are in accord. On this matter. Won't you go, please?"

"There is a meeting tonight at which I might learn of Miss Edwards's location."

"Good God!" Dylan exclaimed. "Then you mustn't go yet! Not until after the meeting, which I will of course attend with you."

Constance battened down on her panic. "Yes, take your cousin with you." And leave her alone to steal away to meet Sir Lorian without detection. "There is safety in numbers."

Saint regarded her, carefully, it seemed. Then he reached for her hand.

"Dylan, allow us a moment alone, will you?" he said.

The baron peered hard at Saint and then at her. "Right! Of course." He popped up and exited.

"If tonight's meeting does not bear fruit," Saint said, his

fingers warm around hers, "I ask you to return to the castle. Shaw is there, and your arsenal of bows and arrows and swords," he said upon a slight smile. "Or go to your cousin at Alvamoor. Though I would gladly absent myself until the murderer is discovered, I will not leave Edinburgh while threat remains to you here."

"I am not under threat. The victims were—"

"I don't trust Hughes, and he has made his wishes clear. Please, Constance. Will you go?"

"Yes. But only with you. This very moment."

"I cannot. Even if I did, they would come for me there."

"You are correct, of course. You must go to your meeting tonight and find her." She withdrew her hand. "Tomorrow, after the indictment, I will leave Edinburgh."

After a moment's silence he said, "You are lying to me."

She stood up. "I needn't tell you the truth. Why didn't you tell me of your brother's bequest? Why did you keep from me Miranda and Patience's secret? After tomorrow you will be gone. I needn't share anything with you if it does not suit me." Her throat was stripped. She moved to the door.

"Constance, stop."

She turned her head and he was standing where she had left him.

"Don't do this," he said, his voice rough. "I cannot—" He covered his face with his hand and breathed hard. He dropped his arm. "*Don't.* I beg of you. Give me your trust, if only for tonight."

Her fingers clamped about the door frame. "What is your meeting?"

"We have been invited back to the Sanctuary. Lady Hughes believes that Chloe Edwards is in Loch Irvine's house."

"*In* the house?"

"When night falls, Dylan and I will go there."

"You will not wait for midnight. That is wise. But how do you hope to enter without Mr. Reeve's consent? Perhaps you should carry one of my hairpins." She forced a smile, but he did not return it.

"You are not insisting on accompanying us." His hands fisted at his sides. "What have you planned?"

"I cannot tell you. You will not—"

He crossed to her in three swift strides, grasped her shoulders, and caught her mouth beneath his. Then his arms were encompassing her, his fingers sinking up into her hair, his lips claiming hers again and again. She wrapped her arms around him.

His hand curved around her face as he lifted his lips from hers.

"If I could stand here kissing you until this night has ended I would," he said harshly. "Don't *do* this to me, Constance. Please."

"I promised him one night."

His chest heaved, his bright eyes searching hers. "One night?"

"In exchange for your safety."

Now he seemed not to breathe.

"He has promised to give me the knife and signed proof of your innocence," she said. "I wish it could be otherwise. Of course I do. But—"

"You've told me. You have just told me your plan."

"Not my plan. *His*. It is the only way to—" She broke away from him. "Why do you smile? Does it amuse you that I—"

"Smile? I could *sing*." Both of his hands came around her face and he uttered over her lips, "You told me."

"I think you are the one of us who is insane after all," she said, holding his waist. "I don't know why I'm trying to save you."

"Because I'm so charming, no doubt." He kissed her. "Wife." He kissed her again. "We do this together." And again. "Agreed?"

"Yes." Her hands on him shook, but she could do nothing for it. He was kissing her neck now, his hands moving down her back to draw her to him. "I have already told him that I will meet him."

"I don't suppose you mentioned the dagger you will be wearing or the parasol you will be carrying," he said against her collarbone.

"No." She stretched to allow him to trail kisses along her throat.

"Nor that you intend to use them on him."

"Not that either, naturally." She wove her fingers into his hair. "I was terribly relieved when I saw the rain clouds gathering this afternoon. It isn't really done to carry a parasol at night, but rain allows me to—"

"My God, how I want you."

"Because I promised a night with another man or because I intend to maim him?" She laughed, but his eyes had sobered.

Gently he stroked the pad of his thumb over her cheek. "You are not afraid."

"My maestro has taught me well. I am ready for this battle." She thought he must be able to see the terror pressing outward beneath her skin. But he only lifted her hands to his lips and kissed them softly.

"We must bring in your cousin to plan," she said and drew away to summon Lord Michaels.

Chapter 33
Sunk In Hideous Night

Constance was obliged to convince her husband that if he went immediately to slay Sir Lorian Hughes in his drawing room he would not only *not* convince everybody he hadn't done away with Annie Favor, but he would be hung for the murder of a man anyway.

"We'll brochette him later, cousin, after you're clear of this tangle," Lord Michaels said, bouncing on his toes. "That'll teach him to knock about with men like us."

They were all agreed she should not accompany them to the Sanctuary. If Lorian got wind of it, he might cancel their appointment. Instead, upon their return they would shadow her meeting with Lorian and, once he had given her what she sought, they would confront him. And in the event that she needed assistance, they would be close by. It was not an ideal plan, but it had the advantage of simplicity.

At the door, Saint took her hand but said nothing, and she let him go. Through the window she watched them ride into the rain-misted darkness.

An hour passed, and another, during which her heart

leaped at the sound of every hoofbeat on street cobbles. The minutes stretched.

They were gone too long.

She wrote letters to the police investigator and the Lord Advocate, and gave them to Aitken with the instruction that if she did not return home he was to deliver them the following morning. Then she penned a brief message to her father. When the clock in the drawing room struck the hour, she called for her horse. Donning her cloak, she drew the hood over her hair, took up her parasol, and went out into the night.

DYLAN HID IN the stable across the drive from Loch Irvine's house as Saint went through the rain to the rear door. As he approached, Miranda opened it.

"You have *come*!" she exclaimed upon a breath of relief. "I watched for you from the window." She ushered him into the unlit foyer and closed the door. "Mr. Reeve is upstairs. We must be quick—"

"You never expect it to be the good-looking ones," Westin said behind him.

Saint's hand went to his sword. He struck and Westin hollered. Miranda screamed. Reeve appeared from the shadows and Saint's blade again connected with bone.

Then the world shattered.

A LIGHT CARRIAGE with a single lantern drew up before the entrance to the royal gardens. Empty of royalty at present, the palace was closed, but the gardens were bursting with summer flowers. Clouds obscured the moon and stars, and rain fell lightly now as Constance watched Sir Lorian descend from the vehicle. He wore a black cloak to his ankles, and his neck cloth was black as well.

She dismounted, drew Elfhame beneath the shelter of a trellis, and secured her.

"My lady," he said, coming forward, "how prompt you are. I half expected you to renege, or at the very least to bring along an escort." He smiled as though he had said something amusing.

"Give me the knife and the letters. Now. Or I will not enter the carriage."

"You are alone." His eyes were lazy. "If I want you to enter my carriage, you will. But I do have your letters." He drew forth two envelopes. "Do you wish to read them now?"

Tucking the parasol beneath her arm, she opened the letters. The first, penned in the same hand as the invitation to the Master's gatherings, declared that he, Lorian Hughes, had mistakenly made accusation against Frederick Evan Sterling in the matter of the murder of Annie Favor, and that he now withdrew the accusation without prejudice. The second letter, written in a rough, careful hand, stated that the writer, Ian MacMillan, had neither sold nor lent any blade to Mr. Sterling except the sale of a single dagger with ivory handle and leather scabbard, and the date upon which he had done so, and that he believed Mr. Sterling an honest, God-fearing man. The letter said nothing of the parasol sword stick, and she could only hope Mr. MacMillan had not told Sir Lorian of it. Perhaps Lorian had blackmailed him. Perhaps the omission in the letter was like the sword stick itself, a hidden weapon the bladesmith had given Saint in apology for betraying him.

Both letters were signed and dated.

Folding the papers, she turned and walked into the garden. When she returned to the entrance, Sir Lorian was grinning.

"You really don't trust me," he said. "It is positively delicious."

"Search as long as you like for those letters. You will not find them."

He came close. "Have you hidden lovers' notes in these gardens before, my lady? And here I had been thinking you so . . ." He stroked a fingertip across her breast. "*Good.*"

"Give me the knife."

A single sandy brow perked upward. "Not yet. I have

plans for that knife tonight." He moved toward the carriage. "But I hold by my promises. You shall have it by morning."

Her feet were blocks of stone on the path. "You killed her. Annie Favor."

He looked around at her. "Of course not. She changed her mind at the last moment. I was remonstrating with her when she stumbled and accidentally fell on the blade. Now, don't be afraid. If you do exactly as I instruct, you will only feel a little prick." He gestured her into the carriage. "Now come along."

The rain fell about them, and she was alone. Her note to her father had told him where to find the letters. But Saint knew where she was now. The longer she delayed here, the better.

"At the last moment?" she said.

He smiled patiently. "Before the ritual."

"What ritual?"

"The equinox ritual, of course."

"Are you mad?"

"No. I am a man of faith, and your husband and Lord Michaels will not come for you now."

Her fingers slid into place on the parasol.

"My wife is a pretty thing," he continued, "but she is astonishingly transparent. Unlike you." He returned to her and stared quite fixedly into her eyes. "Blue. So blue, like the sea, even in this wretched rain. The moment I saw your eyes again I realized Providence had put you in my path. I had been searching, you know. And then you appeared in Edinburgh with your blue, blue eyes. Perfect." He set a gloved fingertip beneath her chin. "Now you have come here of your own accord, suspecting me of all sorts of wickedness. And yet still you have come. Really, you are more remarkable than Styles gave you credit for. But he is a dilettante, after all."

"A dilettante at what?"

"Enough questions. The hour advances and we mustn't be late." He turned again toward his carriage.

The blade snapped free of the parasol handle and sliced his wrist with silent speed.

He shouted and whirled around, yanking a knife from his belt.

"This knife is supposed to remain purified until the ritual," he said furiously. "But I will use it now if you do not drop that."

She gripped the familiar handle, gauged the distance between them, his stance, the terrain, and smiled. "Make me."

SAINT AWOKE TO pulsating pain in his head and a woman shouting.

"You promised not to harm him!" Patience Westin's voice broke through his skull.

"Why do you care?" Westin's mutter was weak.

"He is an innocent man, Robert."

"S'not what Hughes says. God damn it, the son of a devil nearly cut off my hand. Reeve, bring me a tourniquet."

"My husband is a liar," came close by his side.

Saint opened his eyes to Miranda kneeling in the shadowed darkness, her face blotched with tears.

"Oh, heaven *is* merciful! I was afraid you would never wake. I am sorry. I am so sorry. I had no idea they were there."

He flexed his cramped shoulders and rope cinched about his wrists. He was sitting against a wall, his wrists bound to either side and his ankles bound together with leather straps.

"Don't move, Sterling." Westin came into view. "I've got your sword. Stupid fool, Reeve, letting him inside with it, for God's sake. If I had been prepared for that—"

"You would have wet yourself anyway?" Patience said.

"Be quiet, you."

"If you promise not to fight them," Miranda said, reaching for Saint's wrist, "I can untie—"

Westin's fist swung. She fell aside.

Patience leaped on him. "Don't touch her!"

He pinned her arms to her sides.

"Look what you've done, Sterling. Roused the cat." He glanced at Miranda lying motionless. "Well, I'll pay for that. Lorian won't like a bruise on her face."

Patience's body had gone slack in his hold as she stared at Miranda.

"I am sorry, Mr. Sterling," she said. "It was too good to be true, wasn't it? But I am sorry for involving you in it. You will not *harm* him, will you, Robert?"

"Well, what do you imagine I'd do, you little fool? I'm not Lorian to host an all-night ritual, now, am I? Reeve's got it, anyway, as soon as he bandages that eye. Bad form, Sterling, murdering that girl."

"Where is Hughes?" he said through the morass of clouds and pain in his head.

"At the ritual, of course."

Saint blinked hard. Tried to focus. "Ritual?"

"The solstice ritual. She didn't tell you?"

"It isn't solstice yet."

Westin laughed. "Lorian rushed it up. What with your trial any moment now, I imagine he wanted to ensure your wife'd still be in town. He's had his eye on her for weeks now, though I think he imagined she'd be more enthusiastic about it. Now quiet down, Patience. I need a drink."

"*No.*" She struggled against him. "Let me see to her."

"Damn little feline. Do you want me to knock you over too?"

She twisted her head around and bit him on the chin.

"Damn you!" He pushed her away and grabbed his face. "Take a chunk out of me, will you, cat?"

"I will do much worse if you don't help me with her."

Together they hoisted Miranda's limp form from the ground.

"Reeve'll be in shortly," Westin said. "Best of luck with that trial. And don't worry about the ritual. Lorian won't leave a mark on her except the one."

Patience threw him an anguished glance, and then they were gone.

Swiftly Saint studied the room. He was in a bedchamber, presumably still in Loch Irvine's house, furnished simply and lit with only a single lamp, the glow from the sputtering wick casting uncertain shadows about. The ropes around his wrists were tied to iron loops bolted to the walls. Other objects adorned the space: carriage whips, a cudgel, more ropes, and leather straps with buckles. Apparently the Master's guests were not only interested in trading spouses.

He slid his feet to the left and barreled his boots against the ring at his hand. It held fast. He tried again, then turned to the other ring. It proved equally solid.

With fogged eyes and head aching from the pummelling Westin had given it with something far too hard, he studied the floor, furniture, walls, and ceiling and he tried to focus his mind, to drag it away from where it wished to go, to remain in the moment where his first purpose must be to gain freedom.

The door cracked open and Patience slipped in.

"I have already tried the ropes," she whispered. "Reeve tied them too tightly. I cannot pry them apart with my fingers."

"Unbind my ankles, but leave the appearance that they are still bound." She knelt and did so.

"Are you able to reach the door on the landing below unseen?" he said.

"I think so. Robert went into the Sanctuary chamber for a glass of wine. Miranda is still unconscious."

"Beyond that door is a gallery. Beneath the display case you will find a knife. Swiftly now."

She darted to the door and out. He prayed that no one had locked the gallery since Constance had picked the lock weeks ago. And he prayed that wherever she was now, his wife was showing Lorian Hughes precisely what she thought of him.

"Do you see that boy on the pony over there?" Sir Lorian huffed, his panting breaths making clouds of cold mist in the drizzle. Blood seeped from a wound on his chin and his left arm hung at his side. He was so much easier to fight than Mr. Viking; she was downright buoyant.

"I do not," she said, the sword stick poised before her, the closed parasol in her left hand. *Never remove your attention from your opponent.* "Tell me about him, why don't you?"

"He is prepared, at my command, to perform an errand for me." His eyes glittered in the blackness.

"What errand is that?"

"Your husband is at this moment bound like a beast in Mr. Reeve's care. With a single word I can send the boy riding swiftly to give Mr. Reeve permission to put a knife in Mr. Sterling's heart."

"Prove it."

"Boy!" he shouted.

Beyond Lorian's shoulder, in the shadows by the palace wall, a mounted figure appeared.

"Now, will you wager his life against my word?"

Constance lowered her left hand but kept the point of the sword stick aimed at his face.

"What will you do to me?"

"Wise woman." He smiled. "Now the sword."

With the dagger burning against her ankle, she set the sword stick and parasol on the ground and stepped away from them. Knife still raised, he came to her and took her arm.

"I should like the details," she said and allowed him to lead her toward the carriage, where his voice if he shouted would be muffled from the boy's hearing.

"You will see soon enough. I promise, though, that if you behave, you will have a delightful reunion with your husband tomorrow. If he is still alive. Broken bones can splinter and cause infection, of course. Do you know, this all would have been so much easier if you weren't so tiresomely virtuous."

The laughter of hysteria bubbled up in her.

"There is the spirit," he said approvingly. "Come now, into the carriage."

The moment the door closed she reached for the dagger.

She had known he would expect her to resist, but he was quick to grab her. She did not, however, expect him to block her nose, to force her lips apart, and to fill her mouth with wine. Lorian had always been so obvious; she had not anticipated guile from him.

Her father, if he ever knew, would be disappointed.

But Saint, she thought in her last lucid moment, would understand.

THE DOOR SWUNG open and Reeve entered, a cloth tied around his head, bloodied at the eye. He carried Saint's saber like a man who'd never had a sword in his hand before.

"How do you like your handiwork, Mr. Sterling?" he grunted, pointing at his eye. "I'm none too happy with it."

"You attacked me unsuspecting."

"Aye. But you'll be getting yours."

"Where is the solstice ritual?"

He grinned and his crooked nose canted to the side. "Sorry you're not invited?"

"I have a fortune in a bank in London. Free me, and it is yours."

"Sir Lorian said you'd offer money." He swung the saber from side to side like it was a toy. "He said he'd give me twice your offer." He scratched his whiskers. "How much?"

"Forty thousand pounds. That is more than you will ever see in your lifetime. Trust me, I have been a thief. I know. Though I have never been such a stupid thief. You know they will turn on you. As soon as they need a man to take the blame. Westin. Hughes. The Master."

Reeve's brow grew tight.

"The Master's above it all," he said with a round eye. "And I like the other choice Sir Lorian is giving you anyway."

"What choice?"

He tossed the saber aside with a clatter and hefted the cudgel. "A trade: your freedom for your hand."

Saint drew in air through his nose. "Immediate freedom?"

"Aye."

"How can I trust you?"

Behind Reeve, Patience slipped silently into the room.

Reeve swung the cudgel now against his boot. "I could smash both your hands and leave you here all night, if I liked. But he told me I was to give you the choice, and I promised."

Hughes wanted him beaten, maimed, helpless; a shameful prelude to his hanging by mob.

"All right," he said.

Reeve grinned. "Stretch out your hand now."

He flattened it against the wall, his stomach tightening.

Reeve's lip curled. "Sir Lorian said you'd try that. I'll be having the *other* hand, sir."

"Mr. Reeve." Patience came forward. "My husband wishes me to say a word to Mr. Sterling." She halted by his boots. "You will never reach Arthur's Seat by midnight. Do not accept any bargain Mr. Reeve makes for your freedom now." She whirled around. "Mr. Reeve, this is barbarism." In her hand concealed by the folds of her skirt, his knife glittered. "Whatever Sir Lorian has said to you, the Master would not approve of it."

"How would you know what the Master approves of or not?"

"I have spoken with him about such matters. He does not approve of needless violence. If you doubt it, go speak with my husband. He is in the Sanctuary now. I promise that I will not untie Mr. Sterling while you are gone. My husband will tell you that I tried that already, and my fingers are not strong enough. You tie a formidable knot."

He grumbled. But he went, leaving the door open.

She threw herself upon her knees and set to the knot at his wrist with the knife.

"It is too thick," she whined. "There is not time."

"It's a very sharp knife," he said, keeping his voice calm over the drumming of his pulse. "You are halfway through it already."

Reeve appeared in the doorway.

"Patience, go," Saint said.

She dropped the knife and leaped to the side as Reeve lunged and lifted the cudgel above his hand still bound to the wall. Snapping the final strands of cut rope on the other, Saint grabbed for the knife.

The cudgel came down. Swiftly. Twice.

The world spun into an explosion of pain.

He thrust the knife into Reeve's upraised arm. Reeve hollered and the cudgel flew again.

Reality disappeared into agony. Blackness descended.

He fought against it.

"Stop!" Patience's voice, screaming. "Stop!"

A door slamming. Heavy footsteps.

"Mr. Sterling, you must stand up. *Now.*"

Then she was gone, and he was pushing himself up from the cold floor, gripping the knife, cutting the rope about his wrist, blind with pain, sounds all around him—a woman's sobbing, a man shouting. His crushed hand hit the floor and he doubled over.

A fist cuffed his brow. "Not so confident now, eh?" Reeve's voice was thick.

Saint staggered toward a spot of light, found his footing, and reached for the light. His fingers cinched around the lamp handle. He swung.

Reeve crumpled to the floor. Oil spread in a swift circle from the overturned lamp. Fire burst upward, darted across the puddle, and caught on Reeve's clothing.

In the corridor, Patience hung over Miranda. "She is alive, but she won't move."

"We will carry her."

"Your hand—"

"Remove my neck cloth and bind it. As tightly as you can."

She did it without comment and the pain buckled his knees. Constance would have talked, teased, tried to distract him. He needed to hear her voice again. Her laughter.

Smoke rose inside the bedchamber, fire spreading, consuming linens, flying into fury when it found the draperies.

When the hand was bound, he took Miranda over his shoulder and held her with one arm. Inside the bedchamber, Reeve was struggling to his feet, wailing, flames dangling from his coat.

"Miss Edwards," Miranda mumbled. "That door."

He grabbed for the handle. It was locked. Behind them, Reeve ran from the bedchamber and toward the stairs. Flames licked at the bedchamber's threshold.

"Come," he ordered, turning toward the stairs. "Quickly."

"But—"

"*Come*. I will see to her."

The foyer below was now sunk in darkness. He set Miranda on her feet and Patience wrapped her arms around her.

"Go now."

"But, Mr. Sterling, you cannot—"

He turned back up the stairs and into the corridor that was a funnel of heat and smoke. Clamping shut his mouth he went to the locked door.

Like Constance's hairpin, the knife did its work easily in the lock. He shoved the panel open. The air inside was clean, and he gulped it. A young woman stared at him from a chair across the room, a gag tied in her mouth, her eyes round with terror.

"Saint! God damn it, Saint!" Dylan's shout came beyond the flames.

Her eyes flared wider and filled with tears.

He cut the ropes around her wrists and ankles, and hauled her from the chair. She tore at the gag, but he halted her, drawing it swiftly over her mouth and nose against the smoke. Clamping his arm around her, he pulled her from the room as the fire burst into the corridor. On the stairs, she fell upon Dylan with choked sobs.

Outside, rain pummeled the darkness lit by the stable in flames. Its doors were wide open.

Dylan clasped Miss Edwards to him in the downpour. He lifted his face from her hair to meet Saint's stare.

"Fellow came at me with a torch," he shouted through the rain. "The animals bolted."

Patience knelt above Miranda sprawled on the ground.

"Is she all right?" Saint barely recognized his voice.

"Yes. She is breathing."

"You will be fine now." He searched the rain washed darkness for his horse, any horse, pain and desperation tearing at him. "Lord Michaels will assist you."

A window shattered in the house, flames crawling out to battle the rain. His saber was inside. And the knife—dropped when he grabbed Miss Edwards.

"Your sword!" he shouted at his cousin.

Dylan snatched a pistol out of his pocket, soaking it with rain, ruining the powder.

No horse. No weapon.

He ran. It wasn't two miles to the mountain. He had run farther across battlefields strewn with bullets and canon fire, with a bullet in his thigh. He had never run with only one arm. Lodged tight in his waistcoat, his hand had gone beyond pain into hell. After a half mile he gave up and pulled it free, and nearly lost his footing, every broken bone screaming. He sucked in mouthfuls of air saturated with rain, cinched the linen tighter about his palm and fingers, and fell to his knees as darkness surrounded him.

His hand found a fence post. He grabbed it and dragged himself to his feet. Distantly, a horse whinnied over the rain.

Chase down a loose paddocked horse for precious minutes? Or run?

He ran. Scorched from the fire smoke, his lungs burned.

Hoofbeats sounded behind him, then by his side. He slowed, reached out with his hand, and grasped the scabbard of his other sword strapped to the saddle. His horse halted abruptly. Silently blessing the man who had trained the animal, he jammed his foot into the stirrup and, before he was fully in the saddle, urged it across the field toward Arthur's Seat.

Through the rain he saw the torches, high up on the side of the mountain at the ruins of the old church. He dug his heels into Paid's sides and the animal flew.

The path bent to the west on a gradual rise around the other side of the mountain before it doubled back. Too far. *Too slow.*

In the tower of the church at Duddingston afar off, the massive bell tolled the first stroke of midnight, echoing through the rain over the mountain. Pulling Paid's head around and pointing him dead up the hill, Saint snatched his sword from the scabbard and threw his weight forward. Together they climbed.

Chapter 34

The Sacrifice

S he counted.

One . . . two . . . three . .

Her cheeks were wet where Sir Lorian had pulled back the hood of thick satin from her face. Her lips too. Her wrists were bound, palms pressing into the cold stone of the ancient altar.

Idly, distant from her flesh, she wondered what he had done with her gown and petticoat and stays.

Four . . . five . . .

She did not mind it. But Eliza particularly liked that gown.

Delirious. She was certainly delirious.

Six . . . seven . . .

He had removed it in the carriage. All of her garments except her shift. And dressed her in the robe. But he had not touched her otherwise. Strange man. Men. She would never entirely understand the breed.

Eight . . .

And then the torches. And the pain.

Nine . . . ten . . .

Again.

One . . .

The dampness on her cheek seeped between her lips with the rain that pattered all over, filling her ears with sound. Someone was chanting. Peculiar words.

The rain tasted like salt.

Two . . . three . . . four . . .

She must continue counting. The chanting was growing louder.

The clouds in her thoughts slipped, settled, then slipped again. A breath of cold, rain-soaked air stole into her mouth, tickling her nostrils.

Someone was behind her. Touching her. She could *feel* her lips again. Her tongue. The icy rain. Her frigid skin.

She opened her eyes.

Firelight danced on the rain-washed altar upon which she lay. Figures stood nearby, long white robes and rain obscuring them.

"The dead are reborn," Sir Lorian said behind her and she heard it clearly.

The torchlight responded with murmurs.

"The earth bears new fruit," he intoned as her heartbeats stabbed the altar beneath her breasts. The hooded ghosts replied again with mumbles.

"We offer thanks," he declared. "We offer sacrifice."

The caress of cold metal on her exposed calf drove the air from her. She fought against the panic.

He was talking again, his words blurring inside her ears. Her mouth opened, eyes closed, hands balled, body tensed.

Five . . . six . . . seven . . .

Something was different from before, different from when a man had cut her. Something . . .

Her ankles were *unbound*.

She kicked out hard. Her heels met bone.

She kicked again. *Flesh.*

A man was groaning. Another, shouting. The firelight

wavered and a hooded figure jumped backward. Shod hooves beat the earth and clattered upon stone.

She pulled her knees up, twisted, thrust her knee toward her hand, and heard a pop in her shoulder and the scream wrenching from her throat. Her fingers were slippery on the little ivory handle, the rain making her fumble. She grasped it.

A torch dropped to the ground.

Metal crashed to the stone beside her and her hand flew free of the rope. She pulled back her arm, swiveled around, away from the clanging on the other side of the altar. Firelight shifted wildly across the rain. Sir Lorian was doubled over at the base of the altar, his face a pale oval against black.

She leaped at him. He thrust out his arm and knocked her away. Driving her strength beneath the strike, she sliced again. The blade met cloth, jerking her off balance. Her bare feet slipped on the stone, throwing her over the altar's edge, and she fell forward onto him. She struggled, untangling her sodden robe, pushing herself away. She broke free and staggered back. Her hair was a curtain before the rain.

On the ground before her, Sir Lorian was doubled over, writhing. As firelight trailed away with the sound of hoofbeats, he was lost to the dark.

Strong arms banded about her. She jerked her wrist and plunged the dagger backward.

"*Constance*," Saint growled, pressing his cheek to hers. "It is I. It is over. It is over."

She heard the rain's patter all around her and a church bell ringing far away.

Chapter 35

A Sword, Returned

"I've said for weeks now that if you give a woman a weapon she will use it on you. But you refused to listen, of course." Viking whipped a fresh bandage from a pile of pristine linens, draped it across the wound dressed with salve, and began to tie it in place.

Saint shoved his hands aside. With one-handed awkwardness, he tied the cloth around his thigh, pulled his drawers and trousers up, and fastened them. The simple task required far too many minutes. Viking watched, face pinched with superiority.

"You take great relish in my injuries," Saint mumbled. "You know, I did well without a valet for thirty-one years. I am certain I can do perfectly well without one for the next thirty-one."

"Upstart colonial."

"Did you just snort like a pig?"

"I do not snort, sir. That was a 'humph.' I learned it from Mrs. Josephs." Nose in the air, he gathered his medicines and left the room.

Saint eased himself into a chair and closed his eyes, contemplating his pain and the certainty that if he began drinking whiskey now and continued through the morrow he still would not get drunk enough to pretend it wasn't agony to move. But he enjoyed only a moment of this contemplation before a firm knock sounded upon the door and the Duke of Read entered.

"Forgive me if I don't stand."

"May I?" Read gestured to the opposite chair.

He sat forward, ignoring infinite twinges of pain. "Has she—?"

"She is still sleeping. Dr. Shaw believes that her body is allowing itself time to heal from the great quantity of the drug that she ingested. He remains confident she will wake within the day. He requested I remind you that the same philosophy of healing applies to you."

"Isn't it unusual for a duke to act as a messenger boy?"

"No more unusual than it is for a fencing master to wed a noble heiress. Mr. Sterling, when I invited you to Castle Read, I knew that you and my daughter had already been acquainted."

Saint sat back.

"Jack Doreé told me six years ago," Read said. "He wrote to me of what Constance had told him, that you behaved with propriety with her at Fellsbourne despite her impropriety, and that you performed honorably in the duel you fought for her honor. He wrote to me because he did not know what to do. He cared for her, and he knew her character well enough to understand that you were not a momentary flirtation. He wanted her to be happy. I advised him to marry her. I had plans for her that he did not know about. As a marchioness she would have had the influence and authority that I required."

"Plans?"

"To change the law of this kingdom dramatically. To usher in a new era for Britain. After Jack's death I hoped she would wed his brother. When it became clear that she would not, that she would continue to remain unwed—but in seclusion, far from London—I brought you here."

"Not to teach her to fence, I gather."

"To . . . stir the embers, as it were. I hoped that she would finally be inspired to wed. Not to wed you, of course. She forced my hand in that matter."

Saint bit down on his molars.

The duke frowned. "I knew of your exemplary service during the war. But your comportment in my household, your determination to assist Lord Michaels and my daughter, and your letter yesterday, the instruction you gave regarding your fortune, that it was to be entirely my daughter's upon your death . . . You have been a surprise to me."

"Have I?"

"Even at this moment, when I believe you would like to throttle me, you maintain your sangfroid."

"I assure you, my sangfroid at this moment is entirely superficial." He pushed up from the chair. Drawing the antique rapier from its case, he put it in the duke's hands. "This is not mine."

"I gave it to you."

"It was not yours to give."

The duke's nostrils flared. He understood.

Saint nearly smiled.

Read stood. "Thank you for saving my daughter, Mr. Sterling." Taking up the rapier case, he left the room.

Sometime later Dylan woke him.

"They are gone! Every blasted one of them."

Saint began to lift his hand, flinched, and instead lifted the other to rub his eyes.

"Give me that bottle. Who are all gone?"

Dylan uncorked the whiskey. "The members of the Sanctuary. They've all left Edinburgh."

Only six people had been at the ruins atop Arthur's Seat with Hughes, all hooded. He had not seen their faces. He'd seen nothing but Constance stretched out on that rock.

The whiskey scalded his throat.

"It seems Hughes was the only truly bad apple in the bushel," Dylan said.

"Westin hit me in the head with a board." He swallowed another burning mouthful. "I would say that counts as bad, if not entirely rotten."

"I say good riddance to them all."

"You're in fine spirits. Miss Edwards must be well."

Dylan's brow puckered. "She's with her family. She says Reeve treated her unexceptionably. Gave her plenty of books and fine food, and assured her she wouldn't be harmed. He only tied her up a few times, said it was for her *protection*, and apologized when he returned to untie her. I think the fear was the worst for her." His mouth crept into a smile. "But she's said she loves me, and Edwards has promised that we can marry."

"I am happy for you, Dylan."

"Now, all we've got to do is await Constance's awaking, and everything will be just as it ought."

Saint's smile lasted only until Dylan departed. Alone again, he unearthed the packet of papers his brother's solicitor had given him in London, and finally read them. They revealed nothing new. At the bottom of the packet he found a note addressed to him in Tor's bold scrawl.

Saint,

> *You will have discovered already that a portion of my fortune has been tied to the Duke of Loch Irvine's through several ventures. If you do not need the funds in the Edinburgh account, leave them be. As always, brother, I trust you.*

—T. S.

Daylight had disappeared from the room. Saint forced himself from the chair, lit a lamp, and for the first time since he had carried her into the house and laid her on her bed he went into his wife's bedchamber.

Dozing in a chair in the corner of the room, Mrs. Josephs awoke with a jerk.

"She has not stirred. Do go rest, Mr. Sterling. I will alert you to any change."

He stared at his wife's golden hair, neatly plaited, at her strong, capable hands now motionless on the counterpane, at the gentle rise and fall of her chest. And then, finally, at the bandage stretched across her beautiful face.

Dragging his gaze away, he returned to his bedchamber and the bottle of whiskey.

AT HALF PAST eleven o'clock the following day, Viking appeared in the ballroom doorway and said, "She is awake, sir."

Saint ran up the stairs three at a time and nearly collided with Mrs. Josephs.

"The footmen have carried her to the parlor," she said.

"Just now?"

"Twenty minutes ago." She glanced at his bandaged hand. "When she awoke."

"Why—" He halted his words. Twenty minutes ago. Before they told him she had awoken. So he would not try to assist her.

They were six years too late.

The sun cast soft rays upon the woman lying on the divan with her face toward the window, blankets draped over her like mists upon a specter. His footsteps sounded on the floor but she did not turn to him. Her breaths were even and slow, her body relaxed. Asleep again, it seemed.

He lowered himself to the chair beside her, folded his broken hand into the other, and bent his head.

"Constance," he said. "I have not been honest with you. I once told you that an impervious heart makes a man invincible. It isn't true. The deeper you sink into my heart, the stronger I become. Filled with you, I could fight the armies of hell and win."

It was an hour, perhaps, before she stirred. Her hand clutched the blanket.

"I am here," he said.

Her body remained motionless, too still, as though she held her breath. He waited, but she said nothing. Momentarily she relaxed into sleep again.

When dusk fell, he went to his bedchamber to change the dressings on his wounds, and after some minutes heard movement beyond the closet. In her bedchamber he found Dr. Shaw laying her upon her bed. Her eyes were closed and her face turned to the side.

He followed the doctor into the corridor. "What did she say to you?"

"She has said nothing to anyone."

Dylan appeared on the steps.

"How is Miss Edwards today?" the doctor said.

"She's well, given all." His chest expanded. "The banns are to be read this Sunday."

Saint clapped him on the shoulder. The doctor smiled.

"A drink then, to toast my happiness?" Dylan said. "P'raps, cousin, you and I can take the opportunity to convince Shaw here to tie the knot someday too. Don't know what you're missing, doctor, what?"

Dr. Shaw chuckled. "You do not yet know what I am missing either. But I will toast to you. If you don't mind it, Sterling."

"Of course not." He wanted to return to her side and remain there until she spoke. Until she looked into his eyes and smiled again.

"But there is one matter, Saint," Dylan said more soberly now. "Chloe says she's got something to tell you and Constance. After the police left today she said she did not tell them everything. From what I'd told her about Hughes and your arrest, she didn't like the idea of sharing it all with them. But she's eager to tell you and Constance, if Constance is able."

The following morning, she was. Seated in the parlor, wrapped in a voluminous shawl, the bandage stark across her face, she looked at no one but Chloe Edwards as she told them the news she had withheld from the police investigator.

"The day before you came, Mr. Sterling," she said, her eyes wide, "a lady came into the room."

"A lady?" Dylan said. "Lady Hughes? Mrs. Westin? One of the Sanctuary group?"

"No. I never saw any of those people. I didn't even know they were there until you told me. This lady would not tell me her name but she said that she was a friend, and that she would make certain I was freed soon."

"Why didn't she free you?" Dylan exclaimed.

"Oh, she wished to! But I think she hadn't expected to find me there. She said if she were caught in the house all would be ruined."

"What was her appearance?" Saint asked.

"She had gorgeous fiery hair tied back, though very hastily, it seemed, and bright green eyes, like springtime. She was young and quite pretty really."

Not any member of the Sanctuary he had seen.

"And she wore an old cloak," Chloe continued, "with that symbol drawn on it that everybody was talking about all winter, the symbol on Haiknayes Castle. I must have exclaimed when I saw it because she said I was not to worry, that they are both alive and well."

"Who?" Constance's voice was a mere rasp.

"Cassandra Finn and Maggie Poultney."

"Good God!" Dylan exclaimed. "Alive and well, after all!"

"Did she say anything more?" Saint said.

"We heard a noise, and she left straight off and did not return. It was that very night that you found me." She smiled sweetly at him.

Dylan pulled her hand possessively into his.

Holding back his grin, Saint shifted his gaze to his wife. Her eyes were upon him, her beautiful lips curved in a small smile.

THE FOLLOWING MORNING in a light drizzle Miranda Hughes descended from a carriage before the house. Draped in a gown of brilliant pink, a pale smudge of a bruise on her brow powdered over, she did not move to greet him.

"Will you *ever* forgive me for being such a widgeon?"

"Because of you Miss Edwards is reunited with her family." He walked to her. "Are you well?"

"I am wonderful! I loathed him, you know. And now he is rotting in prison, and of course"—her voice dipped—"*incapacitated* in the most fitting manner. How clever of darling Constance to know precisely where a man least wishes to be struck with a dagger." She grasped his good hand. "I did *not* know about those horrid rituals. He never told me. Do you believe me?"

"I do. How is Mrs. Westin?"

"She is at our darling little house. Someday we will repay you, I promise it. Westin won't," she said with a twist of her lips. "He told Patience that he is going to Paris where no one knows his unnatural wife. He intends to get himself a scandalous French mistress to impress everyone. Poor man. I think he is afraid of her. Of my sweet Patience! He has positively no spine." She went onto her toes and kissed him on the cheek. "Thank you," she whispered. "Do you know, Patience wants to name my baby Frederick. I told her that I prefer Evan. Perhaps we will use both. You do have a *frightful* lot of names, darling." She kissed her fingertips and blew across them. "Give Constance my love."

Several hours later, Saint entered his wife's bedchamber to find Eliza Josephs alone. She awoke with her usual birdlike blink.

"Is she in the parlor?" he asked.

"I thought she was with you."

"With me?" His throat tightened. "No."

Constance was not in the family's parlor. Nor was she in the drawing room or formal parlor, or the ballroom or anywhere else. He stood in the foyer as everyone in the house ran this way and that and his heart beat at a hard gallop.

Fingal appeared, dragging his cap from his head.

"Sir, I've juist noticed my leddy's horse be out o' the stable. An' I be wonderin'—"

Saint sprinted to the mews. Elfhame was gone. Paid stood in the stall in which he had deposited him after nearly riding him to death up a mountain, ears cocked in curiosity.

"Fingal!" he shouted, his voice rocky. "Come saddle this horse for me."

Only two places would draw her now. Through the drizzle that became a steady rain as he rode, he went to the nearest.

In the rain she stood amidst the ashes of the Duke of Loch Irvine's house. Her crimson cloak flared out behind her, a brilliant rose blooming from the soot, her milk-white horse standing at the edge of the foundations, the rose's guardian.

He dismounted and walked through the sodden ruins to her. Her eyes were clear, the bandage strapped across her cheek stark white against her skin.

"Constance . . ." The word found no companions upon his tongue.

"You are walking with a limp. I am so sorry that I hurt you."

"I've suffered worse. Much."

"Patience wrote to me of what happened. What you did. Will you be able to hold a sword again?"

He flexed his whole right hand. "At any time my lady requires it."

She lifted her gaze to his. "Saint."

"I don't know," he said. "Perhaps."

"He believed you left-handed, didn't he? Three hundred and fifty-one days wasted," she said, her eyes becoming pools now. "But better that than a lifetime, of course."

"Constance, you mustn't—"

"On that stone I counted to ten. I imagined the positioning of my guard, the angle of my feet, and each movement, each parry and attack. I counted them from one to ten, and when I finished I counted again. I heard your voice telling me to count and I thought, 'Ten is not very high. I can make it to ten.' And when I reached ten each time I began again. Then you appeared." Finally the tears spilled onto her cheeks. "Thank you for rescuing me."

His eyes were hot, but he could not look away from her. "You did not need me to rescue you. You did it yourself."

"I wanted him to die."

"You acted in self-defense."

"Walker Styles. For weeks I wished he were dead. Months."

For many moments there was only the soft thrum of rain on the ruins.

"Of course you did," he was finally able to say.

"I always wanted to be enough," she said. "To be beautiful—*inside*. I wanted someone to look into my heart and to see me, not what he thinks I am, but me, the imperfect girl that is nevertheless worthy of affection." Her shoulders rose as she drew in a deep breath. "I don't forgive him. Not yet. But I don't hate him any longer," she said as though it surprised her.

Pride pressed at his ribs. "You are a warrior, my beauty. Warriors mend."

"My kind, handsome Beast," she said, and reached for his hand.

Chapter 36

A Conversation, with Swords Present

They returned home in silence, she with a pensiveness he did not seek to disturb, and he without words anyway—again.

By the doctor's orders she retired immediately and took dinner with Mrs. Josephs in her bedchamber. In the dining room, the duke reported that Loch Irvine's absence from Scotland during the previous month was confirmed. Since he had departed Edinburgh after visiting the museum, he had been seen in London at Westminster, then in Portsmouth. He had not been in Edinburgh on the date that Constance and Saint attended the Sanctuary or on the evening of Sir Lorian's premature solstice ritual. He was not the Master.

Nevertheless, throughout Edinburgh rumor of the Devil's Duke did not quiet. It was generally believed that Sir Lorian had intended Chloe Edwards for yet another ritual. The prisoner would say nothing, and in the papers and at tea tables theories abounded concerning his use of the symbols on the Haiknayes star.

Reeve could not be found. It was assumed he had fled Edinburgh, along with the other members of the Sanctuary.

"They will be watched," the duke said.

But Saint was finished with it. According to Chloe's mysterious visitor, the missing girls were safe. Constance's mission was accomplished.

Excusing himself from the table, he went to her room.

Mrs. Josephs shooed him away. "That ride exhausted her!"

But he knew his wife. She would not be down for long.

She proved it the following morning when she appeared in the ballroom, where he was wasting time with a sword until she woke. She wore a gown of vibrant hue, which roused her skin to a warm glow, and no bandage on her face. She came toward him but halted at the sword rack.

"Good morning," she said, fidgeting with the hilt of her sword.

"Good morning." Nerves darted around his stomach.

She drew her lower lip between her teeth. He tapped the tip of his sword against the floor. An awkward, uncertain silence crept through the motes of sunlight between them.

She gripped the handle of the épée and brandished the weapon.

"What do you think?" she said, glancing up at him.

"Of that sword? I told you months ago, it—"

"Of my scar." She turned her face so that he could see the angry scarlet slashes on her cheek: three waving lines, crisscrossed with surgeon's thread. "It is still a wound, of course. But soon enough it will be a scar. Does it make me look mysterious?"

"Yes." His throat was a clogged shambles. "Very mysterious."

"Good." She sliced a half circle in the air with the tip of her blade. "Because I like mysterious. I told you that once."

"You did. You were trying to entice me with a display of your martial skill."

"I never try to entice you. You have always found me irresistible."

He lifted a brow. "This is true."

The épée stilled. "I was not ready."

"Ready?"

"Before yesterday. For you to see it."

"You needn't have worried. I've never thought you perfect."

For a moment she only stared at him, her eyes brilliant.

"Why didn't you tell me about your brother's fortune? Rather, your fortune."

"I wanted you to accept me for who I am. For who I have always been. Not because of a pile of gold that someone gave to me. It doesn't matter to me, and I did not want it to matter to you."

With one fine fingertip she traced the golden wings on the épée's guard. "You purchased a house for Patience and Miranda."

"I did."

"Somewhere quiet and safe, where they will not be thought anything but two slightly eccentric ladies of leisure, I hope?"

"In a village on the coast. Westin is now en route to France, apparently, fleeing domestic lack of tranquility."

"Do you wish to go to France too? To found a *salle* in Paris? Dylan told me that was your dream." Her voice was unnatural. Uneasy. "Or will you prefer the West Indies now—now that you are a man of wealth and can do anything you like?"

For many weeks he had dreaded this moment. Now that it had arrived, he found he could not breathe properly.

"Temporarily, perhaps, to see to the property there." He glanced down at the sword in his hand that had sliced through ropes binding her to stone.

He set it aside.

"Constance, I cannot do this."

A wave of panic went through her. For four days she had

lain in bed hoping, praying against this. She had thought it could not happen like this—not now, not *ever*. Yet his shoulders were so rigid, the muscles in his jaw tight. And his beautiful eyes were resolute.

She made herself speak. "You cannot do what?"

"I cannot do as you wish now."

"Oh?" she said with outward poise as inside she crumbled.

"I have done my best to aid you, to serve you these past months as you have needed, and as I vowed. To help you in your mission. But no matter how well I play the gentleman, I am not of this world that you inhabit. I never will be. I cannot let you go. I won't."

"You . . . *won't*?"

"Not this time. Never again."

Air shot from her compressed lungs. "But—"

"I don't care what the laissez-faire standards of apathy and faithlessness are for aristocratic marriages. They are not mine. You are. You are mine. And I'm not letting you go."

"Saint, I—"

"Constance, I love you. I have always loved you. Only you. And you love me. I know you do, even if you're too proud and afraid to admit it. There is nothing on this earth that—"

Her sword clattered to the floor as she threw herself on him. His arms came around her, his hand sweeping up beneath her hair to hold her, and she pressed her cheek to his chest and banded her arms about him. Laughter and tears shook her at once. He kissed the top of her head, settled her more snugly into his embrace, and his voice came muffled against her hair.

"No annulment, then. This is"—he drew a staggered breath—"good news."

She laughed again and heard his heart beating hard and steady beneath her ear, felt it, and she hugged him tighter. Gently he stroked her hair back from her wounded cheek and kissed her brow.

"My lady," he murmured. "You are inside me. You are everything."

She turned her face up. He lowered his lips to hers. Honest and tender, his kiss repeated his words in a caress.

"Tell me you love me," he whispered.

"I love you." She surrounded his face with her hands and met his lips. "Of course I love you."

She withdrew from his next kiss breathless to say again, "I love you," to which he responded with such approval that she was, for quite some time, lost to everything but the perfection of his mouth and the strength of his arms holding her to him.

Finally, breaking away, she flattened her palms against his chest.

"How could you believe that I wished us to *part*?" she demanded.

"You said you did not want to be married," he said perfectly rationally. "You begged me to leave you. Several times."

"I was making a noble sacrifice."

"You did a very poor job of it. I think when we are finished with daggers it might be useful for you to have instruction on effective noble sacrifices, the sort where you don't tear out your lover's heart in the process."

She laughed but her hands clenched in his shirt. "I was *afraid*."

His eyes sobered. "I know."

She ran her fingertips along the scar on his face. "You taught me how to be brave."

"I merely taught you how to wield a sword. The rest was you."

Her palm covered his heart. "I don't mean that sort of brave."

A half smile shaped his lips. "There is only one sort."

"Did Monsieur Banneret teach you that?"

"You taught me that. Six years ago."

"How I love you," she said in wonder. "I did not know that I could be so happy."

He set his lips upon her brow and drew a deep breath.

"Saint, I must tell you my last secret."

"Last?"

"You know all the others."

"I doubt that." His smile was wry. "But do continue."

"Six years ago I joined a secret government agency so that I could gain access to information that would allow me to know where you were. Leam was involved, and he invited me to join it before I even moved to London. He thought I was too unhappy in my mourning. I eagerly accepted. I wanted to help people, of course. But I was also desperate to learn where you were. So I did. I knew when you moved to Plymouth, and when you traveled to the West Indies, and the day you returned to England. I was not allowed to be with you, but I could not forget you. I did not want to forget you."

He stared at her, his eyes very bright.

"That is . . . quite a secret indeed."

She pressed her fingertips into his chest. "And?"

"I admit, I didn't see it coming. You're telling me that you are a spy?"

"Not a spy." She smoothed the shirt linen beneath her hand. "I collected information about missing people so that my friends could help them. A bit like what we have done here, except of course the parts about getting married and noble sacrifices." She smiled. "I saved those for you."

He laughed. "You are mad, after all."

"Mad for you. When you came to the castle, I thought I was dreaming. I knew it must be a dream because in all those years I had only wanted you. Then, despite all— despite my father and your anger—you smiled at me, and I knew. I knew I could not lose you again. So there it is, the unvarnished truth. Will you prepare the attic for me now?"

"Yes." His voice was rough. "And lock myself inside with you."

She went onto her toes as he pulled her mouth beneath his. They were kisses of acknowledged love, spoken love, and they were different—full of trust and hunger and un- restrained joy. She wrapped her arms around his shoulders and he pulled her against him and she felt his body's tension, his passion so powerfully checked.

"I will wait for you to be ready again," he said. "As long as you need. Weeks, months, years, if need be. I will—"

"*Years?*"

"Forever. My God, Constance, I love you."

"But I don't want to wait. I want to make love with you now."

"Now?"

"I am your wife." She trailed her fingertips down his chest. "And you are my husband, to do with what I want. And I want you now."

He scooped her up in his arms.

"Your hand!"

"Your wish, my lady, is ever my command." He carried her from the ballroom, up the stairs, into his bedchamber. Upon his bed he took her in his arms and held her. Then she pushed his shoulders back against the mattress and hooked her knee over his hip.

"Now," she said, rising over him with a glorious smile. "You will be mine."

With his hand in her hair he drew her down and kissed her.

"Now," he said huskily, "I am yours."

Epilogue

The Request

Dear Sir,

As you are already aware, Sparrow has formally resigned from the Club. In the absence of current projects and in light of my father's declining health, I offer you now my resignation as well. It has been an honor and privilege to serve the Kingdom.

Sincerely,
Peregrine

Lady Justice
Brittle & Sons, Printers

Dear Lady Justice,

In sorrow I write to you a final time. The Falcon Club is no more. I beg of you, do not weep for this loss too bitterly. You have other poor souls to badger and other unworthy causes to pursue for the entertainment of your readers. Know, however, that my days will be duller, my nights meaningless, without your correspondence to sustain me. Only, dear lady, do not forget me. For I will most certainly not forget you.

With eternal admiration,
Peregrine
No longer Secretary, The Falcon Club

Peregrine
The Falcon Club
14½ Dover Street

Dear Sir,

I write to you now reluctantly but from terrible necessity. Do not lay down your mission yet. At present, I can say no more to explain myself, except these most difficult words: I need your help.

—Lady Justice

A Note on Disguises, Rogues & Swords

*H*ere is something I find truly sexy: a man who is good, kind, and emotionally strong, and who wants above all else a woman's safety and happiness. Put that man in tight breeches on a horse, and give him a sword, and he's just about ideal.

From the time I first started thinking about Constance's book years ago, I realized she needed that sort of hero. Then as I was writing *I Loved a Rogue*, I discovered how Saint helped the hero of that book, Taliesin, when they were young men. (This happened in the way that characters often tell a writer what to write about them and, if she is wise, the writer obeys.) At that moment, Constance and Saint's love story became clear to me. I knew that he would save her not by slaying the bad guys himself, or even by teaching her how to slay them, but by showing her what honest, generous, true love looks like. If you would like to read the scene where I came to understand Saint, you can find that bonus scene from *I Loved a Rogue* on my website www.KatharineAshe.com. In it, Saint is a very young man, and full of energy, and it marks the moment during his hiatus from war when he picks up a sword again.

Like many of my books, Constance's is a secret identity story of sorts. Beneath her beauty, wealth, and position is a girl who just wants to be loved. Appearances often deceive, don't they? You never really know what's behind the face that a person shows the world. In the next book of the Devil's Duke series, both the hero and heroine are in disguise, which makes for some pretty crazy (and very sexy) shenanigans. Look for *The Earl*, starring Peregrine and his nemesis Lady Justice, coming soon.

Regarding the word "rogue": In the early nineteenth century it carried the meaning of "vagrant" with the strong implication of "idle and troublemaking scoundrel." Social order was hugely important to Britons of this era. The empire was expanding rapidly, and the enormous mercantile and industrial wealth amassed by commoners was upending the traditional power hierarchy that ensured a hereditary aristocracy stayed in charge of everybody else. It was a tumultuous, uncertain time for the landed elite. Additionally, in the post-Napoleonic war years, veterans (many who were seriously damaged from warfare) wandered the countryside searching for work as laborers. These homeless men, along with Gypsies, were called "rogues," and lawmakers, who saw them as forces of chaos in a rapidly changing society that they were desperately trying to control, were not fond of them.

Hanging in my mother's kitchen throughout my childhood was a needlepointed sampler that read, *Home is where the heart is*. I have used the word *rogue* in the titles of my books that feature heroes who are wanderers of one sort or another—pirate, spy, Gypsy, and swordsman—until the rogue finds his home with the woman he loves.

Concerning swords, swordsmanship, and fencing: while most gentlemen of this era learned swordsmanship in their youth, it was relegated to the battlefield and sport. By the beginning of the nineteenth century, gentlemen no longer wore swords as part of their regular dress, and dueling was not only illegal in England; many considered it immoral. If men were caught dueling, penalties included hefty fines, imprisonment, and execution if a duelist killed his opponent. But the origins of the duel went back before even the Middle Ages, and gentlemen had a hard time relinquishing this method of settling disputes of honor. Because death by dueling could not easily be hidden from the authorities, however, most duels between gentlemen at this time were fought to "first blood" only. Nevertheless, men of high rank or position continued to murder their opponents in duels, perhaps because many suffered no punishment for it, especially when the murdered man was of lesser social status than the winner. Tried by their peers in the House of Lords, they were forgiven the murderous deed as the unfortunate by-product of a necessary act of honor.

Laws that significantly hobbled the practice of dueling came into effect only in the middle of the century, but by then so many men of the mercantile class practiced swordplay too that aristocratic gentlemen actually complained of the democratization of dueling. In the meantime, improvements in firearms had made swords less popular on the battlefield. Fencing enjoyed an upsurge of popularity in the late nineteenth century in England, as nostalgic experts encouraged gentlemen to keep swordsmanship in their arsenals of power against socially inferior men. But the great era of the sword had by then come to an end.

A fun fact: in the centuries of public swordsmanship, prize-fighting fencers as well as duelists often fought barechested. This was to prove they wore no protective covering over their vital organs that would allow them to fight more aggressively since they did not fear mortal injury. Essentially, fighting bare-chested proved a man's bravery and honesty in one-on-one combat. It is in this tradition that Saint spars bare-chested.

I modeled Saint's teacher, Georges Banneret, on fencing masters of the era, including the Chevalier Joseph de Saint-Georges, a "creole" from the French island of Guadeloupe who became famous in both England and France for his extraordinary skill with a sword, not to mention his charm and cultivated sophistication. His story is marvelous, and I recommend it to anyone intrigued with this exciting era of revolution (particularly his biography by Alain Guédé).

Saint's words about "calmness, vigor, and judgment" in Chapter 8, and the title of that chapter, come from a short seventeenth-century publication, *The Swordsman's Vademecum*, by Sir William Hope. A concise list of eight rules for fencers, it begins with, "Rule I. Whatever you do, let it always (if possible) be done Calmly, and without Passion, and Precipitation, but still with all Vigour, and Briskness imaginable, your Judgement not failing to Direct, Order and Govern you as to both." All eight rules in this treatise include the words "with Calmness, Vigour, and Judgement." I think this is great advice for life in general, and I couldn't resist including them in Saint's lessons for Constance.

I can never resist borrowing from William Shakespeare when it suits. Fans of the Bard will recognize that the titles of Chapters 32 and 33—"The brave day sunk in hideous night"—come from his twelfth sonnet.

A word on Scotland and castles: *innumerable*. They cover the magnificent landscape. While the Duke of Loch Irvine's principal seat is many miles northwest of Edinburgh, Haiknayes Castle is just a stone's throw from Castle Read, which in my experience of traveling through Scotland is entirely possible. I loosely modeled Castle Read on Castle Fraser, including the grounds. Other details of the Duke of Read's castle are drawn from Abbotsford, the house built with love and at great expense by the popular novelist Sir Walter Scott. Scott was an enthusiast of antique weapons, and the weaponry and its display in Castle Read were almost entirely inspired by the collection at Abbotsford. I am indebted to the volunteer guides of both of these estates for generously sharing their vast knowledge with this humble novelist doing her best to fashion fiction from fact.

The Peppermill, the loch, the church ruins on Arthur's Seat, and many other Edinburgh landmarks in this novel can be found on maps of the era. Some are still there today. One of these is the Sheep Heid Inn in Duddingston, where I spent a delightful afternoon sipping ale, chatting with friendly folks, and plotting Annie Favor's sad fate.

With each book I write, my world of early-nineteenth-century Britain expands. Constance appears in *When a Scot Loves a Lady*, *How to Be a Proper Lady*, *How a Lady Weds a Rogue*, and *In the Arms of a Marquess*; Saint appears in *I Loved a Rogue*; young Dylan makes an appearance in *Swept Away by a Kiss*; and Constance's Falcon Club friends can be found in the other books of that series as well. For a timeline of characters and events in the Falcon Club, the Devil's Duke and all my series, I hope you will visit the Timeline page of my website at www.KatharineAshe.com.

Thank-yous

$\mathcal{M}$y books owe an enormous lot to others. To Marcia Abercrombie, Sonja Foust, and Lee Galbreath, who plucked this story out of darkness and drew it into the light, and to whom I dedicate it, I offer a world of thanks and hugs and munchies and cookies. Thanks to my beloved team of readers—Georgie C. Brophy, Nita Eyster, Donna Finlay, Meg Huliston, Helen Lively, and Celia Wolff—whose generosity and graciousness exceed every expectation of friendship and loyalty and who most certainly made this a better book. Thanks for crucial help also to Diana Bennett for her scene blocking idea; Georgann Brophy, Mary Brophy Marcus, and The Lady Authors—Caroline Linden, Miranda Neville, and Maya Rodale—for love, assistance, and support; Sandie Blaise for emergency counsel; Carol Strickland and the HCRW BiaW writers for camaraderie; Cari Gunsallus, assistant extraordinaire; and Chuck Wendig for lemurs on fire (though not *real* lemurs . . . of course).

I adore both swords and Scotland, so this was pretty much the most fun I've ever had researching a novel. I found the epigraph of this novel in Ben Miller's *Self-Defense for Gentlemen and Ladies* (2015), an excellent collection of Colonel Monstery's newspaper articles from the 1870s on the subject; my thanks to the Reference librarians at the Duke University Library for their assistance in tracking down Monstery's original articles. To Alison Lodge at Castle Fraser for the information she generously shared during my visit there, to the wonderful volunteers at Abbotsford, and to Noah Redstone Brophy for medical consultation, I am indebted. Without consulting Melinda Leigh for her expertise in martial arts I would be lost. And to Jeff Kallio and Jennifer Oldham of Mid-South Fencers Club, Professor Leslie Marx of Duke University Fencing, and Walter G. Green of Salle Green, my gratitude is beyond words.

To my wonderful editor, Lucia Macro, whose work on this book was not only gracious and compassionate, but perfect, I am ever grateful. Indeed, I am enormously grateful to everybody at Avon Books who brings my books to life, including Gail Dubov and Thomas Egner for this beautiful cover; Ellen Leach for copyediting brilliance; Nicole Fischer for making everything so easy for me and for her endless patience; and Pamela Jaffee, Jessie Edwards, and Shawn Nicholls for all of their help and support. To my agents, Kimberly Whalen and MacKenzie Fraser-Bub, and to Meredith Miller and Sylvie Rosokoff, who bring my books to foreign language readers, I send up plentiful thanks.

All accidental mistakes or intentional deviations from historical or technical accuracy in this novel are not to be laid at the capable feet of any of the above, but should be attributed to the faeries who live in the woods behind my house and are growing weary of being referred to obliquely in my books without ever getting starring roles. (Someday, faeries . . . I promise!)

To my readers, who make writing romance an infinitely great joy for me, and whose letters, emails, tweets, posts, and reviews I appreciate more than you can know, I send big hugs and kisses to you all. Special thanks to my Princesses, the best street team in the world, for your love and enthusiasm; I am deeply thankful for you. I love to hear from readers, and I always reply personally. Feel free to contact me via my website or to send a letter the lovely old-fashioned way in the mail.

To my dear husband, son, and Idaho: in these past few years you have taught me more about honest, generous, true love than I had ever thought there was to learn. You are my heroes.